Praise for
Directed Verdict
by Randy Singer

"There is plenty of room in evangelical Christian fiction for fresh voices, and debut novelist Singer is a promising one. Legal thrillers are gaining ground in the evangelical Christian market, and this is an agreeable addition to the genre."

—PUBLISHER'S WEEKLY

"*Directed Verdict* is a well-crafted courtroom drama with strong characters, surprising twists, and a compelling theme: international accountability for religious persecution. Randy Singer's novel is engaging, memorable, and highly significant."

—RANDY ALCORN, author of *Deadline, Safely Home,* and *Edge of Eternity*

"After a string of suspense-filled nights and bleary-eyed mornings, I can personally testify that Randy Singer writes a better legal thriller than even John Grisham. *Directed Verdict* grabs you on page one and never lets up. It is both powerfully spiritual and packed with enough plot twists to make you want to scream. Be prepared for the test of wills when putting the book down at night to go to sleep. And just in case…have coffee on hand for the morning."

—SHAUNTI FELDHAHN, author of *The Veritas Conflict*

"In *Directed Verdict*, Randy Singer gives us not only a fast-paced, beautifully written courtroom drama, but also a glimpse into the hardship our brothers and sisters overseas must endure as they live out their faith in countries hostile to the gospel."

—BILL BRIGHT, founder and chairman of Campus Crusade for Christ

IRREPARABLE HARM

A Novel

RANDY SINGER

WATERBROOK
PRESS

IRREPARABLE HARM
PUBLISHED BY WATERBROOK PRESS
2375 Telstar Drive, Suite 160
Colorado Springs, Colorado 80920
A division of Random House, Inc.

All Scripture quotations are taken from the *New King James Version.* Copyright © 1982 by Thomas Nelson, Inc. Used by permission. All rights reserved.

The characters and events in this book are fictional, and any resemblance to actual persons or events is coincidental.

Grateful acknowledgment is made for the use of select lyrics to "Carried Away," by Steve Bogard and Jeff Stevens, © 1996 Warner-Tamerlane Publishing Corp., Rancho Belita Music and Jeff Stevens Music. All rights administered by Warner-Tamerlane Publishing Corp. (BMI). All rights reserved. Used by permission. Warner Bros. Publications U.S. Inc., Miami, FL 33014.

ISBN 1-57856-634-7

WATERBROOK and its deer design logo are registered trademarks of WaterBrook Press, a division of Random House, Inc.

Library of Congress Cataloging-in-Publication Data
Singer, Randy (Randy D.)
   Irreparable harm / Randy Singer.— 1st ed.
      p. cm.
   ISBN 1-57856-634-7
      1. Cloning—Fiction. 2. Stem cells—Fiction. 3. Attorney and client—Fiction.
I. Title.
   PS3619.I5725I77 2003
   813'.6—dc21

20022155424

Printed in the United States of America
2003

10 9 8 7 6 5 4 3 2

For Charlotte and Darrell, "Duck and Hip," Mom and Dad.
One book can never make up for all the years of mischief I caused as a teen.
But it's a good start.

—◆—

ACKNOWLEDGMENTS

WRITING A NOVEL, LIKE ANYTHING worthwhile in life, is a team effort. I am grateful to the many who have played on this team, making this book far better than it ever would have been coming from me alone. The story has a complex subject matter and plot. To the extent that it hangs together and has a ring of truth, I am indebted to those listed below. The mistakes are solely mine, having successfully managed to slide them by the watchful eyes of so many.

Thanks...

To the first-class team at WaterBrook Press, and particularly to my friend and publisher, Don Pape, and to my editors Erin Healy, Dudley Delffs, and Laura Wright. Thanks for having the courage to address the controversial issues of our day as well as a commitment to excellence in the way you do it. Thanks for patiently pushing and prodding, improving this story one word at a time.

To those who provided technical assistance on the more complicated aspects of the story line: Dr. Kelly Hollowell, President of Science Ministries, who brought a keen eye and powerful intellect to the issues of stem cell research and cloning; Barbara Brownworth, an accomplished linguist at the State University of New York at Stony Brook, who helped me work through the linguistic challenges of a main character who is an immigrant; and Michael Garnier, one of the most capable attorneys I know, who took time from an incredibly busy trial schedule to provide a second opinion on the complex legal issues confronting our characters.

To the many informal reviewers, including Mary Hartman, who enthusiastically checked every Tidewater detail, and the North Carolina crew, who spend summer vacations wading through a rough manuscript of my latest work and providing valuable insights I later claim as my own. And thanks to all the members of the Singer, Wisse, and Rogers families, who have each provided staunch advocacy and unblinking encouragement at every single step in the process.

Finally, in the last but certainly not least category, to my wife, Rhonda, and my kids, Rosalyn and Joshua. I know it's not easy living with an author in the house, especially one who constantly bombards you with his "What do you think about this?" or "Can I get your opinion on that?" questions. Only God knows how many hours you've spent in helping this book come together. And only God truly knows how much I love you and appreciate you for it.

AUTHOR'S NOTE

AS THIS BOOK GOES TO PRESS, the issues of cloning and stem cell research are in the news on a daily basis. Renegade groups claim to have already cloned the first human (though most are skeptical), congress is considering a complete ban on cloning, and scientific advances continue unabated. Writing on these topics presents the unique challenge of creating a story that will not become obsolete with tomorrow's headlines.

To do so, I've anticipated a congressional ban on both therapeutic and reproductive cloning and called it the Bioethics Act. This story takes place approximately eighteen months after passage of this hypothetical ban and at a time when further advances in cloning technology have occurred. I've focused on a particular type of cloning called blastomere separation, which involves the splitting of a very young embryo (less than eight cells) into two or more embryos. It is essentially the artificial creation of "twins" in a petri dish. It differs from the more controversial process of somatic cell nuclear transfer—the process used to create Dolly the Sheep—in both complexity and type. The differences will be detailed in the story.

As I write this note, there are no documented cases of blastomere separation being used to create cloned human embryos for reproduction. Scientists generally agree that the possibilities of genetic defects and the questionable survival rates of the resulting embryos should preclude its use on human embryos at this time. However, a group of Oregon researchers has already used the process to clone monkeys. This story presumes the medical advances necessary to apply this same embryonic technique to humans.

This story also presumes that at this very moment, even months before any ban on cloning goes into effect, a fertility clinic someplace is defying conventional wisdom and using this technology to create the first cloned human embryos. Their future is the story of this book.

SHE WAS ONLY SIXTEEN YEARS OLD. Too young to die. At least that's what her mother kept telling her.

Maryna Sareth shuddered in the rear cargo hold of the rusty Korean freighter. She shivered herself to sleep every night in the bowels of the ship, lying next to her mother, crammed into the putrid container with nearly one hundred other Cambodian and Chinese refugees. They were literally cheek to jowl; if one rolled over, others would move in unison.

Each had paid seven thousand U.S. dollars for the privilege of making this trip. If they arrived safely in America, they would pay ten thousand more.

There were no windows in the cargo hold and only one ineffective fan. It did little to move the stench of urine and fecal matter. The toilets were two buckets, one for men and one for women. Most of the refugees had skin and urinary infections. Maryna was among them. The last time she had been allowed on deck, to wash down with salt water, had been several days ago.

Her eyes stung. They were infected—red and swollen. She could barely see. But at night it was no matter. There was nothing but darkness and the ragged breath of those too cold to sleep. Her only comfort was her mother's bony arm, lying gently across Maryna's back, and her mother's fragile hands, occasionally rubbing Maryna's shoulders to keep her warm.

Maryna could hear the Snakeheads—the Chinese gangsters who ran the human smuggling syndicates—drinking and partying on deck with the Cambodian assassins—the former soldiers of the Khmer

Rouge regime hired by the Snakeheads to guard the human cargo. As the night progressed and the noise crescendoed, Maryna would snuggle closer to her mother, terrified of the inevitable visit. The hatch would creak open, a slit of light would fall across the huddled cargo, and then a cruel game of choice by the Snakeheads and assassins would follow.

On this night, the night forever seared into Maryna's memory, one of the searching flashlights stopped on her. She buried her head in her mother's armpit, hiding her face, hoping that her mother and her own long black hair would provide cover.

But the Cambodian had spotted his prey. She heard him walk across rows of bodies until he stood directly over Maryna, straddling the trembling girl. He pulled her hair and lifted her head up, twisting her neck back, shining the light on her, and catching a glimpse of the elegant young face and the wide brown eyes. Not even the filth, rash, and infection could hide her beauty.

"Come with me," he growled. His narrow eyes leered out from a dark and hardened face covered with hair and sores. He let go of Maryna's hair, and she slowly, obediently, rose to her knees. She did not look up.

But Maryna's mother, thirty-two years old and slender like her daughter, was already on her feet, stepping between Maryna and her tormentor. She began caressing the man's chest, then took a small step back and watched carefully as the man's leer slowly turned from Maryna to herself. She returned his gaze without flinching.

"She's not the woman for you," Maryna's mother said as she unbuttoned the top few buttons on her tattered blouse. She reached out slowly and grabbed the man's callous hand, then turned and began leading him toward the cargo deck.

As her mother walked away with the soldier, stepping around and over the bodies, Maryna reached out for her, tears streaming down her cheeks. But then, as always, her mother was gone, and Maryna was reaching into the darkness.

—◆—

Maryna shivered again, but this time in the sharp night air of the Arizona desert. She had no idea America could be so cold at night, the air so biting, the land so barren.

The Korean freighter had landed in Guatemala in January. Maryna, her mother, and several others were smuggled into Mexico in a tight crawl space under a false floor in the back of a grapefruit truck. In Mexico, three armed "Coyotes" picked up the escort and acted as guides to cross the border. They crossed the desert on foot, with little water and less food. At night, forbidden from starting fires by their Coyote guides, the immigrants held each other for warmth.

On the sixth day, they sliced through a chain-link fence and reached America. The Coyotes had done their job. They had somehow avoided the infrared cameras and the seismic sensors that detected footsteps. They had avoided the helicopters and floodlights of the U.S. Border Patrol. But now, just as the group of twenty-three immigrants prepared to spend their first night on American soil, they had been cornered in the brush by Charlie Coggins, an infamous vigilante landowner who hunted illegal immigrants for sport.

The Coyotes had warned them about Charlie. *"Mexicanos,"* Charlie supposedly bragged, "are the greatest prey on earth." The Coyotes planned to keep the small band just outside Charlie's property. It was a longer route, but safer by far. But the Coyotes had blundered, miscalculating the boundary. Now they were on Charlie's turf and had been rounded up by a pack of hunting dogs.

"Hombre! Hombre!" shouted Charlie into the night. "Come out with your hands up. You're going back to Meh-hee-co!" Then he laughed a heinous laugh.

Maryna and the others huddled tightly together, still as the desert air and terrified to the core. Suddenly a shot rang out, a warning shot fired by a Coyote into the air. Charlie ducked behind his truck and returned fire.

Maryna heard the hiss of a bullet and felt the sand spray up around her. "I love you," said Maryna's mother, squeezing the girl's shoulders and kissing her on the forehead. "You run after I do, but go the other way."

Before Maryna could respond, her mother stood and sprinted from the underbrush, a fleeing shadow in the moonlight. The dogs howled and took up chase, while someone grabbed Maryna's arm and started running in the opposite direction, deeper into the underbrush. Other shots rang out, this time more distant. Maryna glanced back over her shoulder, searching for the slender silhouette in the moonlight. She reached out for it, but it was gone.

The silhouette slowly reappeared, quietly calling her name. "Maryna, Maryna," it said lovingly. It grew and hovered over her, gently shaking and prodding her.

Through the haze, Maryna's eyes began to focus on the figure now standing over her. She tried to reach out a hand, but the muscles would not obey. She blinked slowly...once...twice...trying desperately to bring the object, the person, into focus. The image sharpened, the darkness dissipated, and the light came flooding back.

She blinked again. Dr. Lars Avery, her ob-gyn, was standing next to her bed and smiling.

"Congratulations, Maryna. Everything went well. You're going to have a baby."

Maryna returned the smile then drifted back into a fitful sleep. Even in her dreams her mother's silhouette was nowhere to be found.

Monday, March 29. Six weeks later.

MITCHELL TAYLOR, THIRD-YEAR LAW STUDENT at Regent University in Virginia Beach, Virginia, jogged down the expansive hallways of the law school, his heavy backpack methodically thumping against his shoulders. He darted around students on a more leisurely pace, took the steps two at a time, then slunk into Lecture Hall 230 at precisely 9:04. Class had started at 9:00 A.M.

It was the first time all year that Mitchell had been late. And the first time in months he had not completed his reading assignment. He had considered not coming at all. But the values ingrained during his undergraduate work at Virginia Military Institute would not allow him the luxury of skipping class. Stonewall Jackson, whose lessons still echoed throughout the lecture halls at VMI, would never have condoned such undisciplined behavior.

Still catching his breath, Mitchell pulled his laptop out of his backpack and booted up. He placed his four-inch-thick constitutional law text on the empty seat next to him and opened it to the day's assigned case. He focused on Professor Charles Arnold as the young African American paced the well of the classroom.

"Today," Arnold was saying to the nearly 120 law students, "we will probe the dark recesses of search-and-seizure law—the issue of when the government needs a search warrant to rifle through your personal effects and when it can rummage around without a warrant."

Professor Arnold walked back behind his lectern. The fidgeting, unpacking, and whispering halted for a brief moment of drama as

Arnold's long, thin finger began making its way down the class roster. To a person, the students averted their eyes. It was considered bad form to look up when Arnold picked his prey, so all remained intent on the books and monitors in front of them. Even though these students were second and third years—2Ls and 3Ls in the parlance of the law school—and many, like Mitchell, were just weeks from graduation, they wanted no part of being Arnold's victim for the day. Few escaped unscathed.

Arnold's finger stopped its journey near the bottom of the page, and the professor looked up with a mischievous grin. "Mr. Taylor," he announced, "since you so recently joined us, let's start with you today."

A collective sigh of relief spread throughout the classroom, except for one spot about halfway up the left side, aisle seat, where Mitchell Taylor sprang to his feet. He was not happy about being chosen but decided to make the best of it. The best defense, Mitchell always believed, was a good offense.

"Yes sir," Mitchell announced boldly. He stood ramrod straight with his head held high. He was average height, with square shoulders and a tapered waist. He had close-cropped blond hair, close-knit eyebrows, a granite jaw, and a clean-shaven face. He wiped sweaty palms on the legs of his jeans.

"Did you read the Supreme Court case of *California v. Greenwood?*" the professor asked. This same perfunctory question always signaled the beginning of the interrogation.

"Yes sir," replied Mitchell, a little less loudly, "the relevant portions, sir."

Arnold stopped pacing and looked up at Mitchell, an exaggerated look of surprise on his face. "And what does that mean, the *relevant* portions?"

Mitchell shifted his weight. No use denying it. "I read the majority opinion, Professor."

"I see. And is there a reason you didn't bother yourself with the minority opinion of Justice Brennan?"

It would not suffice to say he ran out of time. "Being that Justice Brennan is a notorious liberal, I find his opinions are seldom well-constructed and never particularly illuminating."

A few students snickered. Mitchell suppressed his own grin. Professor Arnold did not even begin to smile.

"Well then, Mr. Taylor, since you are so fond of the majority opinion, perhaps you could enlighten us on the *majority's* holding in *California v. Greenwood.*"

Mitchell glanced down at his thick book, his eyes focusing on one of the few passages he had highlighted. "Since the respondents voluntarily left their trash for collection in an area particularly suited for public inspection, their claimed expectation of privacy in the inculpatory items they discarded was not objectively reasonable."

He glanced up at Professor Arnold, who was shaking his head. "In English, please."

"Well, uh, the police busted these guys by picking through their trash. The issue was whether the police needed a search warrant. The court said that trash is like, um, abandoned property, and because we don't have a reasonable expectation that our trash will stay private, the police don't need a warrant." Mitchell glanced at some of his conservative cohorts in the class. They were nodding their heads.

"And I take it that you agree with the court?" asked Professor Arnold.

"Absolutely," said Mitchell confidently, "the bad guys went to jail."

"Spoken like a true prosecutor," mused Arnold, his expression taut. He paced for another moment in silence, then stopped and locked his eyes on Mitchell. "Given that you did not take time to read the dissent, perhaps I could summarize Brennan's main arguments and see if it causes you to change your mind."

"Sure," responded Mitchell. He saw a few students grimace. The 3L sitting in front of him typed the words "be careful" on her computer screen in large letters.

The professor started pacing again, head down, hands behind his back as he lectured. "Justice Brennan seems to think that most people expect the contents of the trash bags they place at the curb to remain private. Basically, he says you are what you throw away. If you want to know what's going on in the private lives of people in a community, just go through their trash. A single bag of trash testifies eloquently to the eating, reading, health, personal hygiene, and even sexual habits of the person who produced it. Rummaging through someone's trash can divulge financial status, private thoughts, personal relationships, and romantic interests. Seems to me that looking through someone's trash without a warrant is a pretty severe invasion of privacy." The professor stopped pacing and looked at Mitchell, tilting his head and inviting a response.

"You make some good points, Professor," Mitchell retorted, "but there's a reason Justice Brennan's opinion was the *minority* opinion." This brought some groans from his classmates. The woman in front of him changed the words "be careful" to red.

"When you place those trash bags at the curb," Mitchell continued, "you have abandoned that property. It's common knowledge that garbage bags left on the side of the street are readily accessible to animals, children, scavengers, snoops, and the paparazzi. As the majority opinion pointed out, there's even some rich lady in Westmont who once a week puts on rubber gloves and hip boots and wades into the town garbage dump looking for proof-of-purchase coupons to mail in for manufacturers' rebates.

"With all due respect, sir, when you put that trash bag at the curb, it belongs to the public. As the old saying goes, 'One man's trash is another man's treasure.' In this case, it just happened to be the police who found the treasure."

Mitchell stopped, exceedingly pleased with himself. Being victim for the day wasn't so bad *if* you knew what you were talking about.

"Do you really believe that?" asked Professor Arnold skeptically. "Once you put your trash out, you lose all privacy interests in it?"

"Absolutely," said Mitchell. "It becomes part of the public domain."

"And if it were your trash, you wouldn't feel any differently?"

"Absolutely not."

"Good," said Professor Arnold. He retreated behind his desk and retrieved a roll of clear plastic. As Mitchell and the other students watched intently, Arnold carefully spread the plastic out to cover a large area of the carpet in the front of the class. Then he walked to a small closet near the front of the classroom, opened the door, and pulled out a large green trash bag, bulging with contents and tied at the top.

He placed the trash bag on top of the plastic and looked up at Mitchell.

"On the off chance that you, as our resident law-and-order advocate, might agree with the majority opinion, I took the liberty of asking another resident of the law student housing, who shall remain nameless, to retrieve one of the bags of trash that you left by the curb last Tuesday on trash pickup day."

Mitchell's eyes went wide. There was a general murmur in the classroom.

Professor Arnold began untying the bag. "Now, before I dump this trash out and pick through it in front of the entire class, let me give you one last chance to reconsider the merits of the dissenting opinion."

Mitchell's mind raced through a quick inventory of things he had thrown away. Leftovers from the refrigerator, toiletries, a few old T-shirts, a couple pairs of old underwear—now *that* could get ugly—junk mail, and newspapers that probably should have been recycled. He felt violated and exposed by this stunt. But he was also stubborn. All eyes turned his way. In the split second available for deliberation, he decided to call the professor's bluff.

"Knock yourself out," Mitchell said. "But I'm warning ya—I've already clipped all the coupons."

The class laughed as Professor Arnold untied the bag and dumped its contents onto the plastic floor covering. He spread the trash out and started picking through its contents. The underwear were nowhere in sight. *Maybe that was two weeks ago?*

"Oh, man," groaned a student in the front row, recoiling from the smell.

"Two pizza boxes in one week," Professor Arnold mumbled. "One empty ice cream container and who knows how many Diet Pepsi cans." He placed each item back in the trash bag, as if taking inventory. "Not exactly a health-food nut."

Mitchell forced a good-natured smile. He thought about all the private items the professor would be picking through. He wanted to run down to the front of the class, grab the bag, and scoop up all its contents. He kept his eyes peeled for underwear. But he had a point to make. And he was not about to back down now.

"Here's an old checking account statement," said the professor, holding up an envelope from Mitchell's bank. He ruffled through some of the cancelled checks.

Mitchell, who had been trying to get his financial affairs in order before graduation, felt betrayed. His shoulders sagged slightly.

"And here's a check for the Military Highway Ladies Club," announced Arnold, holding the check aloft. Some students chuckled, knowing that the strait-laced Mitchell Taylor would never go near such a place. But other students fidgeted in their seats, uncomfortable with this display of voyeurism.

And then Mitchell froze. Professor Arnold had picked up a slew of rejection letters, four to be precise, from law firms that Mitchell had recently approached for a job. He had forgotten about *those*.

Until last week, Mitchell had been sitting on a sweet offer from one of the area's largest firms. But in a shocker to Mitchell, the firm had merged with a mammoth New York outfit of more than five hundred lawyers. They would still honor Mitchell's offer, they said, but he would have to work in their New York office. Mitchell knew he would be stuck in the library and not see the inside of a courtroom for five years. It was not the deal he had signed up for. So he was sending out his résumé again, after most of the plum jobs had already been snatched up, with less than stellar results. He had rejoined the ranks of the unemployed.

Arnold looked at the first letter and glanced up at Mitchell. This *was* an invasion of privacy. Rejection letters for the whole class to hear. The professor had made his point. Mitchell wanted to make him stop. But it was also a matter of honor now, a battle of wills, and Mitchell would not be moved. He held his breath.

"And then there's also some junk mail and a slew of other things," said the professor, taking his gaze off Mitchell. "But unfortunately, Mr. Taylor is squeaky clean, and we won't be able to initiate any prosecutions on the basis of this trash." Without a word about the content of the letters, Arnold stuffed them back in the bag.

Mitchell slowly exhaled and allowed himself a relaxed grin.

"But look!" Arnold exclaimed, holding aloft a box of Honey Nut Cheerios. "A proof-of-purchase coupon that he missed."

The class laughed in unison, Mitchell sighed, and Professor Arnold rebagged the rest of the trash and moved on to the next case. Mitchell looked down at his notes and braced himself. He hadn't read the dissent in this one, either.

A FEW HOURS LATER, MITCHELL SAID a quick and nervous prayer before he knocked on the door to the interview room. During the fall interview season, Mitchell had actually enjoyed this process—meeting the lawyers who came to hawk their firms and find ambitious young associates ready to log boatloads of billable hours. And thanks to good grades and a proven work ethic, Mitchell had been in demand. He had owned these interview rooms. The job offers had been numerous and lucrative. But today, just a few short weeks from finals and graduation, the tables had turned. There were few job openings left and plenty of students waiting in line.

To make matters worse, Mitchell had declined an interview with this firm—Carson & Associates—when they had been on campus in the fall. He hoped they didn't remember his name or at least didn't ask why. Although Brad Carson had quite a reputation around Tidewater, Mitchell had never envisioned himself trying plaintiffs' personal injury cases. Until now.

He glanced down the list of twelve students posted on the conference room door and rechecked his time slot. Two o'clock. The prior interview was already running five minutes late. Mitchell heard some muffled laughter behind the door and glanced a little farther down the page. "Please knock when your interview time arrives" the paper said. Mitchell hated this part.

He knocked confidently and wiped his palms on the side of his pants. That first handshake—dry palms, firm grip—was key. More laughter echoed from the room. Mitchell waited a few moments, feeling like a complete idiot, then knocked again. "Just a second," a female voice responded.

He glanced at the list again. Brandon Jackson, a handsome 3L with a quick smile and pitiful grades, was in the 1:30 time slot. *Brandon Jackson,* thought Mitchell, *cutting into my time. Am I desperate or what?*

The door burst open and the laughter crescendoed. Brandon was so busy pumping the lady's hand and smiling with his whole body that he almost tripped over Mitchell as he turned to leave the room. He grunted something that Mitchell took as an apology.

"Don't worry about it," Mitchell mumbled as he sidestepped Brandon and extended his hand toward the lady. "Mitchell Taylor."

"Nikki Moreno," she said, grabbing his hand and smiling. She wasn't at all what Mitchell expected. She had the exotic beauty of a Latin American model, highlighted by long, dark hair, an electric white smile, and dark luminescent eyes. She wore a tight black miniskirt that showed off long legs and a spaghetti-strap top that exposed a pierced navel. Mitchell couldn't help but notice the small tattoo on her left shoulder, although he couldn't make out what it was.

"Have a seat, Mitch," said Nikki, motioning to the chair next to hers. Mitchell lowered himself into it and crossed his legs. He hated the nickname she had just used and had spent three years correcting his classmates. "Mitchell" was much more lawyerly. But you don't start an interview by nitpicking about your name, so he let it go.

"Do you know Brandon?" asked Nikki as she glanced at Mitchell's résumé. He had a hard time not staring at the tattoo.

"Yeah—not real well, but I know him." Mitchell paused. He needed this job, but he knew that Brandon needed it too. "He's a good guy. Pretty sharp."

"Tries too hard." Nikki grinned. "Plus, he doesn't have the grades that you do." She looked up. "Mind if I ask you a few questions?"

Mitchell leaned back and relaxed. He was starting to like Nikki's style. "Sure. Fire away."

For the next several minutes, Nikki spent time puffing her firm and didn't bother asking a single question. Brad Carson, said Nikki, was a successful plaintiff's attorney with a national reputation. The "and Associates" part of the firm was really Nikki, the resident paralegal, and Bella, a pit-bull legal secretary. But Brad was now ready to hire a real associate or two. In fact, they had started interviewing in the fall.

Nikki paused for a moment and looked at Mitchell. "You didn't interview with us last fall, did you?"

Mitchell squirmed. No sense beating around the bush. "No ma'am."

"Ma'am?" repeated Nikki. "I'm not that old."

"Sorry."

"Don't worry about it, Mitch." He cringed at the nickname, hoping maybe she would notice…but no chance—she just flashed another big white smile, lighting up the room, then turned serious. "But do you mind my asking why we didn't talk last fall? And frankly…well, what's a bright guy like you still doing unemployed?"

Mitchell hesitated again and thought about an evasive answer. But integrity won out. "I really didn't think I wanted to do plaintiff's work this fall," he explained. "So I took a job with a large firm that mostly defends civil cases. But they just merged with a big New York firm. I knew I'd never see the inside of a courtroom working for that sweatshop, and I really want the trial work—"

"If you don't want to do plaintiff's work—what *do* you want to do?" Nikki crossed her legs and slumped a little lower in the chair. Mitchell tried hard to focus on the question, not Nikki.

"I'd eventually like to work for the commonwealth's attorney's office. Prosecute criminals."

"You know what those jobs pay?"

"Yeah, I know." Mitchell shrugged. "But money's not the key issue for me."

"Good thing." Nikki studied him for a moment, looking him up and down until the silence grew uncomfortable.

"Did you have any other questions about my résumé?" Mitchell asked politely.

"Nope," she responded, placing her notes and pen down on the table. "That about covers your résumé."

Mitchell looked at her in disbelief. It had only been fifteen minutes—not even half as long as Brandon! But what had he done wrong? He could feel his confusion turn quickly to frustration, bordering on anger. This whole interview process was a sham. Nikki Moreno had already decided whom she wanted to hire, and it wasn't him.

"Sometimes," said Mitchell evenly, weighing each word, "there's a lot more to a person than you can tell from his résumé. No disrespect...but I just don't feel like you know enough about me to figure out what kind of associate I might make for your firm. If I could, I'd like to at least mention a few things." Mitchell paused, waiting for a cue to continue. But Nikki just maintained a cocky, thin-lipped smile, as if she knew something that Mitchell did not.

"That'd be fine if you'd like to," Nikki said finally, "but I know a lot more about you than you think."

Mitchell raised his eyebrows. *Show me.*

"According to your résumé, you grew up in southwest Virginia," said Nikki confidently. "Twenty miles from Roanoke. You're probably an avid country music fan."

An obvious guess, thought Mitchell.

"You've got no ring, so you're not married. And since you played football at VMI and have poster-boy good looks and a body to die for"—the comment, delivered so matter-of-factly by Nikki, made Mitchell's face burn—"you undoubtedly had a serious relationship with a girl during your undergrad days, but she dumped you in law school."

Mitchell couldn't hide his astonishment. Nikki chuckled. "And based on your desire to one day be a prosecutor, your Bible-Belt roots, and the fact that you are at Regent Law School, I'd say you're one of those outspoken Christians intent on changing the world through the law."

"Not bad," Mitchell said skeptically, working hard to maintain a poker face. "Though 'outspoken' may be a bit of a stretch. Now tell me something that's not quite so obvious."

Nikki furrowed her brow as if she were reading Mitchell's mind at that very moment. "Like the fact that you drive an F-150 black pickup and have a bad lower back from an old football injury…"

Mitchell's jaw dropped.

"…and hate being called 'Mitch.'" Nikki tilted her head and grinned.

"What in the world? I mean, how'd you know that?"

"Anybody with grades this good—I check up on them as soon as I get a copy of the résumé from the school," she explained, mischievous eyes sparkling. "Long before the interview, in fact. Brandon's an old friend. And he thinks pretty highly of you."

Mitchell couldn't resist cracking a smile. "Now I know how those FBI candidates feel."

Nikki responded with a chuckle of her own, then quickly turned professional. "There is one thing I really do need to ask about," she said. "If we made you a job offer, would you stick with us long term, or just use the firm as a launching pad to get some experience until something opens up at the commonwealth's attorney's office?"

Mitchell lowered his eyes and studied the floor. Nikki was smart, cutting right to the core issue. Although it would probably kill his chances, his conscience compelled an honest response. "I don't really see myself there long term," Mitchell admitted. "But I would work hard during my time at the firm to make sure you get your money's worth."

Nikki hesitated. "That's what I figured. And much as I like you, Brad would kill me if we hired and trained somebody I recommended, just to watch them jump ship."

"I understand," said Mitchell. "And I don't blame you. Actually, I'd feel the same way."

They sat in silence for a second, then Nikki perked up. "But I do like your style," she said. "And I've got an idea. I used to work for Billy 'the Rock' Davenport. I happen to know he's hiring, even though he doesn't buy into this type of interview process. And frankly, I don't think he'd care how long you might stay. He's desperate for help *now*. I could call him for you."

Mitchell grimaced. The thought of working for the Rock turned his stomach. The king of lawyer advertising. The butt of lawyer jokes all over Tidewater, Virginia. How could Mitchell even consider the possibility? But what choice did he have?

"Thanks," he heard himself say.

"Don't mention it," said Nikki. "There's a reason I'm not still working there." Without giving Mitchell a chance to respond, she leaned forward and quickly changed the subject. "And now that the interview's over, tell me what you're really passionate about, Mitchell."

———❧———

Twenty minutes later, after the next applicant had knocked three separate times, Mitchell found himself smiling as he left the interview room. Nikki was a piece of work. Although he still had absolutely no prospect of working at Carson & Associates, Nikki's boundless energy had somehow buoyed his spirit. He stuffed her business card in his suit coat pocket. He might just call her sometime.

But he hadn't gone to the interview to find a date. He needed a job. And the pleasant thoughts of Nikki soon gave way to the dismal prospect of working for the Rock. "When trouble rolls, call the Rock," mumbled Mitchell as he walked down the hall. It was the slogan that everybody in Tidewater who watched television knew by heart. They even knew the phone number: 1-800-CASH-NOW.

Mitchell felt like he was in a fog. Had it really come to this? All of the hard-earned grades and moot court awards just to work for an ambulance chaser?

Shouldn't he just refuse to consider this option and hold out *in faith* for something better? *It's not like I haven't been praying about this,* he thought as he walked briskly toward the parking lot.

In fact, he had been praying daily about job opportunities. He had felt great peace about telling the New York firm he would not be coming. And since that day he had prayed earnestly for a job where he could really make a difference, where he could leave his mark on the law, where he could impact the lives of others.

But hadn't he also prayed that God would close every door except the one He wanted Mitchell to walk through? Hadn't he asked God to make His will so clear...

No way, he thought. *How could I ever make a difference working for a guy like the Rock?*

And with that question weighing on his mind, and his eyes wide open, Mitchell began to pray. *Oh God,* he said, picking up the pace as he walked, *You can't be serious...*

3

WINSTED AARON MACKENZIE IV THOUGHT he had seen it all. Sixteen years of litigation experience in Norfolk's largest law firm had exposed him to a slice of life that most people only read about or watch on television. He had experienced and exploited the dark side of humanity. Jealousy, greed, ego, and envy. He had seen the large corporate cases come and go. And he had ridden his blue-blood Virginia roots and hard-nosed trial tactics to his share of fame and fortune as the lawyer of choice for corporate execs who played hardball.

But before today, he had never met a man with AIDS, much less allowed one to set foot in his office. And he probably wouldn't have now, except that one of his best clients, Dr. Blaine Richards, CEO of GenTech, had called and asked Mackenzie to personally handle this case. Mackenzie alone had billed GenTech more than two hundred thousand dollars the prior year. He never considered saying no.

"Win," his secretary called from her work cubicle just outside his office, "Dr. Brown is here. Shall I bring him back?"

"It wouldn't do to keep the good doctor waiting."

Win stood behind his oriental teakwood desk and stretched his arms toward the ceiling of his corner office. The desk, the Persian rugs on the hardwood floor, and the wooden Japanese carvings on the credenza gave the office a mysterious Far Eastern flavor. Few visitors could resist commenting on the large picture of samurai warriors that hung on the long interior wall or the collection of samurai swords mounted next to it. Win intended the décor to make a statement. He was not a man to be messed with.

He walked over to a small coat closet and retrieved his suit jacket.

Other lawyers in the firm had adopted a business-casual dress code, but not Win. He slipped the navy blue pinstriped suit coat over his starched white shirt and tugged at his gold cuff links. He methodically brushed each hand over the opposite sleeve, smoothing out any rumples. Then he quickly glanced at his reflection in the samurai picture.

He looked considerably younger than his forty-nine years. Win was the acknowledged pretty boy of the firm—the "face" of Kilgore & Strobel. The wavy brown televangelist hair, sprayed firmly in place, and the pearly white smile fooled most people. The suit coat still hid the few extra inches gathering at his waist. He was, for the most part, the picture of health. A man at the peak of his career, ready to go to battle for the next well-heeled client. *The American samurai.*

"Mr. Mackenzie, this is Dr. Brown." Margaret spoke in her curt professional manner as she ushered the client in.

Dr. Nathan Brown extended his hand. "Nice to meet you," he said flatly.

Win shook the man's hand with his usual vigor. He noticed that Nathan's grip was soft, almost nonexistent. Win half-expected the hand to break off in his own firm grasp.

"Thanks for coming by," Win said with a forced smile. "Have a seat." He motioned toward one of the leather client chairs positioned just in front of his desk. Win retreated to his high-backed leather chair on the other side. The opulent desk would make a nice force field between the samurai and his new client.

"Would you like anything to drink?" asked Margaret from her post just inside the door. Win shot her a disapproving look.

"No, thanks," said Nathan Brown as he took his seat. Margaret disappeared, closing the door behind her. Win wondered about the circulation in the room, released a short sigh, and settled into his desk chair. He unbuttoned his suit coat and slyly wiped his right hand against the outside pocket. It was time to get the suit dry-cleaned anyway.

It was impossible to forget that Nathan Brown had AIDS. His appearance screamed that this man was not well. He was razor thin, with sinewy arms protruding from his short-sleeved golf shirt. His hollow eyes unleashed a molten gaze from black coals surrounded by jaundiced flesh. And Win thought he noticed some telltale scabs on Brown's scalp, partially hidden by his wispy thin brown hair.

Win knew that many people who tested HIV positive looked as robust and healthy as Win himself. He surmised that Nathan must have been sick for some time. Win thought they had drugs to control the progression of HIV these days. But this guy was plainly at death's door.

"I need you to help me revise my Last Will and Testament," Brown said as he reached inside his small leather briefcase and retrieved a sheaf of documents. He placed the paperwork on an empty corner of the desk. Win made a mental note to have Margaret wipe it down later. "Dr. Richards said that you'd be the best lawyer to help me."

"Blaine called me," responded Win crisply. He leaned forward on the desk, then thought better of it and settled back into his chair. "But before I can open a file, there are a few preliminary matters. We'll have to run a conflicts check. My fee is $250 an hour. And we'll need a signed contract, together with a modest retainer, and—"

Nathan Brown held up his hand. "There's only one person you have to worry about in your conflict-of-interest check." Brown's eyes bored into Win, startling him with their dark intensity. "That's my wife, Cameron Davenport-Brown."

"The newspaper columnist? She's your wife?" asked Win. This was something that Blaine Richards had not mentioned.

"Yes."

Win folded his hands. "We do represent the paper," he said thoughtfully, "but technically not the individual reporters and columnists." His mind churned. This might be his chance to dump this dangerously infectious client without alienating Richards. "However, we try to avoid even the appearance of impropriety…"

Brown interrupted again, this time with an outstretched arm handing Win a check—a retainer in the amount of seventy-five thousand dollars.

"You don't have any idea who I am, do you?" Brown asked sharply. "Or why I'm really here?"

Win took the check and placed it on his legal pad. "Just some general information," he admitted.

Brown leaned forward, placing his hands on top of Win's desk, next to the pile of papers he had just put there.

"I am Dr. Nathan Brown, and I am dying of AIDS," he said softly, almost in a whisper. His voice was hoarse, as if even talking was a struggle. "I contracted the disease from a contaminated needle while working in the Norfolk General emergency room. And now"—Brown stopped and coughed, turning his head to the side—"I am about to bring you what could be the most important case of your legal career.

"Within months, perhaps weeks, I will lose my battle with AIDS. I will leave behind a wonderful wife who loves me, and I will leave behind the possibility of a child. I also want to leave behind a legacy."

Brown paused for a moment, closing his eyes in a slow blink. He looked pained, whether from the effects of AIDS or the subject matter he was now sharing, Win could not tell. Brown stared down at his folded hands and continued in a hoarse whisper.

"For several years, Cameron and I could not have children. We tried everything. To complicate matters, she developed a pretty severe case of endometriosis. Dr. Lars Avery, her ob-gyn, suggested a partial hysterectomy." Brown paused and returned his gaze to Mackenzie. "You do know what endometriosis is, don't you?"

"Sure," Win said, unwilling to admit the truth. He was starting to dislike this patronizing doctor.

"After this operation, Cameron could no longer carry a baby—"

"Of course."

Brown shot Mackenzie an annoyed look, exhaled in a grunt, and paused for a long second before continuing. "We really wanted children, so we finally sought help from Dr. Richards and his fertility clinic. Working with Dr. Avery, the clinic harvested two cycles of eggs from Cameron. Do you know how that's done?"

Unwilling to incur more of the doctor's wrath by talking, Win just shook his head.

"It's an intrusive procedure. It requires surgery. It's not the kind of thing you do lightly."

Win nodded.

"Anyway," the doctor continued, "it was not until the third month, after the third operation to extract eggs from Cameron, that the clinic was able to fertilize the eggs with my sperm. At that point we had four fertilized eggs. But Cameron continued to have some pretty severe problems with endometriosis all through her ovaries and fallopian tubes.

"To make a long story short, my wife had to undergo a total hysterectomy with a bilateral salpingo-oophorectomy..." Win furrowed his brow and didn't even try writing it down. Brown didn't seem to notice.

"She was only thirty-one at the time. And now her only chance to have a natural child was contained in those four microscopic fertilized eggs."

As he continued speaking, Brown looked past Win, out the nineteenth-floor window overlooking the Elizabeth River. "But the gods were not done torturing us yet. A few months later I contracted the AIDS virus..." Brown's raspy voice broke off. He sat silently for a moment, then turned his sad gaze to Win.

"She desperately wanted a child, Mr. Mackenzie. She was obsessed with it. It was all she talked about, all she thought about after her operation. I mean, don't get me wrong. I wanted a child too. But not the way she did. It was like she'd be incomplete without one."

Brown stopped and rubbed his forehead.

"We were in a position of needing a surrogate mother. But we also knew that if you implanted four pre-embryos inside a surrogate, your odds are less than 25 percent that any of them would develop. So we did the only reasonable thing under the circumstances."

Brown paused, creating a moment of drama that caused Win to forget his fear of the man's awful disease. Win leaned forward in his chair and fixed his eyes directly on Brown, waiting for the man to continue.

"When the pre-embryos reached the six-cell stage, we used a procedure called blastomere separation. We essentially cloned the pre-embryos, creating multiple copies of them. In essence, we artificially mimicked the natural process that results in twins or multiple births. We then had a total of twelve embryos. Four originals. Eight clones."

Win's eyes went wide. "You cloned them?"

"Keep in mind," said Brown, "that we did this eighteen months ago, before Congress passed the ban. And it's not the kind of cloning that everybody's all fired up about. We didn't do the somatic cell nuclear transfer, where you transfer the nucleus and genes from one person into the egg cell of a second person, thereby creating a carbon copy of the first. That's the kind of cloning that created Dolly the sheep, the kind that this Clonaid group got everyone riled up about. All we did was divide the fertilized egg—the zygote—a few times to increase our odds. We just created several twins, if you will."

Win, now thoroughly confused, scribbled notes on his legal pad. He had a million questions, but he would save most of them. He had done GenTech's corporate work for years but never really ventured into the medical side of things. He could always have an associate research these issues later as long as Win got the terms right. No sense sounding dumb in front of your client.

"What do you call that thing?" Win asked.

"A zygote," repeated Brown. "It's a medical term for a fertilized egg that has not yet been implanted in a uterus."

"Right," said Win, as if he knew it all along. "How do you spell that?"

"Like it sounds. Z-Y-G-O-T-E."

Win scribbled a few more notes. Brown hesitated for a moment then continued his narration. "We took the four original embryos and implanted them into a surrogate mother about six weeks ago. She's a wonderful young girl—an immigrant from Indonesia or some country like that. I'm hopeful she'll deliver a healthy child. Our child." Brown looked down. "Though there's little chance I'll live to see it."

"I'm sorry," said Win without much conviction. He was still trying to figure out what legal issue had brought Brown to his office.

"That leaves eight frozen pre-embryos," continued Nathan. "Cameron wants them preserved in case anything happens to the child that our surrogate is carrying. I want them donated for medical research."

"Why?" asked Win without thinking. On first blush, the wife's position seemed more reasonable. "Why not wait?"

"Two reasons, really. First, I don't want Cameron to feel like she can hang on to me by raising our children. It's not easy coming to terms with your own death. But I've done that. Cameron refuses to accept it. If this first embryo doesn't make it, she'll want the other embryos implanted until one does. This is cutting-edge science, and there's no guarantee that any of the cloned embryos will survive. Even if they do, Cameron will be a single mom raising my child out of a sense of grief and obligation. I don't want that. A part of me hopes these embryos with the surrogate don't make it. I want Cameron free to live again."

Brown swallowed hard and blinked back a tear. Win shifted uncomfortably in his chair and busied himself by jotting a few more notes. After an appropriate pause, he said, "You said there were two reasons."

"There are. I said I wanted to leave a legacy. I want these pre-embryos to be used for medical research on the AIDS virus. They can be cultured into a virtually never-ending source of stem cells, and right now there is an incredible untapped potential for stem cell research. While the president prevented federal funding on new strands, he did not prevent the research itself if it is privately funded. I want my will to donate these pre-embryos to research, and I'm prepared to leave a substantial portion of my estate to set up a trust fund that would support that research by GenTech."

Brown stopped again to take a long labored breath and swallow. "Cameron will probably fight me on this. And though I love her with every ounce of my being, I've got to do it. I want to do everything within my power to prevent others from going through the kind of pain that Cameron and I have endured."

Brown now looked directly at Win and waited for him to finish a note before continuing.

"AIDS is humiliating and debilitating. People treat you differently. As if you're the devil himself. As if by breathing the same air you breathe, they can get the disease." Brown leaned even further forward on the desk. Win looked at his notepad and resisted the urge to inch back.

"I want to fight this demonic disease however I can. This is the only way I know how. It's the right thing to do." Brown said the last statement as if he were trying to convince himself. Then he slumped back in his chair, seemingly exhausted by his own narration.

Win wasn't sure if Brown was doing the right thing or not. But he *was* sure about one thing. If Cameron decided to contest this will in court, it could lead to the most important case of Winsted Mackenzie's illustrious career. And if Cameron made the mistake of running to her dad for representation—the notorious Billy "the Rock" Davenport—an easy victory would be virtually guaranteed. Win had tried a case or two against the Rock even before the personal-injury attorney fell off the wagon, and the man wasn't too hot back then. Surely these days the Rock wouldn't stay sober long enough to be a serious threat on a case like this.

Win looked straight at Brown and was surprised to see wrinkles of worry replaced by deep creases of resolve on the doctor's face. The client was ready. Win glanced again at the retainer check on his desk. Seventy-five thousand dollars. The samurai was ready too.

4

DR. BLAINE RICHARDS, CEO of the GenTech Fertility Clinic, was in his glory. As a result of GenTech's phenomenal growth, he had been spending more and more time administering the company and less time with patients. His days in the lab were almost a thing of the past, replaced by tedious meetings that served no discernible purpose. But today he was in the lab. And he was loving it.

He sat hunched over a micromanipulator, a high-powered microscope used when operating on embryos. Playing the part of an embryologist, a matchmaker between sperm and egg, Richards had already hand-fertilized nearly thirty eggs, and he still had two hours left. The most he had ever fertilized in one day was fifty-two.

Pausing briefly, he ran a hand through his slick black hair, starting at the steep widow's peak that accentuated his long forehead and pointed nose. He brought his hand back to his face for a moment before continuing his work, stroking his jagged chin and rubbing his thumb over the perpetual five o'clock shadow that gave his dark expression the menacing look he preferred. He knew women found the look enchanting, or at least tolerable, in light of his hefty bank accounts and recently divorced status.

Refocusing on the task at hand, Richards deftly pulled a few eggs out of an incubator and placed them on a heating plate at the bottom of the microscope. The minuscule eggs had already been stripped of surrounding tissue by exposure to an enzyme found naturally in sperm. "This enzyme is purified from bull sperm," Richards would tell visiting journalists as he walked them through the process. He knew it wasn't true, but he enjoyed the looks on their faces, especially the women.

With the eggs now in place, Richards turned his attention to an incubator containing the husband's sperm. They were not a hardy lot. In fact, in a perfect Darwinian world, these sperm wouldn't stand a chance. And that, in a nutshell, was the whole reason behind hand-fertilization. Richards used it only for couples where the sperm of the male partner was incapable of natural fertilization. Without Richards and his colleagues, those couples would be childless.

He found a healthy sperm and immediately broke its tail. "If we rough it up a little, it makes fertilization more likely," Richards would say. "Nobody really knows why."

Using the microscope for guidance, Richards collected the wounded sperm in a glass pipette, a precision instrument less than one-tenth the diameter of a human hair. He then placed one end of a long, thin tube between his lips and connected the other end of the tube to the pipette containing the single sperm. Then gently, carefully, skillfully, he positioned the pipette in the heating plate at the bottom of the micromanipulator until its sharp end abutted the cell wall of the egg. Next, he carefully penetrated the wall, then exhaled gingerly into the tube, his air pressure forcing the single sperm into the egg.

Mission accomplished.

As carefully as before, he withdrew the pipette and watched the egg wall immediately reseal itself with the sperm safely inside. Relaxing ever so slightly, Richards tilted his head back and rolled his neck. His breath had once again created a life, or at least the possibility of it, where none had existed before.

A ringing cell phone broke his concentration. He reached into his lab coat and flipped the phone open.

"Richards here."

"Blaine, it's Win. Dr. Brown came by. We completed the will. You'll soon be the proud owner of eight new potential stem cell lines."

"Can you enforce the agreement?" asked Richards acidly. "It cost me nearly a hundred thousand, as you'll recall."

It was a loaded question. The "agreement" was the contract signed by Dr. Brown and his wife when they first came to GenTech's clinic. It was a form agreement based on a contract that Win himself had drafted on behalf of the clinic several years before. In it, Dr. Nathan Brown and Cameron Davenport-Brown both specified that, in the event both parents did not agree on the disposition of any frozen embryos, "the cryopreserved pre-embryos will be donated to the GenTech Clinic for use in medical research and experimentation." If the agreement held, Dr. Brown's desire to donate the remaining pre-embryos and accompanying trust funds to research would become a reality.

"The agreement wasn't drafted to apply to cloned embryos," lectured Win. "Why didn't you tell me you were cloning embryos?"

Richards seethed in silence. He paid this guy $250 an hour. He didn't need his own lawyer second-guessing him.

"What's the difference?" Richards eventually asked. "The agreement says *all* cryopreserved pre-embryos and embryos. Now we get to see if the agreement *you* drafted"—Richards paused a moment to allow the words to sink in—"will hold up in court. If it doesn't, I know plenty of other lawyers who could have drafted a flawed and worthless agreement for half the price."

He could hear Win breathing heavily on the other end of the line. Wisely, the lawyer bit his tongue.

"How much longer does Brown have?" asked Win, changing the subject.

"I haven't seen him for a while, but not long. Maybe weeks. Maybe days."

"Then I'll draft the papers for an immediate lawsuit," Win said, the confidence returning to his voice. "If his wife contests Dr. Brown's desire to donate the embryos, we'll file a Declaratory Judgment action. That agreement will hold. I'll stake my reputation on it."

"You already have," Richards reminded him. "And let's not rush in too fast. Those embryos aren't going anywhere. No sense taking on a grieving widow before the body gets cold."

"You're the doctor. You tell me when the body's cold. We'll have the papers ready to go."

"That works for me, Win. Got to run. There are babies to be made."

"Take care, Blaine."

"Thanks for the update."

Blaine Richards put the cell phone back in its clip. A single stem cell line could be worth millions. But that was just the start. His plans were far more grandiose, far more lucrative. And Win Mackenzie had no idea. He was just a pawn—okay, maybe a knight—to be moved around the board as Richards saw fit. Only Richards had the big picture. Not even his queen could know how this would ultimately turn out.

He turned his attention back to his incubators, repeated the process, and blew life into another egg cell. Dr. Blaine Richards had never felt more like a god.

5

Wednesday, March 31

MITCHELL TAYLOR DID NOT RECOGNIZE Billy "the Rock" Davenport until the man slid into the booth. Mitchell was looking for the Rock he saw advertising his services on television—a tall athletic man with a scowling face that could have been carved out of Mount Rushmore and a full head of thick black hair. Instead, the man who poured himself into the booth opposite Mitchell was an older man, short and squat, with a small ring of graying hair around his balding head. This Rock, the real deal as opposed to the actor, also sported a pair of thick spectacles, red suspenders, and a loosened tie knot hanging halfway down his chest. He had apparently left his suit coat in the car.

"Nice to meet you, Mr. Davenport," said Mitchell. After class he had hustled back to his apartment and changed into his gray "interview suit," a pinstripe affair that made him indistinguishable from every other young lawyer in Norfolk. Looking at the Rock, he suddenly felt overdressed.

"Likewise," said the Rock. "But please, call me Billy or the Rock. Nobody calls me Mr. Davenport. Makes me feel old."

"Yes sir," said Mitchell. For some reason, it was hard to call someone old enough to be Mitchell's father by his first name. And there was virtually no way that Mitchell could call this oversized replica of the Pillsbury Doughboy "the Rock."

"You order yet?" The Rock was already signaling to the waitress.

"Just iced tea."

"I could use something stronger myself," the Rock said absent-mindedly. His cell phone rang and he answered it just as the waitress arrived. Without breaking stride, the Rock talked on the cell phone, ordered a light beer, then ogled the waitress as she left their table. Mitchell felt invisible.

Three cell phone calls and one light beer later, the Rock finally got down to business.

"What's a bright young man like you still doing unemployed at this time of year? Nikki says you're one of the smartest students in the third-year class."

"Well, we both know better than to take everything Nikki says at face value," Mitchell responded.

"You got that right."

"The short story is that I had accepted an offer with Wilkes and Hubbard before they merged with the Patterson firm. After the merger they called and said they wanted me to start as an associate in New York. I figured that I would spend my first six to eight years in the library. Eventually, I want to be a prosecutor. And I know I need courtroom experience to get there."

Mitchell paused and tried to catch the Rock's eye. It was not easy. The man had been following every move of the waitress, listening half-heartedly, if at all.

"You didn't happen to catch her name, did ya?" the Rock asked.

"Her?" Mitchell nodded toward the waitress. She was at least forty-five, wore entirely too much makeup, and chomped her gum furiously. "No, I didn't."

"Hey, gorgeous!" the Rock called. The waitress walked over, smiling. Mitchell noticed the wedding ring on her finger.

"Is lunch on the way?" the Rock asked. They had ordered fifteen minutes earlier. "I'm in somewhat of a hurry."

"I'll check on it," she said. Then pointing to the Rock's empty glass, "Are you good, or do you need another?"

"Let's do one more while we're waiting," the Rock answered nonchalantly. His eyes studied every step as the woman walked away, then he turned back to Mitchell.

"How much?" the Rock asked.

"How much what?"

"How much were they going to pay ya?"

"Seventy-five thousand."

The Rock let out a low whistle. "And you turned 'em down?"

Mitchell nodded.

"Why would I want a lawyer with that kind of judgment working for me?" the Rock asked. Then he threw his head back and laughed. Mitchell smiled politely.

"Tell you what," the Rock said, leaning forward. "You come highly recommended. Nikki says you're one heck of a smart guy. So here's what we'll do. You come to work for me, and you'll get all the courtroom time you'll ever want. I just lost my only associate, so I'm really short-handed. I'll let you personally handle all the criminal defense cases in addition to assisting me on the personal injury claims." The Rock lowered his voice, as if he were about to impart a grave secret. "You want to be a prosecutor? Then beat those boys on a few of these criminal cases I've got in my office and they'll be beggin' ya to join 'em."

The waitress reappeared with the Rock's beer and two sandwich platters. "I'm done working for the day," the Rock said as he poured his second beer. Mitchell sensed the Rock's need to justify his drinking and it worried him. "The case I was supposed to be in court on this afternoon settled."

Without responding, Mitchell bowed his head and said a quick and silent prayer of thanks. He knew the Rock was probably staring a hole in the top of his head. *God, give me wisdom,* Mitchell finished, then lifted his eyes.

The Rock was still gawking after the waitress.

"What kind of compensation package are you offering?" asked Mitchell.

The Rock turned and took a big bite of his tuna melt, letting the mayonnaise drip slowly down his chin. "Thirty thousand first year," he said as he took a swipe at the mayo with his napkin. "Plus 401(k), parking, insurance benefits, and your own office." Another huge bite, then the Rock reached into his pocket and pulled out a one-page document. He slid it across the table to Mitchell, staining it with the grease on his fingers. The paper described the firm's health, life, and disability benefits, as well as the standard 401(k) contribution. "Read all about it."

Mitchell took a long gulp of his iced tea and stared at the Rock. It was either New York City or...*this.*

"Thirty-five thousand plus a health-club membership," answered Mitchell without even looking at the benefits sheet.

The Rock looked up from his food and wiped his mouth again. "Nikki says you took the bar exam in February. That true?"

"Yes sir."

"Did you pass?"

"Sure."

The Rock looked delighted and surprised, as if he had never known somebody who passed the bar on his first try.

"So you could start right away?"

"I graduate five weeks from Friday. Not that I'm counting or anything," replied Mitchell, already starting to have second thoughts.

"Good, then you can start the Monday after you graduate," the Rock announced. He reached out his hand, and the two lawyers shook across the table.

"This requires a little celebration," said the Rock, motioning to the waitress.

"Get my friend here a bottle of whatever he wants," the Rock proudly instructed the waitress, as he gestured toward Mitchell. "He just signed on as the newest attorney at the law firm of Davenport & Associates."

"Congratulations," muttered the waitress.

Mitchell held up his palm and smiled. "Thanks," he said, "but I'm good. I don't usually drink at this time of the day."

"When do you drink?" asked the Rock skeptically, taking another long pull on his half-drained beer.

"Never," said Mitchell.

The Rock nearly choked before he could swallow.

~ ~

On the way back to his apartment, Mitchell dialed the offices of Carson & Associates and asked for Nikki.

"I got the job with the Rock," he announced after they exchanged greetings.

"I'm sorry," said Nikki.

Mitchell laughed. "I may be sorry in a week or so myself."

For the next ten minutes, Nikki told tales about working for the Rock, punctuated by Mitchell's "Are you kidding me?" or "You can't be serious!" or "Unbelievable!" By the time he pulled into the parking lot of his apartment building, Mitchell's already serious reservations had been compounded.

But he's the only one willing to take a chance on me at this late date, thought Mitchell, *knowing that I probably won't stay more than a year or two. After all, how bad can this be?*

6

Wednesday, May 5
Editorial Page, Tidewater Times

AIDS HITS HOME
by Cameron Davenport-Brown

Three times a week in this column I bare my soul and bark my opinions to you, my readers. There is nothing sacred, I say. Nothing off-limits or too personal to be the grist for my keyboard. I will tackle any subject.

Until today that was a lie.

There is one subject that has been too personal and too painful to find its way into this column. There has been one sacred cow, one personal conclave.

Today I broach that subject. And I type on a keyboard wet with tears. This one is personal. This one is about AIDS.

It is one thing to read about the AIDS virus reaching epidemic proportions among the children of Africa. It is another thing to see the devastation among the unfortunate in this country—the druggies, the prostitutes, the poor.

And it is yet another thing altogether when AIDS hits home.

Respectable, white, monogamous, God-fearing, suburban doctors do not get this disease. Or so I thought until eighteen months ago. Then one night, the only man I ever loved uttered a confession that changed my life forever. "I'm HIV positive," he said as he clutched me to his chest. "I've got AIDS."

I know what you're thinking. And that's part of the problem. But sometimes the victims are innocent. Like my husband, Nathan. One minute, a contaminated needle breaks the flesh. The next minute, an emergency room doctor who has devoted his life to helping others becomes a victim of the patients he lived to serve.

"I've got AIDS," he said.

And it changed everything.

At first you fight the disease and you hate anyone who will not join that fight. Decisions to fund or not fund stem cell research, which before were just political decisions to be debated, become intensely personal. You read about every experimental drug. You pin your hopes on stories of other survivors. One year out. Five years out. Ten. You realize that for most people, a combination of AZT and the other antiretroviral drugs work to slow the reproduction of HIV. In other words, it is a disease that can sometimes be managed. But it remains a disease that cannot be cured.

You learn to savor each moment together. And you reserve your hate for those who treat your husband like a leper, like someone who should go around shouting, "Unclean, unclean!"

Some friends stop dropping by. Others whisper when they think you're not listening. You turn on the television and hear hypocritical preachers talk about this killer disease as God's judgment on immoral people. You throw the remote…then pick it up and change the channel. You pick new friends. You start hanging out with others who are fighting the fight.

They say you can judge the soul of a nation by how it treats its least fortunate citizens. If that is the test, I grieve for America. At best, she ignores the victims of her deadliest disease. At worst, she mocks and ridicules them.

There is no good time to lose a husband. And there is no good way for a husband to die. But it is particularly cruel to see your husband struck down in the prime of life, before his first child can ever leave the womb. You think of all the things that will never be. The birthday parties, the long walks at dusk, growing old together. And you ask yourself questions that can never be answered. If it's a girl, who will give her away at the wedding? If it's a boy, who will teach him to hit a baseball? Who will embrace the child with the comfort, encouragement, and security of a father's strong arms?

This was a bad time for Nathan to die. And it was certainly a bad way. The same drugs that stopped the progression of the disease in so many others did not work for us. I cannot remember Nathan as he used to be— robust, playful, full of life. I can only remember the last few months, the relentless advance of this ravaging disease, the melancholy but courageous warrior that Nathan became, the sunken eyes, the flesh hanging from the bones. The helplessness. And ultimately the despair. The desire to die.

Saturday, Nathan's desire became reality.

I should use this column to eulogize Nathan. He deserved it. He loved me unconditionally. He is the kind of man who restores your faith in humanity.

Maybe someday I will write that eulogy. But first, duty calls. And an unfinished fight.

Join me in the battle against AIDS. I will do anything and everything to fight this disease. And equally important, join me in the battle against the prejudice that haunts AIDS victims. This is not a disease that happens only in Africa, in the inner city, and among those who take risks with their sexual conduct. It is a disease that strikes at the core of our humanity. That merits our compassion. That calls for our tears.

It is a disease that sometimes hits home. And like a hurricane, nothing in its path will ever be the same again.

7

Friday, May 7

MARYNA STARED AT THE GRAINY PICTURE on the monitor in disbelief. There, big as life, was the most incredible little bundle of flesh she had ever seen. Cameron's baby!

Fortunately for Maryna, Dr. Lars Avery pointed here and there, giving her and Cameron a guided tour of the little figure on the screen. "Here's the head… We can't really tell if the baby's a boy or a girl yet… See the little body curled around right here? This is called the 'crown-rump length,' which in pregnancies typically gives us a very accurate estimation of the gestational age. Of course with this baby, we pretty much know that already…"

On and on he went, Maryna soon losing focus of what Avery said, as she smiled with contentment at the screen. She watched, mesmerized, as the baby pulsed rhythmically, keeping time with Maryna's own heartbeat.

It's a girl, she thought. *I know it is. Doesn't matter that Dr. Avery can't tell yet. I can feel it. The doctor will learn soon enough.*

A sudden drop in Avery's tone of voice interrupted Maryna's thoughts. She turned from the monitor to the rumpled doctor's grim face and knew immediately, although she had not heard what he said, that he had seen something terribly wrong.

"I don't like the iliac angle of the pelvis," he mumbled, shaking his head and measuring something on the monitor, "or the nuchal skin fold thickness." He turned to face Maryna and Cameron, pausing in an apparent search for just the right words.

"I can't be sure," he said softly, "but there are some critical landmarks that would indicate the need for further screening for Down syndrome. I'd like to schedule a triple-screen blood test and another ultrasound in a week or so."

Standing behind Maryna, Cameron inhaled sharply. "Down syndrome?" she asked. A pause, then, "I bury my husband five days ago and now *this?*"

"I can't be sure," replied Dr. Avery solemnly. "If it looks the same next week, I'd recommend an amniocentesis."

"And then?"

"Let's cross that bridge later, and only if we need to," said Avery. He turned from Cameron to Maryna, who sat in stunned silence staring at the monitor. "Down syndrome is a serious genetic defect," he explained. "A chromosomal abnormality for which there is no cure. Down syndrome children are special kids who bring their own unique set of challenges and rewards."

Maryna felt the force of the words like a bullet to her stomach. A "serious genetic defect," he had said. The same words appeared in the surrogacy contract to describe when Cameron could require that Maryna abort the baby.

A heavy silence descended on the room, broken only by the amplified swoosh of amniotic sac fluids keeping steady time with Maryna's galloping heart. "There's nothing you've done wrong," Dr. Avery added as the tears welled up in Maryna's eyes. "This is a genetic disorder that occurs at the moment of conception."

"Would the other frozen pre-embryos have this defect too?" Cameron asked after another uncomfortable silence. She spoke over Maryna's head, as if the surrogate mother were not there.

"Not all of them. Only the ones that are exact genetic replicas of the implanted embryo."

"Meaning?"

"There are eight zygotes still cryopreserved, and according to Dr. Richards, they were created through the blastomere separation process from four different pre-embryos. Two of the eight embryos would have the same genetic defect; the others would not."

"In other words, " said Cameron, almost matter-of-factly, "if we terminated this pregnancy and implanted the others, we would have a 75 percent chance of having a normal child."

Avery nodded thoughtfully. "If we assume that the cloned embryos don't have any other genetic deficiencies—that's correct."

Maryna winced at this exchange. She couldn't bring herself to look away from the monitor. Her tears blurred the rough image, keeping her from blinking the baby back into focus, but nothing could keep her from feeling pain for this child. In her mind's eye she could see it all too clearly, a sharp profile of the baby, mouth open in awe and wonder, a new life ready to be nurtured in the womb and ushered into a world of endless possibilities.

"We'll work through this," Cameron promised, placing a hand gently on Maryna's shoulder. "One step at a time."

A chill washed over Maryna, and she wondered if Cameron could feel her shiver. But she detected no reaction from Cameron other than a soft sigh. And then she heard Cameron add, almost as an afterthought, "Sooner or later, something good is bound to happen."

8

Monday, May 17

MITCHELL WANTED TO START EARLY his first day at Davenport & Associates but had been told by the Rock to meet Sandra Garrison at 8:30. After this first day, Mitchell would have his own key to the office and could start anytime he wanted. He planned on starting no later than 7:00.

The office was on Military Highway, in an out-of-the-way Norfolk strip mall about ten miles from Mitchell's new apartment. This morning the commute had taken nearly thirty minutes. Tomorrow, at 6:45, with no traffic, he would be there in half the time.

He had no problem finding a parking place, as several of the bordering office and commercial units appeared vacant. An old dry-cleaning shop stood on one side of the law office and an insurance agency on the other. The only establishment that even remotely interested Mitchell was a bagel shop about three doors down. In the twenty-five minutes he had been waiting for Sandra, he had only seen a few customers.

At precisely 8:45, Sandra Garrison arrived and unlocked the office for Mitchell. She was a chubby lady no more than five foot one or two, with rosy cheeks and a quick smile. She had been with Mr. Davenport for more than twenty years, she said, through good times and bad. She claimed that when she started, her hair was "black as coal," but the practice of law "will do this to you." Every strand of her hair, as far as Mitchell could tell, had turned to gray and had the texture of straw. It looked like it needed brushing, but Sandra didn't seem to notice or care.

"Feel free to show yourself around for a few minutes, Mr. Taylor," she said after she had unlocked the doors, turned on the lights, and fired up her computer. "I'm going to get the coffee started, then run down to the bagel place. Want anything?"

"No, thanks." It seemed strange to hear a lady nearly twice his age call him Mr. Taylor. He had an urge to tell her that wouldn't be necessary. But he was a lawyer now. He guessed that was one of the perks.

It would be the only perk he encountered that morning. Over the next several hours, Mitchell Taylor's idyllic first day of practicing law, which he had been dreaming about for weeks, came crashing into the hard and cold realities of the daily grind of a small-firm personal injury lawyer.

His "office," such as it was, consisted of a cramped, windowless room furnished with a pressboard desk, a small credenza, a frayed maroon desk chair that swiveled and tilted to the left, and a wooden client chair. There was a telephone and an old-fashioned 486 computer—the Rock had apparently not yet discovered the Pentium chip. There were boxes and Redwelds covering the desk, the chairs, and nearly every square inch of the floor. There was not one thing hanging on the walls.

Mitchell immediately cleared a path to walk and a place to sit. He went to his truck and brought in a box of framed diplomas and a framed print of Stonewall Jackson leading his troops and earning his nickname at First Bull Run. He unpacked the items and leaned them against the wall. He would hang them later, when he had a few spare minutes. Then he plugged in his laptop computer, grabbed a cup of coffee from the small, dirty kitchen just off the back hallway, and settled in for a full day's work.

During his first three hours, he handled two irate clients who couldn't understand why it was taking so long to win the large settlement the Rock had promised and managed to get chewed out by a defense attorney who called from Norfolk Circuit Court, where the Rock had failed to show for a motion-to-compel hearing. When Mitchell punched the mute button and called out to Sandra for an explanation, she said that the Rock was in Virginia Beach Circuit Court that morning and couldn't possibly be in two places at once. This didn't seem to satisfy the lawyer on the phone, who still swore that the Rock had promised he would be in Norfolk.

Mitchell also interviewed three potential clients, rejecting each of their cases. Sandra was absolutely beside herself with delight, claiming that Mr. Davenport's greatest weakness was that he could never say no to a potential client. Considering the cases, Mitchell didn't really see that he had any choice.

In the first case, a salty old lady in her fifties claimed to have spilled McDonald's coffee on her lap after going through the drive-through. Her case came complete with photos of a burn mark high on her flabby left thigh as well as a receipt from McDonald's that, sure enough, showed the purchase of a small coffee. However, Mitchell happened to know, from his studies in tort class, that after suffering a nationally publicized multimillion-dollar verdict against it for spilled coffee, McDonald's had changed the temperature of their fresh brew so that it couldn't possibly produce those types of burns. Mitchell encouraged the woman to get a second opinion from another lawyer and sent her on her way.

The second person, a high-school senior accompanied by her mom, was determined to sue the tanning salon she had patronized just before going to her senior prom. She still sported the effects of a nasty skin burn, inflicted when she dozed off in the tanning bed while the proprietor chatted merrily to her friends on the phone. Mitchell rejected that case on the basis of contributory negligence.

The third person, an angry man in his late forties, wanted to sue his neighbors for the wild parties that kept him awake until all hours of the night. This loss of sleep, and the man's tendency to compensate by catnapping at work, supposedly got the man fired. Mitchell encouraged him to see a property law specialist and sent him from the office with recommendations.

At 11:30, things started getting interesting. Four more potential clients sat in the lobby, waiting for an intake interview, while the pink phone message slips started stacking up. Sandra, who had been chatting up the potential clients all morning and taking flak over the phone, showed up at Mitchell's door with two small folders in her hand. It was the first time all morning Mitchell had not seen her smiling.

"We don't have much in these files yet," she said apologetically as she placed them on the desk without looking at Mitchell. "Just a police accident report and maybe the physician's notes explaining what kind of treatment they were getting."

"Okay," Mitchell replied suspiciously. Of all the files strewn throughout the office, in his room, the conference room, Sandra's desk, and who knew where else, he wondered why these two files would merit such special attention.

"Did Mr. Davenport talk to you about these?" asked Sandra gingerly.

"No. I haven't seen Mr. Davenport since the day he hired me."

"I was afraid of that," Sandra lowered her eyes but made no effort to leave.

"Are you going to fill me in or keep me in suspense?" he asked.

"Well, these, um, these two files, according to our tickler system, are somewhat time sensitive…"

Mitchell's phone rang. Sandra reached over to pick it up, but Mitchell placed his hand on top of hers, holding the receiver down.

"How sensitive?" he asked.

"Well, I believe the statute of limitations expires…well…today." Sandra said it so softly Mitchell barely caught the words. Still, they hit him like a train.

"And we haven't filed suit yet?" he asked incredulously.

Sandra shook her head.

Mitchell let out a moan from deep in his throat. "You mean to tell me we've had these two cases in the office for two years, and we wait until the very last day to file suit?"

Sandra nodded. "Mr. Davenport has been trying to settle them without filing."

"Oh, man." Mitchell twisted his face in disgust. "Then I've got to draft the suit papers and have them filed by five." He stood up and tried to pace but couldn't find the room. "Cancel all the client interviews. Reschedule the ones waiting in the lobby now. And hold my calls. We've got to prioritize, and these lawsuits are our number-one priority today."

"Yes sir, Mr. Taylor." Sandra still did not leave, and the look of consternation disappeared as quickly as it came. "There is just one other thing, Mr. Taylor, but you're going to like this." Now she positively beamed. "The film crew is here to tape some new commercials. Mr. Davenport said there's no sense paying an actor when we've got a handsome young lawyer like you actually working for us."

Mitchell stared at her and plopped back down in his worn chair. It creaked and tilted precariously. He put his chin on his palm and made no effort to hide his displeasure. The smile quickly left Sandra's face as she scurried out of his office, nearly tripping over some dusty files along the way.

———————

"This isn't working," insisted the platinum blonde with the bright red lips and short black leather skirt. Her name was Lauren Upjohn. Her business card referred to her as a "Marketing Specialist." She was apparently not happy with the third take on the first of the new commercials they were filming for the Rock.

Mitchell glanced down at his watch and sighed. They had been at it for more than thirty minutes and had made little progress.

"Maybe you should just go back to using the actor," he suggested.

"No, honey, you're perfect," Lauren cooed, sizing him up. "You've got those rugged good looks and when you square up that jaw—babe, you look *unmovable.*"

She was animated, walking around the Rock's large office, nearly bumping into her own cameraman. "But you've also got those beautiful blue eyes that scream compassion. It's *perfect* for our new theme: 'an iron fist in a velvet glove.'"

She paused for a moment, making a face, searching for the right words. "It's just that on television, you've got to exaggerate your emotions… You've got to grab the viewers' attention. Show them the iron fist that will hammer the insurance companies." At this Lauren slammed her slender fist down hard on the Rock's desk. Mitchell jerked back, then smiled at himself. "But also show them the velvet glove that says you *care* about your clients." Now Lauren tilted her head to the side and looked at Mitchell with puppy-dog eyes.

"Maybe you should do it," suggested Mitchell. "I'm a lawyer, not an actor."

She walked around the desk and gently held his elbow. "All lawyers are actors, Mitchell. You've just got to let it out." She positioned him, then turned toward her cameraman. "Let's try it again, Rodney."

Lauren stepped away from the desk, and Mitchell picked up the phone.

She nodded her head encouragingly, then held up a finger. "Wait, I've got an idea."

Mitchell said nothing.

"Did you ever play sports?" she asked

"Yeah, I played a little football."

"Wonderful!" she exclaimed. "I figured as much. I mean, you're ripped, babe," she tilted her head and winked. "Anyway, just close your eyes for a second and picture something with me…"

Mitchell felt like an idiot. He rolled his eyes but didn't close them.

"C'mon, Mitchell, humor me."

He let out another sigh and closed his eyes.

"Great. Now picture your archrival, one of those blocker or tackler type guys coming at you, screaming, out for blood. Can you see it?"

Mitchell nodded. He was lying.

"Good. Great. Now that's the insurance company. When you open your eyes, say your lines, but keep that picture. That's the kind of emotion we're looking for."

Mitchell opened his eyes, the phone still clutched to his ear. "No!" he said forcefully into the phone. "Offer rejected! You call that a settlement;

I call it a sellout." Mitchell's jaw was set, the words pouring from his mouth in a fury. He was actually picturing Lauren as the insurance company, rather than some football player from the past, but it was working. "We care more about our clients than our caseload. We'll take this case to the Supreme Court if we have to, but our client will be treated fairly."

As he said the last words, his fist came slamming down on the desk, landing with explosive force, the same way it had a dozen times in the past half-hour.

"Cut! Great! That's just great!" gushed Lauren. "That's definitely a keeper. Imagine this: As your final words come out, we focus in on the fist and show it in slow mo, with a blur of motion behind it, as it slams into the desk. Then the background music and that great tagline: 'Davenport & Associates. An iron fist and a velvet glove.' You like it?"

"I thought you'd never ask," responded Mitchell immediately. Then he paused to gather his thoughts and capture the perfect sarcastic tone. "I think I feel like one of those championship wrestlers on television, screaming at the camera, threatening people. Why don't we just get me a cute nickname, like 'the Cannon' or something. That way we could have the Rock and the Cannon…"

Lauren's eyes lit up, and Mitchell held out his palm. "I'm just kidding."

"Not bad," she injected.

"But this whole approach… It's so phony," protested Mitchell.

"Look," said Lauren, "Marketing is my area; law is yours. In marketing, you've got to have something that distinguishes your firm, makes your brand stand out among consumers of legal services—"

"What's wrong with just the quality of our work?" asked a frustrated Mitchell.

"Hey, if you were getting business just based on the quality of your work, then why'd you hire me in the first place?" Lauren spread her arms, palms turned upward.

"I *didn't* hire you." Mitchell glanced again at his watch, seething. "But it's a question we'll have to take up on another day. For now, I've got to get back to my work, quality or not. Let's reschedule these other shoots."

"Suit yourself, but it's cheaper to do three in one sitting, that way—"

"I know," interrupted Mitchell. "But we really *need* to reschedule." His tone did not leave the matter open for debate. "I'm going to have a long talk with Mr. Davenport about our whole advertising approach."

Lauren apparently got the picture, stepped forward, and briskly shook his hand. "It's been great working with you today," she snapped. "Here's my card. You're going to love this new spot. We should be able to edit tomorrow and have it airing by Wednesday. In the meantime, we'll keep the old ones running."

"Thanks," said Mitchell. He stuffed the card in his pocket, retreated to his office, and pitched the card in the trash. Then the iron fist picked up a pen and went back to drafting pleadings.

9

BY 5:00 p.m. MITCHELL HAD SUCCESSFULLY filed his first two law-suits, one in Norfolk Circuit Court at 4:15 and one in Virginia Beach Circuit Court at 4:45. He had prayed all the way to the Virginia Beach courthouse for favorable traffic. He thanked God several times on his way back to the office.

By 6:30, Mitchell's fatigue began to register. He used his own key to get back into the office, flipped on the lights, and slumped into one of the comfortable chairs in the reception area. Things had to change around the office. It was too disorganized, cases were slipping through the cracks, and the clients were not being served. Mitchell determined that he would work every night until he had leafed through every box and document file, made an inventory of every case kicking around the office, and put together a system to flag significant deadlines and tasks to be done. He was amazed that the Rock had no such system in place. He ordered a pizza, then settled in for a long night of document review.

There was no telling what kind of ticking time bombs lurked in these files, but he might as well find them now. He estimated that there were well over a hundred files at different stages of completion lying around. He would start with the ones in his office.

Mitchell had not even made it halfway through the first box when the telephone rang. At first, he decided to let it go, but then curiosity won out.

"Davenport & Associates," he said.

"Workin' late?" asked a thick-tongued voice on the other end.

"Who's this?"

"Your boss," said the Rock. "Sandra said you got those cases filed. Good work."

"Thanks," Mitchell said. *No thanks to you,* he thought.

"Well, I got somethin' for ya t'morrow." The Rock's words were coming out slurred and distant, as if he weren't holding the phone close to his mouth. Mitchell could hear music blaring in the background.

"What?" Mitchell asked loudly.

"Fer t'morrow," answered the Rock. "Somethin' fer t'morrow."

"What is it?"

"Huh? Oh, it's uh…a case." Muffled shouting came from the background. Then the music fell a notch. "What was I sayin'?"

"Something about a case," prompted Mitchell.

"Yeah, the case." There was a long pause. "Oh, yeah. Uh, supposed t' settle but, uh, Mack Strobel, he's the lawyer…mean as a snake. Well, he got all hard-nosed."

Mitchell heard the Rock yell at somebody in the background again. Somebody yelled back, then the Rock continued. "Where was I? Oh yeah, anyway, now we got to go to trial Wednesday. Can you work it up tomorrow?"

"What's the name of the case?" asked Mitchell.

"Right," responded the Rock. "One of them traffic accident cases. Try 'em in our sleep. Work it up, and I'll let you, um, let you take some witnesses."

"Okay. But what's the name of the case?"

"Parsons versus somethin' or somebody or other." Then the Rock laughed. It was a loud and exaggerated cackle. "Red case file. You'll find it. I owe ya."

"All right," responded Mitchell. "I'll see you tomorrow."

"Hey, kid?"

"Yeah."

"You sure you don't drink?"

"Yeah, I'm sure."

Mitchell heard the Rock yell something like "He ain't comin'" to some folks in the background. Then to Mitchell, "Well, if you change your mind, there's some women down here wouldn't mind meetin' ya."

"I'll keep it in mind," said Mitchell as he hung up.

He stared down at the phone. *What have I gotten myself into?* He absent-mindedly read the pink slip on top of the pile of papers next to the phone. It was marked "urgent," like every other message Sandra had left for him today.

The call was from Cameron Davenport-Brown, and in parentheses Sandra had written "Mr. Davenport's daughter." The phone message indicated that Cameron wanted a return call and had a case she wanted the firm to handle. At the bottom of the slip was an additional note.

"Mr. Davenport would like you to handle. (He and his daughter have not been on the best of terms.)"

I hope she can wait until Thursday, Mitchell thought. Then he started his scavenger hunt for a red case file involving a client named Parsons. He would not wait until tomorrow to start working it up.

10

May 17

My dear little one,
It's been ten days since I've written you. Sorry. But I'm scared and confused.
For ten nights, I cried myself to sleep.

It was not supposed to be like this. And I have no idea what to do. I hope
someday you will read this and understand. I've tried to do the right thing.
Whatever that is.

Ten days ago, I had my first ultrasound. A picture of you in the womb! I
couldn't wait. All those mornings of throwing up, racing to the toilet to unload
every ounce of food in my stomach, saying "good morning" to you while I was
doubled over turning myself inside out, would now be worth it. I would get to
see you! Not real clear, of course, but at least an outline of your little life growing inside me.

The doctor tells me do not expect too much. We were only three months
along. Can you believe it's been that long?! We would see your little head, arms,
and legs. Though the doctor said we would not yet be able to tell, I was certain
you would be a girl (you'd better be!) because Cameron really wanted a girl.
You would be all curled up in a ball. Maybe we could make out tiny fingers and
toes that had just started developing.

I half expected to see more. Cute little round cheeks, big blue eyes and
curly blonde pigtails that I know you one day will have. Okay, I'm a little ahead
of things. But you will be beautiful—I can feel it. I mean, look at your mom. Not
me, silly, I just carry you and protect you for these nine months. I'm what others
call a surrogate. But Cameron, your real mom, she is beautiful! She has striking
outer beauty and a deep inner beauty as well. And she loves you very much.

But you know all this. I've said it all so many times before.

Ten days ago, we got some bad news.

I knew something was wrong a few minutes after Dr. Avery started explaining the ultrasound. He had a serious tone in his voice and sad droopy eyes—I was so scared I could barely focus on what he said.

What I heard pierced my heart.

He couldn't be sure, he said, but there was a possibility that you have Down syndrome. I have heard about that disease, but I have never known what it meant. Tears started clouding my eyes; I couldn't control them; I wanted so badly for this one thing to go right—for you to be a perfect little child.

Cameron, your mom, was pretty upset, which I totally understand. It was not until after she left, that I finally got the courage to ask the doctor some questions.

It is a genetic disorder, Dr. Avery explained, which means you have an extra chromosome in the twenty-first pair. He said he can't be sure just on the basis of the ultrasound. He said it was nothing I had done before or during our pregnancy. It was not my fault, the doctor said, as if he were looking for somebody to blame. He said there are often physical differences between a Down syndrome baby and a normal child as well as some possible medical problems. I asked him to write a few of these things down so I could remember them and look into this further.

Before I left, Dr. Avery scheduled a blood test and a second ultrasound. We'll have that tomorrow. If things still look the same, he will schedule another test—an amniocentesis, say his notes—to decide for sure if you have Down's.

Since that first ultrasound, little one, I've done some research of my own. I've found that they can't really tell much from an ultrasound. I will believe you don't have Down syndrome, but even if you do, I know that everything is going to be all right. I know you are unique and beautiful and very, very special. And you are a fighter. For some strange reason, even though it doesn't make sense, I feel like you got that from me. After all, it *is* my blood flowing through your body.

I've read about mothers of kids who have Down syndrome. Those moms talk about what great blessings their children are—about how full of life and joyful their precious angels are; about how much those moms have learned through the pure eyes of a Down syndrome child; about the victories in the normal things of life.

You *are* perfect, little one—whether you have Down's or not—because the One who created you made you perfectly unique. Together, we will get through this ultrasound and all these other tests. For me to describe how much I love you already—it is impossible. I didn't think I could ever feel this much love. It will be so hard to give you to your real mom after you are born. I'll do it because I know it's best for you—she's more ready to raise a child than me. And she loves you very much. (Have I told you that enough?) I'm only twenty-two, little one, and in times like this I realize how far I am from being the kind of mother that you need—the kind of mother my mom was for me.

I'm scared and I'm tired. So if you wouldn't mind, I'd like to get some sleep tonight. Do you suppose you could keep your wiggling and rooting around to a bare minimum for a change?

Just kidding, of course. I can't really feel you yet, though Dr. Avery tells me you actually started moving at about six or seven weeks. In fact, he says that you are probably swimming around the womb like crazy. I cannot doubt it. If you've got any of my blood flowing through you, then you'll find it hard to sit (or swim) still.

Remember, I love you with all my heart. Now, get some sleep, little one, or you'll be sorry—no more pickles and ice cream.

Maryna put down her pen and stared at the pictures of the Down syndrome babies that she had carefully placed on the table in front of her. She was trying to visualize how this genetic disorder might affect the precious little girl she carried, and the pictures were streaked with Maryna's tears. Now, as she closed her diary, she blinked back a new round, determined to be brave. For this child's sake, it was time to be strong, like her own mother had been. If the second ultrasound confirmed Dr. Avery's preliminary diagnosis, then she would get to know some of the local mothers of Down's children better and learn from them. She would figure out a way to cope.

She could not bear to write in the diary about Cameron's reaction to the ultrasound. Before that day, Cameron had been so good to Maryna. But Nathan's death and the news of the possibility of Down syndrome seemed to be more than Cameron could bear. All Cameron could talk about since the ultrasound was terminating the pregnancy and starting again with the remaining embryos. It would not be fair, Cameron said over and over, to bring "it" into the world under these circumstances. Cameron would be a single mother, she reminded Maryna, and would be unable to provide the increased time and attention a "special-needs" child would require. It would be best for everyone to try again.

Maryna respected Cameron, even feared her. And Cameron seemed to be so sure of the right thing to do. But to Maryna, termination was an unthinkable option. This baby was no longer an "it." Maryna had seen the ultrasound with her own eyes. If nothing changed with the second ultrasound and the amniocentesis, she would summon the courage to confront Cameron and fight for the child's life, regardless of the terms of the surrogacy contract. Maryna knew that's what her own mother would have done—what her own mother had in fact done—when she traded her life for Maryna's.

Thinking about her own mom, Maryna felt alone and wholly inadequate to face the challenges lying before her. She shrank from the task of disagreeing with Cameron and wondered how something so beautiful could turn out so wrong. She absent-mindedly rubbed her stomach, noticed she was doing it, and softly smiled. She was instantly ashamed of the guilt pangs she felt about this pregnancy.

It was beautiful, this miracle of birth. For a moment, she thought only about the incredibly tiny life growing within her, this helpless little thing that was totally dependent on her. And she marveled.

She rose from the small kitchen table and headed across her tiny studio apartment, stopping in front of the dresser. She focused on the small wooden carving of Buddha sitting cross-legged on the top. She focused on the intricate lines of the Buddha's face and drew strength from the look of calm, the eyes of understanding. There was a quiet resolve there, and Maryna's problems seemed to shrink in the face of it.

She found herself repeating the chant of her *metta,* as she had done on so many other occasions. The words, repeated from habit, took on new meaning with this life growing inside her. To terminate this child would be to renounce her faith, her life's commitment to universal compassion and love.

"All beings, whether weak or strong—omitting none—in high, middle, or low realms of existence, small or great, visible or invisible, near or far away, born or to be born," at these words, she paused her quiet chant, lingering there, imagining the life inside her. After a moment she continued, still softly, yet somehow more forcefully, "May all things be happy and at their ease! Let none deceive another, or despise any being in any state; let none by anger or ill will wish harm to another! Even as a mother watches over and protects her child, her only child, so with boundless mind should one cherish all living beings…"

Maryna's voice trailed off. The thought of what she would have to do exhausted her. The words of the chant were beautiful and compelling. But they would call forth a most difficult action. She would have to confront Cameron, and her carved and lifeless Buddha would be of little help during that encounter.

"Go to sleep, little one," she whispered to the child growing within her. She turned and headed back past the kitchen table and straight toward the bathroom to get ready for bed. "You've got a big day coming up tomorrow, and your mom could really use some sleep tonight."

She was so tired, so fully exhausted from work and the weight of her worries that she didn't even stop at the refrigerator for ice cream.

11

Tuesday, May 18

THE PARSONS FILE WAS A MESS. It had taken Mitchell nearly an hour the previous evening just to find all its parts. Only now, after two hours of early morning work under the upward gaze of Stonewall Jackson, whose picture still leaned against the baseboard at Mitchell's feet, was Mitchell finally able to piece it together.

Melinda Parsons was a fifty-eight-year-old fast-food worker who had been involved in a severe traffic accident more than three years ago. She claimed to be proceeding through an intersection on a green light when the driver of an eighteen-wheeler, turning right on red, plowed into the passenger side of her vehicle. The truck driver claimed that he looked before proceeding, saw Parsons coming toward the intersection at a safe distance, and then began his turn. Parsons must have been speeding, the truck driver claimed, or he would have been able to safely make the turn.

This simple case would have been a good file for Mitchell to cut his teeth on, except for the woefully inept level of trial preparation. The Rock had not subpoenaed the police officer who investigated the scene. The Rock hadn't located any witnesses. He hadn't notified the orthopedic surgeon who operated on Melinda and ended up fusing two vertebrae in her back. The medical records and bills, and the documentation concerning lost wages, had just been thrown haphazardly into the file. The client had not even been in the office to rehearse her trial testimony.

By nine o'clock, Mitchell had constructed a list of all the things that had to be done that day—that very day—to be ready for trial the next. If he cancelled all of his appointments, he might have just enough time. He was determined not to be embarrassed on his first case.

Five minutes later Sandra Garrison interrupted his concentration with her cheery humming as she graced the office with her appearance for the day. Mitchell could hear her settling in, checking phone messages, and booting up her computer.

She made her way to Mitchell's office. "Want a bagel or some coffee?" she asked.

"No, thanks. And Sandra, hold all my calls and cancel any client interviews today. I've got to get the Parsons case ready for trial." Mitchell smiled then returned his gaze to the papers on his desk, hoping Sandra would get the hint.

She did not. After a few seconds of silence, with her standing in the doorway and fidgeting, Mitchell looked back up and set his pen down.

"What is it?" he sighed. "Spit it out; I don't bite."

Sandra shifted her weight from one foot to another. She hunched her shoulders, checked her watch, and took a deep breath.

"Mr. Davenport left me a voicemail message last night. You know that important case that his daughter is involved with?" Sandra's eyes darted up just long enough to glance at Mitchell, then quickly returned to the floor. "Well, there's an important meeting with the lawyers for the other side, Kilgore & Strobel, at ten o'clock this morning. Apparently, we're just local counsel. Some lady from the National Right to Choose Committee is lead counsel. But Mr. Davenport said it's pretty important for you to be there."

Sandra hesitated, her face taut, as if she anticipated an explosion.

"Where is this meeting?" Mitchell asked calmly.

"Downtown Norfolk. The main conference room of Kilgore & Strobel," she replied quickly.

"Why can't Mr. Davenport go?"

"He's got court this morning." Sandra raised her inflection, turning her answer into a question.

"Which court? What time does it start?"

Sandra looked down. "I'm not sure."

She was a lousy liar. Mitchell stared at her as she stood nervously in the doorway, her face turning red. He felt sorry for this woman, so loyal to her employer, so quick to cover with a lie.

"Please get me his home phone number," he said evenly.

Sandra did not budge. She did not look up. The only sound in the office was the distant noise from the traffic on the street in front of the strip mall.

"Now!" Mitchell snapped. "Better yet, get him on the line."

Sandra jumped, startled at the outburst, and scurried off to rouse her other boss from a good night's sleep.

～～

"Yeah," said a groggy voice on the other end of the phone.

"I thought you had court today," Mitchell said coldly.

"Huh? Yeah, I do. What the…what time is it anyway?"

"Billy, this is Mitchell Taylor. It's ten after nine. We're twenty-four hours away from a federal court trial on a case that isn't anywhere near ready, and you're scheduling meetings for me today on some new case I've never heard of, and—" In spite of every effort to control his tone, Mitchell's voice rose with every frustrated word.

"Right, right," the Rock interrupted. "Listen, sorry about that. I tried to reach you last night, but I just…" The Rock's voice trailed off.

"That's all right. But look, I don't have time to go to Kilgore & Strobel today for your daughter's case. I don't know the first thing about the case, and I—"

"Mitchell, Mitchell, listen to me, son. You don't have to do a thing. We're just local counsel. Just show up at the meeting and listen, and while you're there see if you can get a quick meeting with Mack Strobel. He's the defense lawyer on this Parsons case, you know."

As the old man rambled on, Mitchell just held the phone to his ear, his neck muscles tense, shaking his head.

"...talk to Mack about settlement in Parsons," Billy continued. "He's offered 100 K. But that's just the insurance company's money. The liability limits are 100, and the trucking company was self-insured after that. See if you can get 150. I mean, for crying out loud, we got a broken back here. The trucking company ought to kick in something. Anyway, I gotta run. Can you transfer me back out to Sandra?"

"Billy, when we get through with this trial, we've gotta talk. Now's not the time, but we can't keep working like this."

"Yeah, I hear ya," moaned Billy. "We gotta talk, that's for sure. Let's schedule lunch on Friday or maybe next week or somethin'. Now, can you get me Sandra?"

Mitchell jammed the transfer button with his index finger, then dialed Sandra's extension. She was on the other line, and he heard her voicemail click in. Without another word, he transferred his mentor into that never-never land.

"I can't believe I went to law school for this," Mitchell muttered.

12

THE OFFICES OF KILGORE & STROBEL were in the heart of Norfolk's financial district, on the top three floors of a bank tower self-described as One Commercial Place. From the firm's lofty environs, the lawyers had a commanding view of the Elizabeth River and the naval shipyards that formed the industrial core of the area's economy. No view in Norfolk was more breathtaking than the one afforded by the ornately decorated Conference Room A with its glass wall of windows that overlooked the horizon stretching beyond the Elizabeth and as far as the eye could see.

Mitchell Taylor entered the conference room without knocking nearly fifteen minutes after the scheduled meeting had begun. Interstate traffic had been a bear. When he finally arrived in the downtown area, he had cruised nearly every side street in the vicinity of the office searching for a place to park. He finally settled on a metered spot that promised to tow his car after an hour. He knew the meeting would last longer; he would have to see if the meter maids were punctual.

As he entered, the meeting came to an abrupt halt for a round of introductions. The exquisitely dressed Winsted Mackenzie shook Mitchell's hand and displayed a broad and plastic smile while he told Mitchell to help himself to the coffee or juice that had been set out on a credenza at one end of the conference room.

A thin and brooding man with a sharp, angular face introduced himself as Blaine Richards and did not bother rising. He simply swiveled in his chair and shook Mitchell's hand as if he could hardly be bothered.

The other two participants were women seated on the opposite side of the table. Mitchell knew this was his team, so he walked around the table to join them. He tried to guess which one was the Rock's daughter but saw no family resemblance in either of them. The shorter of the two was a thick middle-aged woman with short, layered dark hair, rounded shoulders, and an oval face expressing distrust. She wore a gray pinstriped suit designed to impress and rose quickly and forcefully to shake Mitchell's hand. "Nora Gunther," she said, "National Right to Choose Committee."

"Nice to meet you," said Mitchell.

Nora did not respond.

"Sorry I'm late. Traffic was a mess."

"I'm sorry too," Nora said coldly.

The other woman was younger and taller, nearly Mitchell's height, with long blonde hair pulled back in a braid and a handsome face highlighted by deep-set and intense green eyes. She was not pretty in a classical sort of way—there was no softness in her features—but she had an attraction that flowed from strength, the good looks of the neighborhood tomboy who had aged gracefully. She smiled warmly and seemed a little embarrassed by Nora's aloofness. Mitchell found himself mesmerized by the luminous green eyes.

"I'm Cameron Davenport-Brown," she said simply. "Thanks for coming."

"Thanks. Sorry to interrupt." Mitchell took a seat next to Cameron. He was thirsty but noticed that nobody had touched the coffee or juice. It was apparently not that type of meeting.

"Don't worry about it," said Win. "You haven't missed much. Nora was just explaining why she doesn't think the agreement between Dr. Brown, Cameron, and GenTech will hold up."

Win smiled at Nora condescendingly, which she took as her cue to launch back into her legal argument. She leaned forward, elbows on the table, and locked her eyes on Win.

"In the time since Nathan and Cameron signed that contract, everything has changed. Nathan couldn't know this at the time he revised his will, but it appears that the embryo being carried by the surrogate mother has Down syndrome. Under these circumstances, this so-called contract, and the will executed by Dr. Brown, are basically worthless. If you destroy the remaining embryos, you destroy any potential for Cameron to have healthy offspring. No court will uphold your flimsy contract under that scenario."

Nora slid a thick legal document across the table toward Win Mackenzie, apparently returning it to him. Without even looking at it, Win slid it down toward Mitchell.

"This is the agreement your client signed when she and her husband came to GenTech Fertility Clinic for help," Win said to Mitchell. "Part three, section two sets forth in plain language how frozen embryos should be disposed of. You'll notice that, in the event of any disagreement between Dr. Nathan Brown and your client, the contract provides that the frozen embryos will be donated to GenTech for medical research."

Mitchell picked up the lengthy document and started to glance through it. As he did, Win pulled another document from the pile in front of him and slid it toward him.

"This is the Last Will and Testament of Dr. Nathan Brown—" he began.

"Don't bother," snapped Nora. She grabbed the document, then slid it back toward Mackenzie. "We all know what the will says…"

We do? thought Mitchell.

"…but it makes no difference. And Mr. Mackenzie, there's no sense in addressing your comments to Mr. Taylor. He's local counsel. I'm calling the shots."

Thanks for the confidence. Why don't I just slip out and go back to preparing the Parsons case?

Nora drew her lips into a tight, thin line. Win stared back at her in silence, a smirk lingering on his face.

When at last she spoke, Nora clipped her words off with a stiff formality, firing them like missiles at the two men seated across from her.

"Mr. Mackenzie and Dr. Richards, you are both intelligent and resourceful men. And you are both also keenly aware that the United States Supreme Court, for the better part of the last thirty years, has recognized a woman's fundamental right to make her own decisions about whether or not she wants to bear a child. That is why, under circumstances like these—where Cameron has no other options for having a healthy child—we believe that the legislation prohibiting cloning for reproductive purposes will be declared unconstitutional. Thus, Cameron would have a constitutional right to have these cloned embryos implanted in another surrogate. And Mr. Mackenzie, you ought to be ashamed of yourself for even suggesting that these fundamental constitutional rights can be stripped away by your client's flimsy contract. Particularly when your client somehow persuaded Ms. Davenport to sign this unconscionable document at one of the most vulnerable moments of her life—"

"Wait a minute! You listen to me." Blaine Richards was rising from his seat, his finger pointing at Nora. "If you're suggesting for one minute that there was any coercion, undue influence, or—"

"I wasn't finished," said Nora sternly. "Let me finish."

"You let *me* finish," Blaine shot back.

Win Mackenzie immediately placed a calm hand on his client's arm. "Let her say what she came to say," he counseled without taking his eyes from Nora. The smirk was no longer on his lips. Richards gave his own lawyer a look of fierce rebuke, then sat. He stuck out his jaw and stared past Nora, out the conference room window.

"Thank you," Nora said to Mackenzie. Then she turned her glare to Blaine Richards.

"If you fight me on this, I will embarrass you and your clinic in the national media. I'll let the whole world know that you don't care whether a woman like Cameron only has one chance to become a mother. I'll tell every woman who is struggling to conceive that you and your clinic care more about the almighty dollar—the ability to exploit these stem cell lines through research—than you do about bringing healthy babies into the world. You'll be the most reviled man in America, Dr. Richards, the very embodiment of corporate greed."

Richards quit looking out the window, leaned forward, and drilled his eyes into Nora. "Is that a threat?"

Mackenzie touched his client's arm again. "This is not the time, Blaine. Let it go."

Nora snorted. "Take it any way you want, Dr. Richards. I prefer to think of it as a promise. You see, sir, 'threat' implies I might not be able to deliver."

Richards swallowed hard, a vein pulsing visibly on his forehead next to his widow's peak. He continued to stare at the insolent woman sitting across from him.

But Win Mackenzie remained the very picture of calm, the sardonic smile returning to his face. This seemed to aggravate Nora Gunther even more than if he had responded as aggressively as his client. His very demeanor seemed to be saying that he was above her antics, that a man of his immense prestige could not be bothered by her childish shenanigans.

"I know this is an emotional issue for you and Cameron—" Win began.

"*Why?* Because we're women? Because we can't handle it like you *reasonable* men can?"

"No. Not because you're women, but because these are emotional issues: the right to have children and the specter of a possible birth defect." Win spoke slowly now, with condescension, as if he were lecturing a teenage daughter. "But Dr. Richards and I don't have the luxury of responding in a visceral way. We've got a fiduciary duty to Cameron's deceased husband, Dr. Brown, to follow his expressed desires by honoring the original contract. If the shoe were on the other foot, and Dr. Brown wanted to implant the embryos *against* Cameron's wishes, we'd be making the same argument on behalf of Cameron.

"GenTech's clinic is worthless if its patients can't trust it to honor basic contractual commitments on these hyperemotional issues. So, Nora and Cameron, I'm sorry, but our position is nonnegotiable."

"As is ours," Nora shot back, flopping another fat legal document down on the table. "You've got twenty-four hours to rethink your position. After that, I've instructed our local counsel to file suit seeking a preliminary and permanent injunction challenging the legislation against implanting cloned embryos. The suit also requests that the judge prohibit you from destroying these embryos in the meantime and award us punitive damages."

Nora now had Mitchell's undivided attention, as he presumed he was the local counsel she was talking about. He sat up a little straighter in his chair and twisted his face into a nasty scowl.

"You do whatever you've got to do," said Win, as calmly as before. "Our position is *not* negotiable."

Nora stood and started packing her documents, leaving the lawsuit sitting ominously on the table. She then turned to leave, with Cameron and Mitchell following close behind.

On the way out, Mitchell stopped at the credenza and grabbed a bottle of orange juice that he had been eying the entire meeting.

"Thanks for the juice," he said with a smirk. He followed the women as they stalked out of the meeting.

❦

Before leaving the lobby of Kilgore & Strobel, Mitchell received his marching orders on Cameron's case. If he didn't hear from Nora by noon the following day, he should file the lawsuit she handed him and obtain a hearing on the preliminary injunction motion as soon as possible.

"We need a hearing within a week," demanded Nora. "Make sure it coincides with your calendar. I'm working out of our D.C. office, so I'm not admitted in Virginia. I'll need local counsel present."

"And Mitchell, we'd rather have you than my dad on this matter," Cameron said. Her face quickly flushed. "Nothing against my father, it's just that I'm not sure he's at the top of his game anymore. But I called him anyway because I heard he had hired a new associate. I thought that if his firm served as local counsel in this high profile case, it might at least generate some additional publicity. You know, help the firm."

"I understand," said Mitchell. "We appreciate the gesture. I'll handle this myself."

After a few more unnecessary instructions from Nora about the details of filing suit, the women left, much to Mitchell's relief. He asked the receptionist if Mack Strobel was available to meet for a few minutes. She called Strobel's secretary and invited Mitchell to have a seat in the lobby.

Five minutes later, a large and menacing man with a tanned bald pate and a black goatee entered the reception area. He was three inches taller than Mitchell and had broad shoulders and a confident gait. He extended his hand and greeted Mitchell in a booming baritone.

"Mr. Taylor, I presume. To what do we owe this honor of a personal visit?"

"The Parsons case," replied Mitchell. Both men were standing. Strobel was not nearly as hospitable as his partner. "We'd like to settle, but you've got to come up with some money from the trucking company. We'll take 150."

Strobel crossed his arms. "I already knew that. I hope Davenport didn't send you all the way over here just to repeat your prior demand."

"We've got twenty-four thousand in meds," said Mitchell as he reached into his briefcase and pulled out a neatly indexed stack of medical bills. Strobel did not take them. "We've got another twelve, nearly thirteen thousand in lost wages. And we've got a 20 percent disability rating from Melinda's orthopedic. That's thirty-seven thousand in specials with a partial disability claim to boot. She's a likable person. She'll make a good impression on the jury. I'd say 150's a steal."

Strobel threw his head back and laughed. "You've also got some pretty serious problems." His haughtiness made Mitchell's jaw clench in defiance.

"Like what?"

"Like the fact that it's your client's word against my client's word on the speeding issue, and your client's credibility will be severely damaged by a prior conviction for shoplifting."

Strobel paused as Mitchell stoically absorbed this news. Mitchell did his best not to register surprise. *Why hadn't the Rock mentioned that? Did he even know about it? What other surprises were lurking in this file?*

"Like the fact that I'll challenge the necessity of all the medical treatment, particularly the physical therapy, and you don't have her physical therapist under subpoena. Like the fact that I'll challenge the disability rating with a reputable orthopedic that you never bothered to depose. Like the fact that I will invalidate your client's estimate of lost wages because she didn't reduce it to a net present value, and you don't have an accountant on your witness list who could do that."

Strobel paused again and rubbed his chin, studying the expressionless face of Mitchell. "You get the picture."

"Yeah, I do. But you're losing sight of the *big* picture. Your client had the red light. My client was severely injured. There's no dispute about that. Throw in the fact that your client is a big trucking company, and I'll take my odds anytime. All this other stuff," Mitchell made a sweeping and dismissive motion with his free hand, "is just irrelevant detail. Only lawyers care about that stuff. Not jurors."

A thin smile crossed Strobel's lips. He nodded his head for a moment, leaned forward, then lowered his voice as if imparting a grave secret. "Mr. Taylor, it's been my experience from about thirty years or so of trying cases, that trials are won and lost on these issues you cavalierly dismiss as insignificant details. Great cases, like impressive buildings, are built one brick at a time. Lawyers are bricklayers, Mr. Taylor, nothing more, nothing less. And frankly, you don't have your bricks in order to build much of anything tomorrow."

Then, with an air of self-satisfaction, Strobel turned without saying another word.

As he walked away, Mitchell called out after him, "That's it, then? You're not budging from a hundred thousand?"

Strobel stopped and turned back toward Mitchell. "That's a generous offer, Mr. Taylor. You ought to take it and run. And tell Billy if he takes the hundred, I'll also buy him a drink." Strobel laughed, turned again, and disappeared down the hall.

13

May 18

My dearest Dara,

I finally dare to call you by name! How does it sound? Dara. Dara. Dara. I love it.
It was my mother's name.

I wanted to call you that name since the day I found out I was pregnant.
But until today, I was afraid I would jinx myself (and you). But when Dr. Avery
saw the ultrasound early this morning, he confirmed what I knew all along.

"I think it's a girl!" he said. My heart jumped. I don't know if you could feel
it. It just felt like it was beating so hard and fast it was going to come right up
my throat.

"Her name is Dara," I wanted to tell Dr. Avery. "After my mother."

But I said nothing. Your mom was there for a while before she had to leave
for another meeting. You are Cameron's baby really, and she will want an American name, which will be much better for you anyway. But at least for these first
few months, and forever after in my thoughts and heart—just between us—your
name will be Dara.

According to our customs, the name Dara determines many things about
your personality. It means you have a desire and understanding to help others,
but if you are not careful, you will become too involved in the problems of
others and fill your own life with worry. (Who does that remind you of?) You
will desire a home and family of your own, and you will have the ability to
create harmony in your family relationships. You will be caring, forgiving, and
tactful, and you love all children. You will strive never to injure anyone's feelings, even if it means that you suffer greatly. All this, little Dara, I know from
your name. And I know that you will live up to it, even as my mother did.

Forgive my sloppy writing, as I ride the Greyhound bus back from Dr. Avery's office in Norfolk to my apartment in Elizabeth City. It's about an hour and a half ride, and the bus driver, he seems determined to hit every bump in the road. At least no one is sitting next to me. And it's a good thing. I am so emotional today. It's been a roller coaster, really.

We got some good news and some bad news on the ultrasound. First, the good news.

I already told you about the girl part—but I guess you knew that. Anyway, that was exciting for me. And I also got to see you again, a much better picture this time. I just sat there and watched you on the monitor. It was unbelievable!

You are so very tiny. You are only about two or three inches long and weigh maybe a few ounces. Can you imagine? I could hold you easily in the palm of my own hand, and my hands are not very big.

You've got these little tiny fingers, feet, and toes. I couldn't actually see the toes in the ultrasound, but Dr. Avery tells me that you would already have them. And I can make out your skinny little fingers. Listen to this! You already have a heartbeat, your own brain waves, your very own fingerprints and are sensitive to touch, light, and noise. You can even suck your thumb, and I swear that's what you were doing!

Anyway, you were so cute, just all rolled up in a tiny little ball, looking as comfy and secure as anyone could ever be.

Okay, little Dara, now for some bad news. Dr. Avery says that this ultrasound looks a lot like the one he did ten days ago in terms of the angle of that iliac thing and whatever else he looks at to determine Down syndrome. He scheduled an amnio for next week. That test is a little risky and, in his words, will be a "little uncomfortable." Don't you love the way these doctors say things? They are so—what's the word?—underspoken. What he really means is the test will be most painful!

Anyway, the doctor said it would take at least ten days after the test before we can get the results from the laboratory. Then we will know if you have this problem or not. Dara, to me it is no difference. I love you just the way you are. Just the way you were created.

We may be in for a little fight on this, because others, including Dr. Avery, think it may be somewhat unfair to bring somebody into the world knowing that they will have severe physical challenges. He told me I would have to quit thinking about myself on this issue and start thinking more about what's best for the baby and for Cameron. But that's what I've been trying to do!

This is why I'm glad I'm sitting alone right now. Even though I try not to, I get teary-eyed every time I think about this. And I feel like such a fool. Dr. Avery told me not to look at this with my heart but with my head. It sometimes feels like it's just you and me against the world. And honestly, Dara, I feel like we're fighting for your very life. How can you leave the heart out of it?

I'm sorry. I didn't want to burden you with this. But someday, you will be a beautiful young lady reading this diary. And I just want you to know how much I loved you right from the start, how much I believed in you even when things looked dark, and how much I was willing to sacrifice to bring you into this world.

Your real mom, Cameron, loves you very much as well. She only wants the best for you. I know that. Don't ever doubt that, or doubt her love for you, no matter what happens, little one.

There, I've said it and I'm tired. Let's take a nap on this bumpy ride home. We've got to work tonight, which means time on our feet. They'll probably swell up again, but hey, that's life.

I love you, Dara.

Good night.

14

MITCHELL THREW HIS BRIEFCASE into the front seat of his F-150 pickup and breathed a sigh of relief. The meter maids were nowhere in sight. He slipped out of his suit coat and tossed it inside as well. He was already starting to sweat, his shirt sticking to his back. It was nearly ninety degrees, and the humidity was off the charts. His black truck felt like a blast furnace. Too bad the coolest color for a truck also happened to be the one that attracted the most heat.

With sweat beading on his forehead, Mitchell lowered his window and turned the air conditioner on full blast. By the time he hit the interstate, it was just beginning to cool off. He rolled the windows back up.

As he drove with one hand, he reached into his briefcase with the other and withdrew the suit papers that Nora Gunther had handed him. With one eye on the road, he started glancing through the thirty-five-page document. Nora was from the old school of drafting—lots of whereas, heretofore, and hereinafter clauses. The document was hopelessly repetitive and so full of legalese that it sounded like something that Blackstone himself would have written more than two hundred years ago.

But the gist of the suit was just as Mitchell feared. Cameron was trying to preserve her frozen embryos for future implantation. Mitchell could live with that. In fact, he passionately believed that the fertilized embryos, clones or not, were living human beings worthy of all the protection that every other living person enjoyed. Cameron was challenging the contract she had signed with GenTech, which clearly specified that the embryos would be donated for research if either parent objected to their transplantation. Mitchell was in favor of Cameron's position on this too; if these embryos were indeed human lives, then they shouldn't be used for experimentation no matter what the contract said.

But Cameron and Nora were also challenging the federal legislation that prohibited the cloning of embryos for either experimentation or reproductive purposes—the Bioethics Act. And to Mitchell's horror, they were basing their argument on the same principles that initially established the right to abort a child—the notion that there was a constitutional right to autonomy in reproductive decisions that could not be impinged by federal law.

This whole idea of cloning was anathema to Mitchell—so absolutely contrary to everything he believed in. *What kind of Pandora's box will we open if we win this case? What kind of evil will be advanced in the name of science? Will I be responsible for helping to pry open the door for cloning experimentation on the human race? Let's see, I'll take a boy—a blond-haired, blue-eyed, six-foot-three stud just like the Baywatch character. Do you suppose you could clone a few Julia Roberts girls for me while you're at it?*

The questions rattled around inside Mitchell's head as he cruised down Interstate 264, swerving in and out of the right lane, his attention riveted on the pleading in his right hand. It was time for lunch, but he had lost his appetite. His head ached as he tried to think through the implications. Should he refuse to participate? But if he did, what would it matter? The Rock would just serve as local counsel, and the case would go forward without Mitchell. And what of those tiny embryos—frozen in time? He knew there were over a hundred thousand others just like them. But it was only these eight he had been asked to save. Could he refuse? Must he refuse?

He was getting nowhere on his own. The more he thought, and the more he postured arguments and counterarguments, the fuzzier things became in his own mind. He didn't notice the traffic he was whizzing by, the looks from other drivers as he drove erratically, didn't even notice his best-loved country music songs playing on the radio. His mind was lost in a quagmire of legal ethics and his impending duty to play a role he had not auditioned to play.

Suddenly, a thought came with absolute clarity. He needed a second opinion. He should get the advice of a man of absolute integrity and impeccable judgment—an expert in the field of legal ethics. Someone of experience who would pull no punches. He would head east on 64 and exit at Indian River Road. It was time to pay a visit to Regent Law School and borrow the big brain of his old nemesis—Professor Charles Arnold. There was no one he respected more. The professor would shoot straight.

He put down the pleading and started tapping the steering wheel to the beat of the music. He wondered how long the Dixie Chicks had been singing. He hoped the professor was in.

❦

As Professor Arnold finished his appointment with another student, Mitchell nervously paced the hallway outside the office. Time was wasting. He had a trial to prepare. Maybe this was not such a good idea after all.

Finally, it was Mitchell's turn in the small office littered with papers, textbooks, and legal periodicals. The walls displayed pictures of every graduating class that Arnold had taught, his "hall of shame" as he called it, as well as a dilapidated Nerf basketball hoop that looked like it got more than its fair share of attention. After a pleasant "What brings you here?" from the professor, Mitchell got right down to business.

"I need your advice on a case I'm handling, or at least I've been asked to handle, as local counsel," Mitchell explained. He was surprised to find himself somewhat nervous. He licked his dry lips and continued. "It's pretty complicated, but basically I've been asked to represent a client who wants to keep a fertilization clinic from experimenting on eight frozen embryos created from her eggs."

"And her husband opposes this?" asked the professor gently.

"Yes."

"What does the contract with the clinic say?"

Mitchell was amazed at how quickly the professor had zeroed in on the critical issues and picked up the essence of the lawsuit. Mitchell was sure he'd come to the right place.

"The contract says if either parent doesn't want the embryos implanted, then they can be used for experimentation."

The professor nodded. He folded his hands in front of him and squinted at the ceiling. "If I remember right, the courts typically favor the spouse who doesn't want the embryos implanted on the basis that one spouse should not be able to force the other one to bear the responsibilities of parenthood. This reasoning, of course, assumes that the spouses are not already parents, therefore assuming that the embryo is not already a child. I disagree with the whole premise of the argument."

"So do I," said Mitchell. "And in this case, my client would not be able to have children any other way. She's had a total hysterectomy, including the ovaries."

"Why didn't you say so?" asked the professor. "That changes everything.

"You've got a good shot on this one," the professor continued. "To my knowledge, there's never been a case where one of the spouses could argue that this was their *only* chance to have children. I'd take your side of this one."

Mitchell couldn't resist a small half-smile. Professor Arnold had always drilled into his classes that they should never frame their legal arguments until they *completely* mastered all the facts of the case. He had just violated his own cardinal principle.

"I feel like I missed a joke here," said the professor.

"I was just thinking about how you would tell us to master all the facts before framing our legal arguments…"

"Yes."

"Well, a few more details for you: You may want to know that these eight embryos are all clones, created before the Bioethics Act was passed."

Arnold's eyes shot open, and he leaned forward. "Clones?"

"Yep. Every one of them. And in order to win this case and implant the clones, we've got to challenge the Bioethics Act as unconstitutional."

Mitchell pulled the lawsuit out of his briefcase and placed it on the desk.

"Let me see that," said Arnold.

He took the document and began reading it carefully, flipping one page at a time, devouring every word. Mitchell began feeling uneasy just sitting there watching him read for what seemed like forever. But Professor Arnold seemed oblivious to Mitchell or the time, intent only on carefully reviewing every word of the pleading—mastering the facts—before he would speak again.

When he finished, he carefully handed the document back to Mitchell. "Interesting," he mumbled. "Interesting."

"Would you still take my side?" asked Mitchell.

The professor stood and stretched, as if deciding whether he would answer the question at all. He picked up his Nerf basketball and, with a flick of his wrist, banked one through the hoop. Mitchell grabbed it from the floor and tossed it back to him.

"I'm the professor, how 'bout I ask the questions?" Arnold raised his eyebrows, looking for a response. Mitchell nodded his head. Another flick of his wrist, another shot. This time a miss.

"Do you believe those cloned zygotes are fully human?"

Mitchell thought for a moment; he felt like he was back in school. But the nervousness was gone, and his thinking was clear, precise. "Sure."

"Why?"

"They're a union of sperm and egg. They're fully encoded with DNA. If you implanted them in a uterus, they would grow into an embryo, then into a baby, then into a toddler, then into an adolescent, then, if the fates were unkind, into a law school professor."

"They should be so lucky," another shot, this time a swish. "Do you believe in the death penalty?"

"Where'd that come from?"

"Yes or no?"

"Yes."

"All right, Mitchell. Assume you've got eight innocent black clients sitting on death row." Professor Arnold smiled. "Some of my kin, so to speak. Suppose the only way to get them off death row is to challenge the death penalty on equal protection grounds—argue that it applies unequally to men of color like me. You going to make that argument?"

"Of course," said Mitchell, knitting his brow.

"Even though other guilty men might go free based on the same argument?"

"Mmm, I see your point."

Mitchell was pensive now, looking past Professor Arnold and out the window. The professor seemed focused only on his Nerf hoop—shooting, rebounding, pacing, shooting again.

"The way I see it, you've got eight clients on death row," he concluded. "Yeah, I'd still take your side of the case."

"Even if it means overturning—"

"Mitchell." The professor stopped moving and looked at his student with penetrating brown eyes. "You've got to learn something if you want to be a good lawyer." He hesitated, creating a certain tension in the room just by the seriousness of his tone. "There's only one judge in that courtroom, and it's not you—it's the man or woman wearing the black robe. And there's only one Judge in this thing called life, and it's not you either. Get the picture?"

Mitchell nodded. He had heard the rumors about Professor Arnold going down to the boardwalk every Friday night to do some street preaching. He could picture it all now as the professor warmed to his task, morphing instantly from law professor to evangelist.

"Let the big Judge worry about where this is all heading. Who knows? He may use the very line of Supreme Court cases that have justified millions of abortions to now save hundreds of thousands of embryos. Who knows what He'll do? Your job, and your *only* job, is to

represent the cause of your clients—at least the ones that you believe in.
Let the judge with a little *J* worry about how this affects the law, and let
the Judge with the big *J* worry about how this affects everybody else in
the world. You worry about your client. Because all they've got is you.
And they need an advocate, not a judge."

Mitchell sat silent for a moment, nodding his head. "Thanks, Professor," he said at last.

Charles Arnold smiled warmly. "Welcome to the big leagues, buddy.
I think you're ready."

15

IT WAS NOT UNTIL MIDAFTERNOON that Dr. Blaine Richards had a chance to get back inside his large corner office at the GenTech headquarters and close the door. He turned to his computer, ignored the dozens of e-mails that had arrived since that morning, and pulled up his Internet brokerage account with Charles Schwab. The week before, he had transferred $800,000 to the account. It was time to make a move.

He checked GenTech's stock first. It was holding steady at eighteen on a day with relatively low volume. Like many biotechs, his company's stock had experienced a euphoric runup for a few years and then retreated to more rational levels. The government's attempts to regulate the industry, from stem cell research restrictions to anticloning legislation to some proposed national legislation governing surrogacy contracts, had all hurt the profit-and-loss prospects of the industry and thus the price of the stock. Richards himself owned more than three million shares of GenTech outright, and he had lost more than $20 million when the stock took its recent nosedive.

And there would be more rough days ahead if Nora Gunther followed through with her lawsuit. Richards knew that GenTech's stock would take a hit on the announcement of the lawsuit, and it would be a good time to off-load some shares in advance of the suit if he didn't have to worry about the insider trading laws. Instead, he would have to ride out this initial plunge, then figure out a way to get the stock back up over twenty bucks a share.

His magic number: $20 per share. He had thousands of call options that he had earned as bonuses—each was triggered at the $20-per-share price. For every dollar that GenTech's stock climbed over $20, Richards would personally earn nearly $2 million from the options and $3 million from the shares he owned outright. He'd earn $5 million at $21, $10 million at $22, $50 million if he could get the share price to $30! Every time he pondered this, his heart beat just a little faster. And every time he thought about it, he would tick off the particulars of his plan, probing for weaknesses, and find none. He would be a very rich man soon. There could be no stopping him.

And today he decided to grab a little bonus. He pulled up a financial screen on his two main competitors—ProGen and Reproductive Services, Inc. (RSI). ProGen was trading at $46.50. RSI was at $42 and some change. With a few clicks of the mouse, Richards put his money to work. He took out call options on both companies—betting their stock would rise. He bought $400,000 of call options on ProGen at a strike price of fifty, and $400,000 of call options on RSI at a strike price of forty-five. The expiration date on the options was July 19—just two months out.

It was a huge gamble. If the stocks of his competitors stayed roughly the same for the next two months, Richards would lose every dime. Only if ProGen broke through fifty, or RSI broke through forty-five, would he profit. But if they did, he would profit handsomely, and his hundreds of thousands would quickly become millions and even tens of millions. Big risk, big reward.

He confirmed the orders, let out a deep breath, then picked up the phone. In a few minutes, he was talking again to Win Mackenzie.

"I've been thinking about your proposal," Blaine told his lawyer, "to suggest to Cameron that we would preserve the embryos until we find out if the baby being carried by the surrogate mother really has Down's. I agree that if the baby's healthy, this whole issue becomes moot. But I talked to Dr. Avery a few minutes ago, and he confirmed what the Gunther woman said this morning. The blood test and the second ultrasound don't look good. He's doing an amnio next week."

"All that offer would do is delay the inevitable," Richards continued. "We've got to stand on principle here, Win. A contract is a contract. Besides, this Gunther woman drives me nuts. If it were just Cameron, I'd be inclined to try and deal with her. But women like Gunther don't understand nice. If we give in to her here, she'll be back with another client ready to sue our butts next week."

"I can't argue with that," said Win, who had never argued with anything Richards had suggested.

"So let's throw down the gauntlet. Tell them to take their lawsuit *and stuff it,*" Richards said emphatically.

"I may use slightly different terminology," replied Win. "But I get the idea."

"We can't lose this case, Win. I don't care what it costs to defend. But we can't lose it."

"I know," said Mackenzie. His voice sounded less than sure.

In his mind's eye, Richards could see his lawyer sitting in his plush office, staring at the picture of the samurai on the wall, already starting to worry. *It's a good thing I'm not depending on my lawyer to pull this out,* Richards thought. *In a fair fight, I think I'd put my money on Gunther.*

"I've got every confidence in you, Win," Richards said. "And it's a good thing, because this is a bet-the-company case if ever there was one."

Blaine Richards smiled at his own cleverness—his masterful choice of words. He had moved his knight into position. Now it was time to call his queen.

On the way back to the office, Mitchell called Sandra to check for messages. He got her voicemail. No surprise there. She was probably on another of her liberal breaks. He dialed the Rock's extension, which kicked out to Sandra's extension, and landed him in her voicemail again. *What a firm!* A client could be calling with a hot new case in the middle of the day, and they would end up wallowing around in Sandra's voicemail, leaving a message that might never get returned.

As a last resort, Mitchell dialed his own voicemail and worked through the half-dozen messages. Most were left by Sandra, forwarding

to him the clients and other lawyers who had been unsuccessfully trying to reach the Rock for days. One message grabbed Mitchell's attention, and he immediately dialed the number she had left, anxious to
hear a friendly voice.

"What?" said the edgy voice of Nikki Moreno.

"Nice way to answer the phone," replied Mitchell. "You must have
learned that from the Rock."

"Mitchell Taylor?"

"You're in luck."

They talked for several minutes about Nikki's hot new cases at Carson & Associates and about Mitchell's challenges with Billy Davenport.
Mitchell savored Nikki's voice. She was so full of spunk and attitude.
Mitchell let her ramble, sometimes listening to the words, sometimes
just sucking in the energy from the in-your-face perspective she brought
to life. He felt energized by just listening to her. She had heard about his
trial tomorrow—Nikki seemed to know everything—and she had
called to encourage him. And it worked! The challenges he was facing—
his attempts to salvage Billy's law practice, to get ready for tomorrow's
trial—suddenly seemed less formidable while talking with Nikki.

"All right," said Nikki, winding down, "I gotta run. But first, here's
four pieces of advice for your first trial tomorrow. You ready?"

"For the trial or the advice?"

"It doesn't matter, cause they're both coming anyway. Okay. Number one. Don't let Strobel intimidate you. Strobel can be a jerk. Remember, he puts on his boxer shorts one leg at a time."

"Should I be writing this down?"

"Second," Nikki continued, "you're the plaintiff, so you sit at the
counsel table next to the jury box. Knowing you, you'll probably get
there so early that you'll be the first one in the courtroom, and it's
embarrassing when the other lawyer comes in and makes you move to
the other counsel table. Trust me on that one."

"The things they don't teach you in law school."

"Third, I don't care what parts of the trial Billy says he's going to do and what parts he assigns you to do, be ready for everything. At the last minute, he'll say," Nikki lowered her voice and mimicked the Rock's drunken slur, " 'Why don't you take the opening, Mitchell?' or 'Why don't you take this cross-examination, Mitchell?' And by the way, when the judge calls for a bench conference, you go alone. Billy's breath will knock the judge out."

"That's encouraging," Mitchell noted dryly.

"Hey, you can't say I didn't warn you." The sound of a horn blared over the phone. "You jerk!" Nikki yelled. "Where was I? Oh yeah, fourth." She paused for effect. "Are you ready for this?"

"I was born ready."

"Okay. In your opening statement, ask for twice as much money as you think the case is worth. This is especially critical for you, Mitchell, since you said you didn't really want to be a plaintiff's lawyer. This won't come naturally. *But do it anyway!* It's the only way you can compensate your client, to get her justice in a civil case. Remember, she only gets one day in court, one chance to get what she deserves. And when you ask for a big verdict, *try* not to do it with a red face. Maybe a little red on the tips of the ears, but not a red face. Let the jury know that you *believe* in your client and in her cause. That's the most important thing."

"That much," said Mitchell, "they did teach in law school. 'Zealous representation.' Don't worry, Nikki, come tomorrow, you'll think I was a born plaintiff's attorney. And if you have any doubts about that, then you obviously haven't seen my new television commercials. 'The iron fist in a velvet glove…' "

"You're kidding!" Nikki squealed with delight. "They talked you into shooting some commercials?"

"*Forced* me."

"This I gotta see," Nikki said emphatically. "The iron fist and the velvet glove…I love it. With any luck, maybe some Hollywood producer will see it, and you can break into some daytime soaps."

"Shut up," said Mitchell.

Nikki laughed. "That must be the iron fist talking."

16

BY 11:00 P.M., AFTER A FULL EVENING of waitressing at The Surf House, Maryna Sareth was exhausted. As usual, she hitched a ride home with one of the other waitresses, an older woman named Joanne who didn't mind going a little out of her way to help Maryna. Maryna arrived on the street in front of her apartment a few minutes later, tired but content.

She thanked Joanne for the ride, then walked alone down the dark driveway of a single-family home in one of the nicer residential neighborhoods in Elizabeth City. Trees and shrubs lined the long driveway of the stucco home, creating a bizarre mix of shadows from the distant streetlight. It was dark and quiet, the air heavy and moist, but Maryna was used to it. She could hear a faint chorus of frogs and crickets, the occasional car buzzing by on the street in front of the house. She made her way down the driveway by memory, not sight.

There were no lights on in the main residence, which was not unusual. It was actually the second home of some friends of Dr. Nathan Brown, a house close enough to the beach and luxurious enough that they could rent it out most weeks in the summer. The large five-bedroom house had beach décor and a swimming pool out back. Maryna lived in a small but quaint one-room apartment over the attached three-car garage.

She noticed that the small dormer window to her apartment was dark. It was her habit to leave a small reading lamp lit so that she would not have to enter her place in complete darkness. The bulb must have burned out.

Maryna loved her little place. The main room was a combination kitchen, bedroom, and living room. She had a small bathroom with a shower off to one side. An A-frame gave the apartment the trendy feel of a studio loft. And the furniture was all new—a beautiful queen-sized bed, a large-screen television, built-in bookshelves, and a beautiful pine dresser and vanity set. It all came with the apartment; she had bought none of it.

The best thing about the place was the price. She had moved here just before she entered into the surrogacy contract with Dr. Brown and Cameron. For legal reasons, she had to leave Virginia and establish residence in North Carolina. As Dr. Blaine Richards had explained, Virginia required court approval of surrogacy contracts, which would slow down the process unreasonably. The Virginia courts also gave the surrogate mother a certain length of time after birth to assert rights to the baby and, most important, would not allow the real parents to pay the surrogate mother a dime.

By having Maryna move to North Carolina, explained Dr. Richards, the contract could be interpreted under North Carolina law. Maryna could waive her rights to the child from the start, without the court's involvement, and she could also be paid $9,000—$1,000 per month of pregnancy. In addition, Dr. Brown and Cameron promised to find her a place to live in Elizabeth City.

At no cost to Maryna.

As she reached the garage and prepared to climb the outside steps to her apartment, her mind raced with thoughts of her future. For the first time in her life, she was actually getting ahead. With her long and slender legs, wide brown eyes, bright smile, and bubbling laugh, she attracted more than her fair share of flirtatious beachgoers and big-league tips at The Surf House, especially now that the temperatures were warming up and she could wear shorts to work. Plus the colleges were just starting to let out for the summer. The patrons seemed to love her accent, often breaking into a slight smile just listening to her talk. She had made nearly $150 tonight—on a weeknight! She would take advantage of it while she could, before she really started showing, before she had to wear maternity clothes.

She saved every dime. During the day, she studied for her GED. After she delivered this baby, she would take the exam, then get a student visa and go to college. She had no doubt she would pass the exam. School and tests had always been easy for her.

America: the land of dreams and opportunity. It was finally happening for her.

She had spent the last six years becoming as American as possible. She learned the culture and perfected the grammar, purging her vocabulary of all things Cambodian. She spoke nearly flawless English highlighted by her distinct accent. She dressed American. And the more she adopted this country, the more her looks seemed to take on the flavor of the father she barely remembered—an American relief worker who had charmed and seduced Maryna's mother and stayed for another six years before returning to his homeland.

Maryna had spent those years—the first six of her life—in a bilingual home, with talk and dreams of the family one day coming to America. Then her father left without warning, taking the joy of the family and an important piece of her mom with him. But the dream of coming to this land never died. And ten years later, the dream became reality.

In her heart of hearts, Maryna wanted to be an actress, but she no longer allowed those dreams to take root. It was impossible really, and she reminded herself of that often. There were two reasons, neither of which she could do anything about. The first was a matter of physique. She might have the enchanting looks, and she was certainly thin enough, but she didn't have the sensual curves of the American women who made it big. And unlike so many of them, she wasn't willing to have surgery just to fulfill Hollywood's notion of the perfect body.

In addition, acting would mean living in Hollywood. *Los Angeles.* The city of unspeakable atrocities inflicted on her by the Snakeheads who brought her to this country. When she could not pay the remaining ten thousand that she owed them, they made her work it off. She became their slave. And they forced her to do things no sixteen-year-old should ever see, much less experience. It was in Los Angeles that she had learned to disassociate her mind from her body, to become soulless as the disgusting and perverted men had their way. She learned to act the part without *feeling* anything. She could even suppress the contempt and disgust for the men who used her, and the shame at allowing herself to be used, until it was almost as if these indecencies were happening to someone else, and she was just a disembodied spectator watching her own life's play.

She escaped Los Angeles one night under cover of darkness, without ever paying the Snakeheads what they said she owed. She would never go back.

Acting was out of the question.

She would be a teacher, she had decided. She would coach drama, write screenplays, and inspire other actors and actresses, young men and young women who could steal the heart and inspire the spirit. It was her own small slice of the American dream. And tonight, as she turned the key on the door of her apartment, it seemed closer than ever.

―――

Things were winding down early at The Beach Grill, the customers beginning to slowly shuffle home. Not Billy Davenport. The Rock was just beginning to hit his stride.

He sat alone at a barstool, chatting up the bartender and the occasional person who dared take up residence next to him. Tonight's hot topic was the predicted winner of the *Survivor* series from the jungles of South America. The Rock knew it would be the retired CIA agent who was now one of the three finalists. He was willing to bet even money with anyone who wanted to wager against his man. The bartender could hold the bets, the Rock explained, and disburse the funds.

There were no takers.

He thought a time or two about young Mitchell. The boy was determined and bright. And he was so idealistic. Reminded the Rock of himself from his younger days. *Give him a few years,* the grizzled veteran thought, *and the teetotaler will be down here throwing a few down with me the night before a big case.*

The legal profession, especially trial work, would eat you alive. Give you ulcers. The Rock had long since stopped worrying about justice and started focusing on survival. Nobody was ever satisfied. The greedy insurance companies wouldn't pay what the cases were worth. The greedy clients wanted more than they deserved. The judges seemed annoyed if they actually had to try a case when the parties refused to settle. And the defense lawyers—well, the Rock had a few choice thoughts about them as well.

The Rock had learned the hard way about the dangers of getting emotionally involved with the clients. Now he kept them at arm's length. They were just a case number and an attorney's fee.

If he had only known that way back when. He thought about his early days, a young Rock crusading for every client—David against Goliath. Ah, the passion of the young. But the thought of a young Rock always carried with it memories of the Zimmerman case and the exotic allure of Vicki Zimmerman. She had played the Rock, played the entire system really, and made fools of them all. Just a passing memory of the case, of his own daughter castigating his conduct, of how badly he hurt his wife and the embarrassing results—all the memories made his throat constrict and his stomach fill with bile. That was what, twelve years ago? Maybe more? But he still couldn't get away from it. His life, his reputation, his relationship with his family, had never been the same.

Mitchell wants to practice criminal law, he mused. *But on the side of the angels, the good guys, the cops. He'll need experience. And he might as well start tomorrow. I'll give him the opening and, if he does a good job, the closing, too. At that rate, he'll be a prosecutor in no time.*

"One more, Ted," cried out the Rock as he plunked his empty glass down on the bar. "I mean, how you gonna beat a guy who's been trained in the martial arts *and* the fine art of deception? For all you know, the CIA may have already rigged this television show just to get their agency some good PR and a bigger budget."

Nobody argued with the Rock. He could be very persuasive when he was in his element.

17

MARYNA STEPPED INSIDE HER APARTMENT DOOR, reflexively reaching for the light switch on the wall. A gloved hand grabbed her wrist, yanked her inside the dark apartment, and stifled her scream.

The intruder kicked the door shut and threw Maryna back against the wall. She stared ahead in terror, her brown eyes darting, as she desperately tried to bring the shadowy figure into focus. The intruder was in her face, narrow and cold eyes staring out through holes in a ski mask, a disembodied mouth drawing hard breaths through another larger hole.

Her knees went weak, the only thing keeping Maryna from collapsing on the floor was the force of the gloved hand pressing against her mouth, muffling her initial scream and sobs, forcing her head back hard against the wall.

"Shut up!" the intruder hissed.

And then she felt it—cold steel against her neck. She couldn't see it, didn't dare to even try and look down, but she knew it. A knife! She closed her eyes and tried to stifle her sobs. Her breath came in staccato bursts, her heart pounded in her neck, her entire chin quivered in fear.

"Shut up!" the hideous form demanded again. The hand moved slowly away, inches away, from Maryna's mouth. But hard as she tried, she couldn't catch her breath, and she couldn't stop emitting the small guttural sounds of fear.

Her eyes started playing tricks in the dark. Flashbacks. She saw strong and vicious men crawling all over her, abusing her, laughing at her.

"Listen to me!" her assailant demanded. The hooded figure drove the wedge of a cupped hand against Maryna's cheekbones and under her nose, prying her face upward and backward, slamming her head against the wall again. The pain shot through Maryna's brain, and the room started spinning. She tried to focus and calm herself, but she could not bring her convulsive breathing under control.

She felt the knife press harder against her neck.

"Do you know who I am?" the intruder asked in a raspy and measured whisper, pressing his own body forcefully against Maryna, inching his face even closer. Maryna felt vulnerable and shook in fear. She was trapped, defenseless, and terrified. She tried to will her mind to another place.

She shook her head spastically from side to side—small movements —a motion that was more a tremor than an answer.

"You tried to steal from Tsao Vang," the assailant said. "You owed him and you fled. Now you will pay. It's time."

Maryna caught her breath enough to try and speak. "I…didn't…"

In a flash, too quick for Maryna to even react, the intruder stepped abruptly back, released his gloved hand from her face and launched it as a fist into her stomach. Maryna shrieked in pain, doubled over, then felt her head jerked back up and into the wall. The knife was again at her neck, but she could no longer control the loud sobs and groans as the pain consumed her stomach.

"You have ten days," the man said, "to return to Tsao Vang and repay your debts. Ten days."

She searched for the will to protest, to explain that she had already paid for her own arrival, that it was not fair to charge her for a mother who had never arrived. But it was useless. The pain screamed for attention, mocking her efforts to focus on anything else. Cramps gripped her abdominal muscles, setting her stomach on fire.

"We know you are pregnant. You will be of no use to us this way. *Terminate* the fetus, or I will return and do it myself." The intruder now waved the knife slowly and menacingly in front of Maryna's face. Even in the pitch darkness, she saw the glint of steel.

Leaning forward again, the intruder rotated the knife and lowered it, pressing the point tight against the middle of Maryna's collarbone, just below her neck. From somewhere deep inside, she found the will to calm herself and slow her convulsive sobbing. She stilled herself as completely as she possibly could, while fighting for breath and ignoring the fire in her stomach. She returned the cold stare of her attacker.

The intruder's eyes narrowed at this small act of defiance, and he increased the pressure at the point of the knife, slightly piercing Maryna's skin. With surgical precision, he slowly dragged the knife from Maryna's collarbone down toward the middle of her chest—opening a gash four inches long. She shrieked in pain as the blade sliced her smooth skin.

"That is the mark of Tsao Vang," the attacker scoffed. "By the time this heals, you must be in Los Angeles. Tsao may not be so merciful next time; his mark may not be so short."

Maryna watched in horror as the spiteful lips of her assailant broke into a grotesque smile. Then he leaned slightly forward and, in the most degrading act of all, kissed Maryna on the lips, long and hard. "The men in Los Angeles say they are missing this," he mocked.

She wanted to spit, to bite, or somehow strike out at this man who took such pleasure in her humiliation. But she knew that any further act of resistance, no matter how small, would only make things worse and prolong her suffering. So she forced herself to do what she had perfected so many times before—she disembodied her mind and gave her attacker no reaction at all. She willed herself to ignore the pain and emotions of the moment. She focused on happier times—the simple joys she had shared with her mother. She went someplace far away and stared at her assailant with blank and uncaring eyes.

Then, as quickly as it started, the assault stopped. The intruder pulled away the knife, yanked open the door, and disappeared into the night.

She listened, frozen by fear and stunned by her attacker's abrupt departure. Only the slightest chirping of crickets reached her ears.

At that moment, Maryna, free from immediate harm, seemed to rejoin her body and became overwhelmed with the pain and fear of what she had just experienced. She put her face in her hands and slumped down the wall. She curled into a fetal position and sobbed uncontrollably into the darkness.

The pain ached in her stomach and shot from her chest. "Dara, Dara," she sobbed. "Are you okay, my precious little one?"

As her cries echoed throughout the apartment, she squeezed her knees tight to her body and let the tears flow. They dripped down her chin and soaked into her shirt, joining a crimson ribbon of blood.

18

Wednesday, May 19
Final Draft, Editorial Page, Tidewater Times

TO CLONE OR NOT TO CLONE?
by Cameron Davenport-Brown

The undiscover'd country, from whose bourn
No traveler returns, puzzles the will,
And makes us rather bear those ills we have
Than fly to others that we know not of,
Thus conscience does make cowards of us all,
And thus the native hue of resolution
Is sicklied o'er with the pale cast of thought,
And enterprises of great pitch and moment
With this regard their currents turn awry
And lose the name of action.

—Hamlet

Like Hamlet, who lost the nerve to act, so we have allowed our collective "conscience [to] make cowards of us all" on the issue of cloning. We *imagine* unspeakable atrocities, those "undiscover'd countries, from whose bourn no traveler returns," and it scares us away from even considering a technology that can truly change all of our lives and alleviate untold suffering.

We assume that taking one step down this road will inevitably take us to that dreaded country, and so we declare the entire road illegal. We pass the Bioethics Act, effectively banning cloning of every type. And then we smile with smug self-satisfaction while we watch thousands of sick people die and thousands of infertile couples mourn.

It's time we wake up, face some hard facts about the issue, and determine to do the right thing, no matter what the fearmongers say. It's time to realize that we can take a few scientific steps down a road that can heal millions without going so far that we usher in a new world of Frankensteins.

It's time to consider:

First, that people will be cloned. Like abortion, we can't stop it. Fringe groups like the Raeliens will attempt to clone babies, even if they have to go off-shore to do it. The only issue before us is whether we want to force people into a black market or instead regulate this arena and thereby guarantee safety and effectiveness. The cloning procedure is relatively simple; most capable embryologists could accomplish it with some fairly affordable laboratory equipment. Certainly it is better to have our best scientists using the procedure carefully and circumspectly for beneficial purposes than to have a bunch of rogue scientists applying a hit-or-miss process that may endanger thousands of embryos and create thousands of mutants in the process.

Second, we must realize that there are different types of cloning. In the process called blastomere separation, scientists essentially split a zygote— a fertilized egg—into more than one cell. This process simply mimics the natural creation of twins and can be used to increase the chances of conception for infertile couples. It does not create the types of ethical issues associated with what most of us think of as cloning.

The other type of cloning, somatic cell nuclear transfer, does involve the transfer of the nucleus and genes from one person into the egg cell of a second person, thereby creating a carbon copy of the first person. This is the type of cloning that created such an uproar with Dolly the sheep.

Though Congress failed to distinguish between the two procedures and banned both with the Bioethics Act, we can distinguish them. And we should. The first involves none of the ethical dilemmas posed by the second.

Third, we can and should draw ethical lines and then enforce them. By passing the Bioethics Act, Congress quite literally "threw the baby out with the bathwater." Just because cloning could be abused does not mean it should *never* be used in a responsible, moral, and ethical manner. Take the case of an infertile couple, whose only hope of having children lies in blastomere separation of a frozen embryo. (If there are only a few frozen embryos, the odds of implanting them successfully are remote; therefore, additional "twins" may have to be created). Can we really tell that couple that they should go through life childless because scientists are prohibited from creating embryonic "twins"? Or what about the young lady who desperately needs an organ transplant but cannot find an acceptable donor? Can she not create a "clone" of stem cell tissue that could be harvested into a new liver?

Fourth, cloning is an intensely private question of ethics and religion that is not best answered by the government. If we have learned anything from this country's long and bitter debate over abortion, it is that people have diverse and deeply held convictions on these types of matters. Those convictions are based on religion, morals, and life experiences. They concern matters of reproduction and family—intensely personal and private issues where the government should not interfere. I, for one, resent the government playing the moral policeman in matters involving my own reproductive decisions.

These are not just academic musings for me; this is my life. In today's paper, you will undoubtedly read news coverage of a lawsuit I have filed against GenTech and others in which I challenge the constitutionality of the Bioethics Act. In the interest of fairness, our editors have offered this same editorial space in tomorrow's paper to Senator Jeffrey McWaters, sponsor of the Bioethics Act, so that he might defend that legislation.

Please understand that I did not want this fight—I am not on a crusade to be the poster child for cloning. What I did want was the simple yet profound joy that many women have—the opportunity to mother a healthy child who has a strong chance at a happy life.

I am the mother of eight cloned embryos cryopreserved at GenTech's labs. They were cloned at a time when it was lawful to do so. Now a host of strangers trained in the law—with hardly a passing knowledge of bioethics—will decide for me whether the embryos will be allowed to have a chance at life or will be thrown away. In essence, Hamlet's question, "To be or not to be?," is personal and relevant to us all. I pray we have the courage to answer it justly.

~~

Cameron read the draft for the umpteenth time and resisted the urge to make more changes. She realized she would never be entirely happy with the piece, but at some point, she simply had to let it go. If Gen-Tech didn't compromise, and it became necessary to file the lawsuit today, her editor had agreed to preempt the Thursday editorial page and run her column. He had insisted on reviewing it first thing this morning so he could "run it by Legal."

Cameron's shot across the bow would reverberate around the country. She knew that she would be the focus of intense media attention unlike anything she had ever experienced or perhaps ever seen.

She shook her head in resignation and hit the "send" button, catapulting the article through cyberspace to her editor's desk. There. She had done it.

She leaned back, let out a deep breath, and wondered if she was ready. One thing she knew—her life would never be the same again.

19

Wednesday, May 19

AS NIKKI HAD PREDICTED, MITCHELL TAYLOR arrived in federal
court plenty early. He waited fifteen minutes for the clerk to show up
and let him in the courtroom. Court would not start for another forty-
five minutes. He placed his briefcase at the counsel table next to the jury
box and glanced around, turning full circle—almost gawking—taking
in the full sense of the grandiose room.

His first trial. A day he would always remember.

Other participants started arriving twenty minutes later. The jurors
slowly shuffled in, heads down and quiet, and took a seat in the spectator section. Melinda Parsons arrived, looking flushed and nervous. She
packed her considerable frame into a knee-length dress that probably fit
her better ten pounds ago. The court reporter arrived and methodically
set up shop just under the judge's bench, readying her machine and
paper.

And finally Mack Strobel arrived, looking larger than life as he confidently walked through the spectator section to the front of the courtroom. Trailing him was a young and pretty paralegal and a nicely
dressed representative from the trucking company.

Mack came up to Mitchell and shook his sweaty hand.

"I brought my checkbook," Mack said in hushed voice. "The hundred thousand is still there."

"Make it 150 and you've got a deal," replied Mitchell. He spoke
somewhat louder, hoping that a juror might be straining to hear.

Mack smiled. This time he didn't whisper. "Well, at least we tried

to save everybody both the time"—he hesitated for effect—"and embarrassment of trying this case. It's not my style to expose past criminal
conduct unless I'm forced to do so."

Mitchell stiffened. He could sense Melinda Parsons bristling at the
table behind him, and he noticed a juror or two leaning forward.

"Well," Mitchell said matter-of-factly, "if you want to talk about
embarrassment, wait until I reveal that your company didn't even check
your drivers for past DUI offenses."

"What are you talking about?" Strobel snapped. "My guy doesn't
have any DUI offenses."

"Is that so?" Mitchell asked sarcastically. Then he turned his back
on Strobel and started leafing through some of his legal papers.

Melinda Parsons watched intently as Strobel took his seat. Then she
slid over and whispered in Mitchell's ear. "That guy driving the truck
has DUI offenses?"

"I didn't say that, did I?"

She looked puzzled, thought for a moment, then wrinkled her
brow. "No," she said, "I don't guess you did."

❧❧

By 9:15, two critical players were still missing from the Parsons trial. To
nobody's surprise, Billy Davenport had not yet graced the doors of the
courtroom. Every few minutes, Melinda Parsons would inquire about
him, and Mitchell would assure her that the Rock was indeed coming.
"You know how bad Tidewater traffic can be," he would say.

The second player—the Honorable Cynthia Baker-Kline—was in-
dispensable to the proceedings. Although the trial was supposed to start
at nine, the judge was not technically late. As the lawyers who practiced
in front of this judge knew all too well, it was nine o'clock when the judge
entered the courtroom, not a minute before and not a minute after.

"All rise," cried the clerk, "the Honorable Cynthia Baker-Kline
presiding."

She came out, as usual, looking furious. After a few long, loping steps—scowling all the way—she took her seat high up on the bench. She was all arms and legs, her sharp and lanky bones evident even under the flowing robe. She had black hair pulled away from her face, a long hooked nose, and a jaw that jutted outward and downward toward the litigants. The lawyers—behind her back, of course—called her Ichabod. It was easy to see why.

Ichabod settled in and placed her half-moon reading glasses on the end of her nose. Mitchell found himself staring at them, wondering if they might slide off at any moment.

"Be seated," she demanded in a nasal and grating voice. "Counsel, approach!"

Mitchell glanced quickly around the courtroom—still no Rock— then walked tentatively up toward the bench. He was met there by Strobel.

The judge put her hand over her mike. "Why hasn't this case settled?" she demanded.

Strobel cleared his throat. "Judge," he said solemnly, "it's a traffic accident case of disputed liability. Twenty-four thousand in meds, most of 'em bogus, and we've already offered a hundred thousand, our liability limits."

Ichabod turned on Mitchell. "Is that true?"

"The meds are all legit. Plus my client's got a 20 percent permanent disability rating resulting from two fused disks in her back."

"Did he offer a hundred?" Ichabod asked, glaring at Mitchell.

"Yes."

"Settle."

"Judge, with all due respect, we don't think a hundred fairly compensates…"

"Save it," snapped Ichabod, cutting him off. "I can't make you settle, I know that. But let me tell you a thing or two about the realities of federal court." She looked from Mitchell to Strobel, then back at Mitchell. He could feel the hair standing up on the back of his neck, his fighter instincts setting in.

She hasn't even heard the evidence yet! Her job is to try the case, not coerce settlement. If I have to take on both Strobel and the judge to get a fair settlement for my client, so be it.

"Mr. Taylor, are you listening?"

"Yes, Judge," Mitchell said grudgingly.

"Then hear this. I've got more than three hundred asbestosis cases backlogged on my docket. I've got antitrust cases, product-liability cases, drug cases, conspiracy cases, RICO cases. I don't need a traffic-accident case taking up this court's valuable time. You two wouldn't even be in federal court if the parties didn't just happen to be from different states. Now I know I can't make this case settle, but here's what I can do. Mr. Taylor and Mr. Strobel"—both lawyers nodded—"there will be a half-hour break this morning, a one-hour lunch break, and a half-hour break this afternoon. I'm ordering you to spend every minute—every single minute—of those breaks with each other discussing settlement." She paused and let out a deep, prolonged breath—the very picture of patience strained to a breaking point. "Is that clear?"

"Yes, Your Honor," the two men said in unison.

"No meeting with witnesses, no grabbing separate lunches, no phone calls back to the office—you two meet with each other and figure out a way to settle this case."

"We'll try," promised Strobel.

"Mr. Taylor?" Ichabod raised an eyebrow at Mitchell.

"We'll try," promised Mitchell.

"Fine," said Ichabod. "Now let's get started and pick this jury."

Mitchell walked back to his counsel table and took his seat next to Melinda Parsons.

"How'd it go?" she whispered.

"Good," said Mitchell. "I think she likes me."

20

THERE'S NO TURNING BACK NOW, Cameron said to herself as she hung up the phone.

Blaine Richards had rejected their compromise proposal, Nora reported. Nora was going to call Mitchell Taylor and authorize the filing of suit this afternoon. Nora would hold a press conference in Washington, D.C., later in the day. It would be important to begin working public opinion immediately.

Cameron also called Mitchell's office and spoke to Sandra. She explained that Mitchell was in court and gave Cameron his cell phone number.

"They won't let him take it into court with him," said Sandra. "But the marshals will give his phone back as soon as he leaves. It'll be the quickest way to get a message to him."

Cameron dialed the number. Mitchell's voice instructed her to leave a message.

"Um, Mitchell, it's Cameron. Listen, Nora either has called you or will be calling you shortly to let you know that you've got a green light to file my case today. As you can imagine, there's going to be a good deal of publicity generated by this case, and I think it will be critical that we get a jump on it. If we can get our side out there first, we can probably frame the debate in a way that will be more favorable for us.

"So…I hope you don't mind but I've, um, given a few of my cohorts here at the paper a heads-up on the case and have let them know that you are in court this morning. Nora will hold a press conference in D.C. at three, and I've written a piece for the paper. But I thought maybe, if you didn't mind, a few pithy quotes from the steps of the courthouse probably wouldn't hurt our cause.

"Anyway, thanks, Mitchell. I'll talk to you later. Hope your trial's going well."

Cameron hung up and immediately began calling legal reporters at the paper as well as a few close friends at the local NBC, CBS, ABC, and Fox affiliates. She generously parceled out several off-the-record comments about the case. She promised full-blown interviews later.

She was pretty sure that this first round of coverage would be favorable. She could hear it in their voices. They *owed* her for the scoop. They were in her debt.

Big time.

❧❧

At precisely ten o'clock, just as the jury was being seated, the Rock made his grand entrance. He sauntered to the front of the courtroom, empty-handed but nicely dressed. As he approached the counsel table, Melinda Parsons moved over to allow the Rock to sit between her and Mitchell.

The smell arrived a few seconds before the Rock did. Mitchell recognized it from his college days. It was the smell of stale alcohol, and it couldn't be covered even with a heavy dose of mouthwash and liberal amounts of aftershave. The red and bulbous nose, as well as the noticeably bloodshot eyes, confirmed what the breath suggested—the Rock had already been in the bottle this morning. Mitchell suspected that the Rock simply could not face the pressures of a trial without the crutch of a drink.

"Nice of you to join us, Mr. Davenport," said Ichabod.

The Rock rose to his feet, keeping a hand on the table for support. "Thank you, Your Honor." He smiled a distant smile and slowly sat back down.

"Does plaintiff's counsel wish to give an opening statement?" asked the judge.

The Rock started to rise, but Mitchell reached over and put a hand on his partner's arm. "I've got it," he whispered.

He stood and fastened the buttons on his suit jacket. "Yes, Your Honor."

"Very well, then. You may proceed."

For the next fifteen minutes, Mitchell Taylor was brilliant. He felt natural in front of the jury; he was in his element. He had trained three years for this. He had taken trial practice, won moot court tournaments, and prepped a hundred times in front of the mirror. The jury seemed to like him and his confidence rose with every sentence. Soon he was railing against the insolence of the trucking company, pulling on the heartstrings for his client—her life forever changed—and generally imploring the jury to see that justice was done. He even stole an occasional glance at Ichabod, who seemed to be pulled in by what he was saying in spite of herself.

He was winding down—he wanted to keep it short—when he remembered Nikki's firm advice about asking for lots of money. What she had told Mitchell was true. This was Melinda Parsons' one shot at justice. After this trial, life would go on for everyone else. But for Melinda, her life irrevocably changed by the accident, this trial would make all the difference.

Mitchell donned a deadly serious look and lowered his voice to just the right timbre. "This is my client's one chance for justice," he said, looking the jurors squarely in the eye, "and the only way our system has of restoring what she has lost is to require the defendant to compensate her for her injuries.

"Now I'm entitled under the law to suggest a figure that would do that, but let me remind you that it is ultimately your duty to settle on an amount of your own choosing. I've thought a lot about this, and I take this responsibility very seriously. After carefully considering my client's pain and suffering, her inability to seek certain types of meaningful employment, her mounting medical bills, and the very strong possibility of further surgery, I would like to suggest to you that a fair verdict would be no less than $175,000."

Mitchell said it with all the conviction he could muster, but he thought he saw a few jurors blink and some others swallow hard. He would need to justify his demand further to overcome their hesitation.

"You may be thinking: 'Isn't that a lot of money for this defendant to pay? It seems fair to Mrs. Parsons, but is it fair to the defendant?' Well, you should know that the defendant won't have to pay that entire amount. You see, the defendant has liability insurance…"

The words were hardly out of Mitchell's mouth before Strobel was on his feet. "Objection, objection!" he shouted like a madman. Ichabod was banging her gavel and even the Rock, who had been sitting at counsel table with a faraway smile plastered on his face, now had his head in his hands.

"Your Honor, that's highly improper, and I move for an immediate mistrial," Strobel thundered.

In the midst of the uproar, Mitchell turned from the jury to face Strobel and the judge. "Judge, every word I've just said is true. I can't help it if Mr. Strobel wants to hide these things from the jury."

"Approach!" shouted Ichabod. Her face turned crimson as she leaned forward on both elbows. Mitchell wasted no time hustling up to the bench.

"You too!" the judge said sharply, staring at the Rock. The old lawyer rose slowly, gained his balance, then slowly plodded to the bench.

The smell was back. Mitchell tried to position himself somewhat in front—between his partner and the judge.

"Give him room," snapped Ichabod.

So much for that plan.

"Mr. Taylor, I don't know what they teach you in law school these days," Ichabod's voice was at a fevered pitch, nearly cracking, even as she tried to keep the volume down so the jury wouldn't hear, "but that last remark was highly improper. Highly improper." She paused, pursing her lips and forcing a few sharp breaths out of her beak. "You can never—*never*—mention insurance coverage in a jury trial. It's too prejudicial, don't you know that?"

"I've never been told that," said Mitchell despondently. "It's certainly nowhere in the rules of court or rules of evidence."

"Some rules are not written down," said the judge, a little less harshly. She turned her stare to the Rock. "That's why young lawyers need to be taught these things by experienced members of the bar." His eyes were glued to the floor. It appeared to Mitchell that his partner was trying to hold his breath.

"Mr. Davenport?"

The Rock looked up. He kept his mouth closed and breathed through his nose.

"I hold you responsible for this," Ichabod said sharply. "It's your responsibility to explain these types of things to a young lawyer like Mr. Taylor."

The Rock mumbled something in response. Mitchell guessed that the Rock was saying, "Yes, Your Honor," but it was hard to tell since his senior partner seemed determined to talk without parting his lips.

"I'm going to grant Mr. Strobel's motion for a mistrial—I've got to— but Mr. Davenport, I'm also going to sanction you for wasting this court's time. You must personally pay Mr. Strobel for every minute of time he has spent on this case today at his normal hourly rate. Is that clear?"

There was another conciliatory mumble from the Rock.

"Your Honor?" asked Mitchell.

"*What!?*"

"Your Honor, I'm sorry about the issue of insurance, but can't we instruct the jury to disregard the—"

"*No.* The cat's out of the bag. They can't just disregard that."

"All right, Your Honor. But it's not fair to sanction Mr. Davenport for my comments. It's my responsibility, not his."

"I'll be the judge of that, Mr. Taylor. Now, gentlemen, please return to your seats so we can send this jury home."

"Yes, Your Honor," said all three lawyers together.

This time the Rock opened his mouth and said the words clearly. The smell about knocked Mitchell out.

Like scolded schoolchildren, the lawyers turned and shuffled back toward their seats.

"Is that 100 K still available?" Mitchell asked out of the side of his mouth.

"Not on your life," replied Strobel.

———— ◆ ◆ ————

Mitchell was still giving the Rock an earful as he absent-mindedly picked up his cell phone at the metal scanner. The display said Mitchell had received two messages.

I'll check them later, he thought. He still had a thing or two to tell the Rock.

He walked out the front doors of the courthouse, giving the unsteady Rock a piece of his mind, and stepped into the glare of a half-dozen bright television camera lights.

"Are you Mitchell Taylor?" several voices shouted.

The Rock took a little sideways step and pointed. "Here's your man."

Flashes went off, boom microphones were lowered, and the reporters started crowding in.

What in the world?

"Is it true you represent the newspaper columnist Cameron Davenport-Brown in a case challenging the Bioethics Act?" shouted a reporter.

"Are you going to file a lawsuit today?" shouted another.

Mitchell took a deep breath, squared his shoulders, and put on his poker face.

"My client is fighting to save the lives of eight tiny frozen embryos..." he began.

Videotapes started rolling, reporters started scribbling, and the Rock quietly slipped away from the crowd and headed toward his car. Out of the corner of his eye, Mitchell subtly noticed the Rock's quick escape. The old boy looked like he was in serious need of a good stiff drink.

21

BY NOON ON WEDNESDAY, MARYNA was tired of crying. Every sob pulled at the stitches in her chest and stabbed at her stomach. She had cried herself out, drained every tear.

She tried to forget about her nagging fear for a few minutes, but the bile in her stomach would not stop rising. Her mind and heart were consumed with her problems, her loneliness, and the heavy responsibility she felt toward little Dara.

She paced gingerly around her small apartment, stuffing things into a large duffel bag and an already bulging backpack. Every item she surveyed had sentimental value, but she forced herself to make decisions based on logic, not emotion. Was it a necessity? How bulky was it? How much did it weigh? She would never come back. The Snakeheads knew where she lived. Leaving an item behind meant leaving it forever.

She would take her small Buddha carving, but the rest of the items that formed the small shrine on top of her dresser would stay. She could always erect a new shrine at another place. She had no room for pillows or blankets. The CD player that she had purchased just a month after starting at The Surf House would have to stay—which meant the CDs would stay too. One of the hardest things was the shoes. She would wear her Birkenstocks and pack one pair of dress sandals. The rest were history.

She stuffed as many of her clothes into the duffel bag as she could, sat on top of it to pack them down, then struggled to get it zipped. Next she started on her backpack, filling it up, packing it down, filling it up some more. She looked ruefully at the books she had bought and loved. They had been her escape and her education. But they were heavy and bulky. They did not make the cut.

Finally, she placed some pictures of the friends she had made at work and her small spiral diary into one of the backpack's pockets. She dropped the backpack on the bed, winced as she felt the pain in her chest flare, then sat down heavily on the bed one last time. She lay back and stared at the ceiling, afraid to close her eyes.

The events of last night were still a blur. She vividly remembered the intruder, the insidious smile, the dark eyes, the chilling threats, the cutting knife. Every time she closed her eyes, the events replayed themselves in grainy color. His breath, his body, his cruel, salty kiss.

But the rest of the night was a blur. She remembered calling 911. Kind and efficient paramedics rushed her to the Elizabeth City Hospital. She told the healthcare providers her story over and over again, always drawing raised eyebrows and skeptical looks. "I fell down the stairs," she would say, "carrying a knife."

She kept telling the doctors she had no insurance, that she could not afford their help, but nobody seemed to listen. She remembered lying on a gurney and looking up at the caring faces hovering over her, speaking kindly to her. Then the pain medicine kicked in, and night became morning.

She would be all right, her doctors said. A little sore but okay. The baby was fine too. The embryonic sac had not ruptured, and the heartbeat was strong. Maryna's chest required several stitches. They had used the plastic kind that eventually dissolve on their own. She was very fortunate, her doctors said. The cut was shallow and straight. With any luck the scar would hardly be noticeable. "It may reappear a little if you get a nice tan," one of the doctors suggested. "But other than that, you'll need a microscope to find it."

Maryna was glad to be out of the hospital and relieved beyond words that Dara was okay. One of the nurses even gave Maryna a ride home. But when Maryna entered the door of the apartment and noticed the blood, she trembled and sobbed all over again. The room started spinning, and she had to lie down on her bed just to get control.

When she finally felt a little better, her first move was to call The Surf House. It would be awhile before she could work again.

"You'd better not come back," the day manager said in subdued tones. "Two INS agents came by today and asked all kinds of questions. We're afraid somebody reported you."

At that moment Maryna knew she could not stay. The Snakeheads knew where she lived. They knew where she worked. They had hunted her down and trapped her. She knew how they made examples of people. She had seen it during her time in L.A. It was time to run again, she decided, time to start over someplace new.

This time she would be smarter. She had to be. She was not alone anymore. This time she was pregnant. She had a responsibility to Cameron, to little Dara.

She had locked the apartment door, closed every window shade, turned on the television to fill the unnerving quiet, and continued packing her stuff.

Before she left this home forever, she would have to address one last piece of unfinished business. It was something she had been dreading for the last hour, ever since she decided it was something she *needed* to do. It was time to be strong. She could not tolerate any more of her own excuses, her own procrastination. She sat up on the bed resolute and grabbed a pen and some paper.

But before she scratched out the first word, something on the television caught her attention. She could have sworn that somebody said the name of Cameron Davenport-Brown. Was her mind playing tricks on her again? She bolted upright on the bed and stared at the screen.

A camera for the noon news from Norfolk was zooming in on a nice-looking man on the steps of the courthouse. He had broad shoulders, short blond hair, and a determined look on his chiseled face. He spoke slowly and clearly, looking straight into the camera.

"These embryos, like every other embryo, have the full potential to become vibrant members of the human race. The fact that they were created in a petri dish by blastomere separation does not make them any less valuable—their souls any less precious—than an embryo conceived in a woman's uterus. To hold otherwise is to say that all babies conceived in vitro are somehow flawed and less than human."

The picture switched to a screen split between the anchor desk and a female reporter stationed in front of the courthouse.

"Do we have any response from GenTech?" asked the anchorman.

The field reporter shook her head gravely. "No, Bob. A spokesman for GenTech said they would have to review Ms. Davenport-Brown's lawsuit in detail before they could comment."

She had heard right! This was about Cameron!

And she had heard enough. This guy, this young and handsome lawyer, had spoken directly to her heart. He talked about those frozen embryos like they were already babies, as if he felt the same way she felt about Dara. He had even talked about their souls! And he looked so determined, so steadfast in his quest. It was almost as if—what was it about him?—almost as if the issue at hand was a matter of deep religious conviction, a matter of life and death.

Maryna *had* to see him. She had to talk to him, hire him if necessary. He would know what to do. Not just about Dara, but about the Snakeheads too. He would have the answers. And he would have the courage to make those answers reality. She knew it. She could *feel* it.

But as the news announcers droned on, Maryna realized that she didn't even know this man's name. How could she find out? *He has to be listed somewhere in the court documents,* she thought. *Or maybe if I just call Channel 12. They would surely have to know.*

She would find out, even if she had to visit the television station and talk to the reporters herself. Her mind flashed to another thought. *Perhaps the other stations have yet to show this lawyer's face and say his name.* She grabbed the remote and started flicking from one station to the next—she surfed all the major networks—back and forth—*click, click, click.*

One of the split-second images—just a flash, she was surfing so fast—immediately caught her attention. His voice! She backtracked, trying to find that familiar sound.

And there he was! Sitting in an office this time. Talking about insurance companies. Advertising his services. "We care more about our clients than our caseload," he was saying. And then he slammed his fist down on the desk. The special effects showed his streaking fist in slow motion. "Davenport & Associates," said a narrator, "an iron fist in a velvet glove."

Maryna scratched the name and phone number on one of the back pages of her diary: 1-800-CASH-NOW. She stared at the television screen in disbelief. For the first time that day she felt a slight flicker of hope, and she dared to pretend, just for a fraction of a second, that everything might be all right after all. She hadn't even met this man yet, but he was already bringing fresh hope. Her heart was a little lighter, almost as if she could breathe easier without the immense pressure she had been feeling on her chest.

It just can't be a coincidence, she reasoned. *Maybe once, but never twice in a row like this. I mean, before today I've never seen this man, never even heard of him. And now, when I need help the most, he shows up on my television screen twice, addressing the very issue that is ripping my heart out.*

Mr. Whoever-you-are at Davenport & Associates, you're a lifesaver. My lifesaver. Tomorrow I will pay you a personal visit.

But today there was other business to tend to. Hard business. Maryna crossed her legs on the bed, flicked the television off with her remote, and finally began writing the letter she had been dreading so much. She chewed on her pen, searched for just the right words, and choked back the tears.

The right words would not come; perhaps there was just no good way to say this. But she no longer had the luxury of time, so she started anyway.

Dear Cameron, she began.

22

THE OFFICE OF JUDGE CYNTHIA BAKER-KLINE was the last place on earth Mitchell Taylor wanted to be, but he had no choice in the matter, so he waited patiently. He snuck another glance at his watch when the clerk wasn't looking. He had been waiting for more than an hour.

He was just outside her chambers, waiting for a few moments of the judge's valuable time. It was the middle of the afternoon, and he didn't have an appointment, so the clerk made him pay his dues for dropping in unannounced.

"It shouldn't be too much longer," she said without looking up from her work station.

"Thanks." Mitchell glanced again at the thick oak door that separated him from Her Highness. *What in the world is she doing back there? I've got a million things to get done today, and here I sit, doing nothing productive, getting ready to beg a favor from a judge who already thinks I'm a moron.*

An hour earlier Mitchell had officially filed Cameron Davenport's case. But when he tried to get an immediate hearing for an injunction, the docket clerk dismissed him with a wave of the hand.

"You've got to clear that with one of the judges," she said. "I can't authorize that or even guarantee that they'll hear you. Only the judges can schedule emergency hearings on such short notice."

Mitchell knew only one of the judges. *Some local counsel I am,* he thought. So here he was, waiting for that one judge to get off the phone or finish her nap or whatever else she was doing so he could finally set up a lousy hearing.

"Mr. Taylor," announced the clerk after answering a short beep on the phone, "the judge will see you now."

Mitchell rose anxiously, knocked lightly on the door, and walked into the imposing chambers, closing the massive door behind him. Ichabod sat behind her desk on the opposite side of the room, not moving, not even looking up. Her office yawned on all sides before Mitchell, dwarfing him and everything in sight. The judge had plenty of room for her large oak desk, a corner table with several chairs, an oversized maroon leather couch, and a variety of end tables and lamps. To Mitchell's right, several long windows, all covered with ornate drapes and barely letting in the light of day, towered over him.

For a few minutes that stretched to an eternity, Ichabod remained hunched over some papers on her desk while Mitchell waited patiently inside the door. Finally, she looked up, took off her reading glasses, and acknowledged him.

"Have a seat," she said.

"Thanks." Mitchell parked himself in one of the chairs closest to her desk.

"Judge, the first thing I want to do is apologize again for this morning. I thought I was fully prepared for the case, and apparently I wasn't."

Ichabod leaned back in her chair and sighted down her nose at the young lawyer. Mitchell thought he detected a slight softening of her features, even the slightest trace of a smile.

"How long have you been practicing law, Mr. Taylor?"

"Actually, Judge, I just started."

She nodded. "Was this your first trial?"

"Yes ma'am."

"Well, for obvious reasons, I didn't see much of your case. But I did watch the way you handled yourself and the way you gave your opening. You're a natural, Mr. Taylor. You've got real potential. But a good lawyer doesn't get down on himself after one mistake. You learn and you move on."

Mitchell felt himself blushing. He hadn't come fishing for a compliment, especially from a judge notorious for her cynical attitude. But her words encouraged him. Maybe he wasn't ready for the big leagues yet, as Professor Arnold had prematurely announced, but he had a knack for this. He could sense it. He was eager to learn and ready to pay the price.

"Thanks, Judge."

As quickly as her face had softened, the harsh lines returned. "Do you know who you really owe an apology to?" she asked.

"Ma'am?"

"Your client. She's the one who suffers when things like that happen."

"I know. And I have apologized to her. We'll make it up to her, I promise."

Ichabod leaned forward on her elbows and narrowed her eyes. "Mr. Davenport has a serious problem, you know."

"Excuse me?"

"Mr. Davenport has a serious problem," Ichabod repeated slowly and emphatically. "And you aren't helping him by enabling his conduct. Alcoholics get by because their family, friends, and colleagues help them get by—they enable the alcoholic's conduct. They make excuses for him, they cover for him, they pick up the pieces. And all you're doing is exacerbating his disease and prolonging his sickness."

Mitchell looked down at his shoes. The judge was right, of course, but Mitchell felt disloyal even having this discussion.

"Well?" said the judge.

Mitchell hesitated. *What good will it do to continue covering for the Rock? The judge is right. The Rock needs help.* And Mitchell knew enough to realize that the first step toward recovery is admitting you have a problem.

"He needs help, Judge, but I'm not exactly sure how to get it for him. It's not as if he wants any." Mitchell looked straight into Ichabod's eyes. "I'm open for suggestions."

"It won't be easy," warned Ichabod.

"I know," Mitchell said without hesitation. "But if there's anything I can do—"

"Good." Ichabod leaned back in her chair. "There's a program called 'Lawyers Helping Lawyers,' and this is how it works…"

By the time Mitchell left, fifteen minutes later, he had scheduled two further appointments with the judge. A hearing on Nora's preliminary injunction request would take place eight days out—one week from Thursday. Nora would be happy—if that was possible. The other meeting, one that Mitchell had not intended to schedule, would occur the next morning at 9:30. The Rock would not be happy.

Something about the whole plan made Mitchell feel sleazy, like he wanted to take a shower. It did not help him to know he was working in concert with a judge like Ichabod, a woman renowned for spite and guile that exceeded the reputations of most of the criminals she sentenced. And it did not help to know that he was conspiring against his own partner and would be the heir apparent to the Rock's practice if this plan worked.

What kind of lawyer plots against his own partner? Mitchell wondered. *Am I playing the part of Brutus or Nathan? Traitor or healer? Opportunist or friend?*

Time would tell. For now, the course had been set. By tomorrow afternoon, the hardest part would be over.

＊＊

The market battered GenTech shareholders on Wednesday afternoon. Shortly after the broadcast of Mitchell's impromptu press conference on the courthouse steps, the stock plummeted nearly 15 percent on heavy volume, dropping from $18 a share to fifteen and three-quarters. Bargain hunters helped stabilize the price for a few hours while the long-term investors feverishly analyzed the pending legal action. Then Nora Gunther held her Washington news conference blasting GenTech for being insensitive to hopeful mothers like Cameron. Investors began dumping still more shares. The sell-off continued right through the closing bell, spurred on by rumors that the Honorable Cynthia Baker-Kline, a noted feminist judge, had agreed to schedule an emergency hearing on the plaintiff's request for a preliminary injunction.

GenTech's stock closed at less than $14 a share, a dramatic decrease in value that cost shareholders hundreds of millions. Blaine Richards himself had lost more than $12 million in four short hours.

It was not surprising, then, to see GenTech management strike back with a press conference of their own after the market closed. First, Blaine Richards emphasized how grateful the company was to have received the bequest from Dr. Nathan Brown setting up a nearly $2 million trust fund for private research on the new stem cell lines represented by the Brown zygotes. He emphasized how valuable these new lines could become in potentially finding a cure for the AIDS virus or other insidious diseases. He noted that the lawsuit did not challenge the financial bequest in Brown's will, only the donation of the zygotes. He also explained the process of blastomere separation used to create the embryos in question and emphasized that the procedure had been entirely legal at the time.

The company's outside counsel, Winsted Mackenzie IV, followed Richards at the mike. Win made an impressive appearance and emphasized that GenTech remained on solid legal footing. The company was simply honoring the contract that Dr. Nathan Brown and his wife, Cameron, had both signed when this whole process began. Mackenzie confidently quoted from numerous other legal cases where the same type of issue had been decided in favor of the clinic.

By the time Richards and Mackenzie finished calmly answering questions from reporters, the day's events took on a far more rational glow. GenTech shareholders reacted favorably and the stock gained back 50 percent of its losses in after-hours trading. When Richards arrived home for a late dinner, he had trimmed his losses from $12 million to a mere $6 million.

GenTech's competitors also experienced heavy trading volume, with more than twice their normal shares trading hands, but ultimately the companies experienced little movement in price. The stocks bounced around all day, closing slightly higher. ProGen rose half a buck to close at forty-seven while RSI rose nearly a dollar to close at forty-three and a half. Analysts were evenly split on the impact of the GenTech lawsuit. Some feared that this was the first in a rash of messy and high-risk litigation against biotech firms that operated fertility clinics. Those analysts lowered their ratings on the sector. Other analysts were far more upbeat, citing astronomical profit potential from new stem cell lines or from an overturning of the Bioethics Act. Some of those analysts even raised the target prices for GenTech, ProGen, and RSI.

Richards watched the analysts and market gurus until late into the night. They were so predictable, these eggheads. He could have written the script for every one of them himself. They didn't have a clue; they were just bean counters. They understood the finances just fine—the P&Ls, the balance sheets, the market-share numbers—they could recite them forward and backward. But they didn't have the foggiest idea about the science. So they couldn't begin to understand the repercussions of the day's events, couldn't even fathom where all this might lead.

As usual, Richards was several moves ahead of the smartest geeks that Wall Street had to offer. He would have to lead them along, feed them one bite at a time, and make sure they could properly digest what they did not yet understand. This would require great patience. It would not be easy for these boys of limited vision to grasp all the financial implications of the brave new world they were about to enter.

23

WEDNESDAY NIGHT, MARYNA CHECKED INTO a Days Inn located a block or so from Battlefield Boulevard in Chesapeake, Virginia. She was only a half-mile away from Interstate 64 and a few blocks from a bus stop for the Tidewater Transit system. The ride to downtown Norfolk would be no more than thirty minutes. She used an assumed name at her check-in—Mary Sawyer—and paid in cash for a two-night stay.

Early Thursday morning, just as the bright spring sun was chasing the darkness over the horizon, Maryna boarded the express bus for downtown Norfolk. She wore jeans, a high-necked sleeveless cotton blouse, her Birkenstocks, a New York Yankees baseball cap, and a cheap pair of sunglasses. Her long, dark hair was pulled back and up, generally hidden inside the baseball cap, except for the ponytail that poked out through the back and bobbed along as she walked. As inconspicuously as possible, Maryna constantly kept an eye on her surroundings, searching the faces of strangers for any hints of recognition.

She got off the bus in Norfolk, convinced she was not being followed, about four blocks from the *Tidewater Times* offices. It was still early, not quite 7:00 A.M., and there was little pedestrian traffic in the slumbering city. But Maryna was taking no chances. She walked quickly, crossing the street at nearly every intersection. Back and forth she went, glancing around as she waited to cross, ensuring that nobody was following her zigzagging path.

She arrived at the paper's offices a few minutes after seven. She entrusted the letter to the security guard and extracted a promise that he would give it to Cameron Davenport-Brown as soon as she arrived.

Maryna reached into her pocket, swallowed hard, and pulled out a twenty-dollar bill.

"I can't begin to tell you how important it is that Ms. Davenport gets this letter," Maryna said as she stuffed the money into the guard's palm. "Is there a number I can call to confirm delivery?"

"What's this about?" asked the guard suspiciously. He handled the letter cautiously, like it might be contaminated.

Maryna immediately realized that her strident insistence had been a mistake. She was an obvious immigrant, wearing sunglasses, delivering a mysterious letter to a newspaper reporter who had recently become a celebrity. She could read the look of extreme concern on the guard's face and suddenly realized the letter might never get delivered.

"It's a personal matter," Maryna said. She removed her sunglasses and lowered her voice. "Have you read about Ms. Davenport's lawsuit involving the fertility clinic?"

The guard nodded, a vague recognition filling his eyes.

"I'm the surrogate mother for Ms. Davenport. I'm carrying her baby." Maryna patted her small stomach.

"Oh," said the guard. The muscles around his jaw relaxed a little. "I didn't know what this was about... You just never know these days. It's better to be cautious."

"I understand," said Maryna. "If it would help, feel free to call Ms. Davenport's extension when she gets in and tell her you have a letter from Maryna Sareth. You can describe what I look like. That should confirm what I'm telling you."

"I'll do that," the guard said as he placed the envelope on his desk and stuffed the money in his pocket.

"Thanks."

"Don't mention it."

Relieved, Maryna quickly left the newspaper building and retraced her route from the hotel. There was more foot traffic this time, and it made her extremely nervous. *How do I know when they're out there? Every*

stranger, every look, every set of footsteps coming from behind is a possibility.
How can I live like this? And for how long?

At one point during the bus ride, Maryna was sure that a passenger three rows back, a stocky Asian-American male who kept glancing at her, was one of Tsao Vang's operatives. Maryna got off the bus at the next stop, ready to run for her life, but the man did not follow. She boarded the next bus, finally made it back to her hotel room, glanced one last time over her shoulder, and went inside.

She hung a "Do Not Disturb" sign on her door, unpacked her Buddha, and prepared to calm her mind and spirit. Gradually, her short, staccato breaths became deep and relaxing. She felt herself unwind and then begin to float away...

24

Dear Cameron,

You have been so kind to me and so understanding of everything that has happened. It makes it hard to write this letter. But I cannot bear to talk with you face to face about these things. So I had to write.

I am so confused and so very worried right now. I told you and Dr. Brown many sad things about my past when we first met. There were some things too painful to tell you, even though I grew to trust you as much as my own mother. I told you about escaping from Tsao Vang and the Snakeheads in Los Angeles. I told you about their demands for money that I didn't owe and their cruelty to me. What I didn't tell you, couldn't tell you, was how they used my body to pay back their ransom. How they made me sell my body on the streets of L.A. How they made me the toy of vulgar and disgusting men, until I could finally escape their grasp. Only I knew how lucky I really was when all the medical tests we ran in preparation for this pregnancy came back negative.

I know I should have said everything to you, but some secrets are too painful to reveal. And now I feel that everything that has happened is my fault—punishment for not telling you the whole truth.

Tsao Vang's men have found me. One of them came to my apartment and attacked me last night. They want me back in L.A. and I am of no use to them pregnant. They tried to harm your baby, our baby, but the baby is okay.

I will disappear again, I must disappear again, but I will send you letters because I am carrying your baby. Now this is the hard part of this letter, because you have been so good to me.

I can tell you want me to end this pregnancy so that we can try again with another embryo that will not have Down syndrome. But as much as I love you and respect you, I can't do that yet. The doctor says there is still a chance that this baby might be normal, that until further tests are done we won't know for sure. And we've been through so much together, how can we abort this baby now, without knowing for sure?

Cameron, even if this baby has Down syndrome, couldn't we still have her? If I need to, and if it would be all right with you, I can raise her myself. I've read about a lot of mothers that have Down syndrome children, and they all speak about what a blessing those children are. I know you well enough to know that you would make a great mom to a Down syndrome child.

Anyway, if you would think about this, I will find a way to be in touch with you in a few days. I will make sure that the Snakeheads will never be able to track me. I can't go back to L.A., Cameron, no matter what. I would rather die first.

Thanks for being so understanding. I am so very, very sorry.

Love,

Maryna

25

TO THE ROCK, THE TELEPHONE SOUNDED like a nuclear explosion. He pulled a pillow over his head and tried to drown it out. Five rings, six rings. *Doesn't this idiot get the picture? What time is it, anyway?*

Finally, mercifully, the ringing stopped. He cursed, then moaned, and drifted back to sleep.

Another ring brought forth a torrent of profanity from the Rock. He pried open an eye and felt the pounding begin in his head. His mouth was so parched that his lips seemed stuck together. He was lying on his couch, downstairs in his house. He still had on his dress shirt, although partially unbuttoned, from the prior night, as well as his boxer shorts and a pair of silk black socks that covered his calves. His dress pants, suit coat, tie, and shoes were lying next to the couch. The television was blaring.

Ring…ring…

How many times is that? Ten? Eleven? Why doesn't this jerk hang up? Why hasn't my answering machine kicked in?

The Rock sat up on the couch and dropped his spinning head into his hands. He moved slowly and held his head low. His stomach was churning—revolting. Every movement and every ring of the phone pounded at his headache like a jackhammer. Ring…ring… *Finally,* it stopped.

He lifted his head and grabbed the remote. Rubbing his eyes, moving gingerly, he flicked off the television. *Got to control the noise. My gut is killing me.* He glanced around for the phone. *Where did I leave it?*

Ring…ring… This time the sound seemed louder still as it pierced the silence and echoed in his head. Another stream of expletives, then the Rock rose slowly to his feet and waited for the room to stop spinning. *Ring...ring...ring.* There was no way around it. He would have to answer the darn thing.

The Rock staggered to the kitchen counter and found the phone lying among some old dishes from a few nights ago. He picked it up on the sixth or seventh ring. He had lost count. *Who cares?*

"What?" he said. He hadn't intended to whisper, but that was the way it came out.

"Billy, it's Mitchell. We've got something of an emergency."

"For the love of God, Mitchell. Do you know what time it is?"

"It's 9:05, Billy. I waited until I knew you'd be up to call."

The Rock moaned. Still squinting at the light flooding his eyes, he reached for a bottle of Scotch.

"Judge Baker-Kline has insisted that we both appear in her chambers at 10:00 this morning or risk contempt. I guess she had all night to steam about the Parsons trial. She did not sound happy."

The Rock took a long swig. His stomach clenched immediately. "Tell Her Honor to kiss off."

"You'll have a chance to tell her yourself," replied Mitchell evenly. "She insisted that we both be there at ten."

"If I'm not there," said the Rock, "tell her to start without me."

He punched the off button and tossed the phone onto the living room carpet. He lifted the bottle to his lips a second time, but his stomach warned him off.

I've got to get some coffee. Brush my teeth. Maybe a shot or two of rum will still these demons in my head...

———

Mitchell felt his own stomach tighten and churn, the acid eating away at the lining, as he waited in Ichabod's chambers for the Rock to show up. Ichabod sat at her desk, seemingly unconcerned, plowing through some legal pleadings. Cameron was also there, calmly reading the paper.

Sandra Garrison sat on the couch in one corner of the room, nervously wringing her hands together, staring into space. She had already been to the rest room twice.

The tension of the impending confrontation did not bother Mitchell. He was a lawyer. A competitive lawyer, at that. He had been an athlete. Confrontation was in his blood. But Mitchell couldn't shake this nagging feeling of disloyalty. He had misled his employer. And now he was preparing to gang up on the Rock and force the man to do what he had been avoiding for years.

Mitchell was heading up an ambush, no two ways around it.

At ten minutes after ten, Ichabod's receptionist informed the judge that Mr. Davenport had arrived. *Ten minutes late. Not bad for the Rock.*

All eyes turned toward the heavy oak door. Mitchell and Cameron instinctively rose from their seats. For Mitchell, the moment carried the surreal feeling of a surprise birthday party merged with a funeral. He had never felt so uncomfortable in his life.

The Rock entered the room with his shoulders slouched and his head hanging low. He stopped a step or two inside the door and glanced around—his eyes registering his suspicions. He tilted his head a little to the side and focused on his daughter.

"Cameron?" he said, as if he were seeing things. "What are you doing here?"

"I asked her to come," announced Ichabod, rising from behind her desk. "As well as Mr. Taylor and Ms. Garrison."

The Rock seemed to focus for the first time on Sandra, who remained seated, staring at the floor.

"What is this?" he demanded in a gravelly voice.

"Have a seat, Mr. Davenport." It was not so much a request from Ichabod as a demand.

The Rock reluctantly lowered himself into a leather chair that had been placed near the middle of the room. Without saying anything, the others moved chairs into a rough circle with the Rock at one end and the judge at the other, just as they had rehearsed. They took a seat and watched the Rock's eyes dart from one participant to another, trying to make sense of what was happening.

Mitchell, who took a seat to the Rock's immediate right, could smell the vestiges of the Rock's morning Scotch. And Mitchell noticed, perhaps more clearly this morning than ever before, the telltale signs of a serious drinker—the flushed complexion, the red eyes, the bulbous nose, and a slight tremor in the hands.

"What's going on, Sandra?" Rock demanded again. He seemed to sense a weakness in his secretary, but she would not answer him, would not even lift her eyes to meet his gaze.

"Mr. Davenport," snapped Ichabod, "you've got a serious problem with alcohol." She stared intensely at the Rock, who eventually turned his gaze from Sandra to the judge. She softened her voice and continued. "The people in this room care about you too much to allow that problem to continue. We've asked you to come today so we can talk about getting you help."

The Rock's face turned a darker shade of red. Mitchell shifted uncomfortably in his chair. Cameron leaned forward, toward her dad. Sandra stared at the floor.

"Judge, I appreciate your concern. But there's no problem...really." The Rock spoke lightheartedly, as if the whole thing were just a minor communication snafu that his denial could readily resolve. Mitchell half-expected him to rise from his chair, bid the judge "good day," and return to the office. "I have a drink occasionally, who doesn't? But it's nothing I can't control."

"Dad," said Cameron, playing her role to a *T,* "let's be honest. "You're drinking's been out of control for a long time," she paused and licked her dry lips, "ever since you and Mom broke up. And every time we try to talk about it, you just do what you're doing today." Cameron changed her tone, mimicking her dad, "I'm fine... I don't need any help... I'm cutting back... You don't know what I'm going through..."

As the Rock tensed, Cameron's voice choked off. Tears welled up in her expressive green eyes, the strong lines of her face softened by an overwhelming sadness. Mitchell swallowed hard. He felt at once sad and embarrassed to be viewing this poignant moment between father and daughter.

Cameron struggled, but continued. "Dad, I'm tired of living without a real father. Sick of trying to avoid you because I'm worried about what you might say to me if you're drunk, how deeply you might hurt me again with your cruel words. Dad, that's not you." The words flooded out of Cameron's mouth, after years of holding back, and the Rock could no longer look at his daughter. "And Dad, I'm so tired of people finding out that you're my father and saying, 'I can't believe it,' or 'I'm sorry,' or something like that. I know this sounds stupid, but I want to have my father back."

It was the Rock's turn to respond. This aspect of the meeting had been carefully choreographed, and Ichabod had insisted that they wait the Rock out and force him to say something. It was not enough that he *listen,* they must engage him, allow him to air all of his excuses, then reject them one by one.

For an interminably long time, the only noise in the room was the sound of Cameron's sniffling.

"Is that what you really think?" the Rock finally asked, his voice a dull monotone. "The old man's just a worthless drunk. It's all the old man's fault."

"Dad, that's not it at all. You're not listening to me."

"No, Cameron. I think I'm listening just fine. This whole thing was your idea, wasn't it?"

It was more than Mitchell could take, this blame game between father and daughter. He felt sorry for both, saddened by a relationship that seemed beyond hope, and sorry that he had allowed himself to be talked into this idea in the first place. But he was here now, and he wasn't about to let Cameron take the heat. The script said it was not yet his turn, but he decided to ad-lib.

"Billy, you've got your daughter all wrong. This wasn't her idea. She didn't even want to come. And you know why?"

"I'm sure you're about to enlighten me—"

"Because she knew you'd turn on her, just the way you did. It was my idea, Billy. Mine and the judge's."

"Figures," the Rock mumbled under his breath.

"You know what?" barked Mitchell, no longer feeling the slightest bit of sympathy for this man full of sarcastic responses. "It's about time you started taking some responsibility for your own actions. And you ought to start by apologizing to your own daughter…"

The Rock just rolled his eyes, but Mitchell thought he noticed Cameron sit a little higher in her chair, thought he saw a flash of satisfaction in the eyes of the judge.

"I, for one, am tired of covering for you. And I've only been working at Davenport & Associates for three days! How Sandra has survived, I'll never know…"

For the next several minutes, Mitchell took his turn building his case and pleading with the Rock to get help. The Rock responded with more denials and excuses, but at least the sarcasm disappeared. Every excuse conjured up by the Rock was met with a piercing question or two from Mitchell, revealing the hollowness of the Rock's attempt to avoid responsibility. Finally, the Rock gave up the chase and stopped responding at all to Mitchell's questions, shrugging his shoulders instead.

The ensuing silence seemed heavier than before, and it lasted longer, as Sandra Garrison, the Rock's longtime and trusted secretary, drew her courage to speak. She did so in a barely audible whisper, with her eyes still glued to the floor and tears dripping down her cheeks.

"They're right, Mr. Davenport. You don't know how much I hate being here, but they're right. You've been so good to me all these years, Mr. Davenport, and now I've got to do something that will help you." Sandra paused, finding the courage to glance quickly at her boss, then at the others in the room. Mitchell nodded his encouragement. "Please don't hate me for this," she said, her voice shaking, "but we had to do it for your own good."

This time the Rock did not respond. He had nothing to say; he was a defeated man. Mitchell could see it in his posture—his head hanging onto his chest. Mitchell's sympathy returned. Sure, the Rock brought it on himself. But it was still hard to watch a man who believed his friends and family had just turned against him. The Rock had the look of Caesar as he turned to Brutus and saw the dagger.

"We've taken care of everything you need so that you can check into one of the top facilities in Tidewater and get help," said Ichabod, taking control of the meeting again with her commanding voice. "I have personally called the state court judges who are handling your cases and obtained continuances. Mitchell can handle your caseload. Ms. Garrison will handle your finances. And Cameron has packed some clothes and other things you might need. They're over there behind my desk."

The Rock, a moment earlier defeated, was now wide-eyed, his mouth hanging open. To Mitchell, this plan that sounded so reasonable yesterday now felt entirely too heavy-handed.

Mitchell studied the Rock closely and noticed the increased trembling of the old lawyer's pallid hand. He looked pitiful and tongue-tied, angry and confused, defensive and hopeless. Without saying a word, the Rock rose unsteadily from his seat and searched the faces of his conspirators.

"*God* save me from my friends," he said, "*I* can handle my enemies alone."

Then he turned his back and started walking toward the door, his footsteps echoing in the chambers. This scenario had also been rehearsed. And just as the Rock placed his hand on the doorknob, Ichabod's voice rang out one last time.

"If you leave these chambers today, without going straight to rehab, I'll personally see to it that you never practice law again."

The threat caused the Rock to turn and face the judge. And for the first time that day, Mitchell saw fire in his bloodshot eyes.

"How do you think you're going to do that, Judge? You didn't punch my ticket to practice law and you can't unpunch it. Just because you think you're God—"

"Mr. Davenport," Ichabod interrupted as she stood up, "I saw enough, heard enough, *and smelled enough* in the Parsons case to make me very concerned as to whether you can adequately handle your clients' cases without committing malpractice. I am therefore ordering you, on every case you file from this day forward in federal court, to send a copy of this written opinion about the real reasons for the mistrial in the Parsons case to your liability insurance carrier, notifying them of my concern."

As Ichabod walked toward the Rock, Mitchell saw a look of resignation settle in on the Rock's face. A lawyer can't practice law without liability insurance for malpractice claims. And no insurance company would cover a lawyer who had to provide them with a letter from a federal court judge accusing the lawyer of being an alcoholic.

The Rock snatched the opinion from Ichabod's hand and stuffed it in his suit coat pocket without reading it. He stared at the judge for just an instant, seemed ready to turn and bolt out the door, when a desperate cry from Sandra Garrison shattered the tension.

"*Please,* Mr. Davenport. For the love of God, get some help!" And then the pathetic, round little woman, overcome with emotion, put her head in her hands and sobbed.

It was finally enough to break the Rock's fragile emotional stronghold. He walked over to Sandra and put his arms around her, allowing her to cry on his shoulder. Cameron joined them, hugged her dad tentatively, and quietly whispered, "Thank you, Dad."

Mitchell moved slowly over and put a hand on the Rock's shoulder. "You'll be fine," he said. "You'll be back in the office in no time."

The Rock just pursed his lips and nodded grimly. Cameron picked up the gym bag with her dad's clothes from behind the judge's desk, grabbed him by the hand, and started leading him from the judge's office. "I hope you brought a pair of jeans," said the Rock.

Cameron smiled. "I brought two."

Every last detail had been carefully planned. Mitchell would drive Cameron's car. She and her dad would ride in the back. They would stay with him until he checked himself in. Sandra would be free to go home.

"Thanks," Mitchell said to Ichabod, as he followed the Rock and Cameron out the door of the judge's chambers.

He could have sworn he saw a glint of moisture in the judge's cold, gray stare.

ALTHOUGH HE DIDN'T REALLY HAVE TIME, Mitchell felt obliged to buy Cameron a cup of coffee after they left the facility where the Rock would spend the next several weeks drying out. Ten minutes after the last drop of coffee had been drained from their cups, the two were still engaged in lively conversation, avoiding the heavy subjects like Cameron's lawsuit and the Rock's rehab. They focused on each other, oblivious to the other customers at the busy little coffeehouse.

A pause in the conversation gave Cameron a chance to reflect and turn the conversation to the matter that obviously weighed heavy on her heart. "Do you think we did the right thing?" she asked.

Mitchell thought for a moment, raised his empty cup to his lips, and placed it back down.

"We didn't have any choice," he replied. "We couldn't let him go on the way he was."

"Yeah, I know." Cameron made a grim face. Mitchell sensed that she was still trying to convince herself more than anyone else.

"Do you think he'll make it?" she asked.

Who knows? thought Mitchell. But he knew that was not the reply Cameron needed to hear.

"He'll make it, Cameron. Your dad's a tough old codger. He's got a stubborn streak that'll come in handy. Good thing you didn't inherit any of that."

Cameron flashed a broad smile. Her green eyes, still red from the raw emotions of the day, sparkled at Mitchell.

"Can I ask you a personal question?" Mitchell inquired, waiting politely for permission.

"You're a lawyer, it's what you do," Cameron retorted. "Besides, since you're *my* lawyer, you already know more about my personal business, including how many operations I've had and why, than any man should know."

"Okay. Well, I was just wondering—"

"But let me warn you about one thing," Cameron interrupted. "I'm a reporter, actually a newspaper columnist, but that's close enough. For every personal question you ask me, I get to put one to you."

Mitchell scrunched his nose in fake displeasure. "Fair enough. Mine first."

"Bring it on," Cameron said, sitting up straighter.

"What happened between you and your dad?"

Cameron took a deep breath and frowned.

"It's a long story."

"I've got time."

She paused and seemed to be collecting her thoughts. "He used to be a pretty good lawyer. Flamboyant. Colorful. Even tenacious. The clients loved him. He was a sucker for the underdog, always representing David against Goliath."

"I can see that," said Mitchell.

"He and my mom were never close. At least, I never saw any spark there. He worked all the time. Didn't have much time for her or for me. And she wouldn't cut him any slack. After I was on my own and writing for the paper, a blonde bombshell named Vicki Zimmerman hired my dad. If he were telling it, he'd probably say—heck, he has said—that at this point in his life, my mom wasn't meeting his needs. He'd make all kinds of excuses. Anyway, he fell hard for this woman—didn't even try to hide it, really.

"Zimmerman worked as a secretary for a vice president at one of those big manufacturing conglomerates on the Eastern Shore. She claimed her boss sexually harassed her, made all kinds of kinky comments, and tried to grope her every chance he got. She had an especially juicy tale about the office Christmas party when this guy—"

Mitchell looked down from Cameron's eyes, and she apparently noticed. "Am I embarrassing you?"

Mitchell shrugged. "I get the gist, I think."

"You're sweet," Cameron replied. "Old fashioned. Chivalry resurrected."

"I don't know about all that—"

"Well, let's just say that Vicki Zimmerman's boss had a hard time keeping his hands to himself. Okay? Anyway, so did my dad once he started representing this *poor, innocent* little manipulative tease in her sexual harassment lawsuit against the company."

Things were starting to make sense to Mitchell. Unfortunately, it didn't surprise him.

"So my dad leaves my mom because he's fallen for this little bimbo who's about *my* age. It breaks my mom's heart, and she never recovers. My dad wins a ton of money for Zimmerman in her lawsuit. The boss confesses to everything. And then, once Vicki Zimmerman was done using my dad to make her rich, she ups and disappears without ever saying good-bye. Then both my dad and my mom were basket cases."

"I'm sorry," said Mitchell sincerely.

"Wait, it gets better."

"If it's painful to talk about, I don't need to know," Mitchell said.

"Actually, after this morning, it kinda helps to talk about it." Cameron searched Mitchell with imploring eyes. She blew out another breath, then: "I hated this woman for what she did to my parents' marriage. So I couldn't leave well enough alone. I searched all over the country for her and finally found her living in Texas. And guess what?"

Mitchell shrugged. He didn't have a clue.

"She's shacked up with her former boss, both of them living happily together off the money she got from her former company in the lawsuit. Can you believe that? The whole lawsuit was a scam!"

Mitchell edged closer, elbows on the table. *Unbelievable! Talk about a dysfunctional family.* "So what'd you do?"

"What any good reporter would do. I wrote an investigative expose. Vicki Zimmerman went to jail. Amazingly, my dad still loved her, and…well, it's never been the same between us."

"And your mom?"

Cameron paused and looked down at her coffee cup. She had been breaking the rim of the Styrofoam cup into small pieces, carefully placing them into the bottom of the cup. She lowered her voice to a near whisper.

"Suicide. Sleeping pills."

Stunned, Mitchell watched Cameron slowly and methodically destroy her Styrofoam cup. "Wow," he said. "I'm sorry."

"Thanks, Mitchell," Cameron replied, even softer than before. She paused for a beat. "And to be honest with you, I've never forgiven him. And yet, I keep hoping that someday, something will change…"

Cameron gave Mitchell a halfhearted smile. He wanted to comfort her, but what do you say to someone whose mother committed suicide? Every platitude designed to bring comfort suddenly seemed so trite.

Perhaps she sensed his uneasiness, perhaps she just needed a change in subject matter herself. But as if someone threw a switch, Cameron perked up, her voice returning to its normal pitch.

"Now its my turn to cross-examine," she said as she lifted her head and flicked her hair back. "No ring?"

Mitchell looked down at his ring finger as if he had never noticed it before. "Nope."

"Is there a story?" She paused. "Always interested in a good story."

Mitchell shrugged. "You want me to make up something good…or you want the truth?"

Cameron smiled and waited. It was clear she wasn't going to let him off easy.

"All right," said Mitchell. "There's really not much to it. I met a girl when I was an undergrad at VMI. Friend-of-a-friend type of thing—"

"She was a *cadet*?" Cameron raised an eyebrow.

Mitchell laughed. "No. She was at Richmond—met her at a sorority party. Cadets get a lot of invitations to sorority parties." He paused again. "We got serious but decided to wait until after I graduated from law school and she finished undergrad to hook up. So I moved to Virginia Beach and start working my tail off at Regent. I was too busy with the books to notice that we were drifting apart. My last year of law school, she dropped the bomb." Mitchell had been looking at his hands as he spoke, fiddling with his own cup. Now he looked directly at Cameron. "Some guy named Justin."

"Her loss," said Cameron quietly.

The comment seemed so natural from Cameron—more like she was just stating a fact than flirting. Still, Mitchell felt his cheeks turn warm, and he could think of no clever retort—no way to comfortably deflect the compliment.

So again, Cameron bailed him out.

"Thanks for the coffee," she said sweetly. "And for the company."

As she said this, she rose and started picking up her trash. Mitchell took the cue, rose with her, and did the same.

27

May 20

My dearest little Dara,
I almost named you Piseth. That's right, Piseth Peaklica Sareth. I'll bet you're glad I didn't.

Let me tell you why I even considered it. Piseth Peaklica was a beautiful and graceful classical dancer in my country. Most would agree that she was the most talented dancer our country ever knew. She was also an actress, a genuine film star from Cambodia. There was no one else like her.

I wish you could have seen her and marveled at her beauty. She was lovely—long, dark hair, beautiful brown eyes. And she was kind. Everybody in my country loved her. She was the voice of the people, starring in films like *Shadow of Darkness,* speaking out against the wicked Khmer regime.

Then one day, when she was still in the prime of her life, she was gunned down in the marketplace in cold blood. She and her seven-year-old niece were shot several times, the bullets lodging in her spine. She was shot in broad daylight, for everyone to see.

They took her to the hospital and operated. "I did not do any bad thing at all. Why have they mistreated me like this?" she asked.

One week later she died.

The whole country knew who shot her. She was in love with the chief of police. His jealous wife ordered the execution. Poor, beautiful Piseth. No arrests were ever made.

It seemed as if the entire country attended her funeral. My mom took me, we both loved Piseth so much. They say that ten thousand attended. I'm sure there were more.

I had just turned fifteen. The police formed a human barricade and kept us mostly at bay. But I climbed a tree and saw the whole thing. I heard the voices and songs blaring over the speakers. The funeral went on for hours.

I'll never forget what another actor, a man named Daro, said about Piseth.

"Let us speak to the soul of the Lady Peaklica before the fire burns her beautiful body away from us," he said. "She is disappeared from the world, indeed. But the good model of her heroism remains. We shall all remember her forever. Let us say good-bye to our Lady. Good-bye forever...never to see her again."

Then Daro began weeping, and I wept with him. And the whole crowd wept without shame.

And then the most amazing thing happened. A traditional musician, a man named Nol Sobon, rose up to play the flute. He spoke quietly before he played. "I used to play other songs on my flute for her to dance to at national and international ceremonies. But today I play a funeral song for her death. I never expected that."

Then he played. Soft. Enchanting. It was beautiful and it soothed the entire crowd. The sobbing, it was quieted, replaced by peace and resignation.

Then Piseth's husband lit the torch that began the cremation just as a gentle rain began to fall. I heard those murmuring in the crowd say that the rain was accompanying our Piseth to another more peaceful world where she will dance again.

That evening, on the long walk home from the funeral, I decided to be an actress—to devote my life to the study of art. I had seen, no, I had felt, how Piseth captured and elevated the soul of a nation. This orphan named Piseth, through nothing except her kindness, her beauty, and the grace of her performance, rescued our culture from the Khmer Rouge regime. I was searching for something that could transcend the violence and hatred of my country. That day, I found it.

That same walk home is when my mother told me we would leave Cambodia.

"This country does not value life," she said. "How can they kill Lady Peaklica in the light of day on the streets of our city and not be punished? This country is chaos, where evil men prevail."

She stopped walking and turned to face me. She switched from Cambodian to English. "We go to a land where you can dream your dreams without fear. We go to a land that values life, Maryna. We go to America."

My mind raced with a million questions. My friends, my home, my country—how can I leave them all behind? What is America to be like? How can we escape our country? How can we pay the cost?

All my questions, before I could speak them, were erased by the look in my mother's eye. I could no more doubt that look of determination. We were going to America.

So you see, my little Dara, it is because of Piseth Peaklica, one extraordinary woman, that my mom and I found the courage to come to this faraway country. And it is why I almost named you, just for these few months when you are totally mine, Piseth.

But there is another reason I thought about that name. We came to this country to find a land that cares about life. But we found that in many ways, Americans are no different than Cambodians. The strong do not value the weak. The powerful prey on the defenseless.

And so, my little one, there are those in this country who would end your young life before it begins. They would snuff you out, as surely as they did Piseth Peaklica.

I will not let them.

My Dara, you will be safe with me. And someday, you will grow to be a beautiful young woman and perhaps even touch this nation the way that Lady Peaklica touched mine. We will get through this together.

I do not mean to burden you with my problems. But, silly as it seems, sometimes I feel like when I write in this diary, I somehow communicate with your soul. And right now, I need all the help I can get.

I love you so much already. And that will never change.

You are my little Dara. And I dream that someday you will combine the spirit and determination of my mother with the grace and beauty of Piseth.

So you see, Piseth Peaklica is not such a bad name. Even if everybody in this country would constantly ask you how to spell it.

28

THE MAN SLOUCHED LOW in the driver's seat of his Mercedes. He was parked at the far end of the Days Inn parking lot, wedged between two other vehicles, one of them a van. He wore a baseball cap low on his forehead, and a pair of Oakley sunglasses shielded his eyes. He hadn't had time to shave or sleep much in the last two days. But his stubble was covered by the longer and thicker hair from a fake beard; his own short, dark hair camouflaged by a long and full hairpiece. He was blond now with a matching blond beard, although he still had dark eyebrows and darker eyes. When he glanced in the rearview mirror he could hardly recognize himself.

He had been following Maryna since he left her apartment on Tuesday night. He saw the ambulance take her to the hospital. He patiently waited outside the hospital until the nurse gave Maryna a ride home. On Wednesday afternoon, he followed the bus she was riding, at a safe distance, all the way to this hotel in Chesapeake. Then early this morning, Thursday morning, he followed her into downtown Norfolk.

Maryna had been so careful this morning, constantly glancing around, looking right at his vehicle once or twice, that he eventually had to drop back. He watched from a distance as she walked into the offices of the *Tidewater Times*. A few minutes later, he saw her emerge again, and she seemed to look right at him. Spooked, he drove quickly away and went back to the hotel, where he waited. He studied the activities of the hotel maids.

He called in and reported Maryna's actions. The response had been swift and decisive. She was obviously ignoring his threat and hiding from the Snakeheads. Her stubbornness would have its price. They would not wait ten days.

He was told to break into Maryna's hotel room while she was out. Look around some. If it seems she is in the process of setting up an abortion and a return trip to Los Angeles, then let her be. If it seems she is trying to run, trying to hide, then take her out. It would be his call to make.

The stalker watched on Thursday afternoon as Maryna emerged from her room wearing the same baseball cap and sunglasses she had worn earlier that morning. This time, however, she was dressed in a pair of tight-fitting silk slacks and a sleeveless white cotton shirt with a high neckline that clung to her body and accentuated her slender figure. She was trying to impress somebody, he knew. But this time, he would not follow. He had other work to do.

For the next several hours, he continued to watch the maids methodically do their work. They used a master key, entered a room, then left the door open as they changed the sheets and linens, washed down the bathroom, and ran the vacuum. A heavyset woman who looked to be in her midforties was cleaning the rooms on the second floor where Maryna's room was located. She would leave her cart on the covered concrete walkway that ran along the outside doors to the rooms.

His original plan was to wait until this woman left work, follow her until she stopped at home or the store or wherever, and then mug her there, in the light of day. He would take everything she had, including her purse. He really wanted only one thing: the key to the central supply room at the hotel. Located just down the hall from the front desk, he had watched early that morning as new maids would report to work, enter that room, and emerge a few minutes later with their cleaning carts and master keys. He would lift this supply room key, return to the hotel, and find the master keys. If Maryna was not yet back to her room, he had a few tricks to make it easy to get past the chain lock when he would return later that night. If she was already back, he would simply wait until the dead of night, then use the master key on the main lock and a bolt-cutter on the chain lock. Higher risk, but either way, Maryna would be dead by morning.

But now he saw an opportunity that would allow for his preferred plan. He waited until the maid went into a room about two doors down from Maryna's. Then he walked quickly across the parking lot, up the outside steps, and toward Maryna's room. When he reached the room, he took the "do not disturb" sign that Maryna had left hanging on the door handle and quickly turned it over to request maid service. The man glanced around to ensure nobody was watching, then quickly returned to his car.

He watched patiently as the maid methodically worked her way down to Maryna's room, stripping the linens and towels, chatting incessantly to herself as she completed her tasks. The stalker thought for a moment, weighed the risks one more time, then removed his sunglasses, got out of his car, and walked boldly toward room 207.

He entered the room just as the maid finished making the bed.

"How long are you gonna be?" he asked, sitting down on the one chair in the room. He tried to act casual but carefully avoided touching anything.

"Oh, excuse me," said the maid, flushing. "I can come back if you'd like."

"No, that's okay. Why don't you just leave the clean towels and washcloths and that will be fine."

"Are you sure?"

"Yeah. I've got a lot of work to do."

It was that easy. In a few minutes, the oblivious maid was gone, never noticing the absence of a man's toiletries or clothes in the room, never asking a single question of this man who so confidently acted like he belonged here.

When she left, the assailant smiled, shook his head, put on white latex gloves, and began looking around. He was hoping to find a spare key that Maryna might have left in the room. No such luck.

But he did find the diary. He turned to the last page and began reading. "There are those in this country who would end your young life before it begins," Maryna had written to her baby. "They would snuff you out, as surely as they did Piseth Peaklica... I will not let them."

"How sweet," the assailant mumbled. "How stupid."

He carefully placed the diary back exactly as he had found it. He could just wait in the room, hide in the shower, until Maryna returned. But then he would have to kill her in broad daylight and take a chance on someone seeing him leave. Too risky. He would stick to the original plan.

He made a quick trip out to his car, leaving the hotel room door slightly ajar, and returned with a small Nike bag. He closed the door, then slid the small metal chain into place as a safety lock. He reached into the Nike bag and removed a pair of lock cutters. With relative ease, he snapped one of the small metal links on the chain, removed the link, and watched the chain separate and dangle, one side attached to the door, the other side still slid into place on the doorjamb.

Then he reached into his pocket and carefully removed three small pieces of plastic, molded and painted to look exactly like a metal link for the small chain. He snapped them into place on the chain and worked the chain a few times, locking the door and sliding the chain into place. It worked and felt exactly as it had before, but this time the chain had more slack. It also had three plastic links strategically placed so that someone opening the door from the outside would be able to slip a sharp instrument through the cracked door and easily cut the plastic links on the chain.

He inspected his handiwork one last time, admiring his craftiness, then packed up his tools, left the room, and headed back to his car. The only thing left to do was wait until the maid finished for the day and left work. He would look for just the right opportunity, slip on his ski mask, and jump this woman when she least expected it. He would get the master key and pay Maryna one final visit in the middle of the night.

The maid seemed like a nice enough woman. He would probably spare her life. But he would still have to cut her, or at least bruise her up a little, just to make it look authentic.

29

FOR MITCHELL, THURSDAY AFTERNOON had not been very productive. After putting his boss in the rehabilitation clinic that morning, and sharing a long coffee break afterward with the man's daughter, he had finally dragged himself back to the office just after lunch. He was confronted by a despondent Sandra Garrison and a waiting room full of would-be clients.

Mitchell asked all the clients to reschedule, explaining that an emergency prevented the Rock from being at the office that day. He knew that he would never see some of them again; they would simply go to another personal injury lawyer down the block. For that, he would be thankful.

But dealing with Sandra was not as easy. Mitchell tried in vain to cheer her up—he listened, he counseled, he allowed her to sob in silence for a few minutes, he even tried a few lighthearted jokes that fell entirely flat. She told Mitchell she felt like she had betrayed her boss. She remembered the wounded look on the Rock's face as he left Ichabod's chambers. She thought maybe he was suicidal. She was sure it was all her fault.

Sandra compounded her guilt by recounting all the good things the Rock had done before alcohol ruined him. Like the time he had lost an impossible case on behalf of a badly burned young child. It was in the middle of a string of losses, said Sandra, and things were tight at the firm. But two months later, when a big verdict finally came back on another case, the Rock put every dime of his attorney's fees into a trust fund for the burned kid. The Rock nearly lost his house when the firm's creditors found out, said Sandra, blinking back tears. That was the real Rock, she insisted.

By 3:00 P.M., Mitchell gave up trying to console Sandra. She was actually beginning to make *him* feel bad. He felt like he had somehow desecrated the legacy of the firm's patron saint.

Did I judge the man too quickly? Is Sandra now blaming me for trying to take over the Rock's practice?

What choice did I have?

Someday, Mitchell promised himself, as Sandra droned on with another story, *the man will thank me.* But even as the thought flashed across his mind, Mitchell knew he really didn't believe it. He couldn't put his finger on it, but somehow what he had done had a finality to it—a sense that the Rock would never be the same.

Mitchell soon grew weary of Sandra's self-loathing. Knowing that the day was shot as far as any productive work was concerned—Sandra hadn't even answered the telephone in the last two hours—Mitchell finally just sent her home. "Get some rest," he said. "You're physically and emotionally exhausted. Things will seem better when you're not so tired." With a mixture of relief and concern, he watched Sandra, stoop-shouldered and red-eyed, slowly leave the office.

For Mitchell, it was not too late to at least get an hour or two of productive work done. He was tired of talking about the Rock, dwelling on the Rock's problems, wondering if he and the others had done the right thing. What was done was done. It was time to move on.

Mitchell banished his doubts and plowed into some of the old files sitting around his office, losing himself in the endless and thankless job of listing what legal work needed to be done on each case.

An hour later, as he leafed through some unanswered discovery, he heard the outside door of the reception area open and close. A soft and accented voice called out. "Hello? Hello? Is anybody here?"

He thought for a moment that he would just sit tight until the interloper went away. He was in no mood to deal with yet another walk-in looking for quick and easy money through a claim that had been rejected by ten other firms.

"Hello," she cried out again. "Are you open for business?"

Mitchell listened for the door closing behind her as she left, but instead it sounded like the woman had taken a seat in one of the tattered waiting-room chairs. He grudgingly decided to deal with her.

As he entered the reception area, his guest immediately stood from her chair, smiled a nervous smile, and extended her hand.

"My name is Piseth Peaklica," she said. "Are you Mr. Taylor?"

Piseth what? Where in the world did she get that name? And that beautiful accent—where did that come from? He resisted the urge to have her repeat her name.

Her hand was moist, but her grip was firm and confident. The young woman was striking in appearance and exquisite in her posture. Mitchell estimated that she was about five foot six, but her slender build and long, glimmering brown hair made her seem much taller. He was immediately struck by the eyes—large, intelligent, and dark walnut eyes that fixed intently on him. She had the beautiful and soft features of someone from the South Pacific—an enchanting mixture of the Far East and the American continent.

"I'm Mitchell. Mr. Taylor is my dad."

The young woman smiled. The radiance of it, combined with the childlike intensity of her stare, proved hard to resist. Mitchell immediately decided that he could make time for at least one more client.

"Is your father a lawyer?" she asked with an air of formality. Mitchell could not determine whether she was putting him on or not.

"No."

"Then I want to hire you."

Wow, he thought. *A quick wit to match the beauty.*

"All right," said Mitchell. "Let's schedule an appointment when we can talk about it." He walked over to Sandra's desk and checked her Day-Timer. There were chicken scratches everywhere. Indecipherable.

He studied it for a moment, flipped the page and looked at some more hieroglyphics, then gazed back up at the woman.

"What works for you?" he asked.

"It's really something of an emergency, Mr. Taylor—"

"Mitchell," he reminded her.

"I mean, Mitchell. Can we possibly meet for a few minutes right now?"

The mournful brown eyes and pained expression on her face made it seem like she would die on the spot if Mitchell said no.

"Sure, if it won't take long." He actually hoped it would, as he had nothing pressing to do. But he couldn't admit *that*. What kind of lawyer can just be interrupted in the middle of the afternoon and devote a bunch of time to a walk-in client?

"I promise I'll be quick."

"Great, then c'mon back," Mitchell started walking toward his office, then thought better of it and veered toward the Rock's corner office instead. "Can I get you anything to drink?"

"No, thank you."

"What did you say your name was again?"

"Piseth Peaklica."

"That's a pretty name," Mitchell lied. He paused for a beat. "How do you spell it?"

30

OVER THE NEXT HOUR, she told him a lot, but she did not tell him everything. She started with the story of her journey to America. The Snakeheads. The Coyotes. Charlie Coggins and his demonic dogs. She told him about her mother's courageous sacrifices, many times on the boat and one last time after crossing the border.

She was determined not to cry. And so she bravely told her story as if she were narrating the odyssey of someone else. She told it without emotion, not trusting herself to relive the loss of both her mother and her own self-esteem at such a critical time. *I must think clearly,* she told herself. *I must not cloud my thoughts with emotions I cannot control.*

She spoke simply of the misery of her life in Cambodia and the hardship of her journey. As she talked, she reminded herself of the teachings of Buddha. *Suffering cannot be avoided. It is a condition of all existence. It is how we respond that matters.*

Mitchell was an attentive listener. But she noticed that, after a while, he stopped jotting notes and asking questions. He leaned forward with his forearms on the desk, listening intently and returning her stare almost without blinking. When she would pause, he would ask a short question to get her started again. He would nod his encouragement and show great empathy with his expressive blue eyes.

Maryna told him about the unreasonable demands of the Snakeheads once she arrived in Los Angeles. She explained how they had virtually made her their slave, how she had worked for them night and day for nearly two years. She did not say what they made her do. Later, she may have to tell him, but not now. Certainly not at their first meeting. And Mitchell had the grace not to ask.

She told of her harrowing escape from the ruthless taskmasters. How she had come east to start over…fell in love with the Virginia Beach area…got a job…worked on her GED. It was not yet time to tell about the surrogacy contract with Cameron. That, too, would come later. Maybe even before she left, depending on how things went.

Finally, she explained to Mitchell how the Snakeheads had found her in Elizabeth City and had broken into her apartment. Again she held back, weighing her trust in Mitchell against her instinctive need to keep her humiliation private.

"This man threatened me…with a knife." She saw the concern flash in Mitchell's eyes, but she could not bring herself to say that it was more than a threat. "Said he'd be back if I didn't do what he said. The Snakeheads want me in L.A. They reported me to the INS so I would lose my job. The next day, INS agents showed up at The Surf House. That's when I packed up everything and ran. Now I'm staying at a hotel in Chesapeake."

This was hard. All her hopes were pinned on Mitchell Taylor.

"I want to stay in this country. Maybe get a student visa. I studied dancing and drama in Cambodia. I would love to teach drama here in America—especially in the cities. I know there is a great need for such teachers." She paused and gently bit her lower lip to stop it from trembling. She willed herself to stay calm, unemotional. "Mr. Taylor, I mean Mitchell, can you help me?"

For the first time since she had started talking to him, Maryna looked down.

Mitchell took a deep breath and shifted in his seat. "Piseth," he said, "I really want to help you. If I knew the first thing about immigration law, I would try."

She looked up again. She could see the sadness and genuine concern in his eyes. She felt her own eyes start to water, and she blinked hard. She swallowed with difficulty as he continued.

"But I would be doing you a great disservice if I took your case. You need a first-rate immigration lawyer. Someone who can get you a student visa. You've paid a high price to come to this country. And Lord knows we need the inner-city teachers.

"If you can get a visa, then you can go to the police and report this organized crime ring from China. It's despicable, what they do. I'd be glad to help you with that part of it, but you've got to get a visa first. And in the meantime, stay out of sight."

He looked at Maryna and waited. "Okay," she said quietly, still fighting back the tears.

"If you'd like me to, I can call some immigration lawyers for you right now. I can put them on speakerphone and explain the situation, make sure you get a good deal."

Maryna took a quick, sharp breath and nodded quickly. She said nothing, knowing that if she talked, she wouldn't be able to control the tears. Mitchell turned to the phone book sitting on the credenza and leafed through some yellow-page ads. He found what he was looking for and started punching in some numbers.

"Wait," said Maryna, quickly wiping the tears from her eyes. "Before you call another lawyer, I've got to ask you something."

Mitchell stopped dialing and looked up at her expectantly.

"Did you really mean what you said on television yesterday about those frozen embryos that belong to Cameron Davenport?" Maryna asked. "You talked about their souls, remember?"

"Yes," Mitchell said tentatively, his response itself a question. Then he waited. He cocked his head sideways, thoroughly perplexed. He watched Maryna fiddle with her hands.

"My name is Maryna Sareth," she said quietly, almost in a whisper. She looked down at her hands as she spoke, embarrassed for her lies. It had seemed so clever, so necessary, as she was planning this meeting. Now she felt so stupid. "I am the surrogate mother for Cameron Davenport's child."

She glanced up at Mitchell, who was still sitting behind the desk, holding the yellow pages. If he was surprised, he did not show it. Compassion blazed in his eyes.

"Everything I have told you about my immigration problems—they are true. It is probably why Cameron and Dr. Brown choose me to carry their baby. They know I will be totally within their control. I have no ability to go to the courts or the authorities about anything—the authorities will just send me back to Cambodia."

Maryna stopped cold at the thought of deportation. All of her mother's sacrifices for nothing. With a quick brush of her fingers, she wiped at another tear working its way down her cheek, sniffed, and fought to continue.

Without speaking, Mitchell held out a small box of Kleenex. Maryna took one, mouthed her thanks, and dabbed at her eyes and nose. She wadded the tissue in her hands, wringing it as she continued.

"I signed a surrogate contract that says I could terminate this pregnancy if continuing would be a danger to my health and that Cameron could chose to have the pregnancy terminated up to the third trimester if the fetus develops"—she tried to find the word while Mitchell patiently waited—"sicknesses, um, *abnormalities,* I think it says…that would harm its ability to develop into a normal and healthy child. The doctors are telling me that my baby…uh, the fetus, has Down syndrome."

Maryna swallowed hard. *Curse these tears! Keep your head! Think about Dara. Breathe. All humans must suffer,* she reminded herself. *The key is how we handle that suffering.*

Buddha, where are you when I need you the most? How would the Great Teacher handle this? she wondered.

"I think Ms. Davenport wants to abort this baby," she continued. It was the first time Maryna had ever used the word *abortion* out loud. Until now, everybody—Cameron, Dr. Avery, even Maryna—had gently talked about "terminating" the pregnancy. It was time to call it what it really was. "I can't do that, Mr. Taylor. Just because this baby is not perfect does not give us the right to kill this child, throw it in the trash, and just start over again like nothing happened."

She was struggling now to continue. The tears flowed down her cheeks. She pulled out some more Kleenex, dabbed again at her eyes, and unconsciously shredded the tissues.

Her voice choked with the tears, but she went on. "Cameron has been so good to me. I hate telling her that I will not terminate this pregnancy. But if I have to, I will raise this child myself. I thought that as Cameron's attorney, maybe if you agree with me, you could say something, could—"

It was no use now trying to continue. Despair overwhelmed her, and she simply slumped her shoulders, bowed her head, and allowed herself to cry. She hated herself for losing control, but she could no longer keep the emotions in check. The fear of the Snakeheads, nearly dying just two short nights ago. Her life turned upside down. And on top of that, the desperate fight to save her baby from those who had all the power. She had been strong for so long, handled the suffering so well. *Why did I pick this moment to break down? Why do all my faculties betray me now?*

Her chest hurt, the sobbing pulling at the stitches. She stared down at her lap, wondering if she had blown her last chance to save this child.

Then she felt his touch. A strong and warm hand on her small shoulder. He touched her so gently, so tenderly, just placing his hand there as he came over and stood next to her, the soothing feel of his palm partly on her sleeveless shirt, partly on the bare skin of her shoulder. Somehow, magically, like a strong and steady peace flowing from his body to hers, his touch gave her all the answer she needed.

In his other hand, he held the box of Kleenex. Then he did an amazing thing. He squatted down next to her, in front of her, his hand gently dropping from her shoulder to her forearm, all the while maintaining that magical touch. Maryna lifted her head, looked into his eyes, and saw compassion, sympathy, and something more. She couldn't even describe what she saw there, but somehow knew that everything would work out, that fate had touched this man's heart at Maryna's greatest hour of need.

"Hey, everything's gonna be all right," Mitchell said reassuringly.

"I'll talk to Cameron for you. She's a good person. She'll understand. And Maryna…" He paused and looked deep into her eyes. This time there was steel mixed with the tenderness. "I did mean what I said about those embryos."

It was all she could do *not* to reach out and throw her arms around his neck. She had learned to fear men, not trust them. But something about Mitchell Taylor was so very different. He *could* be trusted, he *must* be trusted. She had no choice. *Would it be so wrong to hug this man?*

But then the moment passed, and he was rising from in front of her. He left the box of Kleenex in her lap, and she noticed that her tears were slowing, the sobs disappearing. He squeezed her shoulder, then took a step back and propped himself against the desk.

"I'm sorry to put you in such an awkward position," Maryna said. "I just didn't know what else to do. And then I saw you in that television interview, and it all clicked." She looked at him and forced a smile. "The crying was not part of my plan."

"But a very effective addition," said Mitchell, smiling back. "It's hard to resist a beautiful woman when she cries."

Her heart jumped in her throat, or was it Dara kicking up a storm? The remark caught her entirely off guard, and before she could think, her smile broadened. *Quick, say something witty. Deflect the compliment; show some humility.* She had spent six years flirting with American men. She had seen it all, first on the streets of L.A., then as a waitress in the restaurants on the East Coast. She knew how to play this game. But there was something very different about Mitchell, something more sincere and far more endearing. It caused her brain to shut down, and she felt blood rush to her warm cheeks.

"Maybe I *will* take something to drink" was all she could possibly think to say.

31

BY THE TIME HE ARRIVED back at the Days Inn it was nearly 9:30. The curtains were pulled shut, but the light was still on in Maryna's room. He parked in the back of the parking lot where he could have a good view of her door, slouched down low in the driver's seat, and waited.

He had followed the maid home late that afternoon, but caution won out when she stopped at a bustling pharmacy. Mugging the wench in the light of day might be gutsy, but jumping her in a busy parking lot would be downright stupid. Patience and careful planning were key. He followed her to a run-down section of Portsmouth, where he and his fancy car were definitely out of place. He parked a block away from her row house, barely able to see her parked car from his vantage point.

And he waited some more.

Three hours later, after darkness fell, his patience was finally rewarded. The maid came lumbering out the front door, got in her car, and drove four blocks to a neighborhood grocery store. While she shopped, he used a Slim Jim to break into her car, then climbed into the backseat. He covered his face, his fake beard, and his hairpiece with a ski mask and lay quietly on the floor, waiting for her return.

Fifteen minutes later, the maid came back, opened the trunk of the car first, and unloaded her groceries from the cart. She then closed the trunk, crawled in behind the wheel, and started the car. Without warning, he put a gun to her head and saw her glance instinctively into the rearview mirror. "Drive to that corner of the parking lot," he growled, motioning toward a deserted corner.

When they were in the isolated corner, he made her turn the car off, then he blindfolded her. Still holding the gun to her head, he made her climb over the seat and join him in the back. He almost broke out laughing as he watched the woman, trembling like a fool, trying to haul her considerable girth over the front seat without looking at him. He was lucky to be far enough away from the other vehicles so that nobody could see this spectacle.

Finally, unceremoniously, she joined him in the back.

He duct-taped her hands, feet, and mouth. Talking in the gruffest voice possible, he threatened to kill her if she tried to get out of the car before morning. When he asked if she understood, she nodded her head vigorously.

Then, without warning, he smashed the handle of his gun against her forehead. The blow opened a gash, drove her head against the window, and knocked her unconscious. He holstered the gun, grabbed her purse and car keys, and quickly left.

I probably should have killed her, he told himself. He was sure she would never be able to identify him—not with the ski mask covering most of what she saw—but he probably should have killed her anyway. He remembered how his hand shook just before he delivered the blow to her forehead. She never saw it coming. He struck with all his fury, heard the thud of metal on bone, saw the blood gush out, and felt the rush of adrenaline course through his veins.

He was now a force to be reckoned with. The police would investigate and find nothing. His hair still stood up on the back of his neck when he thought about how he had terrified his victim, the bashing of his prey, her quick groan, and his total domination. It had gone exactly as he had planned.

But still, he probably should have killed her.

With her keys in hand, he had removed the ski mask and returned to the hotel. He parked where he could see the front desk, and waited. When the attendant left the desk and headed into a back office, he walked quickly into the lobby, past the front desk, and just around the corner to the cleaning crew headquarters. He found the right key and let himself in. Using just a flashlight, he searched around an old metal desk until he found what appeared to be the master keys. He slipped out as quietly as he entered, walked right past the front desk, and headed back to the parking lot.

He tested the key on an out-of-the-way room that had been dark for over an hour. He slid the electronic key into the slot, watched a small green light flicker, then opened the door to the empty room. He stuffed the key back in his pocket, closed the door, and returned to his car where he continued his vigil on Maryna's room.

He stared hypnotically for more than an hour until the light flicked off in the room and ended his trance. The room was dark now, except for the fluorescent glow from the television. *More patience,* he told himself.

It was getting harder to wait by the minute. He was ready to do this thing; take care of business. He could hardly sit still. He reviewed the plan one more time in his mind, saw himself fulfilling his deadly mission, and rehearsed every contingency.

He was so very ready.

But still he waited. Another hour, silently watching the shadows on the window formed by the flickering television light. Other guests in other rooms came and went, lights turning off in rooms all up and down his side of the hotel. It was now well past eleven, and the parking lot was still. Another hour passed.

At 12:30, the flickering light from the television stopped, and Maryna's room went completely dark. He could hardly restrain himself. His leg started shaking—small, nervous twitches, constant movement. He forced himself to wait still another half-hour. He watched the sky as the billowy clouds rolled across the face of the half-moon.

It was a sign. It had to be.

He put the wool ski mask on his head, under his Yankees cap, but didn't pull it down over his face yet. He checked his pistol, a Glock 38, and returned it to the holster strapped to his chest. The bulge was noticeable under his blue button-down shirt. But who would see? A quick sprint across the parking lot and he would be at her room. He grabbed a pair of wire cutters in his right hand, climbed quietly out of his car, and carefully closed the door, making hardly a sound.

He walked quickly across the parking lot, checking this way and that, then took the stairs two at a time. By the time he reached the top step, he could feel the sweat pasting his shirt to his back. He worked on controlled breathing as he hustled, not quite running, to room 207. He stopped immediately outside Maryna's door and checked one last time to his left and right, then glanced around the parking lot below. Nobody.

He took out the master key and slid it quickly through the slot in the door. The green light signaled access. He delicately grabbed the door handle with gloved fingers and quietly turned it to the left. There was a small click. He stopped, waited for a split second, then slowly cracked the door open until the safety chain was taut.

Silence inside the room.

He raised the wire cutters and clipped the plastic link in the chain. The snap of the plastic actually made him start—he took a quick half step back—the chain rattled free. In the quietness of the night, it sounded like an explosion. But he was committed now. He stepped quickly inside the door, saw her motionless silhouette in the bed, lying on her side with her back to him. The only sound was the steady rhythm of her breathing.

The assassin exhaled deeply and reached for his gun. In his excitement he had forgotten to pull the ski mask down over his face. He cursed himself silently. *Did anybody see me? Don't be ridiculous. How many times did you look around out there? Concentrate. Don't lose it now. Focus!*

He pulled his ski mask securely into place, breathing deeply of the musty wool, then pulled out the Glock and attached the silencer. His stomach was wrenched in a knot, the sweat now forming under the mask—on his brow and the back of his neck—his heart pounding in his ears. He took a step closer, then one more, the galloping heartbeat driving him insane. His throat was dry. He crouched and grabbed the gun with both hands, pointing it as his victim. *You cannot outrun your past, Maryna Sareth. You had your chance!* His hands started trembling, destroying his aim.

Shoot! His mind screamed at his frozen body. But the fingers would not respond. The hands just shook more violently. *This is your moment! Do it, you fool!*

Finally, he found his nerve and squeezed the trigger. The gun lurched, a bullet flew. Then again. And again. *What an incredible release!* He grinned maniacally as her body convulsed about the bed. He stepped closer, unloaded three more shots toward her head, hitting something. Time slowed down as he squeezed the trigger, each bullet unloading a spasm of pleasure through his own body and metal fragments of death through hers.

As suddenly as he started, he stopped. The room grew still again, darkness cloaking the grizzly scene. Time returned to normal and he calmly, professionally, holstered his gun and silencer. He turned quickly and opened the door, then glanced back over his shoulder at the carnage behind him. Muted rays of light from the parking lot partially illuminated his handiwork. The calling card of a demented killer.

He quickly left and closed the door behind him. He ran down the steps and jogged to his car, leaving the ski mask on as he started the engine and exited the parking lot.

He glanced in his rearview mirror constantly, careful to obey every traffic law as he drove to the Interstate. With one hand on the wheel, he removed the ski mask, the ball cap, the fake beard, and the hairpiece. He put them all, along with the Glock, the holster, and the silencer, into a green garbage bag and sealed it shut. In a few minutes, he would pull over on the shoulder of a high-rise bridge and dump the trash bag into the deep waters of the Intercoastal Waterway. He was five miles down the road before he realized that he couldn't stop smiling.

32

Friday, May 21

BLAINE RICHARDS HATED THE THOUGHT of getting up at 5:00 A.M., but this opportunity was worth it. He pulled into the parking lot of the building that housed GenTech's corporate headquarters—an eighteen-story mirrored-glass building in a Virginia Beach office park— a few minutes after 6:00. He greeted the perky redhead from CNN's Financial Center and her camera crew in the spacious marble lobby. They were scheduled to begin the live shooting of "Breakfast with a CEO" precisely at 7:00.

Although he tried not to show it, Richards had to admit that he was a little nervous. Cameron Davenport's lawsuit and the revelation that GenTech had engaged in the cloning of embryos had dominated the airwaves for the last two days. So far, GenTech's stock had weathered the ordeal well, holding steady at sixteen and a quarter. This morning would be Richards' best opportunity to make his case to the media, buttress that price, and add millions to shareholder value.

His jet-black hair had the normal amount of gel holding it in place, making his widow's peak all the more pronounced. He had last shaved after work the prior evening, and the television lighting accentuated the dark shadow on his face. He wore a pair of tailored microfiber slacks, a monogrammed white shirt and tie, and a knee-length white lab coat. He was a cross between a Fortune 500 CEO and an overworked mad scientist. Precisely the image he wanted.

The interview went even better than Richards expected. There was a definite chemistry between him and this pretty young television face who knew so little about the fertility business. Richards was charming, confident, and professorial. Over eggs Benedict and strawberry parfait he explained GenTech's desire to culture a new line of stem cells from the frozen embryos donated by Dr. Nathan Brown. These stem cells, and the nearly $2 million left by Brown to fund the research, could serve as a catalyst for further grants, allowing GenTech to pioneer possible cures for the AIDS virus, perhaps saving millions of lives. And while he expressed great sympathy for Cameron Davenport-Brown, Richards made it plain that he had a hard time understanding what could possibly motivate the woman to stand in the way of these potential medical advances.

Egged on by his host, Richards also addressed the issue of what would happen if GenTech lost the lawsuit. This part of the interview was, in Richards' humble opinion, certainly his finest hour. With requisite humility, he reluctantly explained that GenTech had far outpaced its competitors in the technical area of blastomere separation. If the court struck down the anticloning legislation as unconstitutional, then GenTech would be prepared to leverage its superior knowledge and help parents avoid the types of hereditary birth defects that sometimes haunt these high-risk fertility lab pregnancies.

"Take, for example, the chromosomal defect that is responsible for Down syndrome," he explained to his television host. "Let's say we harvested and fertilized four eggs from a couple who were having difficulty conceiving. And let's say this same couple consented to blastomere separation of these eggs for the sole purpose of testing for hereditary defects."

The redhead leaned forward and nodded, taking another petite bite of her parfait. The camera zoomed in on the unshaven face of Dr. Richards.

"We could create three or four exact chromosomal copies of each of the fertilized eggs. One or two of those copies could be cultivated and used for chromosomal testing. We allow the specimen embryos to grow in a test tube to the point where the genome pattern can be properly analyzed. If we find a genome pattern in any of the tested embryos that has any type of chromosomal defect, then we reject all of the identical copies of that fertilized egg and implant only the eggs with a healthy genome pattern."

Richards paused for effect and turned slightly to his left. He looked directly into the camera to deliver his punch line.

"We could make Down syndrome and similar birth defects a thing of the past."

The camera angle widened, drawing both Richards and the host back into the picture. "There you have it," said the photogenic host, "the promise and potential of blastomere separation. We'll be back with more, continuing our breakfast with CEO Blaine Richards of GenTech Fertility Clinic."

The red light on the recording camera blinked off, and Richards relaxed just a little.

"Wow," said his host spontaneously, "that's incredible."

—◆—

The market gurus apparently shared the host's enthusiasm. GenTech enjoyed a sharp rise in premarket trading, topping out at seventeen-fifty a share, an increase of about 10 percent. GenTech's stock was now just half a dollar short of where it had been before the lawsuit was filed. Other publicly owned fertility clinic stocks also rallied, although to a lesser extent. ProGen rose from forty-seven to forty-eight and three-quarters, while RSI gained a buck and a half, up from forty-three and a half to nearly forty-five.

Richards' performance caused enough increase in value, just in the premarket activity, to put his call options on ProGen and RSI nearly "in the money." A few more dollars per share for each of his competitors, and Richards would be raking in the dough.

More important, his own company's fortunes had now stabilized. Following his masterful PR breakfast, the market analysts no longer predicted that GenTech's fortunes would rise or fall with the litigation. In fact, some were seeing it as a win-win situation for Richards' company, while others still fretted that the negative publicity could adversely affect shareholder value.

All in all, Richards had to congratulate himself on a very successful interview. He had reaffirmed investor confidence in his company and established great rapport with his host from CNN. He stared down at her business card in his hand and turned it over one last time before he stuffed it in his pocket.

He had checked her left hand carefully for engagement or wedding rings. There were none. That would make it easier.

He would wait a couple of days before giving her a call. No sense appearing too anxious. He would know just what to say; he had already perfected his opening line.

"You've had breakfast with a CEO, now how about dinner?"

33

WIN MACKENZIE WATCHED THE FLAWLESS PERFORMANCE of his premier client on CNN. He marveled as the stock ticker for premarket trading showed a distinct bump in GenTech stock. Richards was a brilliant man. A little demented perhaps, but still brilliant.

Win himself was no slouch, but he had his hands full trying to get a case ready in time for the preliminary injunction hearing scheduled for the following Thursday, just six short days away. *How did Nora Gunther and Mitchell Taylor get a hearing so quickly?* Judges in the Eastern District were not known for being pushovers when it came to scheduling injunction hearings.

In any event, Win knew he needed some high-powered legal help to present the kind of case Richards would expect. He had weighed all the options but kept coming back to the same unpleasant conclusion. The man at Kilgore & Strobel best suited to help Win try this case, the man with the best reputation and greatest level of trial experience, was Mack Strobel.

Win hated the prospect of working shoulder-to-shoulder with Mack. The two were staunch rivals, Mack representing the old school and Win representing the new. And Mack had quirks that made him almost impossible to work with. But Win had to admit, when a client's entire company was on the line, there was nobody Win would rather have on his side than Mack.

Just as long as they didn't have to go out for drinks together afterward.

It was customary to clear this type of thing with a client, so Win waited until just after the "Breakfast with a CEO" piece to give Richards a call. Win knew that Richards would be in a good mood following such a stellar performance.

After a few minutes of gushing about what a great job Richards had done on the interview, Win explained the reason for his call. Although it pained him to do it, he lavished praise on Strobel and explained the necessity of having two topnotch trial lawyers working together to prepare for a preliminary injunction hearing so quickly.

When Win finally stopped talking, silence fell between them. It was not what Win expected to hear.

"You still there?" he asked eventually.

"Yes," said Richards sharply, "but I'm just thinking. And I'm wondering: Why did I hire you, and why do I pay you this enormous hourly rate, if you can't handle this type of hearing?"

"It's not that I can't handle it; it's just that—"

"Bull!" exploded Richards. "I want one lawyer working with me on this case. I don't know Strobel, and I don't trust Strobel. I hired you. Now if you can't handle it, I'll go to another firm."

Win squeezed the phone and tightened his jaw. *The arrogance of this man!* The anger began welling up inside Win, prompting words that, if spoken, he would later regret. He breathed sharply into the silence on the phone, seething at the despotism of this client.

"Well?" asked Richards.

"I hear you," said Win, clipping off the words. He banished the thoughts of what he really wanted to say and swallowed the words that would make him feel better. Part of being a great trial lawyer was self-discipline. And this conversation was taxing every ounce of his.

"Good," said Richards. "I've got confidence in you, nobody else. I don't care how good they are."

Win felt the tightness in his chest as the weight of this entire case descended heavily on his shoulders. He shook his head silently and stared at the picture of the samurai hanging on his wall. As usual, they stared back—the scowls on their faces revealing their obvious displeasure.

34

MITCHELL TAYLOR WOKE WITH A START and sat straight up. A knifelike pain shot through his lower back, his reward for sleeping on the floor in his sleeping bag. The light that streamed through slits in the closed miniblinds caused him to immediately check his watch: 7:45.

His stared down at his black sports watch as if it had betrayed him. He was sure he had set the alarm for six. He rolled onto his side and slowly started to rise. Another shooting pain. Mitchell froze and winced. *I'm way too young to be having these back pains.* He rose slowly and started gradually stretching out the kinks. It took fifteen seconds of stretching before he could even stand up straight.

His orthopedist had told him that eight years of playing organized football like a maniac had taken its toll on the L5/S1 vertebrae in his lower back. It was not just football; it was the way Mitchell played football. A kamikaze defensive back who savored the collisions, throwing his body at bigger men, Mitchell was now paying the price. Keep the back muscles strong, the orthopedist said, and we can probably keep the pressure off that nerve and avoid surgery.

Mitchell rolled up the sleeping bag and stuffed it, along with his pillow, into the closet of the room. He stood in the middle of the "spare" room of his two-bedroom apartment and stretched some more. The room had the musty odor of a guy's locker room combined with a storage bin for old books. He had converted the room into a weight room and littered it with free weights, dumbbells, a bench, and a squat rack. There was a small black boom box in one corner and a television sitting on top of some cinder blocks in the other. He'd stacked piles of law-school textbooks against the walls. There was no room for a bed, which is why Mitchell had endured last night on the thin carpet in a ratty sleeping bag.

He made his way to the kitchen, opened the refrigerator door, grabbed the orange juice carton, and took a swig. He pulled the coffee maker out of a corner of the kitchen cabinet and began making a pot. He never did this just for himself; he preferred the 7-Eleven coffee he could pick up on the way to work. But this morning he was not alone.

He wondered if Maryna even drank coffee.

The thought of her made him smile.

When she first came back to his office early last evening, he thought Maryna had lost it. She was so nervous, nearly hysterical, as far as Mitchell was concerned. He wondered what he had gotten himself into.

She said that someone had broken into her hotel room, she was sure of it. She had left a "Do Not Disturb" sign hanging on the door when she had first come to talk with Mitchell, but someone had entered the room anyway and replaced her towels and washcloths. She called the front desk and they assured her that the maids would never clean a room with a "Do Not Disturb" sign hanging on the door. Maryna also told Mitchell that she had placed a small piece of scotch tape on the outside of the door between the door and the doorframe—out of sight, down near the floor—when she left the room. The tape had been disturbed, broken loose from the doorframe.

"So I checked out and came here," she told Mitchell breathlessly, "but I think they must've followed me."

Mitchell thought she was crazy, or at least overly paranoid, but invited her into the conference room so he could figure out what to do. She eventually calmed down enough so that they could begin exploring alternatives. Other hotels were out of the question. She didn't want to involve any of her friends in this nightmare with the Snakeheads. Besides, they would probably check her friends' places.

Mitchell tried to get in touch with a few female friends from law school, looking for a place Maryna would stay. When he couldn't reach them, he did something that he had promised himself he would never do. But tonight it seemed like the only reasonable alternative under the circumstances. He invited a girl to his place to spend the night. Nothing romantic, he assured himself, just a safe place for her to stay.

She turned out to be a real charmer. It took her a while to warm up, but when that happened, it was worth the wait. She had a great accent, a fun personality, and an enchanting past. She also had great eyes, the dark brown, luminescent kind that expressed a million emotions and drew him deep into her soul. He had caught himself staring at her more than once while they talked into the early morning.

He could have talked all night.

She was very different from any other woman he knew. But after just a few short hours last night, he felt like they were old friends. The more they talked, the more he wanted to make the night last, just play it in slow motion, and study every exquisite line on her face until he had seared it into his memory. Even now, he could close his eyes and see the outline of her beautiful smile.

But eventually, those beautiful eyes began blinking more slowly, and the brilliant white smile she had flashed so naturally earlier in the evening became a lazy half-grin. Mitchell insisted that Maryna take his room, which had the only bed in the apartment. She resisted valiantly, but it was not a decision open for discussion.

He was happy to spend the night in the spare room. A sore back was a small price to pay to see such an alluring face later that morning.

Mitchell began quietly setting two places on the small round table that occupied one corner of his kitchen. He would usually grab a bowl of cereal and eat on the old leather couch in the living room while watching the morning news. But today was not usual. He had a female guest in the apartment for the night, and one he was now hoping to impress.

Cereal would not do. Maryna deserved more. Okay, he would get to work a little late this morning. He would still probably beat Sandra to the office. It would be worth it. Maryna was worth it. He would probably never have this chance again, so he might as well make the most of it.

He would make a run for some hot, fresh, and sugary sweet Krispy Kreme doughnuts. It was all Maryna's fault. She made him feel like a kid again.

He quietly opened the door of the bedroom and silently walked toward his closet. He grabbed an old T-shirt and a pair of sandals to throw on with the baggy shorts he had worn to bed last night. He turned around and couldn't resist gazing, just for a moment, at the woman sleeping in his bed. It was dark, but he could still make out the soft features of her face, partially covered by the strands of her disheveled long, black hair. She looked like a model, posed to show the raw and natural beauty of a woman as she slept.

But she was also practically a stranger, someone with totally incompatible religious beliefs—and someone who was pregnant with another couple's baby. She came to him last night seeking legal help, not romance. It was his job—his duty—to give her the best legal advice he could, uncluttered by the emotions that welled up whenever he looked at her. He would not let those emotions dictate his actions and run roughshod over his common sense.

Steeled, he turned from Maryna and quietly left the room. There could be no future with this girl. But that didn't mean he couldn't treat her to Krispy Kreme doughnuts. Just this once.

❧

When she heard the door softly close, Maryna opened her eyes. She had lain perfectly still and watched through the smallest slit in her eyelids as Mitchell walked toward the closet, grabbed the T-shirt, then turned to look at her.

She wondered if little Dara could keep up with her racing heart. "It'll slow down in a second," she whispered. "He's gone now."

She couldn't let this happen. Falling for Mitchell would only result in more pain, another wound for her crippled heart. He had been so kind last night, so attentive as she talked. But he was probably just being considerate. There was no chance for this friendship to become more.

Mitchell was a handsome young trial lawyer, and Maryna was—what?—an illegal immigrant pregnant with someone else's baby! No, there were a million reasons why a relationship would never develop, and a million more why it could never work if it did.

But try telling that to her heart.

She hugged the pillow and breathed in deeply, filling her lungs with the scent of Mitchell Taylor.

MITCHELL'S MEETING WITH NORA GUNTHER and Cameron Davenport started at 9:30 and lasted nearly three hours. He did not much care for Nora Gunther before the meeting began, and he had absolutely no use for her by the time noon rolled around. From what he could tell, the feeling was mutual.

Nora came to this meeting from D.C. wearing a pair of grubby jeans, an old T-shirt from a cancer walkathon, and a pair of sandals. The T-shirt was too small and too tight, highlighting every unseemly bulge in her squat, middle-aged body. Nora's face was pale and round, with large bags developing under her eyes that Mitchell had not noticed just a few days before.

"We have a critical hearing on our request for an injunction in six days," she announced, as if it were news to Mitchell. "I intend to be ready."

For the first hour, she dictated strategy for the hearing and delegated various menial tasks to Mitchell. Next, Nora and Mitchell started outlining the various legal briefs they would submit to the court prior to the hearing. Then Nora and Cameron began discussing the potential witnesses for the hearing, occasionally pausing to explain to Mitchell why his suggestions about the witnesses were ill-founded. After a while, Mitchell realized he was better off not trying to contribute, allowing the women to ramble on about whether to call this person or that person to testify. Under normal circumstances, Mitchell would have erupted by now, but this morning he was doing everything within his power to preserve what modicum of goodwill might exist between him and Nora. He would need it for the surprise he planned to spring at the end of the meeting.

"Mitchell, in addition to the others we've mentioned, we'll need to subpoena Dr. Lars Avery to this hearing. We also need to issue a subpoena *duces tecum* for all of Maryna Sareth's medical records. We need to have them a day or two before the hearing."

Mitchell grunted his acknowledgment and checked his watch. They had been going nonstop for two and a half hours. The only person to leave the conference room had been Cameron while Mitchell and Nora had discussed the legal briefs.

It was 12:05. Mitchell shot Nora a glance of resentment mixed with admiration. *Doesn't this woman ever pee? What is she, some kind of legal robot—a strange mixture of Janet Reno's looks, Marcia Clark's tenacity, and the Energizer Bunny's work habits?*

Mitchell stood and stretched his back. "I've got to take a short break," he announced.

"Why?" asked Nora without looking up.

What do you mean, why?

"Some of us humanoid types," Mitchell replied calmly, "cannot go for long periods of time without engaging in certain bodily functions—that's why." He started walking around the conference room table toward the door. "Usually when our eyeballs start turning yellow, it's a pretty sure sign that it's time."

Cameron snickered. Nora did not crack a grin, did not even look up from the yellow legal pad on which she still wrote furiously.

"I think we're about done anyway," announced Nora. "Let's just review our task list, then I can get back on the road to D.C."

Torn between the need for a bathroom break and the prospect of having Nora out of his hair, Mitchell opted to hold out a few more minutes. He sat down in the nearest chair and crossed his legs.

Nora meticulously covered each item on her list. It seemed to Mitchell that she purposefully talked slower than she had all morning. After five of the longest minutes he could remember, Nora finally concluded.

"Is there anything else we need to cover before I go?" Nora asked, cramming her papers into an already overstuffed briefcase.

Mitchell sighed and blew out a deep breath. "I've got something pretty critical that's going to take a few minutes. Why don't we take a break, then let me lay it out for you and Cameron."

"Can't we just do it now, I've got to catch—"

"No," interrupted Mitchell as he stood and turned for the door. "We can't just do it now." Before Nora could respond, he exited and slammed the door.

Five minutes later, a clearheaded Mitchell Taylor returned and began explaining the issue. He told them how Maryna Sareth had come to his office the prior afternoon seeking legal advice. He explained how Maryna had been hunted down and assaulted by the Snakeheads just a few short days ago. He detailed Maryna's immigrant status as well as her desire to birth the baby she was carrying, even if she had to raise it herself.

As he talked, Mitchell carefully watched Nora and Cameron. Nora's face contorted with disapproval. She tightened her lips, crossed her arms, and occasionally shook her head from side to side. Cameron, on the other hand, seemed enthralled. She just leaned forward, mouth slightly open, soaking in the details about Maryna's predicament as if she were hearing it for the first time.

Mitchell completed his saga, purposefully leaving out the part where Maryna had returned to his office the prior evening and spent the night at his apartment.

"So here are my two questions," Mitchell concluded, looking between Nora and Cameron. "Would there be any problem if I helped Maryna on her immigration issues, given the fact that she could be a key witness in our case? Also, shouldn't we allow her to give birth to this baby? I mean, how can we come across as the protectors of these frozen embryos at GenTech when we're basically insisting that Maryna abort hers?"

"Are you crazy?" Nora snorted. Her face tightened as she leaned forward. "Do you have the first notion of what a conflict of interest it was just for you to meet with this woman?"

Mitchell threw up his palms. "I didn't see it as a conflict. Her position and ours is—"

"You didn't see it as a conflict?" Nora asked mockingly, her voice hoarse with emotion. "How could you not see it as a conflict?" She gave Cameron an incredulous look, as if Mitchell had simply lost his mind and just reported seeing flying saucers land in the parking lot. "This young woman, living in this country illegally, wants to force our client —your client and mine, Mitchell—to mother a baby that will have Down syndrome—which, in case you hadn't noticed, our client is vehemently opposed to—and you don't see a conflict?"

"She said she'd raise the baby herself if Cameron didn't want to—"

"That doesn't fix a thing!" shouted Nora. "What is it with you?" Her breath exploded from her in short bursts, her voice shaking. "You think this illegal immigrant, who can't even get a legal job, is really going to care for a baby with Down syndrome? Oh, she'll have that child, all right. She'll bring her into this world like a goddess, and then she'll dump her. And then what? Poor Cameron, here, will spend the rest of her life raising this child."

Nora paused, spent by her own anger. She stared at Mitchell, who returned her burning gaze, never blinking.

"What were you thinking?" Nora asked, disgusted. It was more of a punctuation than a question. And she certainly was not looking for a response from him.

The two stared for another long moment as the air between them thickened with tension. Mitchell felt the muscles on his face contract, his hands involuntarily clenching. He wanted to return her fire, match her sarcasm and biting remarks with bitter words of his own. *But what good will that do?* He forced himself to clear the anger that was distracting his thoughts. He needed to think clearly for the sake of both Maryna and Cameron.

"Are you done?" Mitchell clipped the words off in a biting tone, never taking his eyes from Nora.

"Quite done."

"Then you listen to me for a moment, something you're not accustomed to doing." He leaned back in his chair and braced his arms against the table, lowering his tone. "You came to this firm seeking local counsel in a case I have not been comfortable with from day one—"

"Then why didn't you say—"

"*Hey!*" snapped Mitchell. "I let you finish without interruption, now you listen to me."

"Let him finish," commanded Cameron.

Nora sighed and narrowed her eyes.

"I am not eager to help overturn the Bioethics Act and open the door to all sorts of cloning." As Mitchell spoke, Nora harrumphed her disapproval. "But I have given this case my best efforts because I knew that, at the end of the day, we are really trying to save eight tiny embryos. For me, everything else became secondary to that quest."

Mitchell now turned and looked at Cameron, searching her eyes for answers, ignoring the grunted disapproval of Nora. "If our position is that those embryos and the fetus that Maryna carries are only valuable if they're free of defects, well, that's a position I cannot defend. It's the very reason people are scared to death of cloning in the first place; they think it will lead to designer babies." Mitchell could sense that his words were having some impact on Cameron.

"So I'm not trying to play hardball here or issue ultimatums. But if our strategy is to ensure that Maryna aborts this baby, then you'll have to find other local counsel for this case—"

"Of course that's our strategy," snorted Nora. "How can we forcefully argue that they're depriving Cameron of having children if we let this rent-a-mom deliver the one she's carrying now?"

"Do you agree?" asked Mitchell, still looking at Cameron.

Cameron glanced down at the table, then over at Nora. Mitchell saw sadness in her eyes, a reflection of hours spent contemplating the fate of her Down syndrome child. He felt sorry for her and a little ashamed of pressuring her so intensely, adding weight to an already heavy burden.

"Can you give us a few minutes alone?" Cameron asked Nora softly. And with a shrug of the shoulders, Nora rose to leave.

36

WHEN THE DOOR CLOSED BEHIND NORA, Cameron rose from her seat and slowly walked to the single window in the room looking out at the back parking lot. She had her back to Mitchell as she stared out in silence for a few seconds, clasping her hands behind her. Mitchell studied her back, the lean yet muscular frame of a female athlete just past her prime, her curly blonde hair cascading to her shoulders.

"Mitchell, I really need you on this," she said. Her voice was so subdued that Mitchell had to strain just to hear. He leaned forward in his chair, never taking his eyes off the silhouette of the body looking out the window. "Before yesterday, when we put my dad in treatment, you were just another local lawyer…a warm body. But now, somehow, you're much more important than that.

"I know Nora can be a pain, but it's just the way she is. She believes so strongly in this…in a woman's right to choose her destiny when it comes to children. Just think what the press would do if you dropped the case now. Sure, we could get other local counsel. But the press would have a field day. They'd say we were hypocrites—wanting to preserve the frozen embryos in the lab but fighting with our own former local counsel so we could abort the one in the womb…" Cameron shook her head slowly, sadly. "What a mess."

She finally turned to face him, and for the first time, he saw the moisture in her eyes. "If we allow Maryna to carry this child to term, we will lose all the other embryos. They'll be destroyed just like my husband's will says they should be. Don't you see it, Mitchell? Our only argument is that a woman's right to procreate ought to trump the contract that Nathan and I signed with GenTech, and it ought to trump the Bioethics Act and anything else standing in the way. But if I already have a child, even an unhealthy one," Cameron shook her head and shrugged her shoulders, "that argument is gone, and all these potentially healthy embryos will be destroyed for research purposes."

Cameron moved forward and sat heavily in the chair next to Mitchell, facing him. "All my dreams, both mine and Nathan's really, of being the parents of a healthy child…gone forever." She reached out and placed her hand gently on top of Mitchell's hand as it was resting on the table.

"The way I look at it, Mitchell, and the way the law is stacked against us, we can only bring one of the embryos into the world. I have hoped with all my heart that it could be a healthy one. Is that so very wrong?"

Mitchell looked at her but didn't answer—*couldn't* answer.

"I'm asking you as a personal favor, Mitchell." She squeezed his hand and leaned forward, looking so deeply into his eyes that Mitchell was sure she could read every thought. "Will you stay on this case at least through next week's hearing, at least until we get the results from the amniocentesis? If the baby turns out healthy, then I'll be grateful for the miracle and drop this case. But if not, then maybe Maryna will reconsider, and we can all move forward together, fighting for our rights to implant a healthy embryo in Maryna."

He wanted nothing more than to help Cameron; she had endured so much. The suicide of her mother, the death of her husband, an alcoholic father, and now the prospect of a child with a birth defect. What else could life throw at her? And how could he even think of adding to this list of sorrows?

"I can at least wait for the results of the amnio," Mitchell replied earnestly. "I care about you. And I really want to help."

She squeezed his hand and drew a deep breath. "I know," she said softly. Then she leaned forward, whispered a sincere thanks, closed her eyes, and kissed him gently on the cheek. She pulled back slowly, their hands still clutching each other, neither of them saying a word.

This unexpected display of tenderness affected Mitchell in a way he found impossible to describe. This one simple kiss, just the slight brush of her lips against his skin, had bonded them in a way that words never could. There was nothing romantic about it, but still Mitchell had a sense that they had somehow transcended the relationship of an attorney and his client. There was something deeper here, just slightly beneath the surface, drawing them together. He eyed her warily, wondering what this fascinating woman would do next.

"If I could just talk to Maryna, I know we could work this out," Cameron said. "Can you help me make that happen? Maybe even meet with us?"

There was something about the request that bothered Mitchell, but he couldn't put his finger on exactly what it was. He thought for a moment, then sympathy won out, and he reluctantly nodded. She made it hard to say no.

"I'll talk to Maryna and see if I can get her to meet with you."

Cameron flashed a sad half-smile at Mitchell. "You'll never know how much this means," she said. Then she straightened up in her chair, wiped her eyes, and regained her composure. "Now, shall we let Nora back in and tell her that we kissed and made up?"

Mitchell rolled his eyes and smiled back. "Let's not," he suggested, "for fear that she might want to get in on the action."

37

WITH TREMBLING HANDS, MARYNA PICKED UP the telephone and called Mitchell's office. As the phone rang, she stared blankly at the television screen, still unwilling to believe what she had just seen.

On the fourth ring, Sandra Garrison answered.

"Davenport & Associates, can you hold please?"

Before Maryna could answer, she was on hold, listening to elevator music that she didn't really hear. Her thoughts were spinning out of control, alternating between anger and fright. *When will it stop? How can they just kill innocent people, as if life has no value?*

Before calling, she had tried to calm her nerves by focusing on breathing, by repeating the mantras of the Great Teacher, by clearing her mind of all temporal thoughts. Nothing worked. She had to talk to Mitchell.

Finally, the voice of Sandra Garrison interrupted the music.

"Can I help you?"

"Yes, I need to talk to Mitchell Taylor. Right away."

"One moment please."

She was on hold again. The maddening elevator music was back. She stood up from the worn leather recliner in Mitchell's living room and began pacing, the phone propped against her ear. "C'mon… c'mon," she mumbled.

Sandra again. "I'm sorry, were you holding for Mr. Taylor?"

"*Yes.* And please hurry! It's an emergency."

"One moment please," Sandra said cheerfully.

"No!" shouted Maryna. Too late. The elevator music was back.

Finally, a third time, Sandra returned, perky as ever.

"I'm sorry, Mr. Taylor is not available right now. Can I take a message?"

"No, you cannot," Maryna said abruptly. "You tell him that Maryna Sareth is on the line and it's an emergency."

"I'm sorry, but Mr. Taylor said that he didn't want—"

"Just tell him!"

More music. "This is unbelievable," Maryna murmured.

Nora and Cameron had just left when Sandra told Mitchell that a Maryna Sareth insisted on talking to him.

"She's rude," added Sandra. "Says it's an emergency."

"Thanks," Mitchell said calmly, trying to hide his concern. "I'll take it in my office." He closed the door behind him. Sandra was a good secretary, but she somehow thought listening to Mitchell's phone conversations was an important part of her job description.

"Mitchell Taylor." He could hear the anxiousness in his own voice. "It's an emergency," Sandra had said.

"Thank God," said Maryna. He could hear the fear in her fragile voice. "I just watched the twelve o'clock news. You know the Days Inn where I had a room?"

"Yeah."

"A lady was murdered there...shot several times as she slept," Maryna's voice choked with emotion. She hesitated. "Mitchell, that was supposed to be me."

"Maryna, are you okay? Where are you now?"

There was silence on the line.

"Maryna?"

"I'm calling from your place, Mitchell. But I've got to leave. I can't put you in danger. And they won't stop until they've hunted me down..."

Her voice trailed off, the sound of her short staccato sobs filling the phone lines. "I've got to just...leave...get far away from here..."

"Listen to me," said Mitchell. He tried to sound both authoritative and comforting. "You can't leave. Not now."

"I've got to..."

"Listen! They don't know where you are. Think about it. If they had known you left the hotel last night and came to my apartment, they would never have shot that other woman. They thought you were still there. They probably know by now it wasn't you, but they don't have any idea where you are."

The sobbing softened some. Still, Maryna didn't speak.

"The safest place you can be now is right where you're at. If you try to leave the area, well..." He didn't need to finish.

"Okay. I guess I hadn't thought this through." Her voice was still shaky, but she seemed calmer, more under control. "I just don't want to put you in the middle of this."

"Hey. I'm already in the middle of it." Mitchell tried to sound nonchalant, like this was no big deal. "They mess with one of my clients, they mess with me."

Maryna paused before responding. "So I'm a client now?"

"Well, not officially. But I'm working on it."

More silence. Mitchell knew he had disappointed her, but he couldn't mislead her.

"I talked to Cameron and Nora today about your situation. They said they'll wait until after the results of the amniocentesis next week to make any decisions about whether they would agree to let you carry this baby to term. At that point, we can also make any necessary decisions about my role. In the meantime, would you be willing to talk to Cameron about this?"

There was a longer pause as Mitchell waited for his answer. When she spoke, Maryna did so with a tone of quiet but firm resignation. "Mitchell, I just can't. Even if I did, it wouldn't do any good. I told her in my letter how I feel about this."

"All right," said Mitchell, sensing he shouldn't push it just now, "but let's talk about that some more when I get home. In the meantime, don't answer the phone or the door, close all the miniblinds, and don't make any more phone calls. And Maryna?"

"Yes."

"Promise me you won't leave before I get back."

A pause. Then, "Okay."

"Promise," Mitchell demanded.

"Okay, I promise."

Her tone of voice had changed. Mitchell could almost hear her begin to relax.

IT HAD BEEN THE LONGEST twenty-four hours of the Rock's difficult life. The first few hours after admission he had spent in a funk. He cursed his dead wife, his spiteful daughter, and his treacherous new employee. But he was also determined, at least for those first few hours, to dry up. He had signed everything the rehab clinic needed to keep him for the first week against his own will.

Thoughts of suicide were never far away. He would blow his brains out; that would show them. Cameron would be sorry then. Sandra Garrison, that disloyal old hag, would not be able to stop crying. Even Mitchell Taylor and the ice-cold Ichabod would have pangs of guilt, wondering if they had pushed too hard. He would show them all. He would write his own new will, leaving all his money to some mindless charity, something like the People for the Ethical Treatment of Animals, then he would swallow the barrel of a .45 and pull the trigger.

Better yet, he would hang himself. He would ask Cameron to come to the clinic, and just before she arrived, he would hang himself.

After two or three hours of self-pity, a wave of nausea hit him. Then came the cold chills and a blazing headache. By nightfall, despite the drugs designed to mitigate the detox process, he was in the full-blown delirium tremens stage, screaming and running from hallucinations so real he could reach out and touch them. The clinic stationed a guard just outside his door to keep him from doing any serious damage.

When daylight hit, the pain intensified in his stomach, forcing him into a fetal position on the bed. Medication didn't help as the Rock moaned through the morning, wishing he would die. By noon, he was able to sit and even tolerate fluids. His head still pounded. His skin was on fire one minute, freezing cold the next. He shook uncontrollably and the room still spun, but he started thinking that maybe the worst was over. There would certainly be more d.t.'s tonight, but they would subside in their intensity and eventually cease altogether. He had been through this before. He knew.

By midafternoon, the Rock had curled up on top of his bed, watching television in his sterile room, wearing a sweater and huddled in a blanket, the shades drawn to keep out the bright afternoon sun. In a few hours, he would be expected to attend one of those preposterous support-group meetings where he would be further expected to get all touchy-feely and share his emotions with a group of strangers.

Fat chance. The Rock would do this the old-fashioned way, gutting it out on his own, or he wouldn't do it at all. They could make him attend the meetings, but they couldn't make him talk.

An unexpected knock on the door rattled the Rock out of his self-loathing.

"I'm busy," he growled. "Come back later."

The door opened, and to the Rock's surprise, Mitchell Taylor stuck his head in the room.

"Anybody know where I can find a good lawyer?" he asked.

"What do you want?" The question came out guttural and hoarse, like the Rock had just been awakened.

Mitchell stood by the door and looked the Rock over. Then he sheepishly explained that he really needed some advice on Cameron's case, that he was sorry for misleading the Rock about the meeting with Ichabod, and that he would keep the Rock's practice intact until the Rock could get out of rehab and back in the saddle.

When he finished, the Rock sat silently for a long minute. Then, rubbing his temple, the Rock walked over to the sole chair in the room and sat down. He turned and looked at Mitchell with narrow eyes.

"Well?" said the Rock dryly.

Mitchell tilted his head and wrinkled his brow in confusion.

The Rock motioned to the bed. "Well…come on in and have a

seat. Might as well start explaining your problem. Take your time. I'm in no hurry. I'd offer you a drink, but…" The Rock spread his palms indicating his helplessness.

Mitchell muttered his thanks and parked himself on the end of the bed, forearms on his knees. He looked pensive, confused about where to begin, how much to say. He just started talking, and before long he had laid it all out for the Rock to sort out.

When Mitchell finished, the Rock grimaced, his face contorted with the pain of his stabbing headache. He mumbled a few expletives, then leaned forward in his chair, wrapping his arms around his stomach, the blanket falling off his shoulders. His stomach felt like it might explode, and he doubled over for a few minutes, groaning intensely. When the pain lessened, he lifted his head slightly and glanced at the wide-eyed young lawyer sitting on the bed.

He sighed, felt exhausted. "I'm all right," the Rock growled, shaking like a leaf. "Nothin' a few brews won't cure." He pulled the blanket snugly around himself again.

"Would it be better if I came back?"

"No!" the Rock said forcefully, as if Mitchell had insulted him. "Let me just give you two pieces of advice…*ugh.*" He clutched his stomach again but kept on talking. "First, I don't want you touching Cameron's case again until we figure out whether you're going to represent this other woman, this…"

"Maryna."

"Yeah, her. I'll take the role of local counsel for Cameron myself if I have to…in order to avoid a conflict of interest. You stay on that Asian woman's case for now as her lawyer. We'll build the proverbial…ugh…*I hate this stuff!*" The Rock rubbed his forehead with one hand, closing his eyes. He wearily extended the other palm out toward Mitchell—the signal for Mitchell to just hold on. After a few minutes of silence, the Rock opened his eyes and continued. He spoke in slurred and tired tones, the very act of articulating words an immense chore.

"Where was I? Yeah, that's right… We'll build a Chinese Wall between the two of us… Seems to fit doesn't it? You stay away from Cameron's case until this Chinese girl finds out for sure if she's got a defective child…and I'll steer clear of her case. Understand?"

"She's Cambodian, Billy."

"Whatever she is—it makes no difference to me," the Rock shot back.

"Then does that mean I can take Maryna's case?"

"Course not," snapped the Rock. His words were curt, but his voice was tiring, trailing off as he spoke. "But it just means we've got to keep our options open. Then we'll decide later. If we don't do it this way, we could likely get conflicted out from representing either one of 'em. And whether I'm in detox or not, I don't want to lose this high-profile case."

"Not to mention that one of the clients happens to be your own daughter."

"Yeah, that too."

"Okay."

"Now second…" There was another pause as the Rock searched the ceiling for what he was going to say. "Man, I can't remember anything anymore… Oh yeah… Get Nikki Moreno to help you investigate this case. She's the best, knows every angle…"

Mitchell frowned and appeared to be insulted by the suggestion that he needed help on Maryna's case. He started to protest, but the Rock waved him off.

"You're a heckuva lawyer, kid. But Nikki knows how to get things done that you'll never read about in the law books. Just do me a favor and hire the woman." The Rock forced a pained smile. "Not too many men I know would complain about spending time with her."

Mitchell frowned. "All right."

"Third—" started the Rock.

"I thought you had *two* pieces of advice," interrupted Mitchell.

The Rock grunted. "I did. What I said so far was advice. Take it or leave it. Now I'm getting ready to tell you something that you darn well better take to heart." The Rock stared intently at Mitchell, the bloodshot eyes focusing sharply for the first time that afternoon.

"Don't get involved with this foreign girl. She's not even a client yet, Mitchell." The Rock jabbed his finger at Mitchell, emphasizing his point. "And even if she were, love and clients don't mix."

Mitchell bit his lip, choosing his words carefully. "Who said anything about love, Billy? I'm just saying that I can't very well just turn her out on the street."

"Her housing arrangements are not your concern, Mitchell. You're her lawyer, for cryin' out loud. You're not her father. I'm tellin' ya, son, you're playing with poison here…fallin' for her… I can see it in your eyes."

"I'm just trying to find her a place to stay," protested Mitchell.

The Rock doubled over again and groaned. "Agh," he shouted, to nobody in particular, "I hate this stuff. Quick, get me a drink!"

39

ON THE WAY HOME from the rehab clinic, Mitchell swung by the offices of Dr. Lars Avery and his partner, Dr. Elizabeth Strong. Mitchell explained his reason for visiting to the dark-haired receptionist, who acted entirely unimpressed. After waiting nearly forty-five minutes, Mitchell finally managed to get a few minutes of the good doctor's time.

Avery escorted Mitchell down a short hallway bustling with patients and other medical personnel, then ushered Mitchell into a tiny office piled high with medical books, magazines, charts, and files. Avery cleared a pile of books from one of the chairs in front of his desk and offered Mitchell a seat.

The doctor surprised Mitchell with his appearance. For some reason, probably the name, Mitchell expected a tall and handsome blond Swede. Instead, Avery was a short man, no more than five-six or five-seven, with jet-black hair everywhere, including a full head of unkempt hair that looked like it had not seen a comb in weeks. The man had a narrow frame, rounded shoulders, and the quick, precise movements of a high-strung overachiever. Mitchell guessed that Avery was about fifty, although the hair made him look much younger.

"I've got just a few moments," Avery announced, glancing at his watch, "so let's get right down to it." He stared at Mitchell with dark and sunken eyes, shadowed by enormously bushy eyebrows.

Mitchell used the next few minutes to explain that he represented Maryna Sareth, that her life was in danger, and that it was imperative for Avery to reschedule the amniocentesis. The men trying to kill Maryna were undoubtedly aware of the scheduled procedure, warned Mitchell, and going forward on schedule could subject Maryna to great risk. Although Avery was not at all happy about it, he reluctantly agreed to squeeze Maryna into his schedule late Monday afternoon—a full day ahead of schedule.

Mitchell then asked Avery to promise, based on the confidentiality of the doctor-patient relationship, not to tell anyone about the rescheduling. Avery's face tightened at the suggestion, as if Mitchell had greatly insulted him.

"That goes without saying, Mr. Taylor. Nobody will know except the three of us and Cameron."

"No. Not even Cameron."

"It's her child," Avery protested. "You can't be suggesting—"

"That's exactly what I'm suggesting. My client, who also happens to be your patient, is entitled to confidentiality in all aspects of her relationship with you. She is simply requesting that you fulfill your legal duty to honor that confidentiality. Cameron has already consented to the amnio; she can be told of the results as soon as it's over. But my client's life is at risk here, and understandably, she wants to limit the circle of those who know her whereabouts at any given time." Mitchell paused and pinned the doctor back with his gaze. "Now, if you can't honor that request, we'll call somebody who can."

Avery took a moment to make his decision. "All right," he said coldly. "But I will call Cameron just as soon as Ms. Sareth is released from the hospital." The doctor glanced down at the planner on his desk and checked his watch. "Now," he said, "if you'll excuse me, I really do need to get back to my patients."

"Thanks, Doctor." Mitchell stood to leave, first reaching out to shake Avery's hand. The doctor had a strong grip, but the clamminess of his skin surprised Mitchell.

"This really needs to remain highly confidential," Mitchell emphasized. He watched Avery closely to gauge his reaction.

"Yes...yes, I know," said Avery. He was already halfway around the desk and heading for the door. "Tell Maryna I will look forward to seeing her on Monday."

Mitchell watched as the doctor walked briskly down the hall and ducked into an examining room.

"I'll let myself out," Mitchell mumbled.

Lars Avery surveyed the parking lot from behind the blinds of the vacant examining room. He watched Mitchell Taylor climb into his truck and drive away. Then Avery walked back down the hallway, went into his office, and closed the door. He tried not to think about what he had to do.

He took a deep breath and dialed the number from memory. After a curt greeting, he got right down to the purpose of his call.

"An attorney named Mitchell Taylor just came by. Says he represents Maryna Sareth and wants to move the amniocentesis up to Monday."

"Okay," said a contemplative voice at the other end of the line. There was a brief pause. "That doesn't change anything. Everyone knows that an amniocentesis carries a certain degree of risk—including the risk of miscarriage. Am I right?"

Avery just gripped the phone tighter and did not respond.

"Lars, are you with me on this?"

"Yeah, I'm with you," Avery sputtered.

"Just make sure you explain the risks. No sense getting sued for malpractice."

Avery saw no need to respond to the biting comment. His stomach churned at the thought of what he had to do. He couldn't get off the phone fast enough.

40

ON THE WAY HOME, MITCHELL CALLED ahead and ordered Chinese. It wasn't until he was picking up the food that the stupidity of his choice hit him. Maryna would probably think he was a real redneck now. She'd probably assume that Mitchell believed any girl who was part Cambodian would *have to* like Chinese food. *What a dumb choice,* he told himself as he left the restaurant. But he had already paid for it. He would take his chances.

It was worse than he realized. Because Maryna was pregnant, she worried about the MSG in the Chinese food and politely asked if Mitchell had anything else in the house to eat. Chips he had. Hungry Man dinners he had. Pizza he could order. But he had nothing quick and healthy, so they eventually settled on a dinner of cereal and toast. Despite Maryna's protests, Mitchell ate the same thing. He wasn't about to eat beef and broccoli on rice while he watched Maryna eat Raisin Bran.

Although the whole menu thing greatly embarrassed him, it didn't seem to bother Maryna at all. Before long they were smiling and eating and even laughing about Mitchell's selection of Chinese. She placed her palms together in front of her, bowed deeply at the waist a few times, and threw in a lousy Chinese accent.

Maryna's composure amazed Mitchell. She was calm, even carefree. He had expected sullenness and tears. But this girl was resilient. Nobody watching her at dinner would have guessed that a cold-blooded killer was relentlessly stalking her.

Mitchell told Maryna about his visits with the Rock and Dr. Avery. They talked about some ideas to smoke out those who were hunting Maryna and how to keep her safe in the meantime. They talked about possible places Maryna could stay that night. And all the while, Mitchell kept waiting for an emotional breakdown from Maryna that never came. She was so cool and reasonable, they might have been discussing the plot of a movie rather than her own life.

Dinner passed quickly. With Maryna, time always seemed to pass quickly.

"Can you at least stomach the fortune cookie?" Mitchell asked. Maybe it would say something about finding romance.

Maryna grinned. Then her whole face broke into a wide smile, sparkling eyes, dimpled cheeks, everything. She tore into the takeout bag, searching for her fortune.

The doorbell rang.

Her expression instantly changed from playfulness to fear. Her eyes went wide, frozen in time, staring at Mitchell.

He put his hand to his lips and walked around to her side of the table. He leaned down and whispered: "Go hang out in the bedroom. I'll handle it. It's probably nothing."

She rose quickly and without a word disappeared down the hallway. Mitchell walked deliberately to the front door, gathering his thoughts. It was nearly 7:30. *Who could this possibly be?*

Looking through the peephole, he saw two men dressed in suit coats and slacks. One was a short and stocky Asian, the other a taller and older Anglo, thin and wiry, with a pointed face adorned by a long nose angling down and a large forehead sloping back. Both men scowled. The Asian man pushed the doorbell again.

Mitchell took a deep breath and eased the front door open.

The men flashed badges from their suit coat pockets. "Agent Jenkins, INS," said the taller man matter-of-factly. "Can we come in for a minute and ask you some questions?" He was already taking a step forward, as if entering the apartment were a bygone conclusion.

"No," said Mitchell, standing in front of him. He knew the game. If he allowed them into the apartment, then anything they saw in "plain sight" would be fair game in court, even if they didn't have a warrant.

They would claim entry into the apartment had been consensual. "You can ask me any questions you have from right here."

Jenkins looked at his partner, a knowing glance not lost on Mitchell. "Okay," he said. "If that's the way you want to play it." He paused, studying Mitchell closely. "Do you know or have you met a young woman named Maryna Sareth?"

Mitchell swallowed, felt the Adam's apple bobbing in his neck. He looked the man squarely in the eyes. "Yes."

A wry smile. "We thought so. Is she here?"

Mitchell moved his gaze from one agent to the next, never diverting his eyes. He refused to be intimidated by these guys.

"Is she here?" Jenkins repeated.

"I won't answer that," Mitchell said at last.

The Asian agent snorted. "On what grounds?"

"I know my rights," Mitchell spoke calmly but forcefully, "and I refuse to answer that question."

The agent stepped forward. "You've been watching too much TV." His tone was dismissive. "You're not a suspect here. Either answer the question, or we'll take your answer as a no."

"What's your name?" Mitchell asked.

The man scowled. "James Chen," he spit out.

"Okay, Mr. Chen, let me tell you what I know. And this is *not* from TV. If you guys had probable cause for an arrest warrant or your belief that Ms. Sareth is for some reason inside my apartment, then we wouldn't be having this conversation. But you obviously don't, so now you're fishing, trying to get me to provide you with your probable cause to enter. But guess what, guys? I'm not going to play that game. So Mr. Chen, my refusal to answer is just that. It doesn't mean yes, and it doesn't mean no. It simply means I didn't answer."

Chen hardened his gaze and moved closer still. He was now in Mitchell's face, or more properly, just under Mitchell's chin, staring up at Mitchell. "Answer the question," he demanded. "If you say she's in there, we'll make the arrest. If you lie, we'll haul *you* in for obstruction of justice. And if you continue to refuse to answer," here Chen paused and blew out a hard breath, "we'll haul you in for obstruction anyway."

It was decision time for Mitchell Taylor. His mind raced, processing a dozen different alternatives. *Should I answer? Should I call their bluff? Are these guys really even INS agents? At 7:30 at night? Would they really take me down on an obstruction charge? Even if I stonewall them successfully, will they just wait outside the apartment until Maryna leaves?*

Mitchell knew he couldn't lie to these guys. But the truth would be devastating.

Yet there *was* a way out…

"I'm her attorney," Mitchell announced. "Any information she has given me, including her present whereabouts, is protected by the attorney-client privilege."

Jenkins let out a derisive chuckle. "Now I've heard it all." He was shaking his head. "You're her attorney," he repeated sarcastically.

"Yes sir, Agent Jenkins, you've got it correct. I'm her attorney. Now, if you boys will excuse me, I've got some legal work to do."

Mitchell began closing the door, but Jenkins blocked it with his foot. "I'll see you Monday, *Attorney* Taylor—at your law firm, with a subpoena."

"Thanks for the warning," Mitchell shot back, "I'll have the coffee on. Now, if you'll excuse me…" Mitchell looked down at the agent's foot. As soon as he moved it, Mitchell shut the door in their faces, and immediately began second-guessing what he had just done.

He latched the deadbolt and watched through the peephole as the agents turned to leave, the disgust lingering on their faces. And as he walked back to the bedroom to tell Maryna, he kept hearing the words of the Rock ringing in his ears.

Don't get involved with this foreign girl. She's not even a client yet, Mitchell. The Rock's finger was jabbing the air. *And even if she were, love and clients just don't mix.*

Earlier that day, Mitchell had talked to Nikki Moreno about getting involved in the case. After Mitchell caved on the fee negotiations and agreed to an hourly rate that rivaled most lawyers, Nikki had signed on. She assured Mitchell that she would be worth every dime.

As soon as the INS agents left and he talked to Maryna, Mitchell decided it was time for Nikki to start earning her keep.

Unfortunately, when he called Nikki's place, he got her answering machine. No surprise there. It was Friday night, party time. Mitchell left a message for Nikki to call back no matter when she got home.

It was past midnight when she returned Mitchell's call. He could hear the party in the background. She explained that she had checked her home messages from a friend's house.

Mitchell apologized for disturbing her weekend and told her that he was calling about Maryna's case. "I need to know if you'd be willing to have a roommate for the next few days," he asked tentatively.

"Mitchell, I thought you'd never ask. But I'd better warn you, hand-some, the other men in my life aren't going to like it."

Mitchell smiled. "Not me, Nikki. It's for Maryna."

Her laugh came from deep in her throat. "I knew that, Mitchell. But a girl can dream, can't she?"

"You're a mess, Nikki."

"Thanks."

"Can she stay?"

"Sure, Mitchell, I'll take care of the girl."

"Good," he said, letting out a huge sigh of relief.

Nikki picked up on it right away. "Oh," she said, "you mean *really* take care of the girl."

He paused. "Yeah," admitted Mitchell. "That's what I mean."

❦

At 1:30 A.M., no fewer than nine different cars pulled up in front of Mitchell's apartment complex. Soon his apartment was swarming with friends of Nikki. They had brought the party to him.

The madness was Nikki's idea. Everybody would leave at once in the dark. They would all come out huddled together, then split up quickly, hunching over and hiding their faces, and get in different cars. Maryna would slip in with Nikki, other partygoers would also pair up. If anybody was waiting in the parking lot, trying to tail Maryna, they wouldn't know which car to follow. Nikki would make sure she wasn't being followed, then take Maryna to her condo for the next few days.

Before the partygoers left the apartment, Mitchell gave Maryna a long hug and told her everything would be all right. "I'll sneak over to see you tomorrow," he whispered.

"C'mon," said Nikki, hustling people out the door, "this is no time to get sentimental."

41

May 22

My little Dara,

I'm going to tell you some things I was afraid to tell you before. And someday, when you grow up and are ready, I will give you this diary. You must know the whole truth. Only then will you realize how wonderful it is that we even made it.

Sometimes, it's all about survival. I woke up this morning and, as usual, after a few minutes headed straight for the toilet. When will this stop?

But this morning there was something different. I was thankful just to be alive. And thankful you were still alive inside me.

We are staying now with a very strange and wonderful woman named Nikki Moreno. She is helping an equally wonderful person, a man named Mitchell Taylor (who is also a handsome lawyer) handle our court case and protect us from those who are trying to harm us.

It seems like suddenly the whole world has turned against us except for Mitchell and Nikki. A group of evil men who call themselves Snakeheads are trying to kill me. They helped me and my mom sneak into this country six years ago. I paid them everything I owed them but then they said I have to pay for my mom even though she didn't make it. They made me their slave for two years. Then, one day I escaped. And until this week, they did not know where I was.

Now they have found me and they want me to go back to work for them. I won't do it, Dara. I can't even tell you about the things they make me do.

They tried to kill me two nights ago, but thanks to Mitchell, I escaped. Now, they hunt for me again.

They also want to kill you. They say that I must "terminate" my pregnancy and come back to Los Angeles. And they're not the only ones. Even Cameron believes I should terminate my pregnancy. But I believe that someday, when she sees you, she will change her mind and grow to love you very much. If she does, I will rip this page out of my diary before I give it to you. If she does not, I want you to understand that I tried very hard to make things right with your real mother.

The only good thing to happen to us lately is Mitchell. I will tell you more about him later. But right now I will just say that when he walks into the room, you'll know. And hang on. How does 180 heartbeats per minute sound?

I love you, little one. Someday we will look back on these tough times and just shake our heads at how wonderfully it all worked out. But in the meantime, we must try to just make it through.

Some days, as I said, are all about survival.

By the way, if you feel someone rubbing my stomach, it's Nikki. She just can't believe you're down there.

I love you,

Your Mom

42

THE SUN RICOCHETED OFF the bay water and made everything sparkle so bright that Mitchell nearly needed shades *inside*. The condo was beautiful. And the women, despite the threatening circumstances that brought them together, seemed to bask in the rays that reached out to highlight their natural beauty.

They were sitting in the living room of Nikki's condo on the Lynnhaven Bay. Her white leather furniture was complemented by a coffee table and end tables with seashells embedded just under the glass surfaces. Nikki's living room, dining area, and kitchen were all part of the same wide-open room on the second floor, with windows lining every wall and a wraparound deck outside. Mitchell couldn't resist stealing an occasional glance over Nikki's shoulder, looking longingly at the white sand and the relentless rhythm of the waves brushing up against the glistening beach.

Nikki had dressed for the strategy session like a day at the beach, complete with gym shorts and a bathing suit top that exposed as much skin as possible. Maryna, on the other hand, wore shorts and a high-neck cotton T-shirt. Inspired by the barefoot women, Mitchell, who had shown up wearing khakis and a T-shirt with cutoff sleeves, kicked off his sandals as well.

"We can't just hide her forever," Nikki said. "We've got to smoke these guys out."

"Yeah," agreed Mitchell, "but who are they? Where are they? And how do we get them out in the open?" Mitchell propped his legs on the coffee table, leaned back, and put his hands behind his head.

Maryna took a sip of iced tea. "The first part is easy, Mitchell.

They're men hired by the Snakeheads. Who and how many I don't know. And how we handle them, well..." She shook her head and looked out at the horizon over the ocean. "I don't have the foggiest idea. Maybe I should just..." Her voice trailed off.

"You aren't going anywhere without us," said Nikki forcefully. She looked over at Mitchell, who watched the overhead fan as it slowly turned. "What're you thinking, handsome? Something underhanded, I hope."

Mitchell snorted. "I'm thinking that only five people other than us had any idea that Maryna might have been with me last night. One of those five people must have tipped off the INS."

"Cameron, Mr. Davenport, Dr. Avery..." Maryna was ticking off the names on her fingers. "Who am I missing?"

"Sandra Garrison," said Mitchell. He took his eyes off the fan and looked at Nikki. "And Nora Gunther."

"I never trusted Sandra," Nikki responded, ignoring the implication about Gunther. Nikki jumped up and headed to the kitchen to grab another drink. "Nobody can be that nice."

Maryna gave Mitchell a skeptical look. "Are you saying one of them is tied in with the Snakeheads?"

"Not necessarily." Mitchell stood as well and walked over to the window, his hands deep in his pockets. "The Snakeheads want you dead. But somebody else wants you deported. Somebody who thinks they've got a lot to lose if you stay in this country." He turned back around and looked from Nikki to Maryna. No time for implications and innuendoes. "My money's on Nora Gunther. She plays for keeps."

"Okay," responded Nikki matter-of-factly. "Anybody else want anything?" She popped open a light beer.

"No, thanks." Mitchell was disappointed he couldn't get anybody else on board with his blame-Nora theory.

"Let's look at our options," Nikki continued. "We can't go to the feds; they'll just call the INS. We can't hide her forever. Heck, she's got an amniocentesis scheduled for Monday." Nikki paused and the others waited. "I say we get a couple of local hotshots from the Virginia Beach Police Department to follow Maryna around for a day or two. We make her real conspicuous. Mitchell, you take her to some very public places, see who follows her or even tries to make a move against her. Virginia Beach's finest will just lay low until the Snakeheads make a move, then pick 'em up, and we're out of the woods."

Mitchell frowned. There were lots of holes in Nikki's plan. He decided to start with the most obvious one.

"If we take Maryna to all these public places, the INS agents will just pick her up."

Nikki scoffed. "Are you kidding? They said they'd be back Monday with a subpoena. You think they're going to work over the weekend just to bust one illegal immigrant?"

"Okay," Mitchell said skeptically, as he considered another obvious shortcoming. "How are we gonna get authorization to have a few cops at our beck and call the next couple of days to keep watch over an illegal alien?"

Nikki grinned her Cheshire-cat grin. "That's the easy part. Give me a few hours and I'll be back with two cops in tow." Nikki smirked at the surprised looks on the faces of Mitchell and Maryna. "Meanwhile, you two lovebirds enjoy the bay."

Maryna's face reddened, and Mitchell shot Nikki a reproving glance.

"Very funny, Nikki," he said sarcastically.

❦

Nikki located commonwealth attorney Harlan Fowler three hours later, on the back nine of the Virginia Beach Country Club course. With her usual flair, she came riding up behind the foursome in a rented golf cart, then stood quietly beside it as they teed off. Harlan sliced his shot miserably, cursed up a storm, and endured vicious ribbing from the others.

Harlan was a cinder block of a man, short and square, with a flat face and a broad Roman nose. His thick, plastered hair and mean-looking scowl convinced voters he was tough on crime. But Fowler had pretty much become a consummate politician during his tenure as commonwealth's attorney; he had not actually tried a case himself in nearly four years.

"Nice slice," said Nikki as she walked up behind him. "I think you're lifting your front shoulder too early, taking your eye off the ball." Nikki had never played a round of golf in her life.

"Nikki Moreno!" exclaimed Harlan. He extended a hand. The other men just stared. Nikki had traded her swimsuit top for a low-cut tank top, although the switch didn't make much difference. "What brings you out here? I didn't know you were a golfer."

She shook his hand and sized up his compatriots. Good old boys, all of them. Probably campaign contributors. They needed a good laugh.

"You act like you haven't seen me in ages, sugar," she drawled. "I just wanted to let you know that you left your glasses at my place last night."

This brought out a few catcalls and harrumphs from the boys. "Is that all he left?" cackled one.

"Is he playing like he's missing his glasses?" asked Nikki innocently.

"Absolutely."

"I'd be happy to come retrieve them for him," volunteered another.

Everyone laughed, including Nikki. The guy was old enough to be her grandfather.

"Can I speak to you alone for a minute?" she asked Harlan.

"Hooo-yah," his buddies teased. "How can you say no to that?"

He couldn't. When Nikki got him aside, her demeanor transformed from spice girl to professional businesswoman.

"You owe me," she said.

Harlan nodded. "The Hornsberger case."

"It's the only reason you ran unopposed last year," Nikki reminded him. She glanced over Harlan's shoulder at his buddies, then down at the ground. "And I've never asked for anything in return…until today.

If you can help me on this, we're dead even." She looked straight into his eyes and could tell she had him.

Harlan shuffled his feet and paused. "I'll never hear about it again?"

"Never."

Another pause. "If what you need is legal and within reason, I'll see what I can do."

In the next few minutes, Nikki negotiated a twenty-four-hour tail on Mitchell and Maryna. Claiming manpower shortages in the police ranks, Harlan insisted that he could not ask the chief for an hour more than twenty-four. "And even that's a stretch."

Nikki promised to personally keep him in the loop. "We're gonna make you a hero again, Harlan," she promised as she began walking back to her cart. Then, when she was far enough away so she had to yell, she turned back and shouted loud enough for all Harlan's buddies to hear. "See you tonight, sugar!"

This set off another round of teasing and catcalls from the gang. It didn't seem to bother Harlan in the least.

43

THIS IS NOT GOING WELL, Cameron decided. She noticed precious little improvement in her dad. He was still having chills during the day and nightmares at night. He looked haggard and spent. With his two-day growth of gray stubble, he could easily have been mistaken for a street bum. He was focused on only one thing: Did Cameron bring the small flask of rum he had requested? She had told him no over the phone, but he didn't seem to hear.

Cameron had other things on her mind.

"I've got to talk to Maryna, Daddy. Nora says that we need her to testify. And she's got to say that she thinks it is best to terminate this pregnancy if the amniocentesis confirms the Down syndrome diagnosis. Can't you get Mitchell to say where she is?"

"Haven't talked to Mitchell since yesterday," the Rock said in a gravelly voice. "Don't know where he's got her."

"You've got to find out." Cameron's own voice was hard and cold. She was more the stern mother in this relationship than the child. "Call him if you have to. Ask him to come visit you."

The Rock shrugged his shoulders. He kept his gaze fixed on Cameron's handbag. "What's in there? What'd you bring for the old man?" He forced a quick smile.

"Daddy, you'll never get better if I—"

"Don't lecture me," the Rock snapped. Then he shuddered. "In a few more days I can be off the stuff entirely. In the meantime, this cold-turkey routine is for the birds."

Cameron eyed her pathetic father, huddled in the chair, begging for a drink, his bloodshot eyes transfixed on the handbag sitting next to her on the bed. His desperation embarrassed her.

Before she could prevent it, her mind flashed back to her childhood, to images of a charismatic father who everyone loved. And who loved everyone—except his own family. She remembered how desperately she tried to get his attention. "Can I go to the store with you, Daddy? Can you come outside and play with me, Daddy? Can you tuck me in tonight, Daddy?" It was always, "Not now, honey" or "Later, honey" or "Your mama's gonna do that, honey."

And now she could hardly stand to be around the man whose attention she used to crave. She was starting to realize that she didn't really want a relationship with her dad the way he was; she wanted a relationship with the type of dad he could never be.

"Dad, I've got to ask you a favor."

The Rock just stared ahead, shivering, waiting for Cameron to continue.

"You've got to get Mitchell not to represent Maryna. I talked to him myself yesterday but didn't have the heart to make him stop representing her entirely. I told him we would wait and make a decision after the results of the amnio came back. I told him there might not even be a conflict between what I want and what Maryna wants once the test results come back.

"But Dad, then I talked to Nora and she said that was totally unacceptable. We've got to have Mitchell with *us* at next week's hearing. He can't have any split loyalties. I'm asking you, as his boss, to tell him he's already representing us and he'll just have to find somebody else to represent Maryna."

The Rock was shaking his head, and Cameron felt the color rising on her neck. "Can't do that," her dad was saying, "I promised him myself that our office could handle both until the test results..." He shivered again, and his voice trailed off.

"That won't work!" Cameron said sharply. "I'm your own daughter, for crying out loud. You didn't take care of me while I was younger, when I needed you—at least help me now! When is the last time I asked you to do *anything* for me?"

The Rock allowed his daughter's accusation to hang in the air un-answered. Only a ring from her cell phone broke the silence.

"Yes," she said harshly, standing up and listening to the phone. She began pacing around the room, looking concerned. "Just a minute," she said. With the cell phone glued to her ear, she stepped out of the Rock's room and into the hallway, closing the door behind her.

—◆◆—

The Rock couldn't believe his luck.

He rose quickly from his seat. The room spun. He put his hands on his knees for a moment, shaking his head to clear his thoughts as he found his bearings. Then he walked slowly, deliberately, over to Cameron's handbag.

He started rummaging through it, keeping one eye on the door. She kept so much junk in the blasted thing. He could almost taste the rum—the smooth burn of the drink as it slid down his throat and soothed his chest. She would have brought something. He was sure. His hands trembled as he filtered through the items. Lipstick, mascara, a wallet, a wad of receipts, and then...

"What the—?" he murmured. He lifted the item, his hands trem-bling even more than before. He shook his head, a more vigorous shake this time to clear the cobwebs. This couldn't be right. He couldn't be seeing this...holding this... He jammed it in his pocket, hands now shaking violently.

What could it possibly mean?

—◆◆—

Mitchell Taylor visited the Rock later that evening. The Rock was in a foul mood.

"I don't see any way we can represent both Cameron and this Asian girl," the Rock said the moment Mitchell walked in the door. "The whole point of avoiding a conflict of interest is to keep from having divided loyalties. If we continue working on this other girl's case, seems to me we've got divided loyalties."

Mitchell felt a lump of frustration rising in his throat, swallowed hard, then launched into an explanation about the INS agents and the fact that he already told them he was Maryna's attorney. Besides, he argued, the Rock himself had agreed they could work on both cases at least temporarily. But the Rock seemed to be uninterested, glancing around the room, rubbing his temples, occasionally grunting his disapproval. When Mitchell finished, it took the Rock several seconds to respond.

"Is that where she is now? Staying with you?"

"Not anymore," said Mitchell. He decided not to explain further.

The Rock sighed and shook his head in disbelief. "You don't represent her anymore either. Tell her you withdraw."

"I thought you said we'd wait until the results of the amnio came back," Mitchell protested. "I can't withdraw now!"

The Rock stared directly at Mitchell. "I told you not to commit to representing her, Mitchell. I said we were just going to keep our options open. I told you not to get involved with her, Mitchell. Then you go out and totally ignore what I say." The Rock turned up his palms. "I can't have that, Mitchell. I might be an old codger locked up in a rehab clinic, but I still run Davenport & Associates, and I can't have that."

"I'm sorry, Billy," Mitchell said softly. "But the INS agents were at my apartment door, ready to deport her. I had to help her. What choice did I have?"

The two men sat in silence for what seemed like an eternity. The Rock finally spoke, staring at the wall behind Mitchell.

"You really want to represent her?"

"Yes sir, I do."

A long pause. "Then you're fired, Mitchell." The Rock spoke softly, without venom in his voice. "I like you plenty, son. But I can't have someone working for me who I can't trust to do what I say." The Rock's gravely voice softened even further. "Tell Sandra I'll be back Monday—"

"You can't do that, Billy! You're not ready."

But the old man's hand was up, and he dropped his tired face toward his chest. Mitchell realized that arguing further would be fruitless. The Rock was not going to change Mitchell's mind about representing Maryna. And Mitchell was not about to change the Rock's mind about coming back to work. It was a standoff between two stubborn men, Mitchell realized. And it would do no good to argue the point.

Mitchell watched the Rock close his eyes and slowly lean his head back, as if Mitchell had already left. At that moment, Mitchell felt no anger toward the man, just sympathy. Silently, respectfully, Mitchell stood, wanting to shake the Rock's hand but deciding instead to just quietly leave.

For some strange reason, he admired the man who had just fired him. He sensed the Rock was trying to do him a favor, to protect him from something that he could not yet understand. As crazy as it seemed, he would actually miss working for the Rock.

But it was time now to turn his attention to the one client he still had left, Mitchell decided as he headed for the door. And he consoled himself with the thought that if he could only have one client in the entire world, he would pick a beautiful and compassionate young lady named Maryna Sareth.

"Represent that girl, son," the Rock called out, as Mitchell was leaving the room. "But be careful. Nothing in this case is the way it seems."

44

Sunday, May 23

MARYNA FELT LIKE SHE HAD DIED and been reincarnated into another life. She pinched the outside of her right leg, just below the hemline of her skirt, to make sure it wasn't some kind of bizarre dream. She was sitting in church—a *Christian* church no less—next to Mitchell Taylor. The perfect all-American couple without a care in the world.

Nothing could be further from the truth.

Maryna couldn't remember when she had last felt so conspicuous. She kept glancing around furtively, sure she would catch others staring at her. It was all Mitchell's idea. It had even sounded reasonable at the time. "Let's go to my church together," he had said. "Surely the Snakeheads will follow us there, then stay on our trail. The detectives can follow and wait for the Snakeheads to make their move. Where else could we be so noticeable and yet so safe?"

She had not argued. But now she felt like a fool.

For starters, she had overdressed. How was Maryna to know that people didn't dress up for this church? She had dressed at Nikki's condo, and it was obvious that Nikki didn't know the first thing about going to church, either. So Maryna had borrowed a tight black skirt, heels, and a sleeveless cotton blouse that hugged her high around the neck. She had managed to keep the top buttons on her pajamas buttoned the night before. To her knowledge, Nikki hadn't seen the scar.

Mitchell showed up in a pair of dress slacks and a golf shirt. He was apparently too polite to tell her that no one under forty wore dresses to Chesapeake Community Church anymore. "You look great!" he gushed.

Flattered, she had felt her cheeks blush.

Now she felt like a woman wearing a wedding dress at a beach party.

It didn't help to watch everybody singing their hearts out to songs she had never heard before. People closed their eyes, lifted their hands, and sang at the top of their lungs. She watched the words on the screen and mouthed along, wishing at first for the accompanying musical notes. No matter. By the fourth time they sang the same chorus, she could have joined them if she wanted.

Her favorite part so far was the prayer. The man that Mitchell called Reverend Bailey stood up behind the podium and called on the church to bow their heads. When Maryna did so, she felt Mitchell's strong hand gently take hers. She instinctively opened her eyes and tilted her head to look at him, but he kept his own eyes closed. She curled her fingers around his palm.

Touching him was so special, it was impossible to describe. It made her skin tingle and her heart race. A current flowed from Mitchell to Maryna and—she hoped—back to him. She would have to calm down. He probably didn't even mean anything by it.

But a girl could dream. She wished the prayer would last forever.

And it almost did. Reverend Bailey rambled on and on. He prayed about this and that. Sometimes Maryna was sure he was lecturing the church rather than talking to some God out there. But finally he finished with a flourish to a loud chorus of "amens." Mitchell squeezed her hand and let go. *Darn.*

Next, the ushers of the church got busy, and the members paid their dues. Everyone was very discreet about it, stuffing cash into little white envelopes or folding their checks in half so others couldn't see how much they gave. Reverend Bailey had actually said that visitors weren't expected to contribute, but Maryna got the feeling he was just trying to be polite. Although she really didn't have a dime to spare, she reached into her purse and plunked a twenty in an envelope. She placed it proudly in the offering plate, hoping Mitchell noticed.

They sang again, then Reverend Bailey took his place behind the podium to deliver the sermon. This time, everybody kept their eyes open and, to Maryna's disappointment, Mitchell kept his hands to himself.

Reverend Bailey started by reading from an ancient book of the Bible he called Jeremiah. Mitchell impressed Maryna by knowing right where to find it. Maryna followed along as the reverend read.

It was unbelievable, this book of Jeremiah. She felt like the author had been reading her diary. She shot a quick sideways look at Mitchell. He must have been talking to the reverend.

"Before I formed you in the womb I knew you," Reverend Bailey read. "Before you were born I sanctified you. I ordained you a prophet to the nations."

"Wow," Maryna whispered to herself. Then she leaned over to Mitchell, whispering in his ear. "Sanctified?"

"It means purified. Set apart for God," Mitchell whispered.

Maryna nodded her head. Reverend Bailey had her attention. She didn't believe in coincidence, so she listened intently to every word. Although more than a hundred others listened in the school auditorium where this church worshiped, Maryna knew this message was clearly intended just for her.

"Each of us," explained Reverend Bailey, "is 'fearfully and wonderfully made.' We are each unique, special projects of God's creation. And God doesn't make no junk.

"You may wish you had more ability, more intellect, less weight, or a shorter nose. But who are you to question God?" he asked. "God created us. He is the potter; we are the clay. Should the clay argue with the potter? God formed you just the way you are," Bailey argued, "warts and all, handicaps and all."

Did he really say that: "Handicaps and all"? Maryna wondered. *More important, is it true? Does a loving God really create some of us with special challenges in life? Even Down syndrome?*

The reverend must have heard her thoughts. "Have you ever been to a Special Olympics?" he asked. "Have you ever noticed that those kids seem to be happier, seem to be enjoying life more, than those who compete in the international Olympics? And their happiness does not depend on whether they win or not."

His point is true, thought Maryna. She sensed that God Himself was speaking to her, telling her that her feelings about Dara were right. *Before I formed you in the womb I knew you, the Book said.* This Jeremiah, it was like a diary from God to Dara, written to her before she was born—calling her by name, telling her that she was special.

Maryna's mind wandered, and when she returned her focus to Reverend Bailey, he was no longer talking about the Special Olympics.

"Although God created each of us unique, in one important way we are all the same," he said. "He created deep inside every one of us a 'God-shaped vacuum'—an intense longing that can only be filled by a personal relationship with God." According to Bailey, this personal relationship with God was only possible through the provision of His Son, Jesus Christ.

Maryna had, of course, heard the name of Christ many times before, usually in the form of a curse word. As far as she was concerned, Christ was the Western version of the Great Buddha—a wise teacher whose peaceful teachings could help change lives, nothing more.

But according to Reverend Bailey, Jesus Christ was so much more. Christ Himself claimed to be God, Bailey said. He lived a perfect life and died a martyr's death on the cross. On the third day, according to Bailey, Christ rose from the grave and came back to life. He conquered death. It was a proven historical fact. You could look it up.

Maryna stole a quick glance at Mitchell. This man she had learned so quickly to trust, this sharp young lawyer with the analytical mind was soaking it all in, taking notes. *Does he really believe this? Rose from the dead?* Buddha would never make such a brazen claim.

And Bailey wasn't through. Our sins separated us from God, he claimed. *Sins?* Maryna scrunched her forehead.

"Mistakes, failures, pride, selfishness, that type of thing," whispered Mitchell, seemingly reading her mind.

"Because God is holy and pure," Bailey continued, "He cannot welcome us into His heaven when we die unless the price for our sins has been paid. And that," said Bailey excitedly, "is where Jesus Christ comes in.

"He paid the price! By coming to earth and living a perfect life, by obediently and willingly dying on the cross, Christ took our place. God sent His own Son to die for us so that we might accept His sacrifice and have eternal life. The God-sized vacuum is filled when we ask forgiveness for our sins, accept Christ as our Savior, and ask Him to become Lord of our lives."

This information overwhelmed Maryna. Son of God. Savior of man. Conqueror of death. *Just who is this Christ anyway?*

As abruptly as he started, the reverend stopped. And then they were praying again—no handholding this time, it was a very serious mood— and the Reverend Bailey was asking everyone who felt this God-shaped vacuum in their hearts to raise their hand. Almost without thinking, Maryna slowly raised hers. She was drawn by a force outside of her own body, as if she were watching herself in a play. Her heart ached but at the same time pulsed with an intensity she had never known. This deep longing, this yearning to know God personally, this hunger for peace and purpose, was the only thing that was real. She couldn't deny it. She couldn't resist it.

And now the prayer was over, and the entire church was singing. Reverend Bailey, his voice rising above the song, was urging those who had raised their hands to come forward. Maryna knew she should go. She *wanted,* no she *craved,* what he described. But when the reverend glanced at her, she froze. *What will Mitchell think? What will happen if I go? What about Buddha and the faith of my mother? Can Christ really provide a path to God and fill this vacuum?*

And so she stood rooted, seemingly suspended in time and space, as the song dragged on forever. "One more verse," said the reverend, "somebody here is struggling to let go of their sins and come to Christ."

She trembled at the words. He somehow knew. He could see right through her. And Mitchell could probably sense it too. But still she hesitated, sweat starting to bead on the back of her neck and brow. *Relax,* she demanded, *deep breaths, in and out.* She could talk to Mitchell about all this later. Making an emotional decision about religion, in the midst of everything else that was going on, would not help matters. If this was truth, it would still be truth tomorrow. And the next day. Surely, God would give her that much time to sort it out.

And then it was over. The last verse finally sung. Reverend Bailey closing in prayer.

On the way out of the auditorium, Mitchell and Maryna stopped to shake Reverend Bailey's hand. He had positioned himself next to the door, smiling and talking to everyone.

"This is my good friend Maryna Sareth," said Mitchell.

Maryna extended her hand to shake with the reverend. *As if he didn't know,* she thought.

45

Being a lawyer, the Rock knew the clinic couldn't hold him. It didn't matter what he had signed. To hold him against his will would require a commitment hearing, and the commitment hearing would require a showing that he was dangerous to himself or others. It was a showing that neither the clinic nor his daughter could make. And they all knew it.

Not even Ichabod's threat to sabotage his career could stop him. He didn't need liability insurance anyway; he could be self-insured. Sure it was risky, but the Rock hadn't gotten this far by avoiding risk.

And so, after no small amount of arguing, he walked out of the clinic at 3:30 P.M. on Sunday afternoon a free man. He left against medical advice and the pleas of the clinic staff. You never gave it a chance, they said. You'll never be able to live a normal life until you deal with this addiction.

He had heard it all before. The fact that they were probably right didn't even slow him down. This was no time to be sitting and rotting in a rehab clinic. His daughter needed him this week, and he would just have to figure out a way to cope. Somehow, if he could just make it through this one week and help Cameron in her preliminary hearing, maybe things would start to change.

There would be time to dry out in the weeks ahead. But Cameron needed him *now*. And this time, he would be there for her.

The Rock had to wait nearly twenty minutes for a taxi. He chose to wait outside the clinic, preferring the heat and humidity of the outdoors to the scolding inside. He had worked up a good sweat by the time the taxi came. Somebody was jackhammering on his brain, and he could feel the sun frying his bald pate. A minute or two before the taxi arrived, the sky started spinning so badly that the Rock had to sit and close his eyes just to gain some semblance of balance.

The cab driver helped the Rock into the car and asked no questions on the way to the nearest convenience store. For an extra twenty bucks, the cab driver himself bought the six-pack and remained silent as Rock popped the first one before they left the parking lot. By the time they hit the cemetery, the Rock had opened his third.

"Thirty minutes," mumbled the Rock, as he climbed out of the back door clinging to the three cans that remained in the plastic loops of the six-pack. Before closing the door, he threw two more twenties on the front seat as the cabbie pulled away. A few minutes later, the Rock sat dejectedly on the gravestone of Gwyneth Davenport, the sun beating unmercifully on his bald head and the pale, chubby arms that his short-sleeved T-shirt exposed.

"I need your advice," he said, looking down at the flat, carved marble slab that was his chair. "You always knew how to handle her better than I did. And this may be my one chance to redeem myself, Gwyneth, my one chance to win her back." The Rock gazed upward, closing his eyes against the blazing sun. He leaned back on his hands as a single tear crawled slowly down his cheek. "I can't bear the thought of losing you both. What should I do, Gwyneth? What should I do?"

He wiped away the tear with the back of his hand and took another swig of his now lukewarm beer.

❦

Mitchell and Maryna spent most of Sunday trying to be noticed. After church they went back to his apartment so they could both change into shorts, T-shirts, and sandals. Then they stopped by Mitchell's former office, thinking that maybe Maryna's stalker would pick up their trail there. Next they ate lunch at an outdoor restaurant on the boardwalk and took a long walk along the beach.

The whole day, Mitchell glanced around as inconspicuously as possible, always looking for somebody who looked out of place, seemed to be paying too much attention to the couple, or for whatever other reason looked suspicious. He tried not to dwell on the fact that they had intentionally made themselves targets, basically painting a big, fat bull's-eye on their own backs. He reminded himself that two of Virginia Beach's finest—in plainclothes, no less—were never too far behind.

But as the afternoon sun crawled lower in the sky, Mitchell resigned himself to the fact that Maryna's attacker had either smelled a rat or decided for some other reason not to strike.

They had done all they could. Now it was time for some real fun.

As the afternoon turned into evening, Mitchell took another swing by the office and his apartment, picking up a blanket along the way. The last stop of the day would definitely surprise Maryna. Mitchell and Nikki had worked out the details with the detectives but had kept Maryna in the dark. It was not until Mitchell pulled into the parking lot of the Virginia Beach Amphitheater and they saw the signs that Maryna realized they were going to a sold-out George Strait concert— the talk of the weekend at Virginia Beach.

"How'd you get tickets to this?" Maryna asked in amazement. They were sitting in a long line of traffic with other pickups and SUVs.

"Actually, Nikki got 'em," Mitchell said modestly. "They're just lawn seats, but it should be fun. And during the last song, the detectives have it all set up so you can get backstage and head out a rear entrance. Nikki will pick you up and take you back to her condo. If anybody is following us, you'll lose 'em. I'll just leave when the concert's over and go back to my apartment."

"I can't believe this," Maryna gushed.

Mitchell couldn't suppress a big grin. It had not been easy keeping this a secret. "You ever been to a country concert before?"

"No." She returned Mitchell's smile. Then she leaned over and gave him a quick peck on the cheek. "But if I have to go for the first time, there's nobody I'd rather go with."

Mitchell could feel the electricity, and it worried him a little. This was not supposed to be a real date, not with somebody who didn't even share his religious beliefs. Mitchell had a firm rule about that, and this rule was inflexible.

But it's not really a date, Mitchell rationalized. *We're just trying to draw the Snakeheads out.* And he would be careful, he promised himself, not to lead the girl on.

"You know that CD I've been playing all day?" he said.

"Yeah?"

"That's George Strait."

Maryna chuckled. "There's a reason I asked if we could listen to the radio."

"He's better in person," Mitchell assured her as he switched from the radio to his CD player and turned up the volume.

George Strait. Maryna couldn't believe she was here—had now been here all night. And she really couldn't believe she was loving it this much.

At first, she had a hard time enjoying the show. The darkness, the constant glancing around by Mitchell, and the subtle presence of the detectives, all reminded Maryna that her stalker could be lurking behind every smiling face. Yet after a while, the crooning of George Strait combined with the warm, clear night and the nearly full moon to weave a spell of relaxation. Soon enough, Maryna found herself kicked back on the blanket next to Mitchell, feeling as though she didn't have a care in the world.

This was certainly not her type of crowd—she had never seen so many cowboy hats, huge belt buckles, and pointed boots before—but none of that mattered. She was with Mitchell, and he was in his glory. "You'll love this one," he'd say. "It's one of my favorites." He would sing along, and she would just smile and move a little closer.

They talked, they laughed, and they clapped along to the performer's guitar. They made fun of the rednecks and their country girls.

They lay back on the blanket and counted stars. And every second, Maryna wished she could slow the night down and make it last forever.

As the evening wound down, she found her joy replaced by a certain melancholy. The knowledge that her time with Mitchell was short, combined with thoughts of tomorrow's procedure, dampened her spirits and created a lump in her throat.

"You all right?" Mitchell asked. He had caught her staring into the night.

Maryna forced a smile. "Just thinking about tomorrow."

"I really want to be there."

"I know. But Nikki's right." Maryna turned and looked at Mitchell. She leaned closer so she could be heard over Strait's wailing. "If you came, the Snakeheads might follow you to the hospital. We can't take that risk. Nikki will be there with me all day. It's just outpatient. I'll be all right…" She looked down at her hands. In truth, she really wanted him to be there too.

Mitchell leaned so close that his forehead touched hers. As far as Maryna was concerned, there was no one else around, no one else in the world. She closed her eyes and felt Mitchell's arm around her shoulder.

And just when it couldn't get any better, the song ended and the crowd stood and cheered. Mitchell and Maryna joined them, his arm still around her.

The entertainer finally quieted the crowd and started a slow song. Some of the concertgoers sat back down, others rocked slowly back and forth, still others hugged each other close and started dancing.

"When you come around, I get carried away by the look—by the light of your eyes…"

And before Maryna knew it, they were dancing too. Barely moving really. Just holding each other tight, her head lying gently on his chest. She felt his strong arms engulf her, felt each heartbeat, as Mitchell softly hummed the tune.

"Before I even realize the ride I'm on… Baby, I'm long gone. I get carried away. And nothing matters but being with you…"

She could feel his cheek against her hair, her left hand in his, her other hand resting on his shoulder. It was all happening so fast, and yet he felt so *familiar,* so secure, so very comfortable. Did he feel this too? She felt a weightlessness, like she was dancing in a dream, barely hearing the words of George Strait and the soft accompaniment of the piano, everything overshadowed by Mitchell's gentle touch.

"It might seem like an ordinary night. The same old stars; the same old moon up high. But when I see you standing at your door, nothing's ordinary anymore."

The words were so sappy, the tune so down to earth. Yet in some strange way it was so…perfect. Country music. George Strait. She snuggled closer, and the rest of the world faded away.

This was rapidly becoming her favorite song.

❧

Nearly a hundred feet away, the man watched with disgust as Mitchell and Maryna danced. He wore jeans and a black T-shirt, sported a full and unkempt beard that looked real, and peered out from under a baseball cap riding low on his forehead. He could have been one of a thousand George Strait fans, except that he couldn't stand country music. Still, he forced himself to stand and clap with the others from time to time and even smile once in a while so he wouldn't stand out.

He had actually walked behind Mitchell and Maryna earlier, gotten within ten feet or so, just to prove to himself he could do it. They were so vulnerable. And so oblivious.

After the song was over, George Strait took a few bows as if he were done for the night, waited for the crowd to go bonkers calling for an encore, which of course they did, lighters held aloft, then he started in on a song that just about brought down the house. The man watched as Mitchell and Maryna started making their way through the crowd down toward the stage.

He started following at a distance, straining to keep them in sight, standing on his toes, craning his neck as he walked. He bumped into people, rudely pushing his way through the gyrating throng. People cussed at him, but he didn't care.

He felt the panic rising within him as he pushed his way through, searching for the bobbing heads of Mitchell and Maryna somewhere in front of him, somewhere in a sea of cowboy hats and long hair and raised arms. He stopped knifing his way through, surveyed everything within eyesight, and realized he had lost them completely. He cursed loudly, got a few strange looks from those around him, and then returned to his spot in the back of the crowd.

A few minutes later, sitting in his own vehicle in the parking lot, he watched Mitchell climb into the truck alone and join the traffic waiting to leave. Maryna Sareth was getting clever. She had given him the slip.

His lips curled into a smug little smile. It did not matter. Sure, he had been waiting patiently for an opportunity to trap Maryna alone today, away from Mitchell. And yes, that opportunity had eluded him. But he was a patient man. And he had lots of time.

And he knew where Maryna would be tomorrow.

46

Monday, May 24
Editorial Page, Tidewater Times

PRINCIPLES FOR PLAYING GOD:
THE MORALITY OF CLONING
by Cameron Davenport-Brown

It's easy for the fundamentalists to say that cloning is wrong. "We shouldn't play God" is a wonderful platitude. So they fold their arms and close their minds to any consideration of cloning whatsoever. And they condemn innocent men and women to death by depriving them of staggering medical advances that can be achieved only by cloning.

As a society, we are on the verge of recreating a person's own stem cells, which can then be "coached" to become any of the body's essential specialized cells. Through cloning and coaxing the new cell into reproducing, we can create a person's own stem cell line, thereby replenishing damaged brain cells, spinal cord cells, lung cells, or any number of other cells necessary to cure previously incurable diseases. Parkinson's, Alzheimer's, and muscular dystrophy may become diseases of the past. Chromosomal defects like Down syndrome could be avoided by cloning fertilized egg cells, testing the clones, and implanting only healthy eggs.

Is it right to say no to these advances simply because we don't trust ourselves to handle this technology responsibly?

I suggest not. Instead, I believe the morality of cloning could be successfully evaluated on a case-by-case basis, guided by three immutable principles.

First, we should abide by the bedrock principle that love requires us to make every effort to eliminate human suffering and disease. Second, we should value the diversity of God's creation and the uniqueness of each individual. We should never use cloning just to "build" a better baby or construct the "perfect" person. Third, we should recognize that important decisions about procreation are intensely personal decisions that should be controlled by the affected individual and not dictated by the government.

It is on the basis of these principles that I am challenging the Bioethics Act, which prevents any type of cloning under any circumstances. These three principles give us a guiding moral framework to address one of the most promising and troubling issues confronting our society. And I believe that these time-honored moral guidelines, rather than the closed-minded approach of most fundamentalists, will lead us to a balanced and just approach to the issue of cloning.

Would God really want us to turn our backs on the suffering of so many and deny them the only hope they have for a cure? My God wouldn't.

That is why I have challenged the Bioethics Act. I do not want our scientists to play God. But I do not want them to ignore His guiding moral principles, either.

It should be noted that in the interest of fairness, my opponents in the lawsuit were given the opportunity to present their side in today's op-ed piece. For whatever reason, they have chosen not to do so. Thursday in court, they will not have the luxury of silence. Instead, they will be forced to answer the question of why it is morally right to ban the greatest medical hope for our most desperately sick citizens.

I, for one, will be very interested in their answer.

47

IT DROVE MITCHELL CRAZY not to be at the hospital with Maryna as she went through the amniocentesis. He had read enough about the test to be concerned. A long needle would be inserted through Maryna's abdomen and, using an ultrasound as guidance, into the amniotic sac surrounding the baby. The doctor would withdraw about twenty milliliters of amniotic fluid for testing. Maryna would be watched carefully, invited to rest for about an hour, and then be allowed to leave.

It would take several days for the lab to return the results. And according to everything that Mitchell had read, a 2 percent risk of miscarriage accompanied the procedure.

Maryna had bravely said that she'd be fine, and Nikki had promised to stay with her. Still, Mitchell wanted to be there himself to help calm her nerves and walk her through this. He understood why he couldn't go, he knew that at this very minute someone might be following him, but that didn't make it any easier.

Mitchell's guilt was doubled by the knowledge that, contrary to every good intention, he had acted on impulse at the concert, danced with Maryna, and led her to believe there was more to the relationship than could ever be possible. Knowing that he would now have to talk straight with her about this, and explain all the reasons a relationship would never work, haunted him. He couldn't bear the thought of hurting Maryna at this most vulnerable moment in her life and perhaps alienating her forever from the God that Mitchell served. He prayed for wisdom about what to say to Maryna. And when to say it.

Mitchell's first stop of the morning was the office of Davenport & Associates. He arrived at eight o'clock, safely before Sandra Garrison, and cleaned out his desk. He packed up the few personal belongings he had brought to the office the prior week, stuffed Stonewall and the diplomas back into a small cardboard box, and left a sweet note for Sandra, thanking her for her help. He also told her that if a couple of INS agents stopped by with a subpoena, she should just inform them that he no longer worked at the firm and say nothing more. He left his office key on Sandra's desk, turned full circle for one last panoramic view of the little dump where he had started his legal career, then sadly walked out the front door, making sure it locked behind him.

Fifteen minutes later, he pulled in to Regent Law School.

He knew that Professor Arnold's eight o'clock class would finish a few minutes before nine, so he decided to go straight to the professor's office and wait there. Mitchell had no appointment and no guarantee that Arnold would actually go back to his office, but he also had plenty of time. He would find the professor at some point this morning. He was sure of that.

Mitchell knocked on Arnold's office door, not expecting an answer. Then he tried the knob. Fortunately, the trusting professor had left his door unlocked. Mitchell let himself in, grabbed a seat against the back wall of the office next to the door, opened his briefcase, and began reading one of many medical journal articles on cloning that he had in his briefcase.

As Mitchell plowed through the second article, he heard the professor approaching. The man was, from the sound of things, singing softly to himself. Arnold blew through the door without noticing Mitchell, dropped his books on his desk, and whirled around.

"Good Lord!" he yelled. He blew out a quick, deep breath. "You tryin' to give me a heart attack, boy? You *never* lie in wait like that for a black man."

Mitchell laughed as Professor Arnold shook his head, frowning at his intruder. "I've killed men for less, you know."

Mitchell threw his hands up in mock surrender. "I'm just surprised that a man with as many enemies as you would leave his door unlocked."

Arnold laughed and then extended his hand. Mitchell clumsily attempted a soul handshake. This made the professor laugh some more. "Man, you are *so* white," he said.

"Yep," said Mitchell. "Just got back from a George Strait concert. Not a black man in sight."

The professor groaned. "I need to introduce you to some *real* music someday," he teased, circling around to the back of his desk. "*Soul* music."

Mitchell's face turned serious. "Got a minute?"

"Sure."

Charles Arnold listened patiently as Mitchell unburdened himself. He gave the professor a blow-by-blow of everything that had happened the past week—at least everything relevant to the legal issues. Slow dancing with Maryna, his complicated feelings toward her—they were, of course, none of the professor's business.

"Typical first week," said Professor Arnold.

"Right," sighed Mitchell.

Arnold studied him for a minute. "You like this girl, don't you?"

How does he know this stuff? "I'm trying to stay objective," Mitchell said, "with mixed results."

The professor let out a disapproving grunt. "That's dangerous," he mused. "And it complicates things…compromises your judgment."

"I know," said Mitchell.

Professor Arnold's eyes shot around the office, landing on his Nerf basketball. He picked it up and started pacing—shooting at his hoop, popping questions as he moved.

"You going to represent her in this mess?"

"Yes."

"I was afraid of that."

Mitchell didn't respond.

"Have you filed a motion to intervene in Thursday's hearing?"

"No. Should I?"

"Of course. Put your former client, the lovely Cameron Davenport-Brown, between a rock and a hard place. Make her argue that the frozen cloned embryos should be saved but that the one unfrozen embryo growing inside Maryna should be destroyed." The professor stopped shooting for a moment and looked at Mitchell. "How'd you like to make that argument?"

"It'd be tough," Mitchell admitted.

"Then," continued Arnold, "you've got to argue that the surrogacy contract your client signed is void as against public policy because it forces your client to get an abortion against her will."

"Okay," said Mitchell. "Kind of a reverse *Roe v. Wade* argument?"

"It's a long shot…" admitted Arnold, and as if to emphasize the point, he took a behind-the-back shot from behind his desk.

"Nothing but air." Mitchell threw the basketball back, hoping it was not an omen.

Arnold took another shot, missed again, then wrinkled his brow, deep in thought. "Tell me again *why* this girl is getting an amniocentesis done today?"

"To see for sure if the baby has Down syndrome."

"For what purpose?"

"What do you mean, 'for what purpose'? So we'll know for sure. If the ultrasounds and blood test were wrong, if she doesn't have Down's, then there's no longer a conflict between Maryna and Cameron and—"

"What are the odds of that?"

Mitchell thought for a moment, recalling what Maryna had told him. "Not very good, actually. Dr. Avery told Maryna he had never been wrong before—that the amnio had always confirmed his preliminary conclusions based on ultrasounds and the blood work."

Professor Arnold nodded his head. "My point exactly." He stopped his constant motion, emphasizing the advice he was about to dispense. "Right now, there is at least some doubt about whether this baby has Down's. If you *don't* do an amnio and that doubt remains, what are the chances that a *female* federal court judge is going to order this girl to go and get a dangerous test like that done in the first place? If you and your client march into court and tell the judge that your client—what's her name?"

"Maryna."

"—that Maryna is ready to bring this child into the world whether or not the child has Down's, *and raise the child if she has to,* do you really think this judge is going to require her to get an amnio so she can then require her to get an abortion?"

Mitchell leaned back in his chair and crossed his arms. "Never looked at it that way."

"Seems to me," continued the professor, "that by getting the amnio done, you're just playing into their hands, making their case for them. Now they can say, 'See, the baby has a serious handicap, and the surrogacy agreement calls for a termination of the pregnancy under those circumstances.'"

He's right! thought Mitchell. *Why didn't I see that?* Even as Professor Arnold concluded his thoughts, Mitchell started jamming the articles he had been reading into his briefcase. He checked his watch: 9:45. The procedure would start at 10:00 A.M.

"Thanks, Professor," Mitchell said as he pulled out his cell phone and headed out the door. "I've got fifteen minutes to stop this thing."

⚬❧⚬

Mitchell raced down the Interstate, fuming. Nikki would not answer her cell phone. He had already left four messages. He could not get through to Maryna, and the folks in surgical pre-op were entirely unhelpful. Nor could he reach Dr. Avery, although the doctor's office assistant had promised to page the doctor ten minutes ago.

Ten o'clock, and a good ten minutes of driving left. The only thing Mitchell had in his favor was the tendency of every doctor in the world to run behind. He prayed that Avery would be no exception.

Mitchell laid on the horn and tailgated the driver ahead of him. It worked. The woman pulled over, shooting Mitchell a nasty look as he sped on past. After another mile, Mitchell cut into the right lane and swerved into the exit lane.

How could I be so stupid? I never even considered asking Maryna to forgo the amnio. And why not? Is Professor Arnold right—my relationship with Maryna is compromising my objectivity? If he is right, what am I supposed to do? Who else would take this case for what Maryna could pay?

He tried Nikki again, then Dr. Avery's office, and finally the hospital. Ten after ten. He pulled up to the emergency room door, parked near the curb in a towaway zone, and sprinted into the hospital. He stopped a nurse, got directions to outpatient surgery, and took off down the hall, nearly running over an orderly.

He finally found the elevators the nurse had directed him toward, pushed the button several times, shifting his weight from one foot to the next, and impatiently waited for one of the doors to open. He considered taking the stairs but realized he had no idea where they were. Finally, the doors opened, and a car full of people slowly took their time getting off. Mitchell jumped on, pushed the third-floor button, and kept his finger on the "close door" button until the doors slid shut just before an elderly man and woman could get on.

Mitchell paced the elevator as it climbed, darted out at the third floor, took a hard right, a quick left, then raced through two double doors and halfway down a long hallway. He finally arrived at the nurses' station for outpatient surgery and breathlessly asked for Maryna Sareth. The annoyed nurse sitting at the station put her hand up, motioning for Mitchell to wait a minute, and signaled to the telephone.

Mitchell frowned and waited, frowned and waited. "Oh, for goodness' sakes," he blurted out. His impatience proved counterproductive, with the nurse waving him off more vigorously. Just then, another nurse came around the corner, looking far more helpful.

"Can I help you?" she asked.

Before Mitchell could answer, he heard a familiar voice behind him. "Mitchell, what are you doing here?"

He turned to face Nikki. "Where is she? What room?"

"Relax, Mitchell. She's down the hall…resting. They just finished the amnio."

48

THE ROCK FINALLY SUCCUMBED to his alarm when it went off for the third time at 10:30. He popped a couple of Tylenol in an attempt to dull his splitting headache and started getting ready for the office. He shaved off most of his three-day stubble, missing a few fairly obvious places, showered, and threw on a dark gray suit. Prior to rehab, he had dressed casual unless he had to be in court. But this was a new Rock, one deadly serious about his law practice and his daughter's big hearing later this week. The new Rock would dress for success.

By the time he got into his car, his hands were already shaking. He stopped for some coffee on the way to the office and resisted the urge to pull into a nearby liquor store and grab a bottle of Bacardi.

Although he could sense Sandra Garrison's disappointment that he had left the clinic, she worked hard not to show it. Neither of them mentioned the clinic, the confrontation in Ichabod's office, or the Rock's drinking problem. Through the years they had developed an understanding—an unwritten pact of sorts—not to talk about such things. Today they both carefully adhered to the pact.

After explaining why he had to fire Mitchell, also an unpopular decision with Sandra, the Rock settled into his office and began working on Cameron's case. Since he was only local counsel, he would focus on those areas where he could help the most. Nora Gunther would probably hire a few well-paid experts to talk all about the science of cloning and in vitro fertilization. Nora would undoubtedly handle all the witnesses as well as the opening and closing statements. Rock's role would be to sit there and take notes. But maybe he could earn a bigger role by doing some stellar investigative work before the trial.

"Sandra," he called from his office. She appeared at his door almost immediately. "Can we run one of those computer searches on Dr. Lars Avery and Dr. Blaine Richards? I want to know if either one of them has ever been sued before."

Sandra smiled. "Yes sir, Mr. Davenport." She stood there a moment until the Rock looked up. "And if you don't mind my saying, sir—it's good to have you back."

The Rock mumbled his thanks and waved her off. He wasn't very good at expressing his feelings.

But Sandra was good at computer searches. A few minutes later, she had a hit. She placed a single sheet of paper on the Rock's desk. "Dr. Avery got sued in Portsmouth Circuit Court seven years ago," she reported. "The case dragged on for six years. Finally settled out of court last year. Joel Sanger was the plaintiff's lawyer."

The Rock took the sheet and looked it over carefully. "Well...let's get Joel on the phone," he ordered.

"Yes sir," said Sandra excitedly. It looked like she was ready to salute, she was just so happy to have the Rock back in the office and practicing law.

Joel Sanger was a kindred spirit. His advertising budget gave the Rock's a run for the money; the man would sue anything that breathed. The only difference between the Rock and Sanger was that Sanger had figured out a business way to make it all work, with dozens of associates and paralegals running around doing his bidding. And Joel also won most of his cases.

Sandra did her magic and got him on the phone, and the two ambulance chasers shot the breeze for a good five minutes. Sanger especially liked the new "iron fist in a velvet glove" television spots. When Sanger started asking about the Parsons case and Ichabod—the rumors were apparently flying—the Rock interrupted him.

"I've got a couple questions about a case you settled last year against Dr. Lars Avery. What can you tell me about it?"

Sanger paused on the other end of the line. "As part of the settlement, we agreed to seal the case, Rock. Everything's confidential. I'd like to help you, but—"

"Look, Joel, this is really important to me. This guy was my daughter's ob-gyn, and when she decided to do this test-tube baby deal, she apparently recommended him to the surrogate mother. He'll be a major witness for us Thursday in this case dealing with the constitutionality of the Bioethics Act—"

There was a whistle on the other end of the line. "You got that case?"

"Just local counsel for now, but I think I'll end up with a bigger role. It's my daughter who's the plaintiff, you know—"

"Sure, Rock. I just didn't know you and she were on speaking terms."

"That's another story. But can you help me here? I mean, it's not like we'll be using it to ambush Avery. He's our witness, we're just trying to protect him…need to know what's out there."

"Man, Rock, I want to help but…well, you know how tight these confidentiality orders are."

The Rock thought for a moment, silence lingering on the line. He knew he was making Sanger uncomfortable—that was part of the plan. "Let me ask you something, Joel. Does that confidentiality order contain the usual exceptions for lawyers in your own firm who might need to know?"

"Of course."

"Then that's it. Hire me for this phone call and fire me when we're done. While I'm employed by you, tell me about the case."

"Whoa," chuckled Sanger. "The Rock working for yours truly. That just might work."

It took Sanger five minutes to lay out the details of the case. Avery had been sued for medical malpractice when a delivery had gone bad and resulted in a stillborn. As the case progressed, it was discovered that Avery had altered the medical chart, changing the time on a few of the key entries. This had exposed him to potential punitive damages that were not covered by insurance and were not dischargeable in bankruptcy.

The potential punitive damages claim also gave Sanger a chance to investigate the doctor's financial status. He found a medical practice deeply in debt and the doctor himself with enough bad investments to have justified filing bankruptcy years before if his pride would have allowed it. It was the classic case, said Sanger, of a doctor's losing his shirt by getting involved in investment areas like real estate that he knew nothing about.

Because of Avery's financial position and the inability to pay much money for the punitive damage claim, the parties had little hope of settlement. Then, on the eve of the trial, the insurance company threw in their $1 million in coverage, the maximum allowed for simple negligence under Virginia law, and Avery came up with an additional million dollars for the punitive damages claim. Where this money came from, said Sanger, was a mystery then and to this very day. And frankly, Sanger said, he didn't much worry about it as long as the check didn't bounce.

After answering all of the Rock's questions, Joel Sanger promptly fired the Rock and wished him luck. Immediately after hanging up the phone, the Rock put Sandra back to work.

"I want a subpoena issued right away for all of Dr. Lars Avery's financial records, particularly those related to the malpractice case and how he came up with the money to pay off the punitive damage claim. Just for grins, I also want a subpoena issued for all the financial records of Dr. Blaine Richards—that way they won't know that we're onto something with just Avery. And Sandra—"

"Yes sir."

"Hand deliver those today. Would you please?"

"Yes sir."

She turned smartly and left the Rock's office.

It is good to be back, he thought.

49

MITCHELL WALKED ANXIOUSLY toward Maryna's recovery room. Nikki was at his elbow, assuring him that the procedure went fine. When they reached the door of the room, Nikki stepped in front of Mitchell, placing her hands gently against his chest.

"Before you go in there, I want you to know about something."

Mitchell gave her an impatient look. "Okay."

"She's wearing a hospital gown, of course"—Nikki scrunched up her face, apparently thinking about how to phrase this—"and you'll see that on her chest, from about the middle of her collarbone down three or four inches"—Nikki drew a line with her finger on her own chest—"is a scar with several stitches. She didn't want to tell you… It was just too humiliating for her. But, well, I figured you were gonna see it anyway…" Nikki waited to continue, watching Mitchell's reaction.

"How did it happen?" he asked.

"The Snakehead attacker the other night…he did it as a warning—"

Mitchell felt the blood rush to his head, the anger rising in his neck, tensing every muscle fiber in his body. *The coward preyed on an innocent young woman, cut her chest open, humiliated her…might as well have cut her heart out.*

"Then I'll kill him," Mitchell said coldly. There was not a trace of emotion in his voice. He felt his hands curl into a fist, his jaw clench shut. He wished with all his heart that this man, this despicable coward, was standing in front of him right now.

Mitchell glared past Nikki and into the room. She stepped aside to let him pass.

Once inside, at the first sight of Maryna, his anger melted into sympathy and concern. She looked so peaceful and so very tired. Her dark hair was matted against the pillow, her bright eyes closed, her mouth wide open. She was hooked up to purring monitors that registered a strong heartbeat for her and the child. She had her hands crossed just above her stomach, and the hospital gown and bedsheet drooped partway down her chest, exposing a few inches of the scar.

Mitchell walked softly to the far side of her bed and stood there for a moment, just watching Maryna sleep. He bowed his head and said a quick and silent prayer of thanks. Then he leaned over and ever so gingerly pulled up the sheet to the bottom of Maryna's neck, tucking it in around her shoulders. He carefully brushed some hair out of her eyes and traced the outline of her face lightly with his fingers.

"You must be the young man she was talking so much about," said a woman from the doorway. She stood next to Nikki and wore hospital scrubs. She looked young for a doctor, if she was indeed a doctor, with a pretty face and long, curly blonde hair pulled back into a hair clip. Her eyes were her best feature, highlighted by thin brown eyebrows and a long forehead, with high cheekbones that served to underscore those sparkling blue eyes. She was a little overweight, but she moved with an air of confidence that showed she was very comfortable in her own skin.

She walked toward Mitchell and extended her hand. "Dr. Elizabeth Strong," she said. "I'm Dr. Avery's partner."

"Mitchell Taylor," he replied. "Nice to meet you."

"I don't know if Nikki told you," said the doctor as she picked up the chart and started checking the monitors, "but Dr. Avery got stuck in a very complicated C-section this morning. He asked if I would cover this amnio for him, and Maryna said it would be fine."

She made some notes on the chart. "Looks like Maryna and the baby are both doing well."

She walked up to the head of the bed and started gently waking Maryna. "How's Mom doing?" she asked gently.

Mitchell made a face at Nikki behind the doctor's back. He motioned to the doctor and gave Nikki a thumbs-up. He liked this woman. She didn't give him the creeps like Lars Avery did.

This was not a phone call that Avery wanted to make. But, the sooner the better, he figured. He would take his tongue-lashing and move on. He knew from the beginning that this would be the toughest part of his plan.

He found a quiet corner of the hospital, pulled out his cell phone, and dialed the number. "I've been waiting to hear from you," said the gruff voice at the other end.

"It's not good news," said Avery, glancing around to make sure nobody was listening. "I got caught in an emergency C-section all morning, almost lost the baby." He swallowed hard and took a breath. "My partner actually did the amnio."

There was silence on the other end. For Avery, it was worse than getting screamed at. Finally, after an eternity, the person spoke. "So I'm assuming that there was no miscarriage."

Avery hesitated. "That's right."

"Then we all have a very big problem."

"I know," said Avery. "I know."

"You've had one thing to do, and you've messed it up," the other person said sharply. Avery chose not to respond.

"I'll call back later," the person said. "I've got some other ideas."

"Okay," said Avery, then he hit the End Call button on his phone. He let out a huge sigh of relief. He had been asked no detailed questions about the C-section. His story had apparently been accepted at face value. Maybe he was out of the woods.

"What is this subpoena for my personal financial records?" Blaine Richards shouted into the phone. "What does he think he's doing? What does he know?"

"Don't worry about it," said Win Mackenzie reassuringly. "It's just a ploy that guys like Davenport try when they're desperate. I'll get the thing quashed by Thursday—you won't have to produce a thing."

"And the one to Avery too—right? You're gonna quash that one too?"

"I'll do my best, Blaine. There's no guarantee on that one. Davenport is alleging it somehow goes to bias."

Richards snorted. "Win, I'm not paying you to *try*. Quash the thing. How hard can that be?"

"Sometimes harder than you think," Mackenzie responded testily. He was losing his patience. "I don't tell you how to practice medicine, and I don't need your advice on practicing law."

"Okay," responded Richards, lowering his tone a notch, although it was still strained with impatience. "But if you've got to have a triple bypass, you want a doctor who'll get the job done, not one who will try."

"Fair enough," said Win. "We'll quash both subpoenas."

"That's better. Our financial records are none of that jerk's business."

50

MONDAY EVENING WENT EXACTLY as Nikki had planned. She had a long-term strategy for nailing the Snakeheads who were stalking Maryna, but that would take time. For the immediate future, she just wanted to make sure that Maryna could rest in safety as she recuperated from the amnio and nursed her chest wound. And since Nikki had been with Maryna at the hospital, she no longer considered her condo to be safe for Maryna. She would have to take her someplace that the Snakeheads would never suspect, and she would have to do so without being followed.

Immediately after Maryna's release, Nikki took her to the Greenbrier Mall, where the two women roamed the stores for a few minutes, constantly checking over their shoulders. At precisely 6:30, they went into the Interior Designs furniture store, where Nikki talked to a desk clerk about a large mirror she'd asked the store to hold for her the day before. A few minutes later, Nikki and Maryna walked through the warehouse behind the furniture store and out to the loading dock, a recessed area of the buildings next to the parking lot. Anybody who had followed them into the mall could not enter this area without coming through the same loading dock door.

Waiting there with her car running was a friend of Mitchell's from church, a former missionary named Sarah Reed. Nikki also knew Sarah, having helped Brad Carson represent her in a high-profile case the previous year. She knew Sarah to be dependable and savvy, and Sarah had promised to keep Maryna under wraps for as long as necessary. Maryna turned to Nikki, gave her a quick hug, climbed into Sarah's beat-up car, and stared forlornly after Nikki as Sarah drove away.

Nikki turned to the bewildered warehouse worker, told him she had decided not to purchase the mirror after all, and went back into the store to negotiate a refund.

Twenty minutes later she met Mitchell at Regent University's spacious law library. They commandeered a table near the back of the main floor and settled in for an evening of research on the issue of surrogate contracts.

Nikki slapped the *Tidewater Times* front section down on the table between them, open to Cameron's editorial on the morality of cloning. "Have you seen this?" she asked. "This woman has some nerve."

Without a word, Mitchell picked up the paper and read it. Nikki could see the color rising in his face. When he had finished, she started in again.

"Where does this woman get off writing this stuff? How can anyone argue that decisions about procreation should be left to the affected individuals and then turn around and insist that Maryna terminate this child because of the surrogacy contract?" Nikki talked faster with each sentence, really getting fired up. "I mean, you and I are miles apart on the issue of abortion, but I think even we could agree that a contract that *requires* a woman to get an abortion against her will is pretty onerous."

She took a breath, waiting for Mitchell to respond.

"I agree," he said simply. She took it as a cue to relaunch her diatribe.

"This whole scheme—using an illegal immigrant like Maryna, signing the contract in North Carolina so they could avoid the court oversight required in Virginia—this whole thing just reeks of arrogance and abuse…"

Mitchell nodded silently, his gaze fixed on the wall behind Nikki.

"And another thing," she said, leaning forward and grabbing the paper from the table, "she says we should value the diversity of God's creation and the uniqueness of each individual, but she wants to terminate this pregnancy because the baby *might* have Down syndrome. Where's the logic in that?"

Mitchell just shrugged.

"There is none," Nikki continued. "And how can she turn around and argue in support of cloning when that would just create a bunch of babies with mutations and birth defects? You're gonna tear this woman up on the witness stand—assuming we get a chance to intervene."

Nikki noticed that the comment brought a pained expression to Mitchell's face.

"What's the matter?" she asked.

"I guess I just hoped for more out of Cameron," Mitchell said softly. "In the few days I represented her, I really started to like her…"

Nikki tilted her head and narrowed her eyes. *Like her? What does that mean?*

"Not like that," Mitchell said defensively. "But I really thought she was a good person, trying to do what was right in a very complicated case. She's got a jerk for a lawyer, but as for Cameron…well, I guess I'm just disappointed."

Nikki let the silence linger for a moment. But only a moment.

"Maybe we should get another lawyer for Maryna," she proposed. "Someone who doesn't have this history. Someone who will not hesitate to go after Cameron."

She waited for Mitchell's response.

"No," Mitchell said firmly. "I didn't say I *wouldn't* go after her, just that I wouldn't enjoy it."

Nikki leaned back, satisfied. She had just wanted to hear him say it. In truth, she knew that there was no better lawyer for Maryna, nobody who believed more in her cause.

"You may have to take the iron fist out of the velvet glove," she teased.

Mitchell did not smile. "Let's get to work," he suggested. "I'll do whatever I have to do."

51

Tuesday, May 25

BY THE TIME THE ROCK MANAGED to make an appearance at the office on Tuesday morning, three phone messages from Nora Gunther were waiting for him.

"She got madder every time she called," explained Sandra. "Says you have no right to be issuing subpoenas in the case without talking to her. Says you're just local counsel, and she'll tell you if she wants subpoenas issued."

The Rock snorted. "I'll issue subpoenas if I darn well please," he said, not even slowing down on his way to his office. "If she doesn't like it, she can get other local counsel."

Out of the corner of his eye, he noticed Sandra break into a thin smile. She seemed to enjoy the Rock's old feisty self.

"She's lucky I *wasn't* here when she called," he added for good measure as he stormed into his office.

A few seconds later, the phone rang. It started at Rock's extension, then rolled over to Sandra's receptionist desk. Sandra buzzed the Rock on another line.

"It's Nora on line one," Sandra explained. "You want to talk to her?"

"Nah," the Rock tried to sound casual. "You tell her."

"Okay," said Sandra. She sounded reluctant. "She's pretty insistent on talking with you."

"I don't care," the Rock said sharply, nearly yelling. "She doesn't run this firm. I do!"

"Yes sir. I'll handle it."

With that, the sweet voice of Sandra was gone. *I've got to get something for this pounding headache. Hope Sandra's got the coffee ready.*

After a cup of coffee laced with a liberal amount of brandy, the pressure on the Rock's temples subsided noticeably. He almost felt good enough to call Nora Gunther back himself. Instead, he busied himself with some paperwork, his thoughts wandering to a night at The Beach Grill, with plenty of booze and Jimmy Buffet music.

The phone rang, bringing the Rock out of his daze.

"Dr. Lars Avery on line one," Sandra announced.

"I'll take it." The Rock punched the button and cleared his throat. "Billy Davenport," he snarled, sounding rushed and important.

"Mr. Davenport, this is Dr. Lars Avery." The caller paused, and the Rock could hear a quick exhale. "We've got to talk."

❦

The Rock could feel the tension leave his body with each martini, his frayed nerve endings being snipped and fused one at a time. The Town Point Club was one of Norfolk's finest restaurants—with rows of windows overlooking the Elizabeth River—and he was waiting for Dr. Avery. The establishment was reserved for members only, and the Rock certainly did not qualify. But the mention of the doctor's name had earned the Rock a table by the windows and a maître d' anxious to supply the Rock with all the martinis he could drink.

The Rock took a sip of his second, maybe his third, as he patiently waited for Avery. The combination of martinis with the morning brandy returned things to normalcy for the Rock. He remembered fondly how drinking used to make him feel good—give him a pleasant buzz, make him the life of the party. Now he had to drink just to feel normal. It took a lot more drinking to get any kind of buzz now, and a happy Rock seldom emerged after the booze went down. There was only the miserable Rock when he wasn't drinking—the splitting headaches, the churning stomach, the raw nerves.

After a time, things became a little hazy to the Rock, the voices grew a little distant, and everything became muted, like he was in his own private cave, just the way the Rock liked it. Avery was late for his own emergency appointment. He had picked the place and the time. But the Rock didn't care—not about Avery, not about the case, not about much of anything right now.

He motioned to the waiter for one more.

When Avery joined him a few minutes later, the Rock had some difficulty standing to shake the man's hand. The Rock smiled apologetically and clumsily sat back down.

He had met Avery before—the man was Cameron's ob-gyn—but something was different about the doctor today. The Rock squinted a little, trying to bring the doctor into better focus. The Rock had forgotten how short Avery was and how frail looking. Something about the stooped shoulders and the narrow frame gave the impression that a good stiff pat on the back would likely break the man in two. Avery wore a dark gray business suit, but his thick dark hair, as usual, looked like he had just come out of a wind tunnel. He had a five o'clock shadow, as if he had skipped shaving altogether today, and large dark circles under his eyes.

With quick and nervous movements, Avery ordered a glass of Chardonnay, told the maître d' they would not be ordering lunch, then leaned forward and started talking to the Rock in hushed tones.

"I want to help you and Cameron," he said. "But I don't want Dr. Richards and GenTech to know we've had this meeting."

"Fair enough," the Rock said rather loudly.

Avery frowned his disapproval. "Keep it down," he said, glancing around. The Rock nodded knowingly, and Avery continued.

"You're challenging the Bioethics Act, and you will presumably call me as a fact witness to testify about my treatment of both Cameron and Maryna. Specifically, you intend to have me testify that I performed a total hysterectomy on Cameron, who can consequently no longer have children, and that I implanted a fertilized egg into Maryna. You will probably also ask me to testify as to the probability that the embryo implanted in Maryna has Down syndrome, whereas certain of Cameron's other eggs, which are presently cryopreserved, probably do not. How am I doing so far?"

The Rock took this as his cue to take another long hit of the martini and lean forward. This time he spoke in a loud, exaggerated whisper. "So far, you're nailing it."

"Now, that's pretty much the sum and substance of my factual testimony," Avery continued. He fidgeted in his chair, glanced around again quickly, and his eyes somehow became darker, his look menacing. "But what if I gave *expert* testimony about GenTech's other experiences with human cloning? What if I could testify that human cloning is relatively safe based on experiments performed at GenTech? What if I testified that other surrogate mothers have been implanted with cloned blastocytes? What if I said that these other clones have been secretly created, not before the ban on cloning, but after the ban on cloning went into effect?"

The Rock's eyes widened. He leaned forward on the table and worked hard to suppress a smile. *Can this possibly be true? GenTech has cavalierly broken the law, and I have a credible witness to prove it.*

"And what if," Avery continued, "the cloned blastocytes they implanted in these other women were not created by blastomere separation, as they were with Cameron, but what if they were created by a nuclear transfer technique, the way it was done with Dolly the sheep?" Avery paused for what seemed like an eternity. "If I could testify as an expert witness to all those things, would it help your case?"

Wow! The Rock felt like he had just been rocketed into orbit. *Would it help my case—are you kidding?* But even in his disoriented state, the Rock knew that most things that seemed too good to be true usually were. *And why has Avery phrased all these things hypothetically? Why didn't he come forward earlier?* The questions raced inside the Rock's mind—his thoughts swirling like wind-whipped dust.

He shook his head sharply and blurted out the one thought that seemed to dominate right now. "Is it true?" It may not have been clever to ask it so bluntly, but it was something that the Rock certainly needed to know.

He watched as Avery's lips coiled up ever so slowly. The man took a deliberate sip of his drink, then stared directly at the Rock. "What's true is what can be proven true in the courtroom, do you agree?"

"Sure."

"Do you ask all the expert witnesses you put on the stand if their opinions are true? I thought the whole purpose of an expert witness was so they could give their own opinions—"

"Yeah, but I never put an expert on the stand who will give opinions that can be proven to be false…" The Rock thought for a moment. He was on thin ice here, and he had to phrase this delicately. "There are lots of ways to prove or disprove what you just said. For example, Win Mackenzie might ask you, 'Name the surrogate mothers and actual mothers who this has happened to—'"

Avery put up palm, stopping the Rock in midsentence. "I've thought of all that—and I'm no fool. If I simply testify that Dr. Richards *told* me all these things when he asked me to implant the embryo into Maryna, then we're covered. I can say that I didn't ask, and he didn't tell, who the others were. It would be his word against mine. I'm an independent witness with nothing to gain or lose. He's got a lot on the line. Who's a jury going to believe?"

It could work, the Rock thought. The man was handing him the case on a silver platter. And the Rock didn't *know for sure* that this proposed testimony was false. It could have happened just the way Avery was now saying.

But the Rock had never, in his long and sometimes checkered career, knowingly solicited perjured testimony from a witness. And even with everything riding on this case, he didn't want to start now. Still, it was obvious that Avery's opinions were up for sale, and if the Rock didn't lock him down, who would? In the Rock's experience, if a witness was willing to sell his testimony to one side, he was probably negotiating with the other side as well.

The Rock motioned frantically at the maître d'—he needed another drink. He placed his empty glass to his lips and drained the last few drops. He took a deep breath while Avery waited for a response.

"Are you prepared to take the stand and swear under oath that what you just told me about your conversation with Richards is true?" *There. I've asked the question.* An affirmative answer would basically confirm that this testimony was indeed true. Nobody could accuse him of suborning perjury under these circumstances.

Besides, this was, in the Rock's mind, a preemptive strike. He would never actually have to ask Avery to testify about this stuff, but by getting Avery on his team, he would prevent Avery from giving perjured testimony on behalf of Richards and GenTech.

"Of course."

The Rock let out a quick sigh. "Then how much will this *expert* testimony cost me?"

"Seventy-five thousand."

The Rock weighed Avery's expression. There didn't appear to be any room for negotiation. Where he would get the money, the Rock had no idea. But he couldn't pass this up—it could mean the difference between his daughter's winning and losing. And that, in turn, could mean the difference between the Rock having a healthy grandchild or having one with Down syndrome.

The Rock swallowed hard and stared at his empty martini glass. "Sounds fair," he said.

"And does the testimony I described give you what you need?" asked Avery.

"I think that just about covers it," mumbled the Rock.

❧

Thirty minutes later, Lars Avery returned to his office. He still had not eaten lunch. In fact, he hadn't had a bite to eat all day. The mere thought of food made him ill. He hated what he was doing; hated even more the person who was making him do it.

What has become of me? he wondered. *Have I really stooped this low? But then again, what choice do I have?*

That last question was always the one that carried the day. He was in way too deep. He didn't realize that when he had accepted their money nearly two years ago—when they had helped him out of an almost impossible situation—they had not only salvaged his reputation but had purchased his soul.

These days that much was becoming painfully evident.

With the door of his office shut and locked, Avery stripped off his suit coat, his tie, his pressed white shirt, and his undershirt. A white belt lined with Velcro ran around his waist and held a micro reel-to-reel recording device against the small of his back.

The device was called a body Nagra. In terms of both quality and detectability, it was far superior to any other form of microcassette—in fact, it was the top recording device used by the FBI for sensitive under-cover operations. Small wires ran from the device to the shaved places on Avery's chest where he had taped multidirectional microphones. Another wire attached to the recorder ran down inside his pants and up through a small hole he had cut in the bottom of one pants pocket. The wire connected to a small switch in Avery's pocket that operated the Nagra, turning the recording device on and off.

Avery removed the Nagra with all its attached wires and rewound the tape. He listened breathlessly to his conversation with Billy Davenport. He could hear every word. The tape was perfect. Crystal clear.

Avery loathed the machine for performing so flawlessly.

52

Wednesday, May 26

JUDGE CYNTHIA BAKER-KLINE ISSUED three orders in the case of *Davenport-Brown v. GenTech et al.* early Wednesday morning. She had her clerk fax the orders to counsel for Davenport-Brown and counsel for GenTech. The clerk e-mailed them to counsel for Maryna Sareth, since Mitchell Taylor no longer had access to a fax machine. The clerk also placed a copy in the court's file, which in turn was being monitored by the national wire services, CNN, and local news networks. Within minutes, journalists all over the country began reporting the substance of the orders, heightening interest in an already high-profile case.

The first order addressed the petition of various news organizations to telecast the trial live. Baker-Kline had seen so many of these petitions that she used a form order for her reply—changing only the names of the parties. As she did for every similar petition since she took the bench, she denied the request, noting that there was simply no precedent or procedural authority for a live telecast of a federal court trial in the Eastern District of Virginia. She signed that order with a flourish, taking great pleasure in telling the panting media hordes that they could not bring their precious cameras into her hallowed courtroom.

The second order dealt with the *subpoena duces tecum* issued by the Rock for the financial records of Drs. Avery and Richards. Despite Nora Gunther's repeated telephone calls, the Rock had refused to withdraw the subpoena, so it was left up to the judge to decide whether the subpoena should be quashed, as requested by Win Mackenzie, or honored.

This issue gave Baker-Kline no pause. "The documents requested by the subpoena" she wrote, "have no apparent relevance to this case, and the subpoena itself appears to be nothing more than a thinly veiled attempt to harass and embarrass the doctors." Accordingly, the judge ordered the subpoenas quashed, and scolded the Rock for issuing them in the first place. She also noted that even if the financial relationship between Dr. Richards and GenTech were somehow relevant, that information could be obtained from public SEC filings made by GenTech, and therefore the subpoena was unnecessary.

The third order addressed a petition filed by Mitchell Taylor, as counsel for Maryna Sareth, to intervene and participate in the case. Mitchell and Nikki had pulled an all-nighter in order to file the petition on Tuesday. Nora Gunther responded later that same day with a request that the petition be denied along with a further request that Mitchell Taylor be disqualified as counsel of record based on his prior representation of Cameron Davenport-Brown. Win Mackenzie and his large team of associates worked all day Tuesday and most of Tuesday night on a response to Mitchell's petition and put together a doozy. The response, all thirty pages of it, received its final editing touches early Wednesday morning. A runner from the law offices of Kilgore & Strobel was just getting ready to file the impressive document when the judge made it irrelevant by ruling first. As the runner approached the courthouse and heard about the ruling, he wisely tucked Mackenzie's response back in his briefcase and headed back to the law firm to tell the attorneys that all their work had been for naught.

"In the interest of judicial economy," Baker-Kline wrote in the third order, "the court will allow Ms. Sareth to intervene in these proceedings so that all the complex and interrelated issues arising out of the surrogacy contract, the Last Will and Testament of Dr. Nathan Brown, the contract between the Browns and the GenTech fertility clinic, the disposition of the frozen embryos, and the constitutionality of the Bioethics Act might all be resolved in the same proceeding.

"Further, the court finds no merit to the contention that Mr. Taylor is somehow precluded from representing Ms. Sareth. According to an affidavit filed by Mr. Taylor as part of his Petition to Intervene, he swears that he learned no secrets in his brief representation of Ms. Davenport-Brown as local counsel that could be used against her in these proceedings. This court has no reason at this point to doubt the sworn statement of Mr. Taylor. Accordingly, he will be allowed to proceed as Counsel of Record for Ms. Sareth beginning with the Preliminary Injunction Hearing on Thursday."

Mitchell Taylor read the e-mail from Judge Baker-Kline's office on Wednesday morning with a sense of exhaustion, elation, and dread. Two days after officially opening his own law practice, he had just been allowed to intervene as counsel of record in a case the entire nation was talking about. He knew he should be excited—juiced for the opportunity to be a part of legal history.

Instead, he felt a fresh wave of exhaustion wash over his body. He hadn't seen Maryna since the amnio, and he dreaded talking with her about their relationship. Plus, he felt totally unprepared for this hearing and basically out of his league. He had a grand total of about seven hours of sleep in the last two nights and now had less than twenty-four hours to prepare his case. He could research the legal issues, study the contracts, and do pretty well on his feet with the emotional side of the case. But the complex medical issues were a different story. In just under one day, he would have to become conversant in the complex details of ultrasounds and amnios, in vitro fertilization, Down syndrome, and cloning, just to name a few.

Mitchell felt like a crop-duster pilot who had just been thrust into the pilot's seat of the space shuttle. And on board were the hopes and dreams of Maryna Sareth as well as untold other women who would one day find themselves in the same circumstances.

Though he had a nearly endless reservoir of self-confidence and moxie, the prospect of the intervention overwhelmed Mitchell Taylor at 10:00 A.M. on Wednesday morning. But he couldn't waste time lamenting his plight. He didn't have that luxury. He got on the phone with Nikki, divided the research responsibilities, and got right back to work.

They would fight hard to win Maryna the right to carry this child to term. And if they lost, they would at least go down swinging.

⸺⸺

At 2:00 P.M., Dr. Blaine Richards overshadowed the morning's events with a few announcements of his own. He sat stoically at a table in the front of a long room at GenTech's headquarters. He wore khakis, a white shirt, a subdued tie, and a white lab coat. His PR consultant had suggested the lab coat.

Seated on his right, also looking somber but dressed in a custom-made blue suit, was Win Mackenzie. Arrayed in front of the two men was an entire bank of microphones, all bearing the insignias of various news outlets. Reporters, photographers, and cameramen filled the room, elbowing each other and buzzing with excitement.

GenTech's PR consultant called the room to order at a few minutes after two, and the reporters fell silent, pens and Dictaphones poised. Richards cleared his throat and began reading from a prepared statement.

"As you know, beginning tomorrow GenTech and I will be part of a federal court preliminary injunction hearing to decide the fate of eight frozen zygotes and one embryo that has been implanted into a surrogate mother. I will not comment today about that case. Please understand that this press conference is not an attempt to influence that litigation in any way.

"However, I felt compelled to conduct this press conference because there are certain things that will undoubtedly come out in the hearing and will then be distorted by the lawyers in a way that will make it difficult to get at the truth of what is really happening in terms of the science of cloning."

Richards looked up from his written statement, basking in the expectant looks of the media hounds. He felt a certain pride in his ability to command this room and in the fact that everyone there hung on every word, every syllable that came out of his mouth. The chessboard that only he could see was shaping up magnificently. And soon the entire world would be unmistakably aware of his sheer brilliance.

"The plaintiff in this lawsuit, through her lawyers' crafty use of the federal rules of pretrial discovery, has had access to certain proprietary documents that will surely be discussed in court in the next few days. Those documents include references to certain confidential patent applications filed by GenTech that have never before been publicly revealed. Judge Baker-Kline has ruled that the details of the patented processes shall remain confidential, but the subject matter of the patent applications can be brought out by plaintiff's counsel as part of the hearing.

"We therefore thought it would be important for the public to hear from us first as to exactly what these patents are and why we applied for them."

At this point, with calculated drama, Richards let out a huge sigh and turned to look at Win Mackenzie. Just as they had rehearsed, Mackenzie gave him a solemn nod, and Richards returned his intent gaze to the paper in front of him. It was as if Mackenzie had signaled to a reluctant Richards that he must go forward, that it was his sacred duty to inform the public about these earth-shattering advances in genetic research. And then Blaine Richards, ever the reluctant warrior, steadied his gaze and plowed gamely ahead.

"Genetic research contains great therapeutic promise but also presents tremendous challenges. For example, the production of embryonic stem cells created through cloning—by removing DNA from an egg cell, replacing it with DNA from another cell, and then causing the egg to multiply—could provide patients with a fresh supply of cells that match the patients' own genetic code. Transplant failures and immune-suppressing drugs could become a thing of the past. Just as antibiotics and vaccines rid the world of infectious plagues a half-century ago, so stem cells started by the cloning process could eradicate the degenerative diseases of our day, such as cancer, Alzheimer's, and heart disease."

Blaine looked up again, but this time the reporters were fidgeting and looking around. They had heard this stuff before. *That's okay,* he thought, *they're about to hear something that they've never heard before—something that will make their ears tingle with the promise of it.*

"Before Cameron Davenport-Brown came to our clinic, GenTech had never cloned egg cells for reproductive purposes—to implant into a surrogate mother. But the women who have been helped by our clinic, who have conceived the child they so ardently desired, have also donated thousands of unused eggs for research purposes. Prior to the Bioethics Act, this research included attempts by GenTech to clone these cells for therapeutic purposes—to create stem cells, for example. Without creating any more clones since the passage of the act, we have continued to do research on the cloned egg cells that we froze—that we cryopreserved—before passage of the Bioethics Act.

"We have learned that a human egg is unbelievably fragile. It can take hundreds of tries to extract the chromosomes with a microscopic needle without destroying the egg. Then, when the new chromosomes are injected, there is such a small window of opportunity—no more than two hours max—to inject the new chromosomes in a way that will fuse them to the egg cell. But the hardest part of all is the next step in the process. Because no sperm is involved in cloning, we must find a way to make the egg cell think it has been fertilized. We must use either chemicals or electrical current to make the egg grow. Past experiments on human eggs have frequently encountered failure at this point, killing the egg with either the wrong chemicals or the wrong electrical current.

"That's where our first patent filing comes into play. GenTech has discovered, through a systematic process of laboratory testing, the precise mixture and amount of chemicals that interact with a cell's DNA in precisely the right sequence as well as the exact amount of oxygen exposure necessary to cause these cloned egg cells to grow into healthy stem cells. Our success rate, as well as the nonproprietary aspects of our methodology, will be detailed in the summer issue of the *Journal of Genetic Therapies,* where it will receive the exacting scrutiny of the peer review process."

This time, when Richards paused for breath, the pens continued scribbling. The reporters obviously smelled a big story, a scientific breakthrough of undefined proportions, and Richards had not yet even hit them with the good stuff.

He surveyed the crowd and suppressed a smile. "To this point, you may think that this press conference sounds like an advocacy seminar in favor of therapeutic cloning. And in some respects it is. While we will be fighting in court to protect the integrity of the contract signed by Dr. Nathan Brown and Ms. Davenport-Brown, and therefore will be fighting to protect the Bioethics Act from being overturned, we nevertheless recognize that there are great medical advances that could be gained from therapeutic cloning if Congress or the courts choose to reverse course on this issue."

Now Richards paused for effect, working toward his punch line. "But today, it gives me great pride to tell you that the controversy surrounding cloning may in some respects be rendered irrelevant by other research GenTech is presently performing. We also have a patent on file for a technique that might create embryonic cells and eventually stem cells without the need for using an egg cell as an incubator.

"We have been studying for some time the jellylike material inside an egg cell that contains thousands of proteins, which together work to make the old DNA of the parents inside the egg cell young again and ready to develop into an embryo. We have been injecting parts of that material into certain body cells of consenting subjects, attempting to take the cell back in time to an embryonic and moldable state."

As he made this statement, Richards heard a gasp or two, then a buzz of excitement sweep the room. They understood perfectly. He had just described the real-life version of the fountain of youth. The energy level rose as the participants sensed that they were now part of something unprecedented.

"Our ultimate aim, using this technique, is to move beyond the need for cloning by synthetically reprogramming patients' cells so that we can convert them into stem cells and then ultimately into any other type of cell the patient needs. While our work in this area is quite preliminary and not yet ready for publication, we think that the process itself has enormous potential. Most important, we believe this process represents our best chance of finding a cure for AIDS, since we could reprogram certain cells of a patient, convert them into stem cells, and then coax them into the white blood cells needed to replace those destroyed by the disease. If we win this lawsuit, we intend to use the money donated by Dr. Brown, as well as the egg cells donated by the Browns and others, to continue the research on this process."

Richards looked at the mob of reporters in front of him. Most of them were on the edge of their seats and ready to explode with questions.

"Thank you very much," Richards mumbled. Then he and Mackenzie stood to leave. He did not bother to tell them that the preliminary experimental results were not encouraging, or that ProGen and RSI were actually further along on this type of research. It didn't matter. No other company had the public platform and white-hot spotlight that GenTech now enjoyed.

The room erupted with questions as the reporters jumped out of their seats. A hundred flashes illuminated at once. They pushed and shoved, raised their voices, then pushed and shoved some more. But within seconds, the two men who created the uproar were escorted out a back door of the room, the questions bouncing harmlessly off their backs.

"You did good," Richards said to Mackenzie. And then he laughed —a robust laugh from deep in his chest—like he was the only man on the face of the planet who could appreciate such an outstanding joke.

❧

Richards' press conference had an explosive effect on GenTech's stock. The trading had been halted during the conference itself, but as soon as it ended, the stock price shot up. The initial surge took the stock from seventeen and a half a share to nearly twenty. Then the analysts weighed in, praising Blaine for his forthrightness but urging caution on the profit potential of untested scientific procedures.

For half an hour, the traders vacillated between euphoria and caution, with euphoria eventually winning out. By the close of trading, GenTech's stock had topped $22 per share, an astounding increase of nearly 25 percent on the eve of high-risk litigation. Blaine Richards' paper gains based on the GenTech stock alone amounted to more than $25 million. To Richards' way of thinking, his performance at the press conference had earned him about $1 million a minute.

On the theory that one exciting new breakthrough generally spurs others, GenTech's competitors also enjoyed a banner day. ProGen's stock, which had been languishing around $48 per share, suddenly climbed to fifty-two. RSI, which had a share price of forty-five at the start of the day, ended the day at fifty and a quarter. Richards' options were now clearly in the money on both of these stocks, and he would have made nearly $2.8 million if he had decided to cash them in.

Instead, he waited.

Things were just starting to get interesting.

53

May 26

Dara,

Tonight, my life changed forever.

I did not mean for it to happen. But I've learned that the best things in life are usually not planned. Are you ready for this, Dara? Your die-hard Buddhist mother has converted to Christianity. Can you believe it? Actually, I have to be pinching myself, wondering if this can all be really happening.

These last two days we've been staying with this really great woman from Mitchell's church named Sarah Reed. I guess she's somewhat of a legend at Chesapeake Community Church. She used to be a missionary to the Muslims in Saudi Arabia—helping them to understand and accept the Christian religion. She lost her husband and nearly lost her own life when the religious police of that country cracked down on the Christian church a few years ago. But she is so amazing—she is not bitter at all. In fact, once her teenage kids go away to college, Sarah plans to go back to another Muslim country. Under a different name.

At first I thought she was too sweet to be real. But after being with her for two full days and watching her interact with her daughter Meredith (who, as you know, is a handful—don't get any ideas from her), I realize that this woman has something special. I finally got up the nerve to ask her how she could be so full of joy when she had suffered so much. Her answer really got me thinking.

She said that God loved her so much that he sent His only Son to die for her so that she could spend eternity with Him. She said that no matter what happens on this earth, she will one day join her husband in heaven. And she said that because of the sacrifice of Jesus Christ, the very Son of God, her sins have been forgiven and she can know God through prayer and the study of His Word. "How can I not be happy when I think about what He's done for me?" she asked me.

She overwhelmed me with the simplicity of Christianity. I found myself asking question after question while she patiently explained the love and sacrifice of Jesus Christ. I couldn't believe her faith was so pure and so simple. I tried to tell her about the teachings of Buddha, and she seemed genuinely interested, but I realized even as I spoke that Buddha had taught me how to cope with life, not how to conquer death. Sarah's faith promised peace and joy, something I had not experienced much since my mom died.

But I told Sarah that I felt like if I embraced Christianity it would somehow be disloyal to my mom. Sarah assured me it wouldn't. "From what you've told me about your mom," said Sarah, "she only wanted what was best for you. And she wanted you to have a chance to make your own decisions, to be independent and think for yourself. To pursue your own dreams. Isn't that why she brought you to America?"

Sarah was right, of course. And suddenly, I just knew this was part of my destiny, part of the real reason I came to this country. I didn't know it at the time, but looking back on everything that's happened, I could suddenly see that God's hand was all over this.

"How can I have what you have?" I asked.

"I thought you'd never ask," Sarah replied. She told me that God made it so easy to have a personal relationship with Him—all we had to do was pray.

"What if I try that and nothing happens?" I was still skeptical. The truth, Dara, is that I was also scared. I needed this so bad that if it wasn't real, if it didn't work, I didn't know what I'd do. I had been thinking a lot since Sunday about what the reverend said—about that God-shaped vacuum in my heart. I knew it was there, Dara, and the death of my mom and the cruelty of the Snakeheads only made it bigger. I've been so lonely in the last few months, and if it hadn't been for you, I'm not sure I would have had the strength to go on.

But Dara, before I knew it, I was saying a prayer, my first one ever, really. I wasn't very good at it, so I just repeated what Sarah said. I told God that I knew I didn't deserve His love and heaven and all the good things Christianity promised. I asked God to forgive my sins. I asked Jesus Christ to come and live in my heart and be Lord of my life. I knew in my heart that He was real and that God had somehow raised Him from the dead. I knew that Mitchell believed it with all his heart, and I also knew that Mitchell would have weighed all the historical evidence before he believed it.

What I did not know was whether Jesus could also be real for me. But Dara, as I prayed, the most amazing thing happened. There was no flash of light or earthquake or anything like that, but there was this sudden warmth and peace that flooded my whole body. I soon found myself crying as we prayed, and then smiling and hugging Sarah. It's almost like I was floating; the very thought that the God of the whole universe heard my prayer was almost too much to handle. The words that the reverend read from the Bible on Sunday came flooding back: "Before I formed you in the womb I knew you, before you were born I sanctified you..." And I remembered the words of Mitchell: "Sanctified means purified and set apart for God."

And suddenly Dara, I felt pure, I felt loved, I felt...well, I felt forgiven.

And then, almost on cue, Mitchell came by. He was excited so much and so happy when Sarah told him what happened. He almost acted relieved to hear it, like somebody had lifted a great weight from his shoulders. I thought he would hurt me—just pop my stitches right out—he hugged me so hard. He just kept saying how great this was, and then he smiled and shook his head and said he knew it was going to happen, and then he would hug me again just as hard as before. It is kind of embarrassing when you are to be the center of attention like that—but, just between you and me, I loved it. For some reason, I was kind of worried about what Mitchell might think. His reaction was wonderful.

He could only stay for a few minutes because he had so much work to do on the case before tomorrow morning. He said he parked about three blocks away and crawled through backyards just to get here. I cannot believe he would do that much just to see me.

Before he left, he asked if Sarah and I would pray with him. So, I bowed my head, closed my eyes, and listened while Mitchell talked to Jesus like Jesus was an old friend of his. If I ever had any doubt about whether Mitchell really believed that Christ had risen from the dead, that prayer ended it.

And yes, you little smart-aleck, Mitchell did hold my hand during that prayer, just like he did Sunday. It's all kind of overwhelming. I know now how much God really loves me. And I'm starting to think, or at least hope, that maybe Mitchell does too.

Well, Dara, I know I've written a lot of stuff tonight. But this was really a big step for me, for us. It wasn't based on emotion; I've been thinking this through ever since Sunday. It's now nearly 2:00 A.M., and I've been awake for hours just reading something called the gospel of John. It talks all about who Christ was and what He did. I still don't understand everything, but Sarah says I understand enough—that salvation through this Christ is so simple even a child can figure it out.

I can't sleep and I don't care. It's all so new and so awesome and so wonderful. I guess it took the joy of a missionary and the logic of a lawyer to help me see the reality of Christ. Someday, I hope the love of a mother can show it to you.

Good night, little one. Know that as I think of you tonight, I'll probably be smiling. I am sure that everything's going to be all right with the hearing tomorrow. After all, before He formed you in the womb, He knew you. And even now, before you are born, He has sanctified you—He has set you apart for Himself. It doesn't get any better than that.

Your mom loves you. And so does God.

Mitchell felt like a thief as he moved through the backyards of the compact Chesapeake subdivision with its postage-stamp lots. He avoided the lights cast by windows, crouching low as he sprinted from shadow to shadow. The fences were mostly short picket fences, easy to climb over. Most of the taller ones had unlocked gates. The only thing that concerned Mitchell was the possibility of an unfriendly dog.

He still couldn't believe he was doing this—had done this. He couldn't take the chance of just driving up to Sarah's house, fearful that he would be followed. So he had been forced to park down the street and crawl around behind houses like a juvenile delinquent to lose anybody who might have been following him. He knew he didn't have time to be doing this. He would still be up half the night preparing for tomorrow's hearing, and yet he had used two precious hours to drive out here and crawl around the backyards of strangers just so he could spend a few minutes with Maryna.

And the crazy thing was—he was glad he had done it.

Wow, he thought, *What a night!*

Mitchell knew Maryna had been searching spiritually. They had talked for almost two hours on Sunday about the claims of Christ and the teachings of Buddha. And Mitchell also knew that nobody could be of more help to Maryna than Sarah Reed. But even Mitchell, always the optimist, had been shocked when the two women had shared the news of Maryna's salvation. So sudden. So decisive.

God, You are so good. You saved Maryna, and at the same time you saved me from my own stupidity. You kept me from having to give "the talk"…

He stopped in midthought, jerked his head around, and crouched next to the back wall of a small white vinyl house. He was sure he had heard something in a drainage ditch about fifteen yards away. It sounded like footsteps moving through the tall weeds, on a course parallel to Mitchell's path. He stared hard in the direction of the noise. He held his breath and stayed perfectly still. And he listened.

He squatted there for two or three minutes, eyes searching up and down the dark outline of the ditch, scarcely breathing, waiting for another noise. But there was nothing, just the familiar sounds of the night—the crickets, the occasional car driving by, air conditioners running, muted sounds from televisions inside the houses.

Mitchell reached down and picked up a small rock. He tossed it into the drainage ditch, as near as possible to the exact spot where he thought he had heard the noise. Still nothing. He found two more rocks and repeated the throws. He waited. Nothing happened.

Relieved, Mitchell crouched and sprinted across two more yards. He checked in all directions to make sure nobody was around, then emerged from the shadows, rose to his full height, and walked confidently down the street to his dependable pickup.

He glanced around one last time, then climbed in his truck and started it up. He let out a huge sigh of relief and thought again about the feel of Maryna in his arms. Even if nothing good came out of the hearing that started tomorrow, something unbelievably good had already come out of this case.

He dropped his head down against his steering wheel and closed his eyes. "Thank You, Lord," he whispered. He felt lighter somehow; his feelings no longer at war with a biblical principle he had committed to follow.

After a quiet moment, he picked his head back up and shifted the truck into gear. "We've got to quit meeting like this," he mumbled to Maryna, as if she could hear him. Then he put in his favorite CD and began singing along.

"I get carried away..." Mitchell crooned. And for a few short minutes, he did. He forgot all about the fact that he was less than twelve hours away from one of the most important cases he would ever try. He forgot about the mountains of work that still waited for him back at the apartment. He thought only about Maryna and tonight and the first night they met and the George Strait concert.

He had liked this song before. But he absolutely loved it now.

"...by the look, by the light of your eyes. Before I even realize the ride I'm on... Baby, I'm long gone. I get carried away, and nothing matters but being with you..."

He thought about how crazy this all was. The words of the Rock kicked around in his head—*Don't ever get involved with a client.* Despite her conversion, common sense still told him the same thing. *Look at how different the two of you are,* he lectured himself.

But the words of the Rock and the cautions of common sense were easily swallowed up by the soft chords of George Strait's guitar. Sure, Mitchell had only known her for a few days. But Maryna had been through it. And Mitchell had seen her handle the toughest things life could throw at her with incredible class. The woman had character. And she *was* beautiful. And now they shared the same Savior.

"Thank You, Lord," Mitchell mumbled again. Then he hit the button to start the same song over. One more time for George Strait's "Carried Away."

54

Thursday, May 27

WIN MACKENZIE ROSE SLOWLY from his desk, buoyed by the dramatic closing lines of his opening statement. He whispered them forcefully under his breath as he paced the office, reminding himself to talk slowly and to look Judge Baker-Kline directly in the eye.

It gave him goose bumps, this opening statement did. He may have saved his very best work for the most important case of his life. Today he would fight for the very future of medicine and scientific research, for the right to use the money and stem cells donated by Nathan Brown to find a potential cure for hundreds of thousands of victims of AIDS, Parkinson's, and other degenerative diseases.

He would also fight for the principle that a person's word should be a person's bond. How could fertility clinics and researchers in these new areas of medicine operate if the sanctity of contracts wasn't protected? This area of research was risky enough, but if the contracts solemnly signed by patients and clinics were meaningless, just thrown out when a woman changed her mind, then how could any clinic ever hope to operate in this gray area of the law?

But most important, Win would fight to protect the Bioethics Act—to prevent the type of reproductive cloning that society could not yet handle. He knew that most Americans agreed with him on this one. They did not want cloning on demand. Where would it possibly end? Designer babies? Growing fetuses for spare parts? Cloning children so that parents could have another little Johnny if anything happened to the first one?

The mind reeled with the implications of what all this might mean. And only Win Mackenzie stood between this ethical never-never land and the safe boundaries of today's society.

No, Win decided, in a real sense he would not just be representing Dr. Blaine Richards and GenTech. Today he spoke for millions of Americans, for ethical scientific research, for the sanctity of contracts, and against society's playing God.

Thus inspired, he walked over to his closet and pulled out his fresh dark blue Brooks Brothers suit coat. He saved this suit for special occasions—television appearances, that type of thing. He put it on slowly and ceremoniously, as if he were a knight donning a suit of armor. He played with the pocket handkerchief until it fluffed up just right, then he buttoned the top two buttons on the suit coat and smoothed the sleeves.

He would go down to the elegant conference room and practice his opening in front of an appreciative audience of Kilgore & Strobel associates. They would offer polite critiques and tell him how brilliant the opening really was.

He closed the closet door and walked over to face the picture of his beloved samurai. He reached out and gently touched the glass covering the photo with his fingertips, letting the fingers rest on some of the fiercest looking warriors. For a few moments he lingered there, feeling a strength of purpose course throughout his veins. His lips formed a thin, fierce line as he turned away.

In two hours the preliminary injunction hearing in *Davenport-Brown v. GenTech* would begin. And Winsted Aaron Mackenzie IV was way past ready.

⚬⚬

Mitchell slurped down the last few drops of tepid coffee, scribbled a few more notes on his legal pad, and checked his watch. It was almost 7:00 A.M. Nikki would arrive soon. Mitchell tried not to think about how little sleep he had gotten the previous night. By all rights, he should have been exhausted. But the caffeine and adrenaline combined to keep him on edge—he was wired, ready to get this hearing under way.

Sure, Mitchell admitted to himself, he was a little nervous. And the fact that all the news networks had been carrying special reports about the case this morning hadn't helped much. But he had played enough football to know that the jitters went away with the opening kickoff. Once he got inside the courtroom and the hearing started, he would be fine.

At least, that's what he kept telling himself.

Mitchell reluctantly rose from the table and shuffled down the hallway to his closet. He ignored the box sitting on the floor of his closet, containing his diplomas and the picture of Stonewall Jackson. He owned only two suits worthy of a federal court appearance, one gray and the other dark blue. Neither had seen the dry cleaners in a while. He frowned and grabbed the same gray suit he had worn for his interview with the Rock, the same suit he had worn the first time he had disastrously set foot in Judge Baker-Kline's court, the same suit he would have to wear again on Tuesday if the preliminary hearing stretched over the holiday weekend. Then he grabbed a wrinkled white shirt. He sniffed it quickly—not too bad—and plugged in the iron. He made a mental note to hit the dry cleaners over the weekend and to use liberal amounts of aftershave in the meantime.

⚬━⚬

The woman's got to loosen up a little, thought Cameron. She eyed Nora Gunther over breakfast at the downtown Marriott where Nora had set up shop for the trial. Nora had not touched the food in front of her, focusing instead on the yellow legal pad she held in her left hand, her coffee cup in the other.

The legal pad contained her outline for the examination of Cameron Davenport-Brown. This was their third time through it. The strain was starting to show on both women.

"Cameron, you can't use that tone of voice," Nora lectured. "The way you say it is just as important as what you say."

Cameron pursed her lips and bit her tongue. She had learned that there was no sense arguing with Nora. The woman never backed down on anything. She would turn a minor point into a death battle, relentlessly arguing her case until the other person called it quits.

"I'll use a different tone in court," Cameron said flatly.

"All right. Then let's try it again."

After several more questions and answers, none entirely satisfactory to Nora, the lawyer finally put down her pad and took a bite of cold oatmeal. "That's good enough for now," she announced. "We can practice some more tonight."

"Can't you put me on the stand today?" asked Cameron. The thought of another practice session, another twenty-four hours of worrying about her testimony, made her nauseated.

Nora just shook her head. "We've got to start with Richards. He won't be expecting to take the stand so early in the case. I want to get after him before they've had a chance to thoroughly prep him."

Cameron shrugged in protest, but Nora ignored her. "This stuff's terrible cold," Nora complained, shoving the oatmeal toward the middle of the table. Then she checked her watch. "Where is he anyway?"

"Who knows?"

Nora shook her head. "I think it's a great idea to have him on the case as local counsel, *provided* that he understands his role. It makes for great sympathy and drama to have a father and daughter teamed up together. But this stunt about the subpoenas... Where did that come from?"

Cameron didn't answer. She knew she wasn't really expected to answer. Besides, who could ever explain the twisted thinking of the Rock?

———

"Oooooh," the Rock groaned. His alarm blared for the third time that morning. He had hit the snooze button twice, but now the annoying buzzing sound was back. He pulled the pillow over his head and groped around with his free hand for the alarm. His fingers found the snooze button and mashed it again.

His head felt gigantic—five times its normal size. And every inch of it was throbbing. His mouth was so dry that his lips stuck together, fused by the little white crusty stuff caked at the corners. His tongue was cemented to the roof of his mouth, his throat swollen shut. His stomach was wrapped in knots, churning away, raging at the venom that the Rock had poured into it the night before. His liver was probably on overdrive, trying to rid his system of enormous amounts of rum, light beer, and something else he had started drinking about midnight. *What in tarnation was that stuff, anyway?*

There was only one cure for this—a little more shuteye. He couldn't get up just yet and face the world. He could skip the meeting with Nora and Cameron and just meet them at court. He probably should call them, but they'd figure it out. Besides, he was just local counsel. And Nora had made it clear that she didn't really value his thinking.

The best lawyer, he said to himself as he dozed off again, *is a well-rested lawyer.*

55

MITCHELL HAD INTENDED TO ARRIVE at least fifteen minutes early for the nine o'clock hearing. But as usual, Nikki had been running late. When they finally got to court, they had to park two blocks away and then found crammed lines at the metal detectors.

They finally got through security, took the elevators to the third floor, and walked down the long corridor toward the largest federal courtroom in the building. Mitchell was thankful to have Nikki with him, even if she had caused him to run behind. For starters, she looked stunning. Her long, dark hair was braided and pulled back away from her face, highlighting her high, sharp cheekbones and alluring eyes. She wore a black suit, with a skirt that hovered just above her knees, and an expensive white blouse. Heels, a platinum necklace, and matching bracelet completed the look.

"Wow," Mitchell had said when he first saw her that morning.

"What?" Nikki responded.

"You know darn well what," he answered.

Nikki just smiled. She did indeed know.

But she did more than look good. Even though Nikki couldn't handle any witnesses or argue motions, she would be a welcome sounding board for strategy as the trial progressed. And if nothing else, her fearless in-your-face attitude would give Mitchell just the lift he might need, especially since he couldn't risk bringing Maryna to court.

Now, as they made their way through the crush of reporters, Nikki proved her worth. "We'll do our talking in court," she said, as she elbowed her way. Mitchell trailed in her wake. The reporters shoved mikes in their faces and shouted questions.

"Will Ms. Sareth appear and testify? Is it true she's an illegal immigrant? Does the baby have Down's?"

"Excuse me," Nikki insisted as the pushing escalated. "No comment." The reporters shouted more indecipherable questions. "I said no comment." Mitchell noticed Nikki's face grow hard, just a few feet from the courtroom door.

Then one reporter got pushed into Nikki, nearly knocking her off her feet. She caught herself, glared at the man, then stopped in midstride and turned to face the mob.

"Listen!" she screamed, and the intensity of it quieted the crowd. The cameras started rolling. Mitchell moved quickly to her side.

"Our client may or may not appear and testify," Nikki said. "Frankly, I think her privacy has been invaded enough." She paused, and a dozen questions started flying. But Nikki lifted her hand and the questions stopped.

"This is a very simple case, really. We are here not just representing Maryna Sareth, but also the tiny life growing inside her." She gazed evenly and confidently out at the reporters. "If we lose, it will be the first time in recorded American history that a judge forces a mother to abort the child growing inside of her. We don't think that's going to happen."

With those words, Nikki turned on her heels and forced her way into the courtroom. Mitchell turned to join her, but a fierce-looking Asian American blocked his way. The granite block of a man, a full head shorter than Mitchell, was familiar, but Mitchell couldn't quite place him.

"Excuse me," Mitchell demanded. When the man didn't move, Mitchell just glared back for an instant, shook his head, and walked around him. No sense starting a fight in the hallway.

The man let him pass, but something still bothered Mitchell—something he couldn't explain. And that made it worse. His senses screamed danger, but the chaos kept him from focusing on what exactly that danger might be. Still, as he entered the courtroom, he glanced one last time quickly over his shoulder. The man was still glaring.

When Mitchell entered the courtroom, he felt like he had entered another world.

The courtroom was packed, but the atmosphere was surprisingly subdued. The thick oak doors muted the sounds from the raucous hallway. Inside, everyone spoke in hushed tones, respecting the solemnity of the occasion.

The air hung thick and muggy with tension. The calm before the storm, Mitchell knew. But it was also different from anything he had ever experienced. The closest comparison he could make was that moment in the locker room in the preseason, just before a coach would announce who made the team and who was cut. But even that was different. That was just a football team. And football was just a game. Today, Mitchell realized, much more was at stake.

As he walked down the aisle, feigning confidence and feeling sick, he became keenly aware that the eyes of rows and rows of spectators had collectively turned to watch Nikki and him. Could they tell how nervous he really was? Could they sense that he was in over his head—a first-year, no a first-*month* lawyer—playing in the big leagues? Or were they ignoring him altogether, just staring at Nikki as she walked by?

Faith is fear that has said its prayers, Mitchell told himself as he swung open the waist-high doors that separated the spectators from the counsel tables and the well of the courtroom.

And then, in one awful moment, it dawned on him. *There was nowhere to sit!*

Nora and Cameron had spread out on the counsel tables closest to the jury box. Nora was engrossed in some papers before her. Cameron nodded at Mitchell, who nodded back. The Rock was conspicuously absent. He still had five minutes before he was officially late.

On the other side of the courtroom were two long tables, sitting end-to-end, absolutely loaded down with papers and pleadings and books and file folders. Dr. Blaine Richards stood just behind the center of the tables, talking to someone from the spectator section. A slew of Kilgore & Strobel associates—Mitchell quickly counted five—occupied most of the seats at the tables, fussing around and arranging things just right. A quick glance over his shoulder told Mitchell that Win Mackenzie was in the back of the courtroom talking to someone dressed casually and intently taking notes. Probably a last-second media interview.

Not knowing whether to turn right or left, Mitchell just followed Nikki and drifted toward the Kilgore & Strobel tables. Nikki didn't even slow down.

"Gentlemen," she said curtly to the Kilgore associates as she walked in front of their tables. One or two of the young men—there were no women—glanced at her and nodded. The others were too busy to acknowledge her presence.

Then she stopped in front of the second table, at that moment housing two associates and a truckload of paper, and announced loudly, "I believe you're in our seats."

The murmuring that had been pervading the courtroom ceased. Everyone stared.

One of the larger and older associates, a man with a long forehead, wide waist, and well-practiced scowl, snorted at Nikki and pointed toward the tables on the other side of the courtroom. "They've got plenty of room. Sit over there."

Mitchell stiffened, but Nikki just smiled a brilliant white smile. "Fat chance," she said loudly. "Third-party Intervenors are supposed to sit on the defense side of the courtroom—much as I'd prefer not to." And the next second, with blazing speed, she reached out her arm and swept it clear across the top of the table in front of her, sending documents and books and pens and legal pads flying onto the adjacent table. A few scattered on the floor.

"There," Nikki said. "I think we'll have plenty of room now."

All five associates stood immediately. The older man cursed loudly. "What do you think you're doing?" he blurted out, leaning forward.

Mitchell got in the man's face, leaning across the table. The whole courtroom became even more hushed, focusing on the altercation at defense counsel's table. "We're just taking our seats," he sneered. "Now, why don't you move over behind that first table? You and your buddies can sit there."

The associate blew out a hard breath that stank of coffee and breakfast. "That's ridiculous," he said, although not as loudly as before. "We were here first."

"Fine," responded Nikki. Then she turned to the clerk and spoke loud enough so the whole courtroom could easily hear. "Can you go tell the judge we need a few minutes of her time? Even though she said we could intervene in this case, it seems the defendants want us to sit with the spectators."

The clerk, wide-eyed at the litigants' childish behavior, nodded her head, and started back to get the judge.

"No, wait," said Win Mackenzie, walking rapidly through the swinging door and into the well of the courtroom. Then he looked at Mitchell and lowered his voice. "No sense starting on the wrong foot with the judge. She'll not be happy if she thinks we can't even agree on who sits where."

He paused for a moment, glancing around, then grabbed the first counsel table and motioned to one of his associates. "Here, help me move this down a little."

After Win and his associate separated the tables by a few feet, he surveyed his work and forced a smile. "Let's move a few extra chairs behind our table. Mr. Taylor and Ms. Moreno can have that one."

Out of the corner of his eye, Mitchell saw Dr. Blaine Richards give Win Mackenzie a look that could kill. Mackenzie pretended not to notice.

"That will be fine," said Nikki, plopping her small briefcase down on the huge table that she had just cleared. It looked lonely, but she had made her point.

Nikki Moreno had drawn first blood. And for the moment, Mitchell Taylor's butterflies had flown away.

A few moments later, as he and Nikki finished settling in at their newly won table, Mitchell turned to survey the spectators. He was pleased to see a number of young mothers he had dubbed "Nikki's Army" seated anxiously in the second row. Lord willing, they could play a major role in the hearing. But behind them, and directly in Mitchell's line of vision, sat the Asian American he had bumped into in the hallway. This time, Mitchell recognized him instantly, in part because the man sat next to his angular partner, a white man with a long hooknose sloping down toward his lip and a long sloping forehead angling back in search of hair. They were the two INS agents who had come to his house looking for Maryna several days ago. *At least,* thought Mitchell, *that's who they claimed to be.*

He wondered if they had ever followed through on their threat to drop by the Rock's office with a subpoena.

Mitchell turned around to inform Nikki, and found Cameron standing in front of him on the other side of the table. Her face was drawn and pale, the last few traumatic days having taken an obvious toll. She still had strength in the fierce blue eyes, but it was a tired strength, a look of sad resoluteness at the task to be done.

She leaned over and spoke with a soft earnestness so that only Mitchell and Nikki could hear.

"Mitchell, don't do this," she pleaded. "Don't go through with this."

She took a deep breath. This was no act; the words clearly pained her. "If you really believe those embryos at GenTech's labs are live little human beings, help me save them. You and Maryna and I can resolve this out of court. Your presence here"—she paused, struggling for the words—"your intervention against me on behalf of Maryna... It only makes me look bad, and makes it more likely that GenTech can just kill those embryos and use them for research.

"Mitchell, it's my only chance to have a healthy child. Please..." Cameron stopped, choking back the words, working hard to keep the tears at bay. She looked from Mitchell to Nikki and then back to Mitchell.

Nikki kicked Mitchell gently under the table and gave him a quick nod of the head. *Tell her,* the look said.

Mitchell looked down at the table, then up into the sad eyes of his former client.

"I'm sorry," he said softly.

Cameron just stood there for a moment, perhaps hoping that Mitchell would change his mind, perhaps weighing what to say next. Finally, she sighed deeply and stood up straight.

"Then I can't help you," she said. "And I can't help Maryna."

Before Mitchell could ask what that comment meant, she turned and walked away.

"You really told her that time," whispered Nikki. "Yes sir. Really put your foot down on that one." Nikki pulled a few documents and a legal pad from her briefcase and slapped them down on the barren table.

56

THE ROCK WAS ON HIS GAME. Just as the court clerk, in her most commanding voice, ordered everyone to rise—"Court is now in session, the Honorable Cynthia Baker-Kline presiding"—the Rock came blowing through the back doors and shuffled down the aisle. A split second later, Judge Cynthia Baker-Kline came bursting through the front door of the courtroom, wearing a fierce and haughty look, robes flowing behind her. She banged her gavel and called the court to order.

A rumpled Rock hustled through the swinging doors and slid into a seat next to Cameron.

"Nice of you to join us, Mr. Davenport," Ichabod announced, staring him down.

The Rock rose, buttoning his suit coat as he did so. In his haste, his pushed the top button through the second buttonhole, causing the front of the coat to hang at a weird angle. "Thank you, Your Honor," he said. "I had a little difficulty finding a parking spot."

"I'm sure," responded Ichabod.

The Rock sat back down.

A person or two in the back of the courtroom snickered, but they were silenced immediately by a glare from the judge. When she had the complete attention of everyone present, she subtly tilted her head toward the sketch artists, at just the right straight-on angle to hide the enormity of her nose, perched her reading glasses on the end of that prominent feature, and began reading her carefully prepared remarks.

"This is a preliminary injunction hearing. At issue are eight frozen embryos at the GenTech Clinic in Norfolk, Virginia, and one embryo growing inside a surrogate mother, Ms. Maryna Sareth." Ichabod gazed down her nose at Mitchell as if sighting down the barrel of a rifle. "Am I pronouncing that right?"

"Yes, Your Honor."

"Good. Now both the plaintiff in this case, Ms. Davenport-Brown, and the intervenor in this case, Ms. Sareth, are requesting that the court issue a preliminary injunction. The law on this point is crystal clear. I can grant the requested relief only if I believe two things. First, I must believe that the party has a likelihood of success on the merits; that is, I must believe that the party is likely to prevail at the trial of this case. Second, and equally important, I must believe that the party will suffer irreparable harm if I do not enter the injunctive relief. In other words, something bad will happen that cannot be reversed.

"The plaintiff in this case, Ms. Davenport-Brown, says that the eight frozen embryos should be preserved so that they can be implanted in another surrogate mother of her choice. Her claim of irreparable harm is pretty straightforward. If GenTech is allowed to use the embryos for experimentation, then she will lose her only chance to be the natural mother of a child free of genetic disorders. But given the fact that these embryos were created by a cloning process called blastomere separation, and since the Bioethics Act prohibits implanting cloned embryos, in order for the plaintiff to prevail I would have to rule the Bioethics Act unconstitutional. I would also have to override the contract signed by the plaintiff when she first went to the GenTech Clinic."

Although the judge was just stating the facts, the remarks seemed to infuriate Nora Gunther. Mitchell noticed that she scribbled some notes when Ichabod first started speaking, but that now she had dropped her pen and just glared at the judge.

"The defendant," continued Ichabod, "claims that the embryos should be used for medical research, as directed by the Last Will and Testament of Dr. Nathan Brown. The problem with the defendant's position is that this will was written and signed at a time when Dr. Brown was not aware that the embryo implanted in the surrogate mother would eventually develop Down syndrome—at least insofar as the preliminary tests can determine."

Ichabod paused and looked at Win Mackenzie. Mitchell leaned forward slightly and glanced at Mackenzie as well. Mackenzie simply gazed back at the judge—looking stoic, hopeful, and totally unfazed by the court's comments.

"The intervenor," now Ichabod looked at Mitchell, "who is the surrogate mother carrying the plaintiff's child, wants this court to issue an order stating that she may carry the child to term. She claims that forcing her to terminate this child, per the biological mother's wishes, would constitute irreparable harm. The problem with her position is that it ignores the contract she signed with the Browns and GenTech, and it ignores the fact that this is not her biological child. If the intervenor has her way, then the court would be requiring Ms. Davenport-Brown to become the mother of a child with a birth defect, despite the fact that the contract calls for exactly the opposite result."

Mitchell felt a chill run down his spine. He didn't like Ichabod's phrasing of the issue. This was not really about forcing *Cameron* to become a mother—Maryna had already offered to mother this child— it was really about forcing *Maryna* to have an abortion. But for some reason, Ichabod ignored that critical distinction.

"Those are the issues before the court. Although this is only a *preliminary* injunction hearing, for all practical purposes, my ruling at the end of this hearing will decide the matter. This preliminary injunction will remain in effect, unless it is reversed on appeal, for the six months between now and the trial date of this case. By then, the parties will have taken actions that would make any further rulings moot."

Ichabod paused to survey her audience. She put down her papers and removed her glasses. She rubbed her forehead and her eyes, as if struggling under the crushing weight of the seriousness of the case. She lowered her tone so it could barely be heard in the back of the court-room. "The court is well aware of the enormous burden of deciding this

case and the importance of the court's ruling on this request for a preliminary injunction. This case will impact not just the parties before the
court, but perhaps thousands of others around this country." She now
turned to the lawyers seated before her.

"The court therefore implores legal counsel to conduct themselves
in a manner worthy of a case of this magnitude. Let's leave any petty
bickering and gamesmanship aside and stick to the main issues in dispute. I've reserved three days for this hearing—that should be plenty of
time if we conduct ourselves in the manner I've suggested.

"Now, are you all prepared to give an opening statement?"

"Yes, Your Honor," the lawyers replied in unison.

Mitchell felt a knot form in the pit of his stomach. He got the sink-
ing feeling that Ichabod was not exactly approaching this case with an
open mind.

— ❦ —

Mitchell watched Nora Gunther rise to give her opening statement. She
took her place behind the large wooden podium facing the judge and
immediately attacked. Her voice had an edge to it even as she started,
and the longer she went, the louder and angrier she became. The esca-
lation didn't appear to impact Ichabod, who sat with her arms folded,
staring at Gunther with cold, expressionless eyes. Ichabod's unflappable
posture seemed to irritate Gunther even more. The lawyer raised her
voice to a fevered pitch as she continued, her face turning from its normal pale hue to an aggravated shade of red.

"This case is nothing less than a frontal assault by GenTech and its
lawyers on a woman's right to choose," Nora claimed. "The fundamental lesson of *Roe v. Wade* is that every woman has an inalienable constitutional right to choose whether they want to have offspring or not. And
now, thirty years later, GenTech and Mr. Mackenzie have the audacity to
march into this court and ignore *Roe v. Wade* in its entirety—just pretend
it doesn't exist." At this, Nora turned and launched a withering sneer at

Dr. Blaine Richards. "This case has the potential to set women's rights back thirty years."

She returned her gaze to the stone-faced Ichabod. "This is a *critical* decision, Judge, that goes to the core of who a woman is. My client's very right to be a mother is at stake. And who is in the best position to make this difficult moral decision about whether Cameron Davenport-Brown should have a child?" Nora asked caustically. "Is it Dr. Blaine Richards and his giant biotech corporation—the same company that stands to profit by having nearly $2 million funneled into stem cell funding if the court decides against my client?" Nora scoffed, deeming it unnecessary to answer her own question.

"Is it Dr. Nathan Brown, my client's deceased husband? A man who went to extraordinary lengths to become a father—to have a child he could call his own? A man who died not knowing that the embryo he and Cameron had created was inflicted with an incurable genetic disorder? Can anyone really argue with a straight face that if Dr. Brown were alive today and knew about the Down syndrome of the embryo carried by the surrogate mother—that he would still want to destroy the remaining healthy embryos? Forgive my bluntness, Judge, but should we leave this decision to the uninformed Last Will and Testament of a dead man?"

If Nora Gunther was pushing the envelope to get a rise from the judge, it didn't work. Other than a brief scowl, Ichabod's body language remained unchanged. But the remark did cause some disgruntled stirring in the press section of the courtroom, and even Cameron diverted her gaze from the insensitive lawyer.

Not missing a beat, Nora Gunther turned her guns toward Mitchell and his client. "Some would apparently argue," she said with a dismissive wave toward Mitchell, "that the best person to make this decision is the surrogate mother. Here is a person who will apparently not even set foot in this court—her very presence in the country is a violation of our nation's laws. Should a surrogate mother—one who will be emotionally attached to the embryo growing inside her but who will have no legal responsibility for this child once born—should she be the one to make the decision about which embryos should survive and which ones should not?"

Mitchell returned Gunther's disdainful look with an expressionless look of his own. He had learned from watching Ichabod how best to get under Gunther's skin. Gunther turned from Mitchell and glanced down at the notes she had thus far ignored. The momentary pause gave Ichabod a chance to interrupt.

"By the way, Ms. Gunther, who chose the surrogate mother?"

Gunther's eyes grew darker still, as if she couldn't believe that Ichabod had the audacity to question her.

"My client, her husband, and Dr. Richards," Nora said sharply.

"And your client knew that Ms. Sareth was an illegal alien at the time?" Ichabod asked the question without the least trace of emotion.

"Yes, of course."

"Then you probably shouldn't complain about that now," Ichabod said coolly.

The comment made Mitchell smile, if only to himself.

"I'm not complaining," Gunther protested. "But as a practical matter, how can you consider granting the petition of a third-party intervenor who will not even come to court to testify? Especially when granting that petition would require Cameron to allow her child to be birthed and raised by someone who can't even legally hold down a job in the United States?"

Gunther let her question hang in the tense air for a few moments. When it was apparent that Ichabod would not answer, the lawyer glanced at her notes again, reloaded, and plowed ahead.

For the next half-hour she complained about every document that stood between Cameron and her desired outcome in the case. The contract signed by Cameron, Nathan Brown, and GenTech was a "farce," she claimed. After all, it was drafted by GenTech's lawyers and imposed on Cameron during an emotionally vulnerable time in her life. Every lawyer knows that contracts like this one can be invalidated by an unexpected "change in circumstances," Nora asserted.

Gunther harked back to *Krell v. Henry*, a timeless case that every first-year law student studied in contracts class. In *Krell*, Nora reminded the judge—as if she had never taken contracts—the defendant rented a "flat" from the plaintiff for two days, for the express purpose of viewing the procession to be held in conjunction with the coronation of King Edward VII. When the procession was cancelled, due to the king's becoming seriously ill, the court allowed the defendant to get out of the contract based on an unanticipated change in circumstances.

"In this case," lectured Gunther in her shrill tone, "if the fact that the embryo was diagnosed with Down syndrome isn't a change in circumstances sufficient to nullify the contract, then this court will be reversing more than a hundred years of contract law and rewriting every law school contracts textbook in the process."

Ichabod grimaced at these overstatements and the increased stridency of Gunther's arguments, but the lawyer didn't seem to notice. Gunther next took aim at the Bioethics Act.

It was overbroad, she claimed, and in direct violation of a woman's fundamental right to choose as first articulated in *Roe v. Wade*. The problem was that the overzealous congressmen tried to ban even simple blastomere separation right along with the somatic cell nuclear transfer that everyone was so worried about. Who were these congressmen to tell women like Cameron that they couldn't use this simple medical technique to help conceive a child?

If this legislation was not overturned, abortions would be banned and eventually birth control, too. Either a woman had the right to control her own reproductive choices or Congress did, argued Gunther. It was that simple.

By the way, Nora added, Congress could not claim that it had some kind of duty to protect these small pre-embryos. These pre-embryos, or more properly, these zygotes, were not yet a human life, that much was well settled. Otherwise, it would be illegal for mothers and clinics everywhere to discard excess fertilized eggs created by fertility clinics or conduct any experiments on them.

After Gunther had railed against Congress for a while, seemingly without taking a breath, Ichabod finally spoke.

"How much longer do you have, Ms. Gunther? And please remember, I asked for 'brief' openings."

"Just one more thing, Your Honor."

Ichabod sighed. "Make it quick."

"I'll try," Gunther answered, with obvious disgust.

As far as Mitchell could tell, she didn't try very hard.

It took her fifteen more minutes to make her last point: the fact that the contract between Cameron and "the surrogate mother"—for some reason Gunther refused to use Maryna's name—should be upheld. Unlike the other contract Cameron had signed—which of course needed to be ignored—this contract should be punctiliously followed. Why? Because this contract anticipated the very circumstances that now existed. The parties had agreed in writing that the pregnancy would be terminated if continuing the pregnancy would substantially endanger the surrogate mother's health or if the fetus developed any abnormalities during the first two trimesters that would impair its ability to develop into a normal and healthy child. If such defects were discovered, then Cameron could opt to have the pregnancy terminated.

Unfortunately, said Gunther, *that* is exactly what happened here. There were no changed circumstances that caught the parties off-guard with respect to *this* contract. The sad possibility of abnormalities like Down syndrome was discussed when the contract was signed. And now that it had become a reality, there was no reason to let the surrogate mother go back on her word.

As her final pitch, Gunther pleaded with the court to understand that Cameron had nothing against Down syndrome children. She admired so much the incredible spirit and giftedness of such children and the special patience and love of the parents who raised them. But as a result of circumstances beyond her control, Cameron was now a single woman who would have to raise any child on her own while working a full-time job. A special-needs child would require, would deserve, so much more.

"It is a tough call," admitted Gunther, her voice finally lowering. "It is heartbreaking, gut-wrenching. But it is exactly the type of tough call that our Constitution wisely places within the breast of the woman most affected—the potential mother—the one person who will have to live with the consequences the rest of her life. It is a call that Cameron has agonized over and prayed about. It is a call that she is prepared to make. It is the court's job to ensure that she has that chance.

"Any other result, Your Honor, not only causes irreparable harm to my client. It also sets back women's rights in this country by more than thirty years."

Finally, mercifully, Nora Gunther stopped talking. She stared down the judge one last time, then gathered her papers and returned to her seat. The air was thick with the tension created by her combative opening statement. She left no doubt that she was prepared to do battle on every point—with the judge herself, if necessary—to defend her client's right to choose.

"Let's take a break," said Ichabod, "before we hear from Mr. Mackenzie."

57

MITCHELL WATCHED AS WIN MACKENZIE rose majestically for his moment in the spotlight. Win buttoned his suit coat, carefully brushed one hand down each sleeve, smoothing the wrinkles, then grabbed his notes and settled in behind the podium. "May it please the court," he said in a voice that sounded deep and melodic, a nice contrast to Gunther's forceful and fevered tone. He looked down and began reading a carefully scripted opening statement.

Mackenzie started by lauding the same contract that Nora had just dismissed as a "farce." Integrity of contracts is critical to the medical advances being made in this area of biotech research, he claimed.

"How can fertility clinics and biotech firms operate if contracts governing critical issues like the disposal of fertilized eggs can simply be ignored? And why should Ms. Davenport-Brown *alone* decide what happens to these embryos? Instead, shouldn't her husband also have a say? Of course he should. And that's the reason everyone signed the GenTech contract ahead of time. To avoid disputes like this one ending up in court."

Mackenzie then walked a few steps back to his table and took out a large piece of white poster board. On it was a life-sized photograph of the studious face of Dr. Nathan Brown. Mitchell couldn't believe it.

Mackenzie placed the photo on an easel and angled it toward the judge. Dr. Brown seemed to stare at Ichabod, and also catch Mitchell out of the corner of his eye. Mitchell noticed Cameron put her hand on her forehead and lower her gaze to the table, registering her disapproval.

"That's hokey," whispered Nikki. "And insensitive."

"This man is not with us today," continued Mackenzie, his hands gripping the podium, "but his voice should not—cannot—be ignored. The plain fact of the matter is that the contract settles this matter without equivocation and without ambiguity. Under the contract, either the husband or wife can decide to donate the frozen pre-embryos to research. Why? Because neither should be made a parent if he or she is unwilling."

At this juncture, Mackenzie ticked off a long line of cases that had reached exactly the same conclusion—based on contracts remarkably similar to the GenTech document. The courts treated the pre-embryos like property. And like property, the rights to the pre-embryos could be bargained away in a contract.

"Uphold the sanctity of this contract—this legal document signed by all interested parties," urged Mackenzie, "and this case is over."

The arguments seemed to slide off Ichabod like she was Teflon. She took no notes; her face never changed expression. *Is she buying the argument hook, line, and sinker?* Mitchell wondered. *Or is this just her style— let the lawyers have their say in opening statements, take it all in, save her questions for later?*

"Are these small zygotes human beings?" asked Mackenzie, his posture and tone never changing. He still stood clutching the podium, next to the portrait of Brown, his eyes shifting from Ichabod to his notes and back again, his voice one constant note. "Absolutely not. If they were— if the law considered every fertilized egg to be a human being, even those that are not yet implanted—then we would outlaw abortion, we would outlaw IUDs, and we would outlaw most every other form of birth control imaginable.

"Judge, that's not the law, and every first-year law student knows it."

For a moment, Mackenzie seemed to lose his place. He shuffled a few notes, silence filling the courtroom as his face reddened. Then he regained his composure and cleared his throat, putting a finger on the page in front of him to mark his place.

"It's ridiculous for the plaintiff to charge that GenTech is motivated in this case by profit. Absolutely ridiculous! Who could benefit more from overturning the law banning cloning than GenTech? Here is a company that has thousands of frozen embryos in storage and the technology to use them in therapeutic cloning experiments that could lead to unbelievable medical breakthroughs. Yet GenTech finds itself in the unique position today of defending the Bioethics Act—against its own financial interests—simply because it wants to honor the integrity of a contract. Does that sound to you like a company motivated by profit?"

"Well," Ichabod said, with a wry smile, "are you claiming that Gen-Tech won't benefit financially if I uphold this contract and allow the disposition of these embryos suggested in Dr. Brown's will? As I understand it, these cloned embryos could be used to start new stem cell lines for research financed in large part by bequests in Brown's will. Am I wrong about that?" She raised an eyebrow.

"They will…they may…of course there will be some financial benefit," stammered Mackenzie. Mitchell made a mental note to try and keep Mackenzie off-balance and off-script. "But my point is that they would benefit either way, so financial gain is not what's motivating my client."

"Continue," said Ichabod, sounding unconvinced.

Another searching of notes by Mackenzie. Then he set his notes aside, straightened his back, looked the judge square in the eye, and proceeded from memory.

"When Dr. Richards takes the stand, he will tell the court about some of the incredible medical advances being pioneered by Gen-Tech—"

"Are they the same ones that he told the whole world about yesterday?" Ichabod interrupted.

"Um…those and others. Yes. Dr. Richards will testify that this case holds the key to further medical advances in this area. That with or without cloning, GenTech and others are working on ways to develop embryonic stem cells that can be coaxed into becoming healthy new nerve cells and brain cells—possibly holding the cure to diseases like Alzheimer's and Parkinson's. But this research can't be completed, can't even be attempted, if the contracts donating these egg cells for research purposes cannot be relied upon.

"Why are we here today, Judge? Because there are hundreds of thousands of people in this country who are in dire straits—trapped in the burning building of their own body as it deteriorates from Alzheimer's, Parkinson's, and AIDS, just to name a few. Dr. Richards and GenTech have the fire extinguisher—the medical advances and the funding that can save them—but the plaintiff is trying to take this life-saving equipment out of Dr. Richards' hands. Judge, there are only three parties to this lawsuit, but in truth, there are hundreds of thousands who will be affected by it."

Mackenzie paused and took a deep breath. Then he spoke in hushed tones, pleading more than talking. "The flames mount, the clock ticks, the fireman stands ready, the victims cry out. Hear their screams, Your Honor. Give them hope, Your Honor. Save their lives."

For a moment, Mackenzie just stood there, increasing the impact of his final plea. There was a reverent hush in the courtroom, and even Mitchell found himself on the edge of his seat, not wanting to move and draw attention in this suddenly charged moment. He watched intently as Mackenzie silently took down the portrait of Brown, then turned and took his seat. A somber Dr. Richards put his arm on Mackenzie's shoulder and whispered something in his ear.

Nikki interrupted Mitchell's thoughts. "That was weak," Nikki whispered. "Blatant appeal to emotion. Never works with Ichabod."

"Right," said Mitchell. But his mind was elsewhere, rehearsing one last time the emotional appeal he was getting ready to make himself to a judge carved from stone.

The knot in his stomach tightened.

58

"AT FOURTEEN WEEKS OLD," Mitchell began, "this baby is three or four inches long and weighs a couple of ounces. She has developed little fingers and toes. She has a heartbeat, brain waves, fingerprints, and sensitivity to light and noise." As Mitchell spoke, he looked directly into the cold gray eyes of Ichabod. His voice became strong and steady, and the tightness in his stomach faded.

He reached into his pocket and pulled out a tiny pink plastic replica of an embryo. "Though I could hold her in the palm of my hand, she has all the attributes, all of the genetic raw material, all of the potential emotional, psychological, and spiritual makeup of a human being."

"Mr. Taylor," interrupted Ichabod, "I find it most useful when lawyers stick to the law, not emotion." The judge leaned forward, speaking slowly and deliberately. "*Bearing that in mind,* can you please tell me whether other cases addressing similar issues have treated a fourteen-week embryo as a fully developed person? It is my understanding that other courts have governed these situations by reference to property law concepts, treating such a small and undeveloped embryo as more of an organ of the mother than its own independent person."

"I would be happy to address that issue, Your Honor," replied Mitchell, stuffing the plastic replica back in his pocket. "But the truth is that no court has confronted the type of situation we have here today—where a genetic mother is trying to *force* a surrogate mother to abort the baby. Those courts that have addressed the status of an embryo in a surrogacy situation have typically held that the embryo is not, strictly speaking, either a person or property, but is nevertheless entitled to special respect because of its *potential* for human life. That was the reasoning, for example, by the Tennessee Supreme Court in the case of *Davis v. Davis.*"

"Precisely my point," shot back Ichabod. "Wasn't that a divorce case where the genetic mother wanted some frozen embryos implanted but the genetic father did not?"

"Yes, Your Honor."

"And in that case, the court held that the father had a constitutional right not to beget a child—"

"Yes, Your Honor, but—"

"Mr. Taylor," Ichabod's eyes narrowed. "May I finish my question?"

"Yes, of course, Your Honor," Mitchell spit out.

"In that case there was no contract, but the court said, 'I'm not going to force somebody to become a parent if they don't want to.' The court also said that if there had been a contract between the parties, the contract would have governed. Now, Mr. Taylor"—Ichabod took off her glasses and laid them down in front of her—"there is a contract in this case—signed by everyone, including your client. Why shouldn't I honor that contract and require Ms. Sareth to terminate the pregnancy?"

Mitchell hesitated. *Why is she giving me such a hard time? She hasn't asked these types of questions to the others.* When he did speak, his voice had an edge. "May I answer now?"

"You'd *better* answer now, Mr. Taylor."

"Because, Your Honor, the contract in this case is void as against public policy. We all know that contracts that violate strongly held public policy cannot be enforced by the courts. We protect car buyers from unsavory contracts by car dealers on this basis, we protect insured individuals from insurance carriers, we protect home buyers from builders—shouldn't we protect the most helpless individuals of all?"

Ichabod placed her chin in her hand and studied Mitchell with a look of idle curiosity, as if she were a biologist examining a lab specimen.

"What could be more against public policy than a contract that allows a biological mother to reject a baby that doesn't live up to her expectations and force another woman to have an abortion? And why do you think Dr. Brown and his wife hunted down an illegal immigrant to carry this child? They needed someone they could take advantage of—if necessary. Someone who couldn't take them to court and have this unconscionable contract thrown out.

"The contract says the pregnancy will be terminated if the fetus develops any abnormalities during the first two trimesters that would impair its ability to develop into a normal and healthy child. But who defines a normal and healthy child, Judge? This contract is just eugenics—pure and simple. It gives Ms. Davenport-Brown the right to reject a child because it doesn't fit her definition of normal. Judge, that's what the Nazis did, that's what the Chinese do when they abort baby girls. But Your Honor, that's not what we do in America."

Mitchell could feel the eyes of Nora and Cameron boring into his back. He had pulled out all the stops, comparing them to the Nazis, but how could he downplay what they were doing? They, not he, caused this legal showdown. With so much at stake, even though he liked Cameron, he could not worry about hurting her feelings.

"And who does the plaintiff think *she* is? She strides in here and insists that the court order this baby terminated for no other reason than because the child *might* have Down syndrome. Who made the plaintiff God? Why should she alone decide who lives and who dies?"

"Mr. Taylor," Ichabod responded, holding a copy of the contract aloft, "your client gave Ms. Davenport-Brown that right when your client signed *this contract.*"

"She signed it, Judge. But this court now has to decide whether to enforce it. And courts have never enforced contracts that violate public policy."

"And who says it violates public policy to terminate a pregnancy when the fetus appears to have a genetic defect?"

At last. The question Mitchell had been waiting for. Nikki had guaranteed Mitchell that if he hammered at the issue long enough, he would hear this question or something like it. And it was Nikki's idea to be ready in a way the judge would never anticipate.

Mitchell took a deep breath and turned sideways, pointing Ichabod to the second row in the spectator section of the courtroom, a row jammed with the expectant faces and pleading eyes of several young women. "I do, Judge. And so do these mothers of Down syndrome children seated in the second row, each of whom is prepared to testify that their children live healthy, fulfilled, and rewarding lives. In fact, Your Honor, they will say that we could all learn a few things about life from exposure to these very special children."

Mitchell turned back to squarely face the judge.

"Try telling them that genetically screening children does not violate public policy. Try telling them that requiring this abortion does not constitute irreparable harm."

59

"CALL YOUR FIRST WITNESS," Ichabod said to Nora Gunther.

The woman rose, checked her notes, waited for what seemed to Mitchell like an inordinately long time, then announced for the entire courtroom: "The plaintiff calls Maryna Sareth to the stand."

"What?" blurted out Nikki. "That's ridiculous."

"Shhhh," whispered Mitchell, rising. Nikki had spoken loud enough for more than just Mitchell to hear. Ichabod gave her a reproving glare.

"Your Honor, Ms. Sareth is not here today," Mitchell reported matter-of-factly. "We do not plan on calling her as a witness in this case, and we had no idea that the plaintiff would be calling her."

Nora Gunther scoffed and faced Mitchell. "C'mon, Mr. Taylor, you can do better than that—"

"*Counsel,*" snapped Ichabod, "address your comments to the court, not each other."

When both lawyers started talking simultaneously, Ichabod held up her hand. "You first, Ms. Gunther."

"Thank you. Judge. Ms. Sareth injected *herself* into this case. She claims she should be entitled to birth my client's child. She claims she wants to raise this child—a child that suffers from a severe genetic disorder. And she somehow thinks the court can evaluate that claim without ever seeing her, much less hearing from her. How can the court possibly determine what kind of mother she would make?"

All eyes turned to Mitchell. He felt a lot riding on his next few words—the hopes of Maryna, the future of her baby.

"Justice should not require that a woman subject herself to deportation in order to save her child. Ms. Gunther knows full well that my client does not have immigration papers. In fact, we will prove that one of the reasons Ms. Davenport-Brown wanted my client to carry the baby was precisely *because* she is an illegal alien, precisely *because* my client might be intimidated from pursuing her rights for fear that she would be deported. Today, I'm here to represent Ms. Sareth to the best of my ability without her testimony. If she can't testify, that will hurt *us*, not the plaintiff. We're willing to live with that consequence in order to avoid risking her deportation at a critical point in her life."

"Judge, we're entitled to *confront* those who bring claims against us—to cross-examine them in a court of law," Gunther said derisively. "Mr. Taylor doesn't get to say who testifies and who doesn't. I have an absolute *right* to call anybody I want to that stand—anybody within the subpoena power of the court. And by virtue of Ms. Sareth's status as a party in this case, she is clearly within the court's subpoena power."

"But Judge, she's got a right against self-incrimination," Mitchell implored.

"Now I've heard it all," Nora shot back. "May I respond, Judge?"

"That won't be necessary." As Ichabod spoke, she turned to Mitchell. He noticed a softening of her features for the first time in the case. Even her words came out less pointed, as if she were bound by duty to do something she did not relish. "I'm afraid Ms. Gunther is right—I cannot very well allow someone to intervene in a case pending before the court and then have that person refuse to take the stand. Yes, she has a right against self-incrimination, but since this is a civil case, not a criminal case, I am entitled to consider her refusal to testify as part of the evidence. And what else can I conclude, except that Ms. Sareth is an illegal alien who risks deportation if she shows up in my courtroom, quite possibly deportation to a place that could not possibly be in the best interests of this baby?"

Ichabod pursed her lips, took off her wire-rim glasses and rubbed her forehead. She put the glasses back on and looked at Mitchell. "Your only chance is to bring your client in here, let her take the stand, and try to convince the court that she would have the ability to care for this special-needs child in her native country." She paused and grimaced. "Now, I'm not saying that wins the case for you—there are still a lot of other issues to consider—but I'm saying you can't possibly win without doing at least that much. Is that clear?"

"Yes, Your Honor," mumbled Mitchell.

"Then I'll give you until tomorrow to get her in here. In the meantime," Ichabod turned back to Nora Gunther, "call your next witness."

Gunther put on another little show of checking her notes and whispering with her client. When she had everyone's attention, she proudly made her next announcement.

"The plaintiff calls Dr. Blaine Richards."

Mitchell watched carefully as Blaine Richards raised his hand and promised to tell the truth. Richards seemed the very picture of arrogance. His jet-black hair, as always, was slicked back, proudly displaying his lengthening widow's peak. His charcoal suit had a beautiful sheen to it, accentuated by a red power tie, a light blue shirt with a white tab collar, and cuff links that probably cost more than Mitchell's entire wardrobe. It seemed to Mitchell that Richards actually smirked as he took the oath, as if he had anticipated being called to the stand at this very moment.

He climbed into the seat, took a sip of water, and smiled at Nora Gunther.

She glared back.

She clipped through some preliminary questions, trying to establish immediate control of the examination. Richards took his time answering, curling his lips into a patronizing smirk when he wasn't talking. His calm demeanor only caused Nora to spit the questions out faster. And louder.

"You used a process called 'blastomere separation' to split four healthy fertilized eggs belonging to my client and eventually created eight cloned eggs, is that true?"

"Yes."

"And you considered the operation safe at the time?"

"Sure."

"It was successful, was it not?"

"It was."

"And you considered this cloning a safe and effective procedure. You considered the cloned egg cells to be every bit as healthy and capable of producing life as the original fertilized egg cells?"

Richards hesitated and studied Nora's taut face. Mitchell and everyone else in the courtroom knew how Richards would answer, knew how he *had* to answer, but it seemed the witness waited anyway, just to watch the lines on Nora's face grow even tighter.

"I suppose that's accurate."

"Now, you did this because you knew how desperately Dr. Brown and Ms. Davenport-Brown wanted a child, didn't you?"

"Every patient that comes to my clinic wants a child," said Richards calmly. "That's why they come."

"Just answer the question."

"I did."

Gunther looked at Ichabod and spread her hands. "Judge?"

"Answer the question, Dr. Richards," said Ichabod. "We don't need the commentary."

"Sure," Richards sniffed.

"Now, in a surrogate pregnancy, you only implant about four egg cells at a time, right?"

"That's correct."

"But the odds of one of them actually attaching to the uterine wall and developing into a fetus are not very good, are they?"

Richards smiled knowingly. "Actually, at our clinic they are better than most. Still, it's less than fifty-fifty."

"So, if the first four egg cells for the Browns didn't work out, you created others that could be implanted, correct?"

"Yes."

"Is there a point here?" asked an impatient Ichabod.

Gunther shot the judge a look as if she had just questioned whether a priceless work of art had been painted by the numbers. "I'm just about to get to it, Judge."

"By all means, take your time," huffed Ichabod.

"Dr. Richards, isn't it fair to say that the intent of both my client and her husband was to do just about anything necessary to create a healthy child, even if it meant allowing you to clone the egg cells?"

Richards gave Gunther a look of strained patience—the calm, little smirk of a pro being questioned by a rank amateur. "I'm not a mind reader," replied Richards. "I don't know what your client's intent was."

"Were you cloning egg cells just for sport?"

Richards turned to Ichabod. "Do I have to answer that?"

Ichabod shook her head in frustration and looked at Gunther. "You've made your point, now move on."

"And when Dr. Brown made out his will, donating these pre-embryos to research, he was under the impression that the surrogate mother was already carrying a healthy, developing child, isn't that true?"

"I believe that's correct," replied Richards, his chin on his hand. "The Down syndrome was not suspected until later."

"So Dr. Brown's will, in which he donated the eggs to research, was actually the result of a mistaken belief that the cloned egg cells would not be necessary for him and Cameron to have a child free from genetic defects, isn't that right?"

"You know, maybe you've got me confused with Dr. Brown's lawyer," said Richards snidely. "I didn't draft the doctor's will."

This answer drew a long silence from Nora Gunther, while she glared at the witness with withering disgust. "Do you think this is a laughing matter?" she asked, her voice brittle. "Do you think the future of those eight pre-embryos, the inability of Ms. Davenport-Brown to have a healthy child, the death of Dr. Brown from AIDS—do you think these are all just jokes to be laughed off?"

"The only jokes in this courtroom," replied Richards evenly, taking a sip of water, "are your questions."

"Judge—" whined Gunther.

"May I finish my answer?" asked Richards.

Ichabod leaned forward on her bench, glaring at the witness. "Dr. Richards, your job is to answer the questions, not conduct a running commentary on the lawyer asking them." She shifted even farther forward and looked down her nose at Gunther. "And your job, Ms. Gunther, is to act professionally and stop baiting this witness." Ichabod sat back as Nora Gunther rolled her eyes. "And my job is to maintain order in this courtroom, and I'll hold you both in contempt if necessary in order to get it done.

"Now answer the question, Dr. Richards."

The stage had now been set; the witness had the undivided attention of all assembled. He took another long, slow swallow of water, then answered with perfect diction and clarity, letting the words drip like water torture into a silent courtroom. "When Dr. Brown came to me to discuss his will a few months before his death, he believed that the pre-embryo implanted in Maryna Sareth would develop into a healthy child. He told me that his wife, Cameron Davenport-Brown, wanted that worse than anything—a child, a legacy. But Dr. Brown also told me that he wanted to leave behind a very different kind of legacy. He said he wanted to fight the disease that had ravaged his body. He said he wanted to help researchers find a real cure for AIDS, not just more medication to manage the disease. Though he knew he might lose the fight with this disease himself, he wanted to help others overcome. And so he wanted to dedicate his financial resources—*and the eight cloned zygotes*—to AIDS research."

As Richards spoke, Mitchell watched Gunther shift uncomfortably. She had opened the door by asking a broad question about Brown's intent, and Richards was cleverly walking right through it. This witness was shifty, and soon Mitchell would be in Gunther's position, trying to reel him in, trying to make the points that could only be made through Richards without suffering irreparable damage to his own case. Mitchell felt his palms grow sweaty as he thought about his upcoming cross-examination of this brilliant man.

"And Dr. Brown told me," Richards continued, "very explicitly, that even if something happened to the embryo that had already been implanted, he did *not* want one of the cloned embryos implanted into a surrogate mother. If the child was meant to be, then the already implanted embryo would develop into a healthy child. But if not, then Dr. Brown said he would accept that fate as the way it was meant to be as well. He said that otherwise Cameron would live her whole life focused around creating and caring for a child. She would feel she owed it to him, Dr. Brown said. He wanted to free her up. If the implanted embryo didn't work out for whatever reason, he didn't want her saddled with an obligation to a deceased husband to try and salvage one of the frozen zygotes. Dr. Brown knew that the contract he had signed when he first came to the clinic gave either him or Cameron the right to donate the cryopreserved embryos to research. And so he wrote a will that did just that.

"So in answer to your question, Ms. Gunther, it is not as if this whole scenario came as a surprise, or that the Down syndrome would have somehow changed Dr. Brown's thinking. He anticipated it, and he planned for it. He wanted those cloned zygotes to be used for research regardless of what happened to the implanted embryo. And the contract signed by both Dr. Brown and his wife allowed him to do just that." Richards stopped and gave Gunther a knowing look. *Satisfied?* he asked with his eyes.

Mitchell turned his attention to a pale Nora Gunther. She flipped furiously through a couple of pages of notes, hesitated, then flipped another page or two. Richards had just performed expert surgery on her case and neatly clipped out the heart of her argument—that the surrogacy contract and will of Dr. Brown should be negated based on a mistake of fact—and he did it on the basis of a conversation that supposedly took place between himself and a dead man. No one else to contradict or affirm it. *How convenient,* thought Mitchell.

He watched Nora Gunther quickly reevaluate how hard to push

this witness. She took a deep breath as she found some questions that apparently seemed safe enough.

"Does GenTech test for genetic defects as part of your in vitro protocols?"

"If the parents desire us to do so, yes."

"Do those tests include protocols to determine whether the fetus might be at risk for Down syndrome?"

"Yes, of course. The attending ob-gyn would typically carry out those tests."

"Why?"

"So the parents can decide whether to go through with the pregnancy or abort the fetus and try again."

"Now, Dr. Richards, if the genetic parents of this fetus, the ones who would be responsible for raising the child, decide to terminate the pregnancy based on such tests, but the surrogate mother does not want to terminate the pregnancy, what happens?"

"The same contract that I mentioned earlier, the contract signed by your client and Dr. Brown and the surrogate mother at the very beginning, addresses this very question and provides that the genetic parents are entitled to make that decision. These are very emotional decisions, and there is a great danger that the involved parties could agree to one thing at the beginning of the process and then change their minds later. But when you change your mind, it affects many other lives, not just your own. So we hold to the contract. And in this case, the contract says that the genetic parents should not be forced against their will to raise a child with a genetic defect. Therefore, the pregnancy should be ended."

"But doctor," Gunther's voice took on a sarcastic edge, "Ms. Sareth's lawyer claims that this contract is just genetic engineering."

"No, it's just enlightened medical care. You see, Ms. Gunther, we don't check for minor or aesthetic genetic traits, nor would our contract allow parents to end a surrogate pregnancy based on genetic traits that don't suit their liking. But just like in nonsurrogate pregnancies, the fetus is typically tested for severe genetic defects. Then the parents can make a decision about what to do based on their own religious and moral beliefs."

Nora breathed a sigh of relief as she looked down at her notes. She flipped another page and her face hardened.

"Do you believe a woman has a constitutional right to make her own choices, free from government interference, about matters of reproduction and childbirth?"

"Absolutely."

"And it follows, does it not, that my client has a constitutional right to choose whether to bear children or not, whether to have a fetus aborted or not, and whether to have a healthy embryo implanted or not?"

Win Mackenzie jumped to his feet. "Objection. Dr. Richards is not a lawyer, he's a doctor."

"That didn't stop him from waxing eloquent about contract law," shot back Gunther.

"The objection is sustained," ruled Ichabod. "This issue—the constitutionality of the Bioethics Act under these circumstances—is ultimately one for the court to decide. And I don't believe I need any help on the legal issues from Dr. Richards."

"Then I have just one final question," announced Gunther. "If you win this case, Dr. Richards, and are able to conduct stem cell research on these cloned embryos funded by the trust accounts established by Dr. Brown, it could ultimately be worth millions of dollars to your company. Is that true?"

"Yes," said Richards with a thin, tight smile. "And even more important, it could help us take a giant step toward finding a cure for AIDS."

"Fat chance," scoffed Gunther. Then she turned to take her seat.

60

AS MITCHELL STOOD TO FACE the demonstrated brilliance of Blaine Richards, he felt jumpy, his heart racing. It felt like someone was scraping his stomach, churning the acid that gnawed away at the lining. There was so much riding on this, and he wished he'd had more time to prepare.

Nevertheless, he stood ramrod straight and looked Richards squarely in the eye. He had a few interesting questions for the good doctor, and Mitchell would not allow himself to be intimidated by the arrogance of the man. The competitive instincts kicked in. It was time to hurl himself at this crafty opponent, all or nothing, the same way he had always approached football.

"Mr. Taylor," said Ichabod, interrupting his thoughts and freezing him before he could step toward the podium, "as usual, we'll allow Mr. Mackenzie to conduct any direct examination first."

Mitchell felt the stares of the spectators at the same time he noticed that Win Mackenzie was also standing. Mackenzie gave him a condescending smile and walked confidently to the podium. Mitchell slouched into his chair.

"Nice move," whispered Nikki. "Make 'em think you're chomping at the bit to tear into that two-faced liar."

"Yeah," responded Mitchell.

"Ms. Gunther intimates that you are motivated by financial reasons to defend the GenTech contract and the Bioethics Act," began Mackenzie. "Is that true?"

Richards shook his head like a knowing father explaining something for the umpteenth time to a young child. "On the contrary. There is enormous money to be made by GenTech if Ms. Davenport-Brown prevails on her claims. The Bioethics Act stands in the way of the most helpful method to accomplish our mission. Imagine, if cloning becomes legal again, even this most rudimentary form of cloning referred to as blastomere separation, it carries with it enormous potential for good. When a young lady like Cameron Davenport-Brown comes into our clinic, we go through a high-risk and intrusive procedure to harvest her eggs."

Richards shifted in his seat and turned toward the judge. "We normally harvest several eggs at an optimal time of the month. But even if we were able to harvest, say, eight egg cells, the odds of any one of them successfully implanting into the uterine wall of a surrogate mother and then developing into a healthy embryo are not good. What if we could clone those eggs—create an unlimited supply? First, in the near future we will be able to cost-effectively test the cloned eggs to make sure there are no chromosomal deficiencies. And second, we could guarantee that we would never again need to put a woman through the harvesting procedure more than one time. This guaranteed improvement in results would also justify a much higher price."

Richards returned his gaze toward his own lawyer and sighed. "No, Mr. Mackenzie, we are definitely *not* defending the Bioethics Act for financial reasons. As a company with thousands of egg cells available for research, and certain patents pending that give us a substantial head start on this field of research, we would probably benefit more than any other single company if the court struck down the act. We are defending the act because it's the right thing to do. We are defending the act because the sanctity of the contract that we signed with Dr. and Mrs. Brown requires no less. We want our patients to know that when they sign a contract with us and have our word, we will do whatever it takes to fulfill that word."

"One other question," said Mackenzie, sounding pleased with the witness. "Ms. Gunther tried to make it sound like your company was trying to make reproductive decisions for Ms. Davenport-Brown, especially with regard to the frozen pre-embryos. Is that true?"

Richards scoffed. "Absolutely not. The plaintiff and her husband decided together what they wanted to do with the frozen pre-embryos. We explained all the options. They then decided that either one of them would have the right and the ability to say that the frozen pre-embryos could be used for research. In other words, *they* decided, not us— *them*—that if they both didn't want the frozen embryos implanted, then the frozen embryos wouldn't be implanted. Dr. Brown could not force Cameron to become a mother of these pre-embryos, and Cameron could not force her husband to become a father. It was their choice, and they signed a contract confirming that choice.

"Mr. Mackenzie, we're not trying to make this choice for the plaintiff. We're just trying to carry out the choice that she and her husband already made. To allow her to change her mind now, after all the parties relied on her previous decision, would be grossly unfair."

"Thank you, Dr. Richards, that's all the questions I have for now," said Win Mackenzie. Then, turning to the judge: "We'd like to reserve the right to recall Dr. Richards as part of GenTech's case in order to provide further detail of some of the medical advances by GenTech in the area of cloning."

"Very well," said Ichabod. Then Mackenzie took his seat.

Mitchell waited to rise until Ichabod looked at him and nodded.

"No prisoners," whispered Nikki.

———————

"This baby growing inside Maryna is now approximately fourteen weeks old. True?" asked Mitchell with a scowl.

Richards crossed his legs and took a slow drink of water. "Yes. That's true. The *fetus*…" Richards let the word hang in the air for a moment, like a brief slap at Mitchell, "is approximately fourteen weeks old, give or take."

"And you heard my opening, didn't you?"

Richards nodded.

"You must say yes or no," Mitchell lectured. "The court reporter cannot pick up head nods."

Richards smiled at the court reporter. "Then the answer is *yes*," he said. Turning to Mitchell, "Unfortunately, I had to sit through your opening."

Mitchell decided to ignore the insult, although he could feel the arrogance of Richards already getting under his skin. "You heard my description of this *baby* in my opening—how it already has little fingers and toes, a heartbeat, brain waves, fingerprints, and a sensitivity to light, noise, and pain. Is that a fair description of a fourteen-week-old *baby?*"

Richards thought for a moment, running his hands down his cheek and bringing them together off the end of his chin. "In a manner of speaking. But generally, when you refer to a fourteen-week-old baby, you are saying that it has been about fourteen weeks since the first day of the mother's last menstrual cycle. That's how weeks of pregnancy are measured. But conception actually occurs approximately two weeks after that date. So technically, by the time conception occurs, a woman is already two weeks pregnant. Because this embryo was already fertilized when it was implanted into your client fourteen weeks ago, some would say this is a sixteen-week-old baby."

Huh? Mitchell knit his brow, thoroughly confused. He shook his head quickly and tried again.

"In my opening, did I properly describe the *approximate...*" he paused, letting that word hang out there, "uh, the *approximate* fetal development of this baby?"

The smug witness didn't hesitate. "There is some controversy as to whether the fetus really has any sensitivity to pain at this very early stage of the development process. But there are some documented reactions to light and noise. Your description is close...for a layman."

This act is already getting old, Mitchell thought. He removed the plastic replica of a fourteen-week-old baby from his pocket. "And this is about the size of the *baby* who is growing, even as we speak, safely inside the womb of Maryna Sareth. Is that correct?" Mitchell extended the two-inch plastic replica toward Richards carefully, cradled in the palm of his hand, as if it were alive.

Richards snorted. "No, that cheap cereal box insert you have there is nothing like the fetus inside Ms. Sareth. For one thing, that cheap imitation in your hand does not mimic the one thing that brings us all to court this very day—the fact that Ms. Sareth's fetus has a debilitating and life-changing chromosomal deficiency that cannot be cured." Richards shook his head defiantly at Mitchell. "It cheapens the reproductive and fetal development process for you to trot that plastic doll in here for sympathy purposes and oversimplify everything that is occurring inside the embryonic sac of your client."

Mitchell could no longer keep from raising his voice. "*I'm* cheapening the reproductive process? *You're* the one experimenting with babies like they're some kind of widget from a factory line, constantly in need of tinkering so they can fit your all-knowing and unbending mold of what a perfect little *fetus* should look like." Mitchell glared at Richards, wishing it were just the two of them so that he could knock the cocky little smirk off the witness's face.

"Objection," called out Mackenzie as he sprung to his feet. "That's not a question; it's a juvenile outburst."

Ichabod looked sternly at Mitchell. "Mr. Mackenzie's right. Name-calling may be appropriate on the playground, but it doesn't help us much here."

Stung, Mitchell thrust the plastic replica back inside his pocket. He fingered it there for a moment, regrouping his thoughts, remembering why he was here in the first place. He willed himself to calm down. He would have to be more careful, more controlled. Maryna and her child deserved a lawyer who would not lose his cool.

"You don't know for sure that this child has Down's, do you?"

"We're fairly certain. Dr. Lars Avery, whom I highly respect, has conducted two ultrasounds and a triple-screen blood test that all confirmed the possibility of Down's." The witness took another slow drink of water, running his tongue along the inside of his lips when he finished.

Mitchell made a mental note of the gesture, then zeroed in on the issue. "Ultrasounds and blood tests can be wrong, can't they? I mean, we won't know for sure until the amniocentesis comes back—right?"

Richards' tongue repeated its journey across the inside of the lips, barely visible as he repeated the unconscious habit. "I have never known Dr. Avery to be wrong on the basis of these screening tests," he said.

There's something here, Mitchell thought. *Something that's making Richards extremely nervous.* Mitchell hesitated and studied the witness, waiting for another sign of nervousness, searching desperately for what was causing it in the first place. To his credit, Richards never looked away and resisted mightily the urge to snatch another drink of water for his parched lips and mouth.

"Mr. Taylor," Ichabod said after a few seconds, "do you have another question for this witness?"

"Sorry, Your Honor." Mitchell kept his eyes on Richards. "But you would admit that in some cases the ultrasound and blood test can lead to an improper diagnosis, and that is the very reason that Dr. Avery suggested an amnio in the first place—am I right?"

The tongue made its round again, followed by a quick sip of water. "I don't know what Dr. Avery was thinking when he ordered the amniocentesis. But I can tell you this. An amniocentesis is a high-risk procedure. You don't order one unless you're absolutely convinced that there is a high probability of a defect. In a few more days, we should have the definitive results."

"Speaking of defects," said Mitchell, "there is no guarantee that the cloned embryos do not also have genetic defects—is there?"

"Highly unlikely."

"But you can't rule it out, can you?"

Richards glanced at his water glass but did not reach for it. "This is cutting-edge science, Mr. Taylor. You can't rule anything out."

"Do you need more water?" asked Mitchell, pointing to the half-empty glass.

"I'm fine," snapped Richards.

"Good, because I've got some questions about why you used Ms.

Sareth as a surrogate mother, and I want you completely comfortable as you answer them."

"Objection—"

"Sustained."

Mitchell never changed expressions. "Do you respect the legal rights of surrogate mothers at your clinic?"

"Of course. If we didn't, we couldn't exist."

"Then whose idea was it that Ms. Sareth move to North Carolina during this pregnancy?"

"We all decided together."

"And you did that in order to circumvent the Virginia law on surrogate contracts and deny Ms. Sareth her rights under Virginia law, didn't you?"

"We did that," answered Richards with a tone of patient condescension, "so that Ms. Sareth could be paid."

"Which is illegal under Virginia law, isn't it?"

Richards shrugged his shoulders.

"Come now, Dr. Richards. Are you telling this court that you are the CEO of one of the world's largest fertilization clinics, located right here in the Commonwealth of Virginia, and yet you don't know the law of your state governing surrogacy contracts?"

"I didn't say that."

"Then answer the question," demanded Mitchell.

Mackenzie rose to his feet and spread his palms. "Judge—"

"The witness will answer the question," Ichabod ruled without hesitation.

"Yes, it's illegal to pay a surrogate mother in Virginia."

"And you are also familiar with Virginia Code Section 20-162, which provides that a surrogate mother will have a full twenty-five days after a child is born in order to determine whether she wants to relinquish her parental rights. Isn't that true?"

Richards kept a level gaze and even tone as he answered. "Unless the surrogacy contract has been approved by the court in advance. In that case, the surrogate mother would have only those rights set forth in the contract."

"Oh," said Mitchell, feigning surprise. "Then I'm assuming you had this surrogacy contract approved by a Virginia court in advance."

"No, we did not."

"And why not?"

Richards lowered his voice a notch. "Because the surrogate mother was living in North Carolina."

At this, Mitchell actually smiled and shook his head. It was time to move in for the kill.

"The real reason you tried to circumvent Virginia law was because you knew a Virginia court would *never* approve a surrogate contract with an illegal immigrant. You knew that under Virginia law, courts could only approve contracts for surrogate mothers who are married, have had at least one prior pregnancy, and can be recommended for an additional surrogate pregnancy by a mental health professional. Am I right about that?"

Richards hesitated and shifted in his seat. Mitchell took a step toward counsel table and was handed a document by Nikki Moreno, which he waved at the witness. "Do you need to see a copy of the Code?"

Richards made a face. "No. I know full well what the Code says. But in this case, your client wanted to be paid for her services, and the Browns wanted to pay her. So we had her move to North Carolina."

Mitchell felt his own anger bubbling up. *The arrogance of this man!* "So you thought by paying her a measly $9,000 for nine months of pregnancy you could strip away her rights under Virginia law? And you also knew that since Maryna was an illegal immigrant, she could never challenge that in court."

"It was a price we all agreed was fair."

Mitchell nearly laughed at the absurdity of it. He noticed Ichabod hunch forward on the bench, her brow deeply furrowed.

"Nine thousand bucks for nine months of pregnancy," Mitchell exclaimed, "for hours and hours of birth pains, for the emotional turmoil of birthing a child that you then give to someone else—how did you describe that price again, Doctor?"

Mitchell saw Ichabod shaking her head. Then he watched with satisfaction as Richards' tongue made its quick and nervous round, followed by another drink of water, and this time, a brief flash of panic in the eyes. But the composure returned as quickly as it left. "It's nine thousand more than she would have received under Virginia law," he sneered.

"How generous," Mitchell said flatly.

"Judge…" whined Mackenzie.

"Sustained."

A conservative lawyer, thought Mitchell, *might be tempted to quit on that one. But being conservative is not what got me this far.* "One last question, Doctor. And I'm sure it's a question that a lot of young women might like to have answered. Is it still your testimony that you respect the rights of surrogate mothers at your clinic, that you did everything possible to protect and preserve the rights of Maryna Sareth in this case?" Even before Richards could answer, Mitchell decided to add the one last dramatic flair that his law school professors had always warned him against. "And let me remind you, Dr. Richards, that you have taken an oath to tell the truth."

This time Richards did not hesitate. "The truth, Mr. Taylor, is that your client was more interested in obtaining payment for her services than she was in protecting her ability to birth and raise this child. She wanted to live in North Carolina since that's what it took for her to get paid. If she has now changed her mind, she ought to at least have the guts to come into court and tell us."

The answer hit Mitchell like a hard fist to the midsection. He recognized too late that he had fallen into the trap of every rookie lawyer. Greed. He had asked one question too many.

"Nothing further," Mitchell managed, as he turned to take his seat.

61

THE ROCK LEANED OVER SLIGHTLY, patted his daughter's knee, and gave her a patronizing smile. "Old Mitch didn't do half-bad for a rookie," he whispered. "Like to think I taught him a thing or two."

The Rock thought he said it softly, but that didn't prevent Nora Gunther, seated on the other side of Cameron, from rebuking him with a loud "Shhhh!"

The Rock grunted in response.

"You may step down," Ichabod said to Dr. Richards, "your testimony has been most enlightening."

Richards nodded at the judge and stood proudly. Bowed, slightly bruised, but not beaten.

Not so fast, thought the Rock. He stood. The room started a slow spin. The Rock steadied himself with one hand on the back of his chair.

Showtime.

"I've got a few questions for the witness before he's done," announced the Rock. Out of the corner of his eye, he saw Nora bolt to her feet. Cameron's jaw hung open. "I believe, since we called the witness, we're entitled to recross."

"We have no recross," said Nora. She stared at the Rock, shooting darts with her eyes. Although he could see her out of his peripheral vision, the Rock decided to ignore her.

Ichabod looked from one lawyer to the other, then said, "Mr. Davenport, please have a seat. Ms. Gunther is lead counsel, and she says there will be no recross."

"Thank you, Judge," said Nora.

This actually made the Rock smile. A chance to poke both Ichabod and Gunther in the eye at the same time. *Nobody* should have this much fun trying a case.

The Rock walked slowly…purposefully…carefully so as not to fall…a few steps to the podium. He grabbed its sides and steadied himself. Lesser men would need notes for an intense examination of a major witness. Not the Rock.

"Mr. Davenport, did you hear what I just said?" asked an astonished Ichabod.

"Sure, Judge." He decided to keep smiling—keep it friendly. "But I'm local counsel on this team, and the only lawyer on our team actually licensed to practice before you. If Ms. Gunther doesn't let me examine this witness, then I'll withdraw. And then, well, the court will have to recess this case while she searches for another local lawyer."

The Rock saw a look of consternation cross Ichabod's face, the lines growing tighter. His stomach gurgled, loud enough, he was sure, to be heard the next courtroom over.

After a long pause, Ichabod spoke. "Okay," she said bitterly, "but keep it short."

"Judge, you can't let him," protested Nora.

"Who chose him in the first place?" shot back Ichabod. That silenced Gunther, who reluctantly took her seat.

The Rock could have used another shot or two of rum to calm his nerves and put out the fire in his belly. On the other hand, the witness was already a little blurry, and his tongue felt just a tad oversized. And he had just enough lubrication in his system to keep his confidence soaring. Drunk or stone-cold sober, he was still twice the lawyer of anybody else in the courtroom.

"How you doin'?" the Rock asked the witness.

"Fine," Richards said with no small amount of contempt.

"You actually ever had a baby yourself?" asked the Rock. *Clever,* he told himself. *Clever and cute at the same time.*

Richards just snorted, as if the question didn't even deserve an answer.

"Then you can't really say what's going on inside the heart and mind of"—the Rock suddenly drew a blank, what was her name again?—"um, that Oriental girl, can you?" *Oops. That didn't come out right.*

"Nobody can. That's why she needs to either come in here and testify herself, or drop her case."

Maybe I ought to stick to defending my own client...

"You know what undue influence is?"

"Yes."

"You know that a will made under duress or undue influence is invalid."

"There was none of that here."

"Dr. Brown was dying of AIDS, wasn't he?"

"Obviously."

"Made him a little weak and vulnerable emotionally, didn't it?"

"That's ridiculous."

"At the same time, your company—its stock price was flounderin'. Tanked at about eighteen bucks a share. Hadn't moved for months—isn't that right?"

Richards went for the water glass. He clearly didn't like this subject. Just watching Richards take a slow, calculated drink...the Adam's apple bobbing up and down...smooth liquid coating the mouth and windpipe... It made the Rock incredibly thirsty himself...

"I wouldn't call it in the tank," said Richards calmly, as if he were reassuring investors that very moment. "It had a nice little runup for a few years, and like most other stocks that have dramatic runups, it needed to stabilize at those new levels for a while."

The Rock coughed. Something caught in his throat. He could feel his face turning red, his eyes watering, the eyes of the courtroom on him throughout this little coughing spell.

"You okay?" asked Ichabod.

He waved her off. "Just fine," he said. He shook his head a little to clear it. Smiled at the judge. Stepped over to his own counsel table...carefully again...and took a quick little drink.

There, that's better.

"Some of this testimony is just a little hard to swallow," he said, smiling. *Clever,* he thought.

Nobody laughed.

What's wrong with these people?

"Anyway, whether or not you would characterize it as 'in the tank,' the fact of the matter is that you had stock options—thousands of 'em—that would kick in at twenty bucks a share. If the stock stayed below twenty for the next six months, they would all be worthless—isn't that a fact?" As he spoke, the Rock was shuffling through some papers he had unloaded earlier on his counsel table. He had a hard time focusing on the tiny print, wavy black lines blurring together. "It's right here somewhere…in your company's 10Ks and 10Qs," the Rock mumbled.

Richards let the Rock fumble around for a few moments, then: "Don't bother looking for it… This is all a matter of public record. I did have stock options that vested at twenty, and about three million common shares as well. If you're trying to prove that I would personally make money if GenTech's stock went up"—Richards flashed an arrogant grin—"guilty." He paused for a beat. "Like every other CEO in the country, I might add."

The Rock's stomach growled at the answer even as he stepped back to the podium. Richards was not making this easy.

"Are you saying that this is all just a big coincidence—your stock is in the tank, then Dr. Brown just happens to draft a will that generates a giant lawsuit and immense publicity for your company…your company just happens to have a number of patented stem cell research procedures that come to light under the white-hot media attention this case generates…your stock just happens to take off over twenty bucks a share, and you just happen to make millions of dollars? You're saying that you didn't plan this, didn't coerce Dr. Brown or entice him into drafting a will that would generate all this publicity, that instead of wise and deceptive planning…this just happens to be your lucky day?" The Rock harrumphed as he delivered his punch line, exceedingly pleased with the question.

He watched Richards' expression tighten, the Adam's apple bobbing its displeasure. Richards' impatience started to resonate in the tone of his voice. "Mr. Davenport—"

But Mackenzie was on his feet. "Don't answer that question," he commanded the witness. Then to the judge, "I object to this whole line of questioning, Your Honor. This witness is not on trial here. There's nothing wrong with owning stock in your own company. And besides, this court earlier quashed a subpoena for Dr. Richards' personal financial records, ruling that those private matters were not relevant to this case, and now—"

"I've heard enough," snapped Ichabod. She turned and glared at the Rock. "Mr. Davenport, you're about six inches from earning yourself a contempt citation. Mr. Mackenzie is right. I've previously ruled that these private financial matters are not relevant. Do you understand what that means?" Ichabod paused and pronounced her words slowly, emphatically, *"Not relevant."*

The Rock nodded.

"Six inches, Mr. Davenport," Ichabod repeated.

The Rock nodded again. *At least I've got her attention. And if she liked that…she'll love this.*

"Then let's talk about the financial situation of Dr. Lars Avery… about his bankruptcy, about who helped him get out of Chapter 11—"

"Objection!"

"Sustained!" Ichabod slammed her gavel. "Two inches, Mr. Davenport. You are now two inches from contempt."

Whoa! That gap closed fast! Better get to the bottom line quickly.

"My daughter's egg cells…ah, I mean, Ms. Davenport-Brown's egg cells are not the only ones you've cloned, are they?"

"I prefer not to use the word 'cloned' in this context, because it has other connotations. But it is true to say that Ms. Davenport-Brown's zygotes are not the only ones on which we used the process of blastomere separation. As you know, this is simply the process of splitting the zygote into two identical parts—creating twins, if you will. Prior to the passage of the Bioethics Act, we used this process occasionally so that we wouldn't have to subject women to numerous operations of harvesting egg cells if the first attempt at implanting a number of those egg cells was not successful."

The Rock smiled at this answer, as if he knew something that nobody else in the room did. He let the silence linger in the air for a moment, building the desired sense of drama. Then he began to step out from behind the podium, felt the walls start to move just a little, and decided to stay put. It wouldn't be quite as effective, but he would deliver his bromide from right where he stood.

"I know what blastomere segregation is," said the Rock, with an exaggerated air of authority, "and I'm not talking about that. Isn't it true, sir"—he pointed accusingly—"that you used the process of nuclear transplantation…or whatever the heck it's called…the Dolly the sheep process…the process that will create a genetic gallery of horrors because it's so unreliable… Didn't you use that very process both before *and after* the passage of the Bioethics Act?"

The Rock got the response he wanted. A murmur in the courtroom. Mackenzie on his feet and shouting, "That's ridiculous!" The witness shaking his head in fierce anger, saying, "That's *absolutely* not true!" And Ichabod banging her gavel.

"Those are strong accusations," Ichabod hissed, after she had restored order. "Criminal accusations." Her eyes lasered in on the Rock. "And you'd better be ready to back them up with something other than your active imagination."

"Your Honor," said the Rock proudly, "tomorrow I intend to call a witness who will do just that."

He couldn't resist a sideways glance at his client…his daughter. The young lady he had so irresponsibly let down so many years before. Today he had stood tall for her. And tomorrow he would stand even taller. He had grabbed his chance at redemption and made the most of it.

After all, dads were supposed to be heroes, not cowards.

But when he looked at Cameron, he did not see the eyes of a beautiful young lady doting on a brave dad. Instead, he saw frustration. Resignation. It was a look of pain and pity accompanied by a subtle but sad shaking of the head.

The look told him everything he needed to know, but still he sat down and stared at the single sheet of paper that Cameron had placed on top of his other piles. He looked, squinted, then looked again to make sure he was reading it right. "You're fired," the paper said. It was signed by Nora Gunther…and by his own daughter. He squinted again. The words were blurry, but unmistakable. She had signed her name in a way he had never seen before. The signature said simply "Cameron Brown."

62

RICHARDS PUSHED HIS GRAY BMW to the limit, flying like a bullet past the other cars on the Interstate. Smooth tunes from a favorite jazz CD coated every inch of the soft beige leather and beautiful wood trim. The digital readouts and pulsating graphs from the dashboard display created an almost hypnotizing light show—soothing, relaxing—mimicking the gentle rhythm of the music.

Oblivious to the tune, Richards slammed the heel of his hand against the steering wheel. He cursed Billy Davenport. *What does he know?* Richards wondered. *And who betrayed me and told him?*

Billy was *supposed* to know about the other alleged incidents of cloning. That part was a setup, a neat little trap that Billy had stumbled into. But the questions about finances—and not just Richards' finances but Avery's as well—those questions had Richards worried.

And furious.

Either Davenport was very good—no, that couldn't possibly be the case. Davenport was incompetent…a drunk. He had to have had help. Somebody was talking.

More expletives as Richards took another shot at the steering wheel. All this planning—every contingency covered. Plans and backup plans and reserve backup plans. Now the whole thing risked being screwed up by an old lush who didn't have the sense to come in out of the rain.

Billy Davenport knew too much. He was unpredictable. Dangerous. It was time to take him out.

Richards could handle that. In fact, he had planned for it. What bothered him, what kept him driving longer and faster and harder as he considered his options, was the person who had provided Davenport with the information.

Once again, he considered every alternative. He studied each possibility clinically, like he would a laboratory rat. He dissected them, turning them over and over in his mind, poking and prodding the possibilities from every angle. Each time, he came to the same inevitable conclusion.

He picked up the phone and dialed. Lars Avery answered on the second ring.

"Hello, Blaine."

"Meet me at my office at nine o'clock," Richards ordered. "And bring the tape with you." He subconsciously licked the inside of his lips. "We've got to do something about Billy Davenport."

The Rock was just beginning to feel a good buzz—the kind that made all the conversation and noise around him run together like the constant hum of a car engine. Background noise. The whole world just became background noise—indistinguishable and unimportant.

Plus, he floated just a little. Not literally, of course. His rear hadn't left that same barstool more than once or twice or was it five times— who remembered? who cared?—in the last two hours. The last time he had gotten up, he practically swam to the men's room, steadying himself on the backs of chairs and tables along the way. He had a vague recollection of pinching some cute girl, of getting snarled at, of laughing it off.

He slouched a little lower on the stool, forearms leaning heavily on the bar, and slid his empty glass forward. Ted would know he needed another. No words necessary.

That's the thing he loved about The Beach Grill. When he got a good buzz on, he would usually get funny—David Letterman would have nothing on him—and the boys at the bar would laugh along. But sometimes, like tonight, he would just get mellow. Real mellow. And the boys would leave him alone.

"You sure?" asked Ted, as he grabbed the Rock's beer glass and slid it under the tap for another Corona.

The Rock nodded. "First one tonight." He gave Ted a melancholy smile. "Got nothin' to do tomorrow anyway."

"She's crazy, that Gunther woman," Ted said as he poured out some foam and topped off the beer. "The six o'clock news says you nailed that witness. GenTech stock lost a buck fifty a share just based on your questions."

"Yeah, yeah, yeah," Rock said as he took a swig. Ted always had a way of putting things in perspective. Ted had been working on cheering up the Rock since the Rock announced his own firing a few beers ago. "Wanna know something?" The Rock motioned for Ted to lean forward, halfway over the bar, so they could have a word in private.

Only problem was, the Rock forgot to lower his voice. "I think that Gunther woman and Ichabod are…" the Rock wiggled his hand and raised his eyebrows. "Know what I mean?"

"No kidding," said Ted.

"I could tell," said the guy on the next stool.

The Rock shot him a glance, ending that conversation, then retreated back inside his shell. He focused on the beer, little bubbles darting their way to the top. He tried to figure out the pattern.

"She's definitely got a screw loose," said Ted. "Anybody'd fire you, ain't thinkin' right."

The Rock tended to agree but felt no need to respond.

Millions of bubbles and a few beers later, the Rock decided he'd had enough. The endless buzz of noise all around him—loud music and louder conversation—started to pen him in. The walls of this place were shrinking. He needed some fresh air.

The next time Ted walked by, he slid the empty toward the barkeep, but held up a palm.

"Had enough?" asked the image in front of the Rock.

"Guess so," the Rock rubbed his face, then slipped off the barstool, stumbled, and caught himself. He grinned. "What do I owe ya?"

"It's on the house. Let me call you a cab, buddy."

The Rock shook his head vigorously. "Don't need no cab. And I'm not a charity." He reached deep in his pants pocket and felt some wadded up bills, a snot rag, some folded notes, change, keys, who knows what else. Ted could sort it out. He grabbed a handful of everything and dumped it on the bar.

Ted separated out a few of the bucks and some change. "You sure you're okay?"

"Never better."

"What's this?" Ted had pulled something out of the little pile. "Birth control pills?"

The Rock's head started spinning. This was not good. "Give me those," he said. He crammed the small, round container of pills, his keys, his change, and everything else back into his pocket. Nothing worse than a nosy barkeep.

He grabbed what felt like two quarters from the stuff he had put back in his pocket and slapped them on the bar. Talk about a stingy tip! Maybe next time Ted would mind his own business.

The Rock turned to swagger out of the place. Instead, he grabbed a barstool, steadied himself, then lined himself up to make a beeline for the door. It would not be easy. Somebody kept moving the darn thing.

———

The Rock believed he actually drove a little better after a few beers. Alcohol loosened him up a little, lubricated the reflexes. Tonight, as usual, he cruised toward home almost on automatic, like his Audi could basically drive itself.

He took the long route, a few extra side streets to avoid the Interstate until absolutely necessary. The cops liked to patrol the Interstate and pull you over for no apparent reason. Although he could handle the driving, those pain-in-the-rear Breathalyzer tests failed to distinguish between experienced drivers like the Rock, who could handle themselves, and teenage drunks, who were a danger to society.

He watched the streetlights, big blurs of hazy lights, as they blended into the occasional headlights of oncoming cars—more big balls of fuzzy lights. All the lights, even the ones that were attached to the street poles, were moving. He blinked several times to sharpen the lines. This only caused the dashboard lights, green and orange running together, to bleed into the outside lights, like one big psychedelic display.

He drove without thinking, without feeling, really. Yet still he drove carefully. More carefully, he thought, than those nights when he was stone sober. He could drive a lot faster if he wanted to, but still, better safe than—

Without warning, everything happened at once, too fast to react, yet almost in slow motion. Big, bright lights coming straight at him, the distant sound of a horn. His mind screamed *danger,* sensed a need to act, but his hands and feet seemed to reside at the end of interminably long limbs, big hands and big feet…clumsy, controlled by someone else.

In that split second, just before the lights came bursting through his windshield, the noise stopped, the lights faded, and he seemed to swim underwater. The uncooperative hands had finally pulled the wheel hard to the right, the world spinning fiercely, yet slowly…a tree growing larger, a last flash of light in a split second that lasted forever.

He felt a blow—more like an explosion—but before he felt pain, he succumbed to darkness.

63

"WHY WOULD AVERY DO THAT?" Mackenzie asked, staring at the ceiling in Blaine Richards' lavish office.

The attorney leaned back in his chair, his body mirrored by the dark floor-to-ceiling window behind him. Blaine could actually look right past Mackenzie and admire the serene look on his own face. His composure contrasted nicely with his lawyer's, a man gallantly trying to act unfazed. But when Mackenzie locked his hands behind his head, a small half-moon of sweat creased the underarms of the same starched white shirt he had worn to court. *If the stakes weren't so high, this would almost be fun,* Blaine thought. He crossed his legs.

"Who knows," Blaine responded, checking his watch. "Money… probably. I mean, unless you've got a better theory." 9:10. Avery was late. "That's why I asked him to come out here tonight."

Mackenzie brought his arms down, ran a hand through his hair, and shook his head. "I don't know. This whole thing is so…"

"Bizarre?"

"Yeah. Bizarre."

The two men sat in silence for a long minute, Mackenzie staring at the floor, Richards studying his own reflection in the window. The loud ringing of the phone—one long ring, an internal line—broke the spell.

"Yeah," Blaine answered.

"There's a Dr. Avery here to see you," reported the security guard.

"Send him up."

Richards nodded to a worried Win Mackenzie. "Avery's here."

Richards stood and stretched. "You mind if I meet with him alone for a few minutes first? He might be more inclined to open up a little if there's no attorney in the room."

"Okay," said Mackenzie, sounding relieved not to be included in the initial confrontation.

"You can just hang out here," Richards motioned. "I'll come get you if he says anything helpful."

Without waiting for a reply, Richards headed down the hallway, leaving Mackenzie staring into space. Richards greeted Avery at the elevator on this top floor of the GenTech building—eighteen stories, nearly as tall as the office buildings in downtown Norfolk. After a firm handshake, "Thanks for coming, Lars," Richards ushered Avery into the conference room.

The room featured a large oak table with about twelve swivel chairs positioned around it. The interior wall contained an array of what the designer had called "classic" art, abstract paintings that Richards could never quite figure out. No matter. He had been told they cost more than the paintings hanging in the main conference room of the Kilgore firm. The exterior wall was really just one huge window, thick-paned glass, floor to ceiling, with a few decorative vertical metallic pieces to break up the width of it.

Avery, looking more pallid than ever, his dark hair shooting everywhere, slouched into a seat with his back to the massive window. He placed his thin black leather briefcase on the table. He looked pathetic, thought Richards, sporting the thin, rounded shoulders and sunken eyes of a beaten man.

Richards walked toward the serving table at one end of the conference room, talking as he moved. "We're in some kind of bind in this case now, Lars. People think that maybe old man Davenport took a good bite out of me today. You heard any of that?"

"Not really." Avery sounded unconvincing.

Richards picked up a glass bottle of sparkling soda from the serving table and began filling two small glasses. "Davenport's dangerous. They say that stuff about illegal cloning's got the market spooked."

"So it seems."

Reaching down and opening a door to the cabinet, Richards removed a small bottle of Scotch, Avery's drink of choice. He poured a generous portion into each glass and brought them back to the conference table, sliding Avery's across the table toward the nervous little man.

Avery held up his hand in protest.

"Nonsense," snorted Richards, taking a large swallow. "Got your first choice of drink here, and it's going to be a long night." He stared hard at Avery, saw fear shooting out from eyes under the heavy black eyebrows. "I need you relaxed."

Avery picked up the drink, couldn't quite hide a small tremor, and took a sip. "I'll be relaxed when this whole thing is over."

"You got the tape?"

Avery reached into his briefcase and removed a small cassette player that he placed on the table.

"Great," said Richards, as he watched Avery take another sip. "Let's hear it."

For the next few minutes, the men listened in silence to the conversation between Lars Avery and Billy Davenport: Avery's offer to perjure himself about illegal cloning at GenTech in exchange for seventy-five thousand and Davenport's acceptance, labeling Avery as an expert witness.

"Nicely done," commented Richards. He took a last swallow from his drink and plunked it down with authority on the table, a subtle message to Avery that he was falling behind in the drinking department.

"I take no pride in it."

"Nor do I. But it was necessary. It was insurance. Now, with Davenport sniffing around my finances…and yours, we need to use it."

Another swig by Avery. Things should be starting to blur for the man soon. *This will be the most critical and difficult part,* Richards reminded himself. *And I could use a little luck.*

Under the table, out of Avery's sight, Richards reached into his pocket and pulled out a small microcassette recorder, the same one he used every time he worked in the lab to dictate notes. He laid it on the chair next to him, not yet turning it on. With his free hand, he reached out to grab the cassette recorder on the table that had just finished playing the tape brought by Avery.

"If the amnio had gone according to plan," Richards said, looking sternly at the smaller doctor, "we wouldn't need to use this tape—the fetus would be terminated, and this whole ugly business with Maryna would be moot."

At that instant, the very instant "moot" crossed his lips, Richards flicked a switch and put his own hidden microcassette into the Record mode.

Avery looked down at the table and spoke softly. "I told you the truth. I mean, what do you want from me? My schedule was…well, it was one of those days. Beyond my control."

Idiot, Richards screamed in his thoughts. *Not at all what I needed.*

He subtly turned the hidden machine off, hit Rewind, got ready to record again. Avery took another hit on his drink, nearly finished it off. Richards thought he saw the eyes roll back just a little. *Not much time. He takes hardly a sip for five minutes and now he practically chugs it!*

Nearly panicked, Richards still kept his voice calm…and stern. After all, he didn't really need this new tape. It was just more insurance. Still, it would be nice to wrap this whole plan up in a tidy little package with a bow on top.

He hit Record.

"I can't begin to tell you how much that disappointed me," Richards lectured. He paused, let the words sink in. Avery refused to give him eye contact. "But at least you've got this tape. Now"—another pause; Richards' hands started to sweat—"are you ready to do what you have to in order to make this right? Are you ready to march into court tomorrow, tell the judge that you lied to Davenport about this alleged illegal cloning just to see if he'd pay you for saying it? Are you ready to tell the court that there really wasn't any illegal cloning going on at Gen-Tech at all?"

Avery contorted his face and pushed the glass a little on the table. "Blaine, I don't know about this...don't know if I can go through with it..."

"*Hey!*" Blaine caught himself and toned it down. "You're the one who created this whole mess. Either you testify about this tape, or I'll bring it to the attention of the court myself."

Avery seemed to shrink back at the suggestion, retreating further inside the hooded eyes. A look of painful recognition dawned on his face. It was, Blaine thought, the moment that Avery realized how deep he was into this whole thing, how little choice he really had.

Blaine kept a finger on the Record button. *Is now the time to shut it off? What I have is pretty good. Should I chance one more sentence?* He hesitated, and the choice was made.

"Don't guess I have much choice," Avery mumbled. "But I don't like it."

Perfect, thought Blaine. *Absolutely perfect.*

"No, I don't guess you do," Blaine responded. "And it's the right thing to do—the only thing to do under the circumstances."

Pleased, he turned off the recorder and watched the haze begin to roll in over Avery's eyes. Avery reached out slowly, lethargically, and tried to push the glass away.

"What did you—" he slurred the words, looking up at Blaine with slowly registering panic. Avery began to rise, leaned heavily on the table, sighed and sat back down. His head drooped forward, slowly at first, then practically banged on the table.

"Lights out," said Richards.

Then he stood, pulled two latex surgical gloves out of his pocket, and put them on. He stretched his fingers as only a surgeon would know how to do, and the gloves snapped into place.

64

MARYNA HAD CAUGHT A FEW NEWS CLIPS about the trial earlier that evening. The commentators thought that Mitchell and the Rock had carried the day; that they had made some serious headway against a headstrong Blaine Richards. The business channels said that GenTech's stock had fallen. And rumors about illegal cloning now filled the airwaves.

But one of the legal experts had added that Maryna would now be forced to testify. Maryna hoped—no, she prayed—that the commentator had made a mistake. But now, sitting across the kitchen table from Mitchell at Sarah Reed's house, she learned the terrible truth.

"So the bottom line," Mitchell said, "is that the judge has basically ordered you to testify or we will lose the case." He gently covered her hands on the table with his own. Compassion filled his eyes. "We don't have a lot of choices here. If you don't testify, we lose. The INS will still try to track you down for deportation. If they or anybody else finds you," Mitchell hesitated, then continued in a voice even softer, more compassionate, than before, "they could force you to terminate the pregnancy and then be deported."

Maryna had sworn she was ready for this news. She had been thinking about this awful choice the entire three hours since the six o'clock news. But even as gently as Mitchell delivered the truth, it still grabbed her heart, squeezed it hard, and twisted it, ripping the very fabric of her soul. Her infant faith tested so severely, so soon.

Be bold, she told herself.

"And if I do testify?"

"The INS would still try to deport you. They'll probably be waiting in the courtroom tomorrow. But maybe the baby…"

Maryna felt a flicker of hope. Dim, but undeniably there. *What about my baby?*

"Maybe we could argue that the baby is destined to be an *American* citizen—a daughter of American parents. Maybe if you testified and we won the case, we could then convince the immigration court to allow this child to at least be born here...to stay here."

With who? wondered Maryna. *Cameron? The woman who wants to abort Dara?* Maryna shuddered. Two weeks ago, that's all she wanted. Now, how could she turn this baby, *her baby*, over to a woman who fought so hard to keep Dara from ever being born?

Mitchell squeezed her hand softly. "Maryna, are you okay?"

She would *not* cry. She had already decided, before Mitchell even arrived, sneaking as usual through the backyards, that crying would not help. The tears came unbidden anyway, but she blinked them back, focusing on something far away. She would speak bravely, logically, about this difficult but necessary choice. But her throat constricted as she began, choking back the words, and all she could do was nod.

"No, you're not," said Mitchell. "And I don't blame you."

Then he did the most amazing thing, the one thing she wanted more than any other. Without another word, he got up from his side of the table and came over to hers. Maryna stood, nearly collapsing into his open arms, embraced him totally, and lost herself in his strength. She felt a soft kiss on the top of her head and the gentle stroking of her hair.

From the day that she lost her mother, she had always handled things alone, put them in perspective, forced herself to deal with reality. Emotions didn't help. She could switch into survivor mode, ignore emotions, detach herself, and move on with life. But now, with Mitchell, things had changed. She wanted him, *needed* him, to walk through this with her.

The tears she had fought so hard to keep back now spilled from her eyes onto his chest. "I can't terminate this pregnancy," she struggled to get the words out. "And I can't give up this baby. I'll take her with me to Cambodia if I have to—away from this judge, away from the INS, away from the Snakeheads…"

She couldn't finish the sentence because she couldn't bear the thought. *Away from this judge, the INS, the Snakeheads…and away from you!* Just when things seemed to have turned her way, just when she had found a new faith and a man unlike any she had ever met, she would lose it all. Her mother sacrificed her own life so that Maryna could live in America and chase her dream. And find a man like Mitchell. Now Maryna had to choose between that dream, that man, and the baby growing in her womb.

For the first time in her life, she knew—not just intellectually but from the depths of her heart—why her own mother had done it, had given her life for the life of a child. Maryna knew that a mother really had no choice. No matter the cost. Maryna knew that Dara was her first responsibility, her first instinct. Everything else must yield to this over-whelming need to protect and keep her child. She would birth Dara. Raise Dara. Love Dara. Even if she had to do it in Cambodia.

Everything else must yield to the good of Dara. *Everything.*

Her heart ached, it hurt so bad, the fist around it squeezing tighter and tighter as she considered the unthinkable consequences of the action she was about to take. She took a deep breath and tried to stop herself from crying. She needed to take a step back and face this diffi-culty like she had so many times in the past. But for now, just a few more seconds, she would lean into Mitchell and allow herself to cry a little harder.

He felt so helpless, holding her tight but not being able to stem the flow of tears. In a way, he had caused it. And he would do anything to take this burden from her. He would pay any price.

She had him, he knew. It had all happened so quickly, so unex-pectedly. Somewhere, and he didn't even know where, she had gone from client to friend to…something much, much more. How much, he

didn't know. Didn't even dare ask himself. But this much he did know:
When she hurt, he hurt. And right now, every tear ripped his heart open
a little more.

Mitchell was no stranger to love. He had been charmed before,
smitten before, giddy in love one day and over it the next. He had dated
prettier girls, possibly smarter girls, although he wasn't quite sure, and
girls with personality by the boatload. But he admitted for the first time
while he stood there holding Maryna against his chest, he had never
been *drawn* to a woman like this before. This bond was deeper. Faster.
Stronger. He had known Maryna for what—a week? Ten days max. But
that ten days felt like forever. As if she had been there his entire life,
somewhere deep inside of him, a soul mate brought to the surface who
in turn brought out the best in him.

This is crazy! I don't even know this girl.

"I'll think of something," he found himself saying. "There's got to
be a way."

He felt Maryna place her palms against his chest and move her
cheek slightly away. She looked up at him with those big, beautiful, glistening brown eyes.

"Can we pray about it?" she whispered. "Maybe Sarah can pray
with us. I know what I've got to do. I just need the strength to do it."

Mitchell felt his knees go weak. He was the one who had been a
Christian for years. He was the one who should have suggested prayer.

"Sure," he said. Then he put a hand gently under her chin, brought
her lips to his, and kissed her as if it were the most natural thing in the
world.

It took a few minutes before they called Sarah to join them in
prayer.

65

BLAINE RICHARDS KNEW HE NEEDED to move quickly, precisely. Fortunately, adrenaline pumped through his body, temporarily overcoming the fatigue that had dogged him after a long day in court. This much adrenaline would make most people jumpy, muddle their thinking. But being a surgeon meant you learned to control the adrenaline and channel it into positive energy, crisp thinking, and extraordinary strength.

He had rehearsed these steps in his mind a dozen times earlier in the day. First, he grabbed the shot glasses—his and Avery's—as well as the two half-empty bottles of sparkling soda and walked out into the hallway and a few doors down to the kitchen. He had checked the offices earlier that evening. There was nobody left on the floor at this hour except Mackenzie, and he was in Blaine's office on the opposite hallway, half a building away.

Richards poured the contents of the soda bottles into the sink, rinsed the bottles, and threw them in the trash. He washed both shot glasses in the sink, rinsed them, and dried them. Then, checking carefully in both directions, he left the kitchen and took the glasses back to the conference room, replacing them in the cabinet.

As expected, Avery hadn't moved. He breathed deeply in and out, alive and well, but deeply unconscious. His face lay flat against the table, mouth partially open, hair naturally disheveled, looking for all the world like a sloppy drunk who had simply passed out.

Such was the beauty of gamma-hydroxy-butyramine. GHB. Called by some the "ideal sleep-inducing substance." Although it was not generally available in the United States, even by prescription, qualified research labs like the one owned by Richards had no problem obtaining

the drug. Richards chose it tonight because there would be no metabo-
lite released in the bloodstream, no trace of the substance even if someone went looking for foul play. And he chose it because it guaranteed
three hours of sound sleep.

Not that he would need even a fraction of that time.

He hooked his arms under Avery's armpits and dragged him out of
his seat, lowering him cautiously to the floor. He checked the room one
last time, making sure he didn't miss anything. Then he stuck his head
out into the hallway. It was quiet. Clear both ways.

He came back in, took a deep breath, picked up the swivel chair
that Avery had been sitting in and smashed it with all his might against
the thick glass of the window. The glass shattered, but did not break,
surprising Richards with its resiliency. The blow reverberated through
the conference room, sounding much louder than Richards thought it
would, and for the second time that evening, Richards bordered on
panic. He took a step back, lifted the heavy chair again, and this time
flung it as hard as he could against the shattered windowpane.

To his great relief, the chair burst through the window, creating a
jagged and gaping hole, and then plunged eighteen stories to the concrete below. Without waiting even an instant, Richards grabbed Avery
under the arms and dragged him next to the window and halfway up
on the windowsill. Richards crouched his legs then swung Avery up and
over with all the adrenaline-fueled strength he possessed, tossing Avery
like a bag of feed out the window to a certain death.

He listened. He waited. And he heard a sickening thud echo up
from eighteen floors down. With no small amount of willpower,
Richards resisted the urge to lean out the window and gawk at the sight.

He quickly checked his own hands and arms for cuts, found none,
then pulled the self-addressed manila envelope out of his briefcase. He
took off the surgical gloves and sealed them inside. Then he grabbed the
precious cassette tape that Avery had brought with him to the building,
put his own microcassette recorder in his pocket, and calmly walked out
of the conference room. On the way across the hall lobby, he slipped the

envelope into the mail drop slit on the wall near the reception desk, smugly imagining the letter falling the same eighteen stories that Avery had just transgressed, but landing softly in the mailbox at the bottom of the drop.

On his way down the hall to his office, Richards wondered how long it would take before somebody discovered the body. The noise of impact, the thud of the body, or the sound of the chair hitting hard concrete might carry through the first-floor lobby and alert the guard. But then again, Richards knew that the guard working the front desk at night was an avid television watcher. There was a fair chance he might not even hear such a loud noise from the back.

Richards returned to his office and placed both tapes on his desk. Mackenzie stood, eyes expectant.

"Just as I thought," Richards said. "The jerk had agreed to perjure himself for Billy Davenport. Davenport agreed to pay Avery 75 K for spouting a bunch of lies about our illegally cloning other egg cells." Richards watched Mackenzie's eyes widen with disbelief. "Fortunately for us, and unknown to Davenport, Avery secretly recorded the deal. Are you ready for this?"

Mackenzie nodded, apparently speechless.

"It's all right here on tape," Richards said, tapping the cassette that Avery had played in the conference room. "I can't believe he taped it."

Richards sat down, and put on a display of indignation and exhaustion. He furrowed his brow. "Are tapes even admissible in court?"

"As long as one of the parties consents to it being taped, the other one doesn't even have to know." Mackenzie eyed the tape for a moment, then almost to himself said, "This will knock the Rock right out of the case. Subornation of perjury, for starters."

Then he looked at Richards again, jamming his hands in his pockets. "What's this other tape?"

"Oh. Avery doesn't know it, but after he started confessing, I used my little Dictaphone to secretly record *our* conversation. I told Avery he would have to confess in court, tell the judge everything. He seemed reluctant. So, just in case he tries to deny it later, I've got *our* conversation on tape too."

"Great thinking," gasped Mackenzie. "Is Avery still down there in the conference room?"

"Yeah, and we better get to him right away to prepare his testimony…before he has a change of heart," Richards paused, hearing the faint sound of a siren in the distance. Avery's grizzly suicide had apparently been discovered quickly.

"He seemed pretty torn up about it," Richards added for effect.

"Wouldn't you be?" asked Mackenzie. He took his hands out of his pockets and gingerly picked up the tapes.

"It's all pretty unbelievable," mumbled Richards. He stood, and Mackenzie, still clinging to the treasured tapes, dutifully followed Richards through the door.

66

HE REALLY WASN'T MUCH OF A FATHER, Cameron reminded herself as she hustled through the front door of her home, car keys in hand, on her way to the hospital. Strange then, how this call managed to shatter her world. "He's been in a car accident," said the caller, somebody at Virginia Beach General. Cameron couldn't even remember who called or how they said they got her number.

She always knew that sooner or later a call like this would come. But why now, of all times?

"It's not life-threatening," she remembered the person saying. Some broken bones, a bad concussion, something about keeping him for observation. His life was not in danger. Still, Cameron's world was now a blur. After all, he was her father. The car had been totaled. He was lucky, said the caller, to be alive.

She backed her car out of the drive, pressed the accelerator, and raced down the street. Her own tension—the quickness of her breath, her death grip on the wheel—it caught her by surprise. *Why do I even care? He really never was much of a father.*

But all her attempts to conjure up the anger brought about by his desertion, his irresponsibility, his utter selfishness, were quickly washed away in the lingering memory from late this afternoon. Her own dad standing there, trying mightily to defend her in court, proud of his bold attempt to cross-examine Blaine Richards, then crushed by the note waiting for him at counsel table. She could still see the hurt in his eyes. Deep pools of pain and confusion. She couldn't stop reliving that split second when his countenance dropped, when the drunken old fool realized that the cross-examination he took such pride in performing was just another hopeless failure.

There had been happier times. As a little girl, she had been in love with him. He would swing her around in circles, carry her on his shoulders, tickle her till she squealed her surrender.

So she had been told. She remembered none of this. Only the hurt of his betrayal. And the ensuing separation.

And now she had returned that hurt, she knew. With cold calculation, she had snipped the last fragile emotional thread that held them together. She had disowned him. Impaled him on the cold steel of her words and twisted. But now, because of what she had done in court, she felt responsible for his physical pain, for the very fact that he was lying wounded in the hospital. She had driven him to it as surely as if she had been driving the car herself.

Stop it! I can't do this. I won't...shoulder this load. This man has caused enough pain for two lifetimes! He's not the victim here. I am! And he never was much of a father.

She parked in the lot nearest the emergency room entrance, still debating whether she was doing the right thing. Although visiting hours had ended an hour ago, at 9:00 P.M., she acted like she owned the place, sweet-talked a few nurses, and eventually wound up just outside her father's room. She wondered again if she was doing the right thing, realized he would do the same for her, hoped that he was not awake, took a deep breath, and entered the room.

She was not prepared for what she saw.

His eyes were closed, thank goodness for that. But he looked so pale. And so helpless. He had a tube attached to his right arm as well as one coming out of his nose. A blue splint covered his left leg. His mouth hung open, sucking air in fitful bursts. A deep gash ran along his left temple, and the eye on that side was outlined in purple. Cuts and scrapes, puffiness, a nasty bruise or two. He was lucky, all right. And he looked so...helpless. That's what surprised Cameron the most. The ornery man who had never needed anybody's help, the one guy who would never take anyone's advice, the man whose theme song was "I Did It My Way."

He looked so pathetic. And vulnerable. Almost like a child.

She walked toward him as if drawn by some irresistible force. She thought about staying. She would just sit there. And she would be there when he woke up.

Then she thought about leaving a note. She could share her feelings. Say all those things she really wanted to say. She had a chance to mend fences. A chance to say that she never meant to hurt him. A chance, maybe her last, to apologize.

For what?! What have I ever done to him? What did I do to deserve being abandoned? Tossed away like yesterday's trash?

As always with her dad, she wrestled the warring feelings. Emotions of guilt and indignation. Sympathy and shame. Duty and revenge. She despised him, yet needed his approval. Shunned him, yet wanted more than anything to find security in his arms. To at least be his friend.

She thought for a moment about how great it would be to get some sage fatherly advice at this very moment. With everything going on in her life, how she needed someone to confide in. But it could never be him.

Like all of life's other challenges, she would face these difficulties alone.

She stood there, motionless, staring into his stubbled face. She studied the cut on his forehead, the dark stitches holding the skin together. It would probably leave a scar. She watched the fitful breathing. And she realized that this man, like so many times before, was oblivious to her presence and removed from her pain. He was hurting. But she was hurting too. And, as always, there would be no comfort in his arms, no assurance from his lips.

Oblivious. That was her dad.

And this night, he was also helpless. Like a child.

And so, as one would with any child, Cameron bent over and kissed him on the forehead, right next to the gash, tucked the thin hospital sheet gently around his neck, and whispered, "Everything's gonna be all right."

She lingered there for a moment, as if she half expected him to answer and somehow acknowledge her presence. But he didn't, and she turned to leave.

They say that parents have a sixth sense about their children, she thought on her way out the door. *Even when he's unconscious, a dad knows if his child comes to visit.*

Most dads.

But not mine. He's just oblivious.

And he never really was much of a father.

67

NIKKI MORENO IMAGINED THAT SHE LOOKED like Rene Russo in *The Thomas Crowne Affair.* Younger and firmer than the actress, of course, but with that same sense of alluring dangerousness. Sleek. And dark. She wore a pair of black stretch leggings and a skin-tight, black spandex top. Black latex gloves covered her hands, black sneakers her feet. She was ready to conduct high-level espionage, ready to face down danger and assume risk in a provocative manner perfectly suited to the big screen.

Who was she kidding? Nikki Moreno was preparing to scrounge through Cameron Davenport's trash.

And she had never felt more like a redneck.

For this job, she drove Mitchell's F-150 pickup. She had traded her Sebring for the night. She actually liked the way she rode up high in the truck, like she was sitting on top of the world. But still, the engine growled and rumbled along, and it handled…well, like a truck. Not a very good getaway vehicle.

At least it was black. And at least it didn't have a gun rack in the back window or a Rebel flag on the plates. But everything else about the vehicle screamed "bubba."

On the way to Cameron's house, she reset each of the automatic buttons for the radio. No sense having them all kick you straight to country stations. Mitchell needed a little variety. Jazz. Hard rock. Hip-hop. Oldies, against her better judgment. Anything but country.

Nikki had visited Cameron's neighborhood and Blaine Richards' neighborhood earlier in the week, as soon as Nikki and Mitchell learned they could intervene in the court hearing. Both Nikki and Mitchell felt they were missing something but couldn't quite put a finger on it. Richards' neighbors said the trashman had already come for the week on Monday. But according to Cameron's neighbors, trash pickup for that neighborhood was on Friday. Most everyone wheeled their big green plastic trash cans—standard size provided by the disposal company—to the curb on Thursday night.

When she learned this, Nikki thought about tacking a note on everyone's door in the neighborhood earlier in the week telling them that the trash would actually be picked up on Wednesday. But Mitchell had talked her out of it. Thursday night is soon enough, he said. If we find anything, we can still use it on Friday.

So here she was, at 1:00 A.M., driving a conspicuous, huge, rumbling black pickup truck down a regentrified portion of Norfolk where everybody drove foreign compacts.

The streets seemed to grow smaller as Nikki approached Cameron's neighborhood on East Granby. Cars lined both sides of the street, barely leaving enough room for other cars to get out of their driveways. There was hardly enough room in the street itself for two cars to pass in opposite directions. The houses, these huge Victorian models with big white pillars and gingerbread roofs, seemed to be squeezed into too-small lots, so tight that it seemed to Nikki the neighbors could actually open their windows and shake hands with each other.

Nikki turned onto East Granby and slowed down to get her bearings. The street was deserted and, as a bonus, dimly lit with streetlamps placed too far apart. Nikki traveled about half a block and found Cameron's address on her right: 250 East Granby. The large white Victorian with a wraparound porch was dark, the green trash can sitting dutifully by the curb. Nikki left the truck running in the street, turned off the headlights, leaving only the parking lights on, jumped out, and hustled over to the trash can.

She pulled back the lid and starting slinging green plastic bags of trash into the back of the pickup. A white kitchen trash bag joined the loot. Nikki dug deeper, finding newspapers and plastic milk jugs scattered throughout the trash. *Hypocrite,* thought Nikki. *If your readers only knew.* Cameron Davenport, champion of environmentalism, friend of the earth, tree-hugger. Cameron Davenport, a woman who doesn't even recycle paper and plastics.

Two more bags and Nikki would be on her way. But as she twisted back toward the trash can, she caught some faint movement out of the corner of her eye. She pivoted and focused on a form lurking in the shadows a few feet up the sidewalk.

Just shoot me.

A stooped older lady—she had to be at least seventy—with a bushy head of unruly gray hair, and wearing some kind of gaudy-looking flowered housecoat, was out walking her dog. A Chihuahua, of course. At 1:00 in the morning!

The lady had stopped in her tracks, no more than thirty feet away, dropped her jaw halfway to the ground, and commenced staring at Nikki. The dog stopped as well, thrust her pointy little nose up in the air, and yapped.

"Hush, Suzzie," said the lady, as if maybe Nikki wouldn't notice them if the dog shut up. But Nikki glared at the woman. And Suzzie kept yapping.

"Hush," said the lady. Then to Nikki, in the shrillest of accusatory tones, "May I ask what you're doing here?"

Nikki let her eyes roll back in her head, then forced them a little cross-eyed, a trick she had learned in grade school. She managed to let a little drool slip out the corner of her mouth. "You live in this neighborhood?" Nikki slurred.

"Yes," the lady said primly.

Nikki sneered. "Figures." She reached into the trash can and tossed a couple of milk jugs into the back of the pickup. "You know how much you can get for these things?"

The lady shook her head. Suzzie snarled.

"Figures." Nikki reached in and grabbed an armful of paper. "Recycling. Five cents for every jug and can. Penny a pound for the paper."

She tossed some newspapers into the bed of the pickup, scattering them on top of the garbage bags. "Not everybody can afford to just throw this stuff away, you know."

Nikki took a step toward the lady, staggering for effect. "You got any trash out here I can dig through?"

Grandma seemed to hesitate, then recovered her poise. She thrust her chin in the air, matching the snotty little Chihuahua, and pulled her housecoat tighter around her waist. Without answering, she harrumphed, turned on her heel, and headed back down the sidewalk.

"Nice talkin' to ya," called out Nikki. At this, Suzzie barked and yanked just a little on her leash, as if she would have attacked Nikki if the lady would just let her go. Since Grandma's back was now turned, Nikki took a quick and aggressive step toward the little yapper, showed her own teeth, and watched the dog scurry back to her master's side.

Satisfied, Nikki hustled back to the trash can, threw the last two bags into the back of the pickup, and drove away. Only in this neighborhood could you get away with pretending to be a tramp when you drove a shiny F-150 pickup truck and dressed like a movie star.

A few miles away, Nikki pulled into a deserted church parking lot and stopped directly under a street lamp. For forty-five minutes she picked through the trash. A cereal box, an apple core, fast-food bags, and junk mail. Receipts, soda cans, rotten grapes and frozen dinners. Bag after bag. Junk and more junk. *This is pointless. Time to get some sleep.*

At a few minutes after two, Nikki opened the third large, green trash bag and poured out the contents. The bag obviously contained items from a bathroom trash can. Empty toilet paper rolls, used Band-Aids, an empty shampoo bottle, rumpled Kleenex. Personal stuff. Gross stuff. Nikki moved aside a piece of plastic—dry cleaning plastic—and blinked.

Her eyes popped open—*this can't be*—and she spread the items out carefully, gingerly, in the bed of the truck. She stared at them for a long time. With renewed vigor, she sifted through the rest of the bag, then checked and rechecked every drugstore receipt and grocery store receipt from the other bags. An hour flew by before she knew it. Nikki was jazzed, full of energy as she considered the possibilities. At 3:00 A.M., having pored through every single shred of trash, she finally allowed herself to dwell on the more sinister scenarios that she had suspected all along.

She called Mitchell Taylor.

He didn't pick up for four rings. Even when he did, she had to wait another couple of seconds before he said anything.

"Hello," said a gruff and groggy voice.

"Put some coffee on, I'm coming over."

"Huh?"

"The trash, Mitchell. You won't believe what I found in the trash."

68

Friday, May 28

THE ALARM SOUNDED DISTANT TO MITCHELL, like maybe it was just a dream. A bad dream. He tried to roll over, felt a shooting pain in his lower back, and winced. He pulled the pillow over his head—anything to make the obnoxious beeping go away.

It would not. If anything, it seemed to grow in volume. He cracked an eyelid and looked at his wristwatch. Six o'clock. His eyes bolted open, glancing around the room—the *living* room. *That's right. Fell asleep prepping for court. Where's Nikki?* Over Mitchell's protests, she had insisted on staying to help him prepare for court.

He rolled from the couch and stepped over the papers that he had scattered like confetti around the place. More sharp pain, like a knife. Worse. He grimaced and froze. A few seconds later, the pain subsided a little. Bent over, he padded back to the bedroom to silence the alarm.

Nikki lay sprawled on top of his bed, still wearing her black secret agent outfit, minus the shoes, which she had kicked off next to the bed. She smelled like garbage. Two pillows covered her head, her face buried deep underneath, so that only her long dark hair poked out the sides.

Mitchell found the button and shut off the alarm.

"What took you so long?" she mumbled, as she came out from under the pillows, then curled into a ball and placed one of the pillows under her head.

Mitchell stared at her for a few seconds, resisting the urge to argue this early in the morning, then sat wearily on the side of the bed. He still wore the khaki shorts and tank-top undershirt he had thrown on when Nikki arrived three hours ago.

"Good morning to you too," he said. Man, he felt terrible—the woozy feeling that comes from getting just three hours' sleep. His eyes especially—red and sore and swollen. And the smell wafting over from Nikki didn't help. But still, he had this incredible sense of anticipation about the day.

He stretched his back…twisted a little to the left, a little to the right, slowly… "Aghh," he moaned as he tried to stand.

Nikki squirmed a little—short, violent movements, no subtle message to Mitchell to quiet down so she could sleep.

"C'mon, sunshine," Mitchell said. He hit her gently with the one free pillow. "It's a big day."

She shrugged it off. "Call me at noon," she snarled. "And let me know if she shows up."

"Does that mean you're not going to iron my shirt?" Mitchell asked as he gimped toward the bathroom to shower.

"Ouch!" Another sharp pain in the back—this one from Nikki's sneaker, which she had just sent hurtling across the room.

❧

Nearly three hours later Mitchell joined the other lawyers and litigants in Ichabod's chambers. Everyone else was already seated when the clerk showed him in. The others sat eerily silent, some reading, others whispering. When Mitchell took his seat, Judge Baker-Kline glanced up from her desk.

"Is this everyone?" she asked the clerk.

The young man nodded with his whole body. "Yes, Your Honor."

He left the room, closing the door behind him.

"It's been quite a night," Ichabod said wearily. "First, I've been informed by Ms. Gunther that Mr. Davenport had a car accident last night…"

The words slapped Mitchell. He felt a grinding in the pit of his stomach and looked at Cameron. She sat stoically, her face an expressionless mask.

"I understand that he's been released from the hospital," continued the judge, "with a broken femur and several stitches in his face and arm. Nothing life threatening."

"That's correct," Nora Gunther said as the judge looked at her for confirmation. Nora turned to her left and motioned to a young man in an expensive charcoal black suit with a baby face, wavy blond hair, and wide shoulders. "This is Oliver Price. He will take Mr. Davenport's place as local counsel."

Mitchell caught Cameron's attention for a moment. "Sorry," he mouthed. She nodded her head in thanks.

"That would be enough tragedy for one night," Ichabod continued. "But unfortunately, there's more. Mr. Mackenzie?"

Win Mackenzie cleared his throat. He looked down as he talked, showing none of yesterday's bravado. "Last night, Dr. Lars Avery came to GenTech's offices to prepare for his testimony today. While he was there, Dr. Richards confronted him about the questions that Mr. Davenport had asked during his cross-examination of Dr. Richards yesterday. You see, Blaine felt that somebody had provided Billy Davenport with false information about GenTech, especially as it pertained to alleged illegal cloning. I wasn't in the room at the time, so Blaine can take it from there."

All eyes turned to Blaine Richards, the one man in the room sitting straight up in his seat. Unlike Mackenzie, Richards spoke with confidence. "Dr. Avery confessed to me that he had spoken with Davenport and offered to perjure himself on the stand for seventy-five thousand. He was prepared to testify that GenTech had illegally cloned embryos, when of course we had not, and he was going to testify that I had made illegal payments to Avery to keep him quiet in the past. Last night, Avery decided he couldn't go through with this fraud…"

Richards paused, apparently collecting his thoughts. It sounded to

Mitchell like Richards' voice caught just a little, and now he heard a sniffle. He watched as Richards quickly licked dry lips, then continued.

"Lars was a friend…and I was shocked. It's all just been"—Richards struggled for the words while Mitchell thought about how quickly he had gone from confident to broken up—"so unbelievable. Anyway, Lars had secretly taped the earlier conversation with Davenport. He played it for me last night."

Richards dramatically dropped the tape on the judge's desk. "This second tape," he said, "is a partial tape of my conversation with Lars. When I realized what he was saying, I turned on my own microcassette recorder. You'll hear me tell Lars that he has to bring this information to the court and come clean about his deal with Davenport. You'll hear me tell him just how disappointed I was in him. You'll hear him acknowledge responsibility and say that he didn't know if he could go through with it."

Now Richards paused and drew a dramatic deep breath. "When I left the conference room and walked down the hall to get Win Mackenzie, Dr. Avery jumped out the window of the eighteenth-floor conference room."

Mitchell felt the air flee his lungs. *Suicide!* This couldn't be happening! The shock of it rattled Mitchell, and he felt his own thought process shutting down, like he was dropping into some impenetrable fog.

Perjured testimony. Suicide. Things spinning out of control.

"Mr. Taylor," Ichabod was saying, "do you need a continuance? Other counsel thinks it is better to proceed—that by suspending this hearing we just draw more attention to it."

Mitchell shrugged. He tried to process it all but couldn't quite focus. "Let's proceed," he said mechanically.

In the next several minutes, the lawyers agreed that the judge would start court by briefly mentioning the suicide of Dr. Lars Avery. The judge would also announce, without providing details, that she had been made aware of conclusive evidence to show that there had been no illegal cloning at GenTech and that the issues of financial motivation hinted at by Mr. Davenport in his questioning the prior day had no merit. Although Mitchell objected to the last part of the instruction, he had no evidence to support the Rock's allegation, and he was summarily overruled.

Everyone else believed that this general statement by the judge would put these extraneous matters to rest in a way that would do minimal damage to the reputation of the deceased Dr. Avery. Mitchell just shook his head in disbelief as he left the court's chambers.

And I thought I was the one with the big surprise.

69

ICHABOD'S ANNOUNCEMENT STUNNED everyone in the courtroom. A reverent hush descended on the place, as if Ichabod had asked for a moment of silence to honor the dead doctor. Mitchell took advantage of the opportunity to scan the crowd.

There, about halfway back on the other side, sat Mutt and Jeff, the INS agents. What were their names? Chen and Jones, or something like that. They knew that Maryna would have to testify today or lose the case. They were practically drooling.

Nikki's Army, the group of Down syndrome mothers, was present and accounted for in the second row. Many of them had made a point of stopping Mitchell after the first day of court to tell him what an outstanding job he had done. Their presence today brought him no small degree of comfort.

Nikki had not yet arrived. She would be there, Mitchell knew, about midmorning. In the meantime, he felt a little lonely at the large counsel table that Mackenzie's associates had dutifully avoided on this second day.

After reading the stipulation about the lack of evidence on illegal cloning and financial self-dealing, a stipulation that had the reporters scribbling furiously, Ichabod turned to Nora Gunther.

"Call your next witness."

As she did the first day, Nora stood and waited until she had everyone's undivided attention. In a strident voice that to Mitchell seemed even more obnoxious than the day before, a feat he would have previously thought impossible, she declared: "Our next witness is Ms. Maryna Sareth."

At this pronouncement, all eyes turned to Mitchell, who busied himself carefully writing his client's name on the empty legal pad in front of him.

"Mr. Taylor, is your client present today?" asked Ichabod.

Mitchell stood, buttoned his suit coat. "Yes, Your Honor. In the hallway."

The marshal walked down the aisle to get Maryna, and Mitchell stole a glance at the INS agents. They sat on the edge of their seats, a folded paper in the Asian agent's hand—presumably deportation papers.

The marshal returned with Maryna in tow. *She's never been more beautiful,* thought Mitchell. He watched as Maryna walked gracefully to the front of the courtroom.

<hr>

For the most important occasion of her life, Maryna wore her favorite dress. It was a little loud, a little bold. But she was done hiding. Today was different. Today she would make a statement.

The dress was casual and colorful, a sleeveless shift with a small floral pattern: reds, oranges, and yellows. Sarah said it brought out the color in her eyes. A small ruffle at the hem hit just above the knee. The V neck plunged a little, revealing the scar inflicted by the Snakeheads. Maryna was not proud of the scar, but she would no longer hide it. *It's who I am,* she reasoned, *take me or leave me.* Today was a day for putting the whole truth in the open for all the world to see. She wore a pair of comfortable sandals and a small silver cross necklace that Sarah had given her the night before. She pulled her hair back in a tight braid, accentuating the sharp lines of her face.

The person who mattered most to her—the handsome young lawyer she had completely fallen for—had already told her that she looked beautiful the minute he laid eyes on her that morning.

What a great way to start the day. What else could she ask for?

As she took the oath, she knew she should be nervous. There would be so much riding on her testimony. The courtroom was huge. Formal. Cold. Intimidating.

But still, she really didn't feel at all nervous. Sarah and Maryna had prayed for peace. This morning, she knew their prayers had been answered.

Maryna took the stand, cast a tender look at Mitchell, and crossed her legs. She locked her eyes on the lawyer about to question her. She assumed it was Nora Gunther, a lady that Mitchell said was cold as ice. "She would just as soon gut you as look at you," he had warned. Maryna figured he was playing it up a little, just to keep her on her toes.

"Your Honor," called out the Asian INS agent from the audience, "may I approach the bench?"

"Who are you?" asked the judge. Mitchell had referred to her as Ichabod, and Maryna could see why.

"Agent James Chen, Immigration and Naturalization Service," the man said with a condescending air of authority. "I have deportation papers for Ms. Sareth."

Maryna's throat constricted a little. This had been expected, but still…

"Your Honor," said Mitchell, jumping to his feet, "Ms. Sareth has decided to take the stand today, even though she knew these gentlemen would be here. Shouldn't we at least allow her to be heard? If they still want to try and serve her with those papers after her testimony"— Mitchell turned and shot a look at Agent Chen—"there's only one way out of the courtroom."

"I agree," ruled the judge. "I, for one, am impressed that Ms. Sareth even came here to testify. That tells me a lot. I think we ought to at least hear from her before we let you begin the deportation process."

Chen sat down heavily. Maryna breathed a short-lived sigh of relief. Nora Gunther flashed a look of venom. This was not going to be easy.

"You may proceed," the judge said to Gunther.

"Thank you.

"You think you can raise a Down syndrome child on your own in Cambodia?" Gunther demanded, right out of the blocks. No "How are you." No "Nice to meet you." Not even a "Please state your name" or any such thing. *What an attitude!* Maryna began to think that maybe Mitchell wasn't exaggerating about this woman. "You think the best thing for this fetus is to let it fully develop and be born to a single, unemployed mother in a country where it will be almost impossible to get the care it needs?" Gunther pressed.

"No ma'am."

The unexpected answer seemed to freeze Gunther, if just for a moment. "Did you say, 'No ma'am?'"

"Yes," answered Maryna calmly, "that's what I said."

"So you agree with me, it's not the best thing for this special-needs child if you go hauling it off to Cambodia."

Softly, "Not the best thing. But better than an abortion."

The lines on Gunther's face tightened. A pause. A stare. "You are an illegal immigrant, correct?"

"No ma'am." Maryna wanted to explain, but Mitchell had told her a hundred times to keep her answers short and not to explain anything unless she was asked.

"Judge," Gunther turned to the lady on the bench, who was now scowling right along with Gunther. "This is ridiculous. Do I have to put the INS agents on the stand here? Maybe if we remind Ms. Sareth about the penalties for perjury—"

Mitchell jumped from his seat, palms spread wide. "Judge, if Ms. Gunther wouldn't be so anxious to skewer this witness before she even completes the preliminary questions, then we wouldn't be having these problems—"

"What are you talking about?" spit out Gunther.

"Why don't you give her the common courtesy of stating her name for the record?" shot back Mitchell.

"Why don't you conduct *your* examinations and let me conduct *mine?*"

"Counsel!" snapped Ichabod. *"Children."* She studied the notes on her legal pad for a moment. "It's common protocol to ask the witness her name for the record. It doesn't look to me like you did that—"

Gunther snorted, whirled, and made no effort to hide her disgust. "Please state your name for the record."

Maryna looked at Mitchell and caught the subtle nod.

"Maryna Sareth…" She paused, looking at Mitchell again, and couldn't help but smile. It felt so good to say it. "Maryna Sareth *Taylor.*"

A gasp from those present, then a swinging of heads from Maryna to Mitchell and back again. Cameron Davenport caught her breath in astonishment—a quick and sharp intake—and covered her mouth in disbelief.

"Unbelievable," muttered Blaine Richards.

———❦———

Mitchell looked at Maryna, her deep brown eyes gleaming, every inch of her face beaming with the pleasure of announcing that she was in fact Mitchell Taylor's wife. *She's gorgeous,* he thought. *So cute. And so proud to be mine.*

He felt the same sense of pride swell in his own heart, and a wave of gratefulness wash over his body. In a few short days, he had found his life partner.

And he knew beyond any doubt that he had done the right thing.

70

May 28

Dara,

It's not even half over, but this is already one of the happiest days of my life. I'm a bride now. *Mrs. Mitchell Taylor.* You won't believe how it happened. It's almost like a fairy tale.

It all started late last night.

Mitchell snuck out to Sarah Reed's house and told me I had to testify today or lose my case. If I lost the case, I would lose you, too. And I knew I couldn't let that happen. But I also knew that if I testified, the INS agents would be here in court, and they would send me—send us—back to Cambodia.

But still, I had to try.

I told Mitchell that I knew what I had to do, that I just needed the strength to do it, and then—are you ready for this?—he kissed me. Not a normal little kiss on the cheek (I'm going to have to wait longer than I first thought to give you this diary), but an electric kiss on the lips. It was at that moment, for the first time ever really, that I kissed a man who I loved with all my soul and I knew—I just *knew*—that he loved me just as much. Mitchell didn't even have to say anything. From the minute he kissed me, I knew everything would be all right.

I know it sounds sappy, Dara, but what can I say? It's hard to describe; it's beyond words really, and you will only understand when someday it happens to you.

After Mitchell kissed me, we prayed for a long time with Sarah Reed, then Mitchell asked if he could speak to me in private for a moment. And that, Dara, was a moment I'll never forget. If I close my eyes right now I can still see it, as if it is happening again, in all its Technicolor detail, right before my very eyes.

He was standing in front of me, just a few inches away, holding my face gently in his hands. Another kiss, I thought. I hoped. My skin tingled. I began to close my eyes.

"Marry me," he said.

What?!

"Marry me." He said it again. Softly, but with such passion. The words stopped my heart, sent my head into orbit. I had to blink just to make sure it was real.

And Mitchell, wonderful, patient Mitchell, just waited without breath. My heart screamed yes!

But my lips said no. I wanted this so bad, but I knew why he was asking. It was the one sure way to make me a U.S. citizen, to keep me from being deported back to Cambodia. It was not a good reason to promise someone forever.

Before I knew it, I was saying things in Cambodian that Mitchell did not understand. Dara, I was so shocked, I just couldn't even think straight.

"English," said Mitchell. "Tell me yes in English!"

"Mitchell, I know why you're doing this..."

"It's not what you think." He said it with such intensity, Dara. He promised me it wasn't about the case, about citizenship. It was, he said, about being with the only person who had ever made him feel this way.

I just stared down at the floor, Dara. I had to. What else could I do in the face of such unflinching love? But I also had to tell him.

"It's not just that," I said. "You don't know what happened in California." I searched for the right words, feeling so exposed, "What they did to me, what I did for them. How could anybody want me after that?" I choked on the words, and tears filled my eyes.

Then he gently pulled my chin up so I was looking right at him, and he said something that for the rest of my life I will never forget. Ever. He said he didn't care about the Snakeheads or what I did with them. "It's not about the past," he said, "it's about the future. Our future." He said he couldn't bear the thought of not having me with him. "I've only known you for ten days," he said. "I wish we had more time to sort things out, but we don't. I just know this—I can't face tomorrow if you're not with me."

Then he did the most amazing thing, Dara. He put his finger to my lips, and he told me just to listen. He told me again how much he loved me. He made me promise not to tell him yes or no just then. He said that he had already talked to the Reverend Bailey at the Chesapeake Community Church. The Reverend Bailey agreed to meet us the next morning—*today*—at seven o'clock. Mitchell asked me to think and pray about it last night.

"I'll be at the church at seven," he said. "If you show up, we'll spend our lives growing old together. You, me," he reached down and patted my stomach, "and Dara. And if you don't show up..." he kissed me softly, then he said, "I'll understand. But I don't think I'll ever stop loving you."

And a few minutes later, he was gone.

Of course I couldn't sleep. Sarah and I talked for hours. Then I tossed and turned half the night, and prayed the rest. But I never really considered not showing up. The thought of Mitchell, my Mitchell, standing alone at the altar, was more than I could take.

I started getting ready at 5:30.

Sarah went with me to be my maid of honor. Nikki came with Mitchell to take pictures. The Reverend Bailey lectured us for a full thirty minutes. We took our vows, we kissed, and we walked down the aisle while Nikki hummed the traditional wedding march. Mitchell was so full of himself, he picked me up to carry me across the threshold of the church, and then immediately yelped from a pain in his back. Dara, I only weigh a hundred and fifteen pounds! Anyway, he placed me back on the floor rather quickly, I almost tripped, and Nikki about fell over from laughing so hard.

Not exactly the way I had planned my wedding day.

But the groom, that's a different story. He's the man I'd been dreaming about my whole life. My prince.

And his parents—though I've never met them and only talked to them on the phone this morning for the first time—I can already tell they're so sweet. It was physically impossible for them to get here from the corner of southwest Virginia in time for the wedding, but still they sounded so supportive. Mitchell's mom welcomed me to the family, called me the newest of the Taylor women, and said that she knew I must be a wonderful girl if her son chose me.

It sounded like something my own mom would have said.

Okay, I only have a few more minutes before court starts again. More details about the wedding and Mitchell's parents later. That's the fun part. My dream.

But now, let me tell you how my dream became a nightmare.

After our wedding, we went straight to federal court where I testified in this hearing to determine whether Mitchell and I will get to keep you. It all started out great—you should have seen the looks on their faces when I announced that my name was Maryna Sareth *Taylor*. And Mitchell still insists that I did just fine on the witness stand the rest of the morning. But I know better. I just about lost it during the questions by this female attorney named Nora Gunther.

She made a big deal out of the fact that Mitchell and I did not get married until this morning. She called it "interesting" that I had told him no last night and then showed up this morning. She called it a "marriage of convenience" and then hinted that since we had not yet spent the night together, we would probably just have it annulled as soon as the case was over. She made it sound like we had just done it for legal reasons, like it was some kind of strategy to help us in the case—nothing more.

Dara, she made me so mad. I was on the verge of tears throughout my entire time on the witness stand. I just wanted to strike out at her and I really wasn't thinking very clearly. She twisted my words, made it sound like I had promised one thing to Cameron Davenport and now wanted another. She wouldn't let me explain what it was like having a baby growing inside me, how much that changes *everything*.

Then Cameron Davenport took the stand the rest of the morning and sounded so sincere and so sophisticated. I've never felt so stupid in my whole life.

So, it's been quite a day. And it's not over yet. In a few minutes Mitchell, my *husband,* will be asking Cameron Davenport a few questions of his own. That's why he's not with me now—he's getting ready for that.

Oh Dara, I know all this stuff is way beyond you. But I also know that Mitchell, your *daddy,* will want to read this diary soon, to help him understand how my love for you has grown. And when he does—well, truthfully, today's entry is meant not just for you but also for him. It's my own silly way of letting him know how much I love him now...and forever.

Thanks for believing, Mitchell. Thanks for loving me in spite of my past. And thanks for doing everything within your power to make the three of us a family.

I love you, Dara. I love you, Mitchell,

Your doting mom. Your adoring wife.

71

"LOOK AT THESE WOMEN seated in the second row," Mitchell demanded of the witness, "and tell them you don't think this baby growing inside Maryna ought to be given a chance to live."

Mitchell steeled his gaze at Cameron Davenport, then turned and motioned toward Nikki's Army. The women stared intently at Cameron, hard lines creasing their faces.

Cameron did not return their stares but looked instead at Mitchell. "It's not easy raising a special-needs child. These women that you have brought into court... I admire them, though I think it's shameful that you would parade them in here this way."

Mitchell blanched. A few seconds ago, he had actually felt a little sorry for Cameron, knowing what he had to do. Her comment chipped away at what little empathy he had left.

"But they're not me. And the essence of the right to privacy, as I understand our Constitution, is that we have the final say over our own reproductive decisions. In my case, as a single mother in a demanding career, I know there is no way I could do what these brave women are doing—"

"And you don't think Maryna could either?"

"*Mitchell,*" Cameron said it imploringly, like an exasperated old friend. For some reason, this breach of formality, this level of intimacy, aggravated Mitchell. "She's a young, single...well, at least until this morning she was single. Let me rephrase it. When this case started, she was a young, single woman, an illegal immigrant with no clue about how to raise a special-needs child. Ask your friends in the second row if it's easy, if they think this would work. It's *not* easy, Mitchell."

"Said like someone who has actually tried," Mitchell shot back. After his comment, Cameron's eyes flashed briefly, then returned to their detached poise. He could feel the thin emotional bonds that had connected him to this woman snapping one at a time, the walls of an adversary rising in their place. "And things have changed for Maryna now. Haven't they? Are you saying you're still uncomfortable with her ability—with *our* ability to raise this child?"

Cameron let slip a derisive little chuckle. "More so than ever. Her decision—heck, your decision—is not exactly the model of careful family planning. *If* the marriage is real, and not just a sham—and that's a very big *if*—it still has virtually no chance of working." Mitchell couldn't believe Cameron was saying this, judging him so cavalierly. It was his job to get under the witness's skin; instead, just the opposite was happening. "And a failed marriage relationship—a divorce—would only make things even tougher on a Down syndrome child. I mean, how could the child possibly make sense of all that?"

Calm down. Mitchell forced himself to take a deep breath and pause for a beat. He could feel the anger closing in and blurring the lines of his reason. Anger, or at least indignation, would have its place in this case, but…not yet. First, it was time to spring Professor Arnold's little dilemma.

"You write a column for the *Tidewater Times* newspaper, is that right?"

"I do."

"And in that column, you are an unfailing supporter of women's rights. Isn't that true?"

"I'd like to think so."

"You believe those things you write in that column, do you not?"

"Of course I do."

"Then why don't you tell this court how it is consistent with your high view of women's rights to force Maryna to have an abortion—to rip this child out of her womb against her will?"

Nora Gunther sprang to her feet. *Good,* thought Mitchell, *I hit home.* "I object," Gunther complained. "He's badgering the witness."

Ichabod thought for a moment. "Overruled, she may—no, she *must*—answer the question."

"But, Judge—"

"*Sit down,* Ms. Gunther."

With pleasure, Mitchell watched Nora Gunther drop to her chair in disgust.

But Cameron didn't bat an eye. "I believe in a woman's right to choose," said the cool customer on the witness stand, "and will defend that right with every ounce of my strength. Maryna had that right here, and she *chose* to sign a contract that said if there was any significant genetic disorder with this child, any such harm with *my* child, Maryna agreed to terminate the pregnancy. Yes, Mr. Taylor, I certainly believe in Maryna's right to choose. I just want her to follow through on the choice she has already made."

Take that, her look said to Mitchell. It seemed to him that Cameron considered this just a game, a high stakes battle of wits. A battle in which she was plainly holding her own.

But he was not finished. In fact, he had anticipated this answer, so he and Nikki had rehearsed what to do next.

"Stick with her choices," said Mitchell sarcastically. "She should stick by her choices…just like you did? Is that why you're asking this court to overturn the contract *that you signed* that allows either you or your husband to unilaterally donate the frozen embryos to research?"

Cameron began to speak, paused, then stared pensively ahead. "That's different," she said, after a few beats, "and you know it."

"Because?"

"Because of a change in circumstances that my husband did not anticipate. Because I know he wouldn't have signed a will donating these embryos to research if he knew that the embryo implanted in Maryna had Down syndrome." Her tone became more strident.

"Because if he were alive today, he'd be right here with me, fighting so that we could parent a healthy child."

"I see," said Mitchell, hoping that the judge would find the answer as unpersuasive as he did. Then, to the judge, "May I have a moment?"

"Sure."

Mitchell leaned down and whispered to Nikki, who had arrived in court just before lunch. "Are you sure about this?"

She gave him a stern look. *"Do it,"* she whispered.

Mitchell returned to the podium carrying a small see-through plastic sandwich bag.

"Is it your testimony that you should be allowed to have the frozen embryos implanted because it would be your only chance to have a healthy child?"

Tentatively, "Yes."

"And that's because Dr. Avery performed a total hysterectomy due to some problems you were experiencing with severe endometriosis?"

Cameron looked wary. "That's right, we introduced his surgical note as Petitioner's Exhibit 12...or something like that."

"Fine." Mitchell scratched the back of his head and scrunched up his nose in a demonstration of idle curiosity. "Did I see you wearing some Band-Aids on your ankle yesterday?"

This brought a frown from Cameron. She looked at the judge. Ichabod shrugged.

"Yes. I nicked myself shaving."

"May I approach the witness?" asked Mitchell.

Ichabod nodded.

Mitchell walked forward and handed Cameron the plastic bag. It had two used Band-Aids inside. "Are these Band-Aids yours?"

Cameron shot Mitchell an incredulous look. "You're kidding, I hope."

"Nope. My paralegal pulled them out of your trash last night. I just want you to confirm whether they're yours."

If a bomb had exploded under Nora Gunther's seat, she wouldn't have been up any faster. "I don't believe it!" she wailed. "He went through her trash? What kind of sick man—"

"*California v. Greenwood,* Your Honor," Mitchell replied. "When you leave your trash in a collection area, it becomes abandoned property. You lose all reasonable expectation of privacy. One man's trash becomes another man's exhibits."

"That's perverted," responded Gunther.

The fight was on.

For nearly ten minutes, the lawyers argued about the propriety of searching trash for potential exhibits. Gunther staked out the moral high ground, but Mitchell had a Supreme Court case in support. In the end, Ichabod had no choice.

"I don't like it either, Ms. Gunther, but I can't just ignore this case." Ichabod turned to Mitchell. "Proceed, counsel, but watch your step."

He turned to Cameron. "Are they yours?" he asked coolly.

Mitchell thought he saw a quick look of panic in her eyes and a small bead of sweat form just above her lip. He watched her eyes dart—the bag, her lawyer, Mitchell. She handed the bag back to Mitchell and drew a deep breath.

"They look like mine," she said nonchalantly.

Mitchell looked back at Nikki. She nodded.

He turned to face the judge, shoulders straight, chin held high.

"No further questions at this time."

72

"WHAT'S THE BIG DEAL about the Band-Aids?" Ichabod asked as she took off her robe and hung it on the back of her office door. She had invited all the parties and attorneys into her chambers at the conclusion of the day's hearing to discuss settlement. Mitchell knew that the disrobing, so to speak, was a ploy to put the parties at ease.

He stiffened in his seat.

"We'll link it up next week when we call Ms. Moreno to the stand," he said guardedly.

"And keep us all in suspense in the meantime, I suppose," mused Ichabod. She took a seat behind her massive oak desk. Mackenzie, Richards, Cameron, and Gunther had arrived first and claimed the seats immediately in front of Ichabod's desk. Mitchell and Maryna had been delayed a few minutes, so they squeezed in next to the dashing young Oliver Price on a leather couch situated along a side wall. The sun streamed through the open curtains on the tall windows to the side of the couch, hitting Mitchell in the eyes and causing him to squint.

Ichabod sighed and looked around the room. "Monday is Memorial Day. We'll resume Tuesday at nine. Ms. Gunther, how many more witnesses?"

"We rest with Cameron, Your Honor."

"Mr. Mackenzie?"

"Two."

She tilted her head and looked over at Mitchell. "Mr. Taylor? And don't even think I'm going to let you call all those women in the second row."

"Three or four, then."

This brought another Ichabod sigh. "It's been my experience," she said, "that cases like this should be settled out of court. All these witnesses. Plus, if I have to rule"—she paused to glance around the room—"I'm going to make some parties very unhappy. I mean, we're talking about the future of an embryo in the womb, the zygotes in the lab, the validity of the Bioethics Act. Isn't there any way you can agree to some temporary disposition of these issues until we can have a full-blown trial?"

"No way," huffed Nora Gunther, as if it were the dumbest suggestion she had ever heard. "No *possible* way we can settle this mess."

Ichabod pinched her eyebrows in obvious displeasure, glaring at the lawyer. "Ms. Gunther," she said curtly, "would you mind checking something at the window for me?"

Nora gave Ichabod a puzzled look and didn't move.

"The window," Ichabod repeated, as if maybe Gunther simply hadn't heard the first time.

Gunther shrugged her shoulders and slouched over to the tall windows a few feet from the couch. She peered out quickly, then turned back to Ichabod, screwing her face into a look that said she didn't have time for games.

"Is that the sun pouring through that window and causing Mr. Taylor to squint?" asked Ichabod.

Gunther glanced briefly at Mitchell then back at the judge, uncomprehending, as if the judge had just spoken Greek.

"Is that the sun?" repeated Ichabod.

"Of course."

"Thank you. You can return to your seat."

At that moment, the punch line apparently dawned on Gunther. Her eyes narrowed, shooting flames at the judge. She walked back to her seat and plopped down in stony silence.

"I just wanted to make sure you weren't going to argue with every single thing I propose," said Ichabod calmly. "Your affirmation that the sun is indeed shining through that window gives me new hope. Now"—

she paused and swept the room with her gaze—"let me ask again, and this time request that you give it some serious thought. Is there any way this case can settle?"

All the lawyers but Gunther shuffled in their seats and stared at their shoes. Gunther simply stared back, shaking her head.

"How can we settle this case, Judge?" Nora eventually asked. "I mean, Cameron wants, more than anything in the world, a healthy child. Even if GenTech wanted to let these zygotes be implanted in another woman, they couldn't. As you know, the zygotes were created by cloning. Implanting them now would be a violation of the Bioethics Act. So what I'm saying, Judge, is that until you rule on the constitutionality of the Bioethics Act, settlement's impossible."

Another pause, then: "I agree," said Mitchell, although it pained him to agree with Nora. "Nora's right about the Bioethics Act. Plus, there's no way on our own that we can reach an agreement about the baby Maryna's carrying."

"Mr. Mackenzie?"

"Same, Judge. It just can't be settled."

Ichabod waited, studying the faces in the room one more time. "That's what I figured," she said at last, "but it never hurts to ask. Okay, we'll have one more day of testimony on Tuesday. Mr. Mackenzie, you get to take the morning for your witnesses. Mr. Taylor, you get the afternoon. I'll rule Wednesday."

The lawyers all murmured in unison and started to rise.

"Wait," said Richards, who sat unmoving, his chin resting on his hands tented in front of him. "This may be improper protocol… I'm not a lawyer, but can we go off the record here?"

"Settlement discussions are always off the record," replied Ichabod. "What do you have in mind?"

As the others sat back down, Richards laid out a proposal. "Your Honor, GenTech and I have not been fighting Cameron's lawsuit because we think the Bioethics Act is constitutional, or even a good piece of legislation. We're fighting it because our contract with Cameron and Nathan allowed either of them to donate the zygotes for research, and Nathan did that in his will.

"At the same time, I can understand why Cameron would want those zygotes implanted in another woman. Also…" He turned and looked at Maryna. "I can understand why this young lady would want to keep the child growing in her womb. I think there's a win-win here, but it would require the court to first overturn the Bioethics Act."

Ichabod leaned forward, interested. "I'm not sure I'm ready to declare the act unconstitutional. And even if I did, how does that create a win-win?"

"Well," said Richards, leaning back and crossing his legs, "if you declare the act unconstitutional as applied to Cameron because it prohibits her from having a healthy child—you know, invades her right to privacy or however that reasoning goes—then we could actually split the eight remaining frozen zygotes. Four could be used for research, along with the money donated by Dr. Brown; the other four could be implanted in another surrogate mother. There's about a 25 percent chance of the zygotes attaching to the uterine wall, so Cameron would have a strong possibility of being a mother. In exchange, Cameron would have to agree to let Ms. Sareth keep the embryo growing inside her. I mean, it's not perfect, but…"

Ichabod raised her eyebrows in approval. "It's *not* perfect, but I haven't heard a better solution yet."

For the next several minutes, Mackenzie and Gunther weighed in on the settlement proposal. The lawyers all had a chance to confer with their clients.

Gunther announced that she and Cameron would accept the proposal based on one condition. Remember, she said, that two of the cloned zygotes presumably had the same genetic defect as the fetus growing inside Maryna. The other zygotes, because of the unproven nature of blastomere separation in humans, could have defects as well.

Chromosomal testing at this early stage of pre-embryonic development, as Gunther understood it, would destroy the ability to implant the embryo. She looked briefly at Richards, who did not argue.

In light of this, Gunther proposed that four of the zygotes be implanted into a new surrogate mother. If one attached and grew to an embryo that did not test positive for Down syndrome or another defect, the remaining four would be donated to research. If one of the first four did not attach, or if the resulting fetus tested positive for defects, then the remaining four would also be implanted into a surrogate mother.

This brought another round of huddling, after which Win Mackenzie announced that such an agreement might be acceptable to his client, so long as the research money went to GenTech under either scenario.

"Then settlement all depends on whether I'm prepared to hold the Bioethics Act unconstitutional as a violation of the reproductive rights of Ms. Davenport-Brown, is that where we stand?" asked Ichabod.

Maryna slid a little closer to Mitchell, wrapped her fingers in his, and whispered in his ear. "I'm still not sure about this. Can't we get a little time?"

Mitchell gave her his best *Are you crazy?* look, then reluctantly spoke up. "Not so fast, Judge. I'm not sure *we* could agree to it."

Heads swung in his direction, revealing puzzled looks. "You get what you want," said a frustrated Gunther. "How could you object?"

Good question, thought Mitchell. "Because I don't know if we can agree to a settlement that is contingent on the Bioethics Act being overturned. This is all happening so quickly. We just need a little time to process this." Maryna squeezed his hand in appreciation.

"Never satisfied," Gunther said under her breath, loud enough for the others to hear.

"If they're taking the weekend, we'd like to take the weekend as well," announced Mackenzie after whispering to Richards. "I'm not sure if we can agree to make all eight embryos available for implantation, especially after what Dr. Brown said in his will."

In a huff, Gunther stood to leave, her displeasure evident in every movement. "Now you know, Judge, why we haven't settled this case."

—◆—

As soon as Richards got in the car, he dialed her number—his friend at CNN who had hosted their little breakfast with a CEO chat.

"Are we off the record?" he asked.

"Sure. Have you got something for me?"

"The parties are close to settlement." He lowered his tone for effect. "It's complicated, but it would involve an overturning of the Bioethics Act. Remember all those research advances that we talked about?"

"Sure. You guys have a patented way to clone donated eggs and test the clones for chromosomal defects, eliminating any possibility of things like Down syndrome in these test-tube babies—"

"And we've also developed those patented advances in therapeutic cloning," Richards reminded her. "Looks like all those scenarios could be realities by next week. The patents I announced a few days ago will skyrocket in value."

"Can I go with this today, quote you as an inside source?"

"Will you reconsider my dinner invitation?"

The line fell silent as she hesitated. "Just kidding," said Richards with a chuckle. "Of course you can go with it. Just protect my anonymity."

—◆—

The hot news lit a fire under GenTech's stock in after-hours trading. The rumors of settlement, told and retold over the airwaves until they became fact, generated endless debate about potential advances in cloning technology. This in turn fueled even more speculation about the value of GenTech's patents, particularly the ones dealing with therapeutic cloning techniques. The commentators opined that GenTech's process on coaxing a cloned egg cell into reproduction, even without the introduction of a sperm cell, was plainly the most advanced process in the business. This meant that GenTech could clone egg cells and create an endless supply of stem cells for young women, which could be frozen and later coaxed into replacements for any diseased cells in the body. The technology would be particularly useful for those women who already had egg cells cryopreserved at a GenTech clinic.

Buyers responded to this onslaught of commentary by snatching up shares of GenTech, pushing the stock to over $24 per share. And just to make sure they weren't backing the wrong horse in this brave new world, investors also helped themselves to healthy portions of GenTech's main competitors, driving up prices for both RSI and ProGen.

Through it all, Richards sat back in smug satisfaction, watching as the buying frenzy he had caused resulted in personal net gains of more than $11 million.

73

DRIVING HOME FROM COURT WITH MARYNA, Mitchell found himself unable to keep his eyes on the road, unable to keep himself from looking at his wife. *My wife. How strange does that sound? How strange does this feel?*

When they hit the Interstate, he put his arm on the back of the seat—around Maryna—and she slid as close as the stick shift would let her.

"Not exactly the babe-mobile," she said.

He squeezed her shoulder, *God, how I love her,* and leaned over for a kiss. "Worked for you, didn't it?"

He caught her smiling out of the corner of his eye. "Anything to get my citizenship," she teased. He laughed, pushed her playfully away, and watched with satisfaction as she slid back.

They rode in silence for a few minutes, Mitchell switching on the radio—the country stations—and Maryna wincing. Then she turned to him, "What are we going to do for our honeymoon?"

"Do I have to spell it out for you?"

"Mitch-ell!" She punched him playfully, and he grinned to himself. "I meant, are we going out to dinner to celebrate or anything?"

"I know a good Chinese place…"

After ten minutes of driving, unwinding, and stealing kisses, the talk finally turned to the settlement offer. "How can we not do this, Maryna? I mean, it guarantees that we get to keep your baby"—he smiled—"*our* baby. It's why we intervened in the first place."

Maryna responded with silence, looking ahead at the traffic. Then finally, "I know."

"Then why did you say you needed more time? Why do you seem so...saddened by it?"

Another uncomfortable pause. Then Maryna turned toward Mitchell, staring at him with those irresistible eyes. *Mesmerizing eyes,* thought Mitchell.

"Do you remember why I came to you for this case? The very first time?"

Mitchell nodded.

"I saw you on television," Maryna continued, "and you were talking about those cloned zygotes the way I felt about Dara...like they were real people...with a soul. It's what Buddha taught, really. It's what Reverend Bailey said when I went to church with you—'before I formed you in the womb I knew you.'

"I think that applies to all those tiny little pre-embryos created in fertility clinics. Hundreds of thousands of them. And if we allow this cloning ban to be overturned, it might create millions of them. And for what, Mitchell? So that they can be used for scientific experiments?" Maryna caught her breath, slowed down, lowered the volume. "How can we allow that?"

The traffic slowed, and Mitchell removed his hand from behind the seat, downshifting. "But Maryna, there's no guarantee the judge won't strike down the law even if we don't settle. At least this way, we'll—" He suddenly realized he was in lawyer mode, with his own wife. This was no way to start. "Let's not argue about it right now."

"No, Mitchell. I need to know what you're thinking."

"Okay." He took a deep breath and turned down the radio. "I'm thinking that I've only got one client in this case—and that's you. I'm thinking that you and I only have one child involved, and that's Dara. When I represented Cameron, it was my job to focus on those other embryos. But now...now, I've got to focus on my wife and my daughter. You and Dara are my first responsibility.

"And I don't think God wants me to risk sacrificing our child just for the possibility, just for the *potential* to help unknown others who have not even been born yet."

As Mitchell shifted, Maryna put her hand gently on his. "God did," she said softly.

Maryna suddenly had his head swirling. Mitchell chewed on her words for a minute. *Is she right? What about the things that Professor Arnold said—"You're not the judge, Mitchell; just take care of your client, Mitchell, and let God worry about the rest."*

Slowly, a smile crawled across Mitchell's face.

"What's so funny?" Maryna asked.

"Our first fight," said Mitchell. "And we've just barely been married twelve hours."

"Yeah," said Maryna. She grinned now too. "And I'm undefeated."

"Not yet, you're not. I've got someone I want you to meet."

74

MITCHELL AND MARYNA TRACKED DOWN Professor Arnold on Atlantic Boulevard in Virginia Beach, where he was setting up his sound equipment for a night of street preaching. It was one of the things that had earned Arnold legend status at the law school: suave professor during the week, street preacher on Friday nights.

Arnold wore khaki shorts, sandals, and a T-shirt with the sleeves cut off, looking more like one of the boys from the hood than a law school professor. He greeted folks as they passed by with a "s'up," or a silent extended fist touching the fist of a familiar passerby. A few folks gathered around as Arnold busily plugged his karaoke boom box into his Kmart car battery and started hooking up his speakers and mikes.

This was not exactly the quiet scene Mitchell had hoped for—just the three of them and coffee someplace—but Mitchell needed advice *now,* and so, after he introduced Maryna, the two of them followed Arnold around as Mitchell explained their disagreement about the proposed settlement.

"I remembered what you told me when I was thinking about representing Cameron even though I might have to argue that the Bioethics Act was unconstitutional. You told me it was like I had eight little clients—those cloned pre-embryos—on death row and I should only worry about representing them, not where all this might lead. You said I was a lawyer, not a judge."

Professor Arnold tapped on a mike, "Testing, one, two, three. Stick around, people, we're gonna have church in a minute." A few of the curious who had watched Arnold set up now started wandering off. Arnold grabbed the mike and called after a couple of young men: "Was it something I said? Maybe God figured if some of you couldn't find His house on Sunday morning, He'd just go ahead and bring it to you on Friday night."

He turned to Mitchell. "So you just want me to explain to the new Mrs. Mitchell Taylor that whole concept about the lawyer and judge thing, just let her know how right you are—is that it?"

Mitchell shrugged. "I just thought it might help for her to hear your perspective."

Arnold bent over and fiddled with the boom box. Soon a song blared through an attached speaker. "He's an on-time God…oh, yes He is…"

"She's right, Mitchell," Arnold spoke loudly over the blaring music. *Huh?*

Some of the regulars started clapping. Then Arnold apparently spotted somebody he knew. "Hey, Serita," he said into the mike, "c'mon up here, girl, and lead this choir."

She came up, gave him a hug, took the mike, and started swaying. Soon she had several others singing, clapping, and swaying along. Professor Arnold pulled Mitchell and Maryna off to the side. The music blared so loud they had to shout.

"How does that jibe with what you told me earlier?" asked Mitchell. He was confused about the professor's last comment and suddenly felt out of place on Atlantic Avenue in his white shirt and dress slacks. Maryna still had on the dress she had worn to court.

"First," said the professor, "let me congratulate you on your choice of women." He looked Maryna up and down. "How did a fine girl like you get hooked up with a dude who drives a pickup?" Maryna smiled, a little embarrassed.

"Don't let that sophisticated Asian look fool you," said Mitchell, "she's country all the way."

"Yeah, and so is P. Diddy Combs." Then the professor turned serious. "When you're trying the case, Mitchell, you've got to focus only on your client… You're an advocate, perhaps the only thing that stands between your client and some real bad stuff. But when a settlement is thrown on the table, the rules change. A settlement is something you voluntarily do, you *compromise* your case to do it. Now, you're not just fighting for your client against her adversaries in the court system, you're advising your client on the wisdom of a possible settlement. And you'd better consider *all* aspects of it."

Just then a truckload of white southern boys came cruising by, prowling slowly down the street in the flow of traffic. They wore cutoff T-shirts that exposed bulging biceps and barely covered their generous guts. One stood in the bed of the pickup. "Hey, Preacher Boy," he yelled, making an obscene gesture. "Preach this."

Arnold just shook his head, not dignifying them with a response.

"Regulars?" asked Mitchell.

Arnold glanced over his shoulder at Serita and the gathering group, who were also ignoring the rednecks and swaying together like a gospel choir. He turned back to Mitchell. "I thought they were friends of yours," he deadpanned.

"Actually," replied Mitchell, "cousins."

The professor smiled, then turned serious again. Mitchell sensed one of those Socratic questions coming, and the professor did not disappoint.

"Let's say that you're negotiating with one of these terrorist cells of the al Qaeda network for the release of nine American hostages. It's your job, Mitchell, to obtain their safe release. Now, let's say that the terrorists agree to release the hostages as long as you give them the blueprints and security plan for Three Mile Island and every other nuclear facility in the United States. You gonna do that, or are you gonna send in your special forces?" Arnold tilted his head and raised his eyebrows.

Mitchell cracked a small smile, not nearly as large as the one now adorning Maryna's face. "I send in the special ops boys—hostage rescue unit—and I blow them away, probably losing the hostages in the process."

"Of course you do, and you know why—other than your obvious fascination with guns and explosives? Because the cost of compromise is just too high. Not for the hostages, but for millions of others."

Maryna cast a satisfied look in Mitchell's direction.

"Hmm...I see your point."

"Then that's your answer."

The three chatted for a few more minutes while the street crowd grew with a few curiosity seekers. Professor Arnold apparently decided it was time to preach. "The crowd beckons," he said and turned. He hesitated for a moment. "I really pray you get to keep that baby," he said to Maryna. Then to Mitchell, "Did you cancel that amnio like we discussed?"

"Actually, no. I got there a little late. We're supposed to get the results tomorrow. The doctor is coming in on Saturday so we can have the results before Mackenzie starts his case."

"Oh," said the professor, plainly disappointed. "Well, either way, I wish you both the best. And Mitchell, I'm proud of you."

He patted Mitchell on the outside of both arms, then turned to join in the singing.

Mitchell and Maryna stuck around for a few minutes—the professor's form of interactive preaching, questions and answers, actually drew quite a little crowd—then the two honeymooners left and strolled back to their truck, hand in hand.

"I like that guy," said Maryna. And then, after a few more steps in silence, almost under her breath, "Undefeated."

He followed Mitchell and Maryna to Jason's on Rudee Inlet, a jazzy little seafood place with an ocean view and a loyal Friday night crowd of beach lovers. The restaurant was trendy and, in his opinion, probably over-priced. But it was also squeezed tightly onto a prime piece of real estate with limited parking and therefore required the services of a valet.

Perfect.

He watched Mitchell hustle around to open Maryna's door—how sweet, that would last about two days—and then hand the keys to the valet and enter the restaurant with his wife. Two or three minutes later, he pulled up in his own car and asked the valet if he had seen his friends yet—and described Mitchell and Maryna. The valet nodded and said that the couple had just arrived.

Next, he entered the restaurant, hung out for about five minutes at the bar, then headed back outside. He waited for the same valet, explained that Mitchell had left something in his truck—"You know, the black F-150"—and then waited nervously as the valet brought the truck back around.

The man tipped the valet for the hassle and climbed into the driver's side of the truck. He made a show of leaning over and checking the glove compartment, then quickly, efficiently, pulled out the clay and made a quick mold—first one side, then the other—of both keys dangling from the carabiner attached to the ignition key. He was pretty sure which one was the apartment key, but there was no sense taking any chances.

He got out of the truck and smiled at the valet. "They just got married," he explained. "My friend can be forgiven for being a little distracted."

75

Saturday, May 29

NIKKI ROLLED OUT OF BED just before eleven, then called to check on the lab tests. "The blood work's done," said the lab tech. "And the blood was a match."

"Okay. I'll be by about two or so to pick up the report."

"That's fine. And Ms. Moreno?"

His tone of voice caused a lump in Nikki's throat.

"Your hunch was right about that other issue." He hesitated, as if afraid to say anything more over the phone. "I'm sorry, Ms. Moreno."

Nikki thanked him and got off the phone as quickly as possible. She immediately called Mitchell, then took a long hot shower, digesting the possibilities.

After a quick lunch, she headed down to East Granby Street and parked about a block away from Cameron Davenport's house. Using a tiny set of binoculars, she spotted Cameron's car in the driveway and decided to wait it out.

Two hours later, she followed Cameron, at a distance, to the store and back. At 4:30, she followed Cameron to the Harbor Point Athletic Club, a swank gym where Cameron spent about an hour and a half. After following Cameron home, then spending another two hours watching the house, Nikki began to think she was wasting her time.

Stakeouts were just that way, she knew. Hours and hours of inactivity, followed by a brief bathroom break, which was always when the subject would decide to move. It was now nearly 8:30 on a Saturday night—a *summer holiday weekend* Saturday night—and the party scene would be swinging into high gear in just a couple hours. Without Nikki.

That was hard to imagine and harder still to swallow.

Maybe she would just give it another hour. Things didn't *really* get swinging 'til ten or eleven anyway.

At just about that moment, somewhere between Nikki's *should I go or should I stay* ponderings, Cameron emerged from her Victorian home looking like a woman on a mission. For men. Nikki adjusted the binoculars, caught Cameron in just the right combination of twilight and streetlight, and immediately confirmed her suspicions. Cameron wore a pair of short shorts and a skin-tight, low-cut spaghetti-strap top with the outline of her bra clearly visible. Her hair was clipped back, and it looked like her makeup was carefully applied—just the right amount of natural hues—to suggest a casual look. Nikki, no slouch in the makeup department, knew that this subtle look required as much effort as a more formal presentation. Cameron had dressed to impress.

Juiced again, Nikki followed her from the streets of Norfolk to the Virginia Beach expressway to the back roads of Pungo and eventually to the beach community of Sandbridge. At least twice on the way, Nikki thought for sure that she had lost Cameron, only to reestablish sight at the next red light or intersection. She didn't think Cameron had noticed the Sebring following her, but then again, you could never be sure.

At about 9:15, Cameron pulled into the driveway of a Sandbridge beach house, one of those cedar-shingled buildings on stilts just a block or two from the Atlantic. Like most of the houses in this beach resort area, the ground "floor" was nothing more than a storage shed and driveway under the main house. The second floor generally contained the sleeping quarters, and the top floor consisted of the living room, kitchen, and dining area, with tons of windows and lots of decking.

Nikki pulled over a half-block or so from the house, until she was sure that Cameron had sufficient time to get out of her car and climb the stairs to the living area. A few more minutes of waiting, then Nikki drove slowly by. The second and third floors were both well lit. There was one car besides Cameron's in the driveway. A gray BMW.

Nikki called in the address of the house to a friend who worked for an investigative firm that had software containing the city directory for all Virginia cities. Whether the residents had a listed phone number or not, they were all catalogued in this directory: names, addresses, and phone numbers. Just to be safe, Nikki also called a state trooper friend who could run the license plates.

A few minutes later the first friend called back, and Nikki promised she would return the favor someday. Without waiting for her second phone call, Nikki immediately dialed Mitchell's home number and was only half surprised when nobody answered.

"Honeymooners," she murmured. Then she remembered what Mitchell had told her. He had quit answering his home phone during the preliminary hearing. Too many prank calls. And those had started even before Maryna announced in open court that she and Mitchell had married. No telling how many calls he was getting now.

She tried his cell phone. This time, he picked up on the second ring.

Nikki made him write down directions to the house she was watching. "Get out here right away," she demanded, suddenly realizing how pushy she sounded. After all, the guy had only been married one day. "I mean, *please* get out here right away."

"What's the big emergency?"

"Looks like Cameron's having a little rendezvous with Dr. Richards at a rental place he runs in Sandbridge, and I'd like for us to be the first to greet her after she leaves."

❧

Maryna double-checked the deadbolt and the lock on the door handle, then retreated to the bedroom. She climbed up on the queen-sized bed, found the remote, and flicked on the television. Background noise. Anything to keep her mind off the Snakeheads.

Although they were still out there, she knew she couldn't live her life in fear. She had a new faith and a new husband. She felt totally safe when Mitchell was around. Maybe the Snakeheads would figure out that she would not come back, under any circumstances, and eventually leave her alone. Maybe the fact that she was now in the national spotlight would scare them off for a while. Wishful thinking, she knew.

She heard a noise, at least she thought she did, out in the living room. She got up slowly, walked tentatively down the hallway and checked around. She glanced out through the peephole and saw nothing. She checked every closet, turned on every light in the house, and returned to the bedroom. This time, she turned the television off and listened.

I can't live like this.

Determined to do something normal, something to calm her fears, she grabbed Mitchell's Bible and her diary. She had already learned from Sarah that the book of Psalms had some great words for frightened hearts. But first, she wanted to let Dara know how wonderful married life was.

May 29

Little Dara,

What a great day! I've got some really big news to tell you about. But first, let me tell you about your daddy.

I've already talked to you about your genetic father, Dr. Nathan Brown. He was an emergency room doctor. A very smart man and very nice man who spent his whole life helping others and then got a disease for which there is no cure. I'm sure he would have been a great dad for you and would have loved you very much. Unfortunately, Dara, you'll never have the chance to meet him. The disease took his life several weeks ago. He died without the opportunity to ever tell you or show you how much he loved you.

But God knew all this would happen, and He sent you another daddy. And Dara, you are one lucky girl. Actually, Sarah Reed tells me we're not lucky, we're blessed. And you, blessed one, will have something I always wanted, someone to call Da—

She saw a blur at the door and dropped her pen. She sucked in a sharp breath, tried to scream but couldn't, tried to scramble off the bed, but he was on her *so fast*. In a rush, he had her, the black glove stifling her renewed effort to scream. Then he slapped her hard across the face, bouncing her head off the headboard. He clamped one hand over her mouth and straddled her, up on his knees, towering over her, the same hooded figure who had invaded her apartment—she could smell the same putrid mix of cologne and sweat—his gun pointed at her forehead.

He smiled wickedly, the lips and teeth mocking her through the small slit in the ski mask. She trembled beneath him.

With his free hand, he grabbed his ski mask and pulled it off.

"Hello, Maryna," he said. "How's Dara?"

76

CAMERON SIGNED BOTH COPIES of the document, then lifted the narrow glass with the long stem in a toast.

"To sheer brilliance," said Blaine Richards. She watched him over the top of her glass as she pretended to sip the dark, full-bodied Merlot. His eyes never left hers.

As always at his beach house, the coverless picture windows surrounding the third floor made her feel like she was sitting in a fishbowl. Although there was a fair distance between houses, and the neighbors kept to themselves, still...

She placed the glass back on the coffee table that separated them, leaned back, and crossed her legs. She could read lust in his eyes, the lust she had used to her advantage on prior occasions. It kept him off-balance and gave her the edge. She needed him passionate, muddleheaded. But she would not let him touch. Tonight, she wanted no part of him.

"What price?" he asked.

"ProGen at fifty-six, RSI at fifty-two, and GenTech at twenty-three and a half." She smiled. "GenTech almost hit twenty-four—but I wasn't that patient."

"Never your strong suit." Richards gazed at her for a moment with fire in his eyes. The look, designed to entice, revolted her. "You're sure the transactions can't be traced."

Another sip of wine, a little more dangling of the legs. "I'm sure. All those dummy corporations you set up—I can barely keep track of them myself. Go ahead and check the Belize accounts, if you don't believe me. It's all there."

"You touch those buttons and you're a dead woman," Mitchell said to Nikki as she reached toward the radio. She had just left her Sebring to join Mitchell in his truck. He grabbed her hand. "It's taken me two days to get things right since the last time you drove my truck."

"So one-dimensional." She smiled and pulled her hand back. "I'll bet you don't even know that your wife prefers classical."

Mitchell gave her a sideways look. "Classical?"

His cell phone rang. The display showed his home number.

"Hey, babe."

Maryna hesitated, and even in the split second before she spoke, he could sense something was wrong. "Uh, Mitchell, I need you to come home right away… I've got…um, I'm not feeling good at all… *Please*."

He heard the distress in her voice; knew it must be serious. He felt a rising tide of panic, of helplessness. "Do you need me to call 911?"

"No, Mitchell, not yet. I just need you to come—"

"Is it the baby?"

"Please, Mitchell, just hurry."

Cameron's assurance that the money was tucked safely away in an off-shore account that required both of their signatures seemed to relax Blaine Richards a little. He leaned back, throwing an arm up over the couch. "I never liked to mix business and pleasure." He tried sounding casual. "But now that the business is done…" He gave her that look again. He was almost too predictable, too easy.

She placed her glass on the table and stood. He came to her—you always make them move—and placed his hands on her hips.

"One more piece of business first," she said coolly. "Lars Avery. Why?"

Richards dropped his hands from her sides, his face changing instantly from seduction to suspicion. Distrust and contempt flashed in his eyes. "You're wired."

She tensed, then trembled a little from this unexpected outburst. *Where did that come from?* She shook her head quickly. She needed to regain control. She tried to force a smile, but Richards' face went even more taut. He grabbed her face in the vise of his strong right hand, squeezing against her cheeks.

"Don't move," he whispered.

He lowered his hand and made a show of patting her down, every inch of her body—*where would I hide anything?*—and then returned his hands to her face. "Avery lost his stomach for this," Richards whispered. "He had to go. Your father was nibbling around the edges." Then he slowly leaned forward and started kissing her forehead, her face, her cheeks, her lips. "Enough business."

She wanted to vomit. But she was scared, and she knew that she had somehow sent him over the edge with her last comment. He became more aggressive, but she gave him nothing in return.

Abruptly, he stepped back, tilted his head slightly as if trying to understand this latest insult, then slapped her hard across the face. "Get out!" he hissed.

She recoiled from the sting and tasted the blood inside her mouth, her cheek bubbling with pain. With trembling hands, she reached down and picked up the document. *How did the tables turn so quickly?* She would leave, but not like this, not while she was shaking like a child. This man was more volatile, more *deranged,* than even she had appreciated. But she could not let him intimidate her. They were equals. He would learn.

She stood straight, resisted the urge to strike back, and returned his penetrating stare. "If you want your money," she warned, "you leave my father out of it."

Richards just glared at her, not saying a word. She let him stare for five or ten seconds, matched him eye-to-eye with a glare of her own, then stalked out.

She slammed the door behind her as she stepped out onto the deck, then let out a deep breath she didn't realize she had been holding. She ran her tongue along the inside of her cheek, wincing when she touched the spot that Richards' slap had ripped open.

She spat a mixture of saliva and blood on the wood deck and headed for the steps.

⎯ ❧ ⎯

When Cameron came out of the house, the man next door breathed an incredible sigh of relief. Through his binoculars, he had seen the slap and, as quickly as possible, started down his own stairs to come to her aid. He had made it as far as his driveway when he saw Cameron emerge onto the deck. He watched from the shadows as she walked down the stairs, climbed into her car, and drove away.

77

NIKKI SAW CAMERON PULL AWAY from Richards' beach house and immediately changed her plans. Following Cameron until she was a safe distance from Richards' house and then confronting her might not be the best move. What if Cameron denied that Richards was even at the beach house? What if Cameron said that Richards was there with his attorney or any number of third-party witnesses who might later lie for her?

No, thought Nikki, *there's only one way to really nail this down.* She put the Sebring in gear and pulled into Richards' driveway. She could confront Cameron later. First, she would have to confirm that Richards was actually at this house at this time and that he was alone. And while she was at it, she would pose him a few questions as well.

She walked boldly up the outdoor steps, all the way to the third-floor deck, and knocked loudly. After a moment, Richards answered the door, looking grim. He wore brown shorts, a blue golf shirt, and Birkenstocks.

He stared at her, unspeaking, and in that moment Nikki realized that she didn't have the foggiest idea what to say—how to get this conversation started. "How's Cameron Davenport doing?" she blurted out.

Richards did not blink. "Fine."

This led to another uncomfortable silence. *What the heck, there's no easy way.* Nikki toughened her look, hardened her voice.

"You're involved with her, Richards. I just saw her leave. You're pretending to be her adversary, but in fact you're working in collusion to defraud my client and the entire court system." She paused and leaned an arm against the doorpost to show him how casual she was. No fear. "How am I doing so far?"

The small smirk she saw curling on his lips infuriated her.

"Smile all you want, Richards, but these are felonies. And you'll do time."

Now the smirk had actually become a smile—broad and sure. "Is that what you think?"

"It's not what I *think*—it's what I know. What I saw."

"Sounds like I've got some explaining to do," he smiled some more and stood aside. "Cup of coffee?"

Against her better judgment but fueled by the curiosity of what she might find—something unintentionally left lying around perhaps—Nikki stepped inside. She found her way to a small kitchen table with a beautiful wooden top—alternating strips of light wood and dark. She took a seat while Richards silently went about the business of fixing coffee. She had no desire to initiate any small talk with this man and couldn't think of a thing to say even if she had wanted to. She watched as he messed with the coffee, then grabbed something from the counter and turned back to the table with a cutting board and a pineapple.

"You like pineapple?" he asked.

"I'm not in the mood."

"No problem."

He placed the cutting board and pineapple in the middle of the table. He then walked over to the family room and returned with a typed document. He flopped it down in front of Nikki, next to the pineapple she had tried to refuse.

"You need to join one of those conspiracy clubs," he said confidently. "No telling what you could do with the assassination of JFK."

As Nikki picked up the document and started glancing through it, Richards turned and walked a few steps back to the counter. *Darn it.* She felt stupid. And confused.

She read quickly through the terms of the "Release and Settlement Agreement." The Bioethics Act would be declared unconstitutional. Cameron would get custody of the four zygotes for implantation in a surrogate mother. If the first procedure didn't work, she would get the remaining four zygotes to try again. GenTech would get the money bequeathed to it by Dr. Nathan Brown in his will. Maryna would get custody of the embryo developing inside her. The document was signed by Blaine Richards, as CEO of GenTech, and by Cameron Davenport-Brown. There was a blank signature line for Judge Baker-Kline and one for Maryna.

Richards returned to the table, a large, black-handled cutting knife gleaming in his right hand. The blade had to be at least seven inches long with a sharp serrated edge. *For pineapple?*

"I figured if just Cameron and I could meet, keep the lawyers out of it—especially Gunther—we could reach a deal."

"The same deal you rejected yesterday?"

Richards leaned over the table, palms of his hands on the table, the knife under his right hand. "Yesterday, I wanted to keep the second set of zygotes. Remember?" He blew out a hot breath smelling of wine. "Today, I had a change of heart. Now the only small hitch is whether your client will agree to this." He stood back up straight and focused on the pineapple. "And why not? She gets everything she's after."

He grabbed the pineapple with his left hand, flexed his right forearm—bringing the veins to the surface—and sliced easily through the pineapple, decapitating the stem. He turned the pineapple quickly and effortlessly lengthwise, a few more flashes of the knife—the quick and skillful strokes of a former surgeon—and the pineapple was cut in quarters. With practiced ease, he cut out the core, sliced off the skin, and cut the pineapple into bite-sized squares.

It might have been the look in his eyes, the skill of his cuts, or the strength of his hands, but whatever it was hit Nikki like a hard slap as she watched the dissection. Maryna's scar! The surgical cut from collarbone to breastplate. A surgeon's straight line and a surgeon's carefully calibrated depth—deep enough to bleed, shallow enough to heal.

The blood rushed to Nikki's head, the walls started closing in. She pushed her chair back just a little, got her bearings. *My back to the kitchen counters, Richards between me and the door, no other knives within easy reach.*

"It was you, wasn't it—Maryna's cut?" She braced her hands against the table, ready to jump back and dive right, anxiously gauging the reaction on his face.

In a flash he switched his grip from underhand to overhand, brought the knife up, the blade reflecting the light. Nikki gasped and pushed back as the blade came flying down.

78

IT WAS A VERITABLE PARADE of women into the beach house tonight. First Cameron. Now Nikki. But this time Richards had a knife, and Nikki obviously had no idea what she was getting into.

He placed his binoculars on the table, took another quick swig of the rum and coke, and speed dialed the number on his cell phone. "Same drill as before," he mumbled. "Ten minutes. This time, it's Nikki Moreno." He ignored the excited chattering in response and hung up the phone.

He shook his head in disbelief and headed next door for the second time that evening.

Whack!

The point of the knife stuck straight in the cutting board, the knife now standing on end. Richards let go of the knife, reared back his head, and laughed.

"What an imagination," he sneered, popping a piece of pineapple in his mouth. "Sure you don't want any?"

Nikki caught her breath, unable to speak.

He leaned forward again, and seemed to relish towering over Nikki. "I'll tell you the truth," he whispered. "I wasn't on the grassy knoll."

He sneered, then turned to get the coffee. When Richards had his back turned, Nikki stood quietly, yanking the knife out of the cutting board. Richards turned slowly around to face her, a cup of coffee in each hand.

This time, she was standing. And this time, she had the knife.

"I thought you didn't like pineapple," he chuckled, keeping his distance. Nikki walked slowly out from behind the table, the knife held low at her side. Richards turned his head a fraction to the left and gave her a curious look. He put the coffee cups back on the counter.

"I want answers," she demanded and took a menacing step toward him.

He kept the tone light. "I have no idea what you're talking about." She looked deep into the eyes—no trace of fear.

She had no idea what to do next and certainly had no intention of attacking the man in his own kitchen. He couldn't be intimidated, that much was obvious. But she wasn't about to let go of the knife either.

She rotated back to the table, cut one of the pieces in half, and pinched it in her mouth. "I like mine cut smaller."

Richards grinned and picked up the coffee again. Just then, Nikki heard a loud knock on the door. Relieved beyond measure, she placed the knife gingerly on the table. "I'll get it," she said, and practically sprinted toward the door.

She opened it and stood face-to-face with the Rock—crutches, plastic leg cast, and all. "You okay?" he asked.

"Sure," she said, totally confused.

The Rock looked over Nikki's shoulder and scowled at Richards. "I've called a friend of mine," he warned, "and told her to call 911 and send the police to this address if she didn't hear back from me in ten minutes." The Rock stopped, pleased with himself.

Richards smiled politely and shook his head in bewilderment. "You and Nikki here ought to get together," he said. "Lee Harvey Oswald could've used you two."

❧

As the Rock hobbled down the driveway, Nikki at his side, he handed her his cell phone and asked her to call Sandra. No sense sending out the cops for nothing.

"How'd you know I was in there?" Nikki asked.

The Rock nodded to the place next door. "I rent that place."

"Quite a coincidence."

"When I did the asset search on Richards, I found out about his second house at the beach. That's when I discovered the…uh…" The Rock pulled his crutches to a halt, thinking. "Let's just say I had a suspicion that maybe Cameron was involved with Richards somehow…can't say how. Well, I decided to do what any red-blooded American father would do—rent the place next door and spy on 'em."

He started hobbling along again, still a little out of breath. "You were just a bonus, Nikki, but I probably saved your life." He was breathing hard, and she could smell the rum on his breath as it mixed with the humid saltwater air.

"You probably did, Rock. You probably did."

79

MITCHELL UNLOCKED THE APARTMENT DOOR and burst through it, sensing immediately that something was wrong. He had tried to call Maryna at least a dozen times on the way home, but the line rang busy. He had worried about the Snakeheads, then banished those thoughts. Call the police? An overreaction, he decided.

But now, in the stillness of the living room, he sensed real danger. "Maryna!" No answer. He started down the hallway, half walking, half running. He needed to get his hands on his hunting rifle—a Remington 700, in the bedroom closet. "Hey, babe, you here?"

He hit the bedroom doorway and froze.

The sight of Maryna, held hostage and sobbing uncontrollably, paralyzed him. Her ankles had been duct-taped together with what looked like several layers of the wide durable tape. Her wrists, similarly bound, were wrenched behind her back. Worse yet, her captor had wrapped layers of duct tape across Maryna's mouth and around the back of her head—outside of her hair, pulling the tape so tight that it bit into the corners of her mouth and distorted her face.

The man stood behind her, with his left arm wrapped over Maryna's shoulder and across her chest. In his right hand, he pointed a gun at her temple. A sleek black handgun, a five-inch barrel—*probably a Smith & Wesson*, thought Mitchell—*with a silencer.*

Mitchell forced himself to focus quickly, assessing everything with a quick glance. This was no time to freak. Maryna's life—his own life—depended on quick thinking. Clear thinking. His fear quickly gave way to anger, an emotion harder for Mitchell to control. He saw red—hated this man who threatened his wife. Took a step toward them. Two.

"Far enough," said the madman.

Mitchell lifted his hands, palms open. No threat here. He took another step. *God, help me kill this man!* He took another step and watched the man begin to drag Maryna along the other wall. His wife's eyes, huge with fear, tried to tell him something. *Focus!* He demanded of himself. *What does this man want?*

"That's close enough!" the man barked. Mitchell stopped dead; it hit him so suddenly. That face! A flashback to court. Win Mackenzie's little poster. The face was thinner and angrier, but unmistakably the same.

"What do you want from us, Nathan?" asked Mitchell as calmly as he possibly could. He started moving again, tiny steps, feeling that if he could just keep moving, circling even, narrowing the distance, he could eventually make a move.

"I want you to watch your wife die. I want to see the look in your eyes before *you* die." Nathan Brown paused, breathing heavily. "Cameron and I had it all—the perfect little American dream couple— until some jerk in the ER took it away, left me an outcast, a leper, a sinner in the eyes of folks like you." He wrenched Maryna tighter. Her body shuddered.

Mitchell instinctively reached out a hand, he was still too far away, fifteen feet maybe.

"Stop!" yelled Brown, swinging the gun in Mitchell's direction. Mitchell recoiled but noted the reaction. *If I could just get a little closer.*

Brown turned the gun on Maryna again. "One more step, *one more!*" he yelled—then lowered his voice to an even more frightening level—"and she buys it." The gun started trembling, and Mitchell knew he meant it.

"What's all that talk about the emergency room got to do with us?" asked Mitchell. *Keep him talking. It's our only chance.*

The eyes scared Mitchell the most. They were devoid of emotion. A man with nothing to lose. "Cameron and I lost it all, then we began to rebuild," Brown said, almost in a moan. "We figured out a way to raise the money for AIDS research, to fund the best lab in the country, even to free up stem cell research on thousands of frozen embryos—medical advances that can save my life—and who would be hurt?" His voice shook with rage. "Who would be hurt? And then you…and this witch…" He pushed the gun harder against Maryna's temple, the barrel marking her flesh.

Mitchell began shaking his head. He needed to speak calmly, matter-of-factly. The tone would matter more than what he said. *What causes a man to lose control? How do you reason with a psychotic?*

"It was never that way, Nathan. Maryna and I didn't spoil anything. It was never that way."

"Shut up." This time Brown sounded fatigued, not angry. Afraid, perhaps, to hear the truth.

"Cameron doesn't care about you, about finding a cure for you." Mitchell gauged the doctor's eyes; saw a glint of resignation. He prayed he was saying the right thing. "She's already sleeping with Blaine Richards. You two were history long before us."

Mitchell expected another outburst, prepared to lunge, but feared he was still too far away.

"You will go to your grave with lies on your lips—"

"I can prove it. I saw her tonight. Nikki Moreno was with me." The words came pouring out, Mitchell couldn't leave time for a response. "She saw her too. I'll call her, ask her yourself…" As he talked, Mitchell reached gingerly for his cell phone, with two fingers, quickly unclipping it from his belt, and pushed the number two with one quick motion.

"Drop it, you idiot," ordered Brown.

Mitchell held it for another second, still pushing the number two, Nikki's speed dial, then dropped the phone gently to the floor. He watched it bounce, face up, and prayed that she would answer.

◆◆◆

"I've got to go," Nikki said to the Rock. She had nursed one cup of coffee and forced the Rock to drink two. They had plotted and schemed the demise of Blaine Richards, but none of the plans really made much sense. And by now Nikki had concluded that none of the plans they concocted at this time of night, with the Rock already three sheets to the wind, ever would make much sense. Richards certainly covered his tracks. And honestly, Nikki felt lucky just to be alive.

She would worry about bringing down Blaine Richards in the morning, but now she was tired. She was never too tired to party until two or three in the morning. But conversations with the Rock were another matter. She thanked the Rock again and prepared to leave the beach house. She wondered what in the world had happened to Maryna. She would call Mitchell and find out as soon as she got into the car, where she had left her cell phone.

"It just hit me," declared the Rock. "One more cup of coffee. Please. This one will really work."

Nikki sighed. The night was already shot. "All right. One more cup." She thought one more time about calling Mitchell but realized she didn't have his cell phone number memorized. Who needs to memorize numbers when you can just program them into your phone?

～～

"Put the gun down now," pleaded Mitchell, still at fifteen feet, "and we'll help you out with the commonwealth's attorney. Think this through. You can't just kill us in cold blood. If you cooperate on Blaine Richards and Cameron—"

"The Snakeheads," interrupted Brown. "It's not me, it's the Snakeheads. It'll be the first thing they consider. I'm dead, remember? Case closed. Cameron and I take off for the Bahamas. Richards works on a cure."

Maryna's eyes, wet with tears, caught Mitchell's. She rolled them toward the nightstand, and nodded ever so slightly in that direction.

"You don't get it, do you?" Mitchell argued. "Cameron learned this whole scheme from her dad. You've got the fraud-on-the-court part down cold. But you've forgotten that in the end, Cameron takes off with the other man—the man she sued."

"Enough talking. Your wife dies first."

"Wait! One more thing!"

Brown locked his eyes on Mitchell, and Mitchell sensed this was his last chance. "Your baby. Cameron's baby. She's all right. A healthy little baby girl. The amnio came back this morning. Look, on the night-stand…" Mitchell pointed, then saw Brown start circling back in that direction with Maryna. "The test results. We just got them back today."

As Brown moved, Mitchell moved. Slowly, circling, watching the man's eyes. Ten feet. "Did Cameron tell you about that?" Mitchell asked, his voice rising. "Did she tell you that she paid Avery to say otherwise, to kill your own child with the amnio test? Your own healthy child…"

Suddenly, Mitchell saw it, that slight flinch just before an inexperienced shooter pulls the trigger. A quick blinking of the eyes.

"No!"

Mitchell braced and dove, his body stretched in a desperate flying tackle, his right hand aiming for the barrel of the gun, his shoulder hurtling toward Brown's head. But at the last possible second, just as Brown flinched and Mitchell dove, Brown also swung the gun and pulled the trigger—one smooth, fatal split-second decision that sealed the fate of three innocent lives.

To the naked eye, the time between when the bullet left the barrel of the gun and when Mitchell smashed his body into Brown would seem like no time at all. But in the slow motion calculus that determines life and death, those milliseconds were more than enough for the bullet to find its mark and explode through flesh and bone.

MARYNA FLINCHED, TWISTED IN ANGUISH, then fell to the floor. "God, no!" her cries were muffled by the duct tape. "Mitchell! Mitchell!" The name became more stifled sobs.

She expected pain but felt none. Then she saw him, crawling toward her, his face and chest covered in blood. *Thank God, he's still alive.*

She squirmed toward him, convulsing, her eyes flooded with tears. She felt his arms engulf her. She buried her head in his chest, the sobs coming harder. He fumbled with the tape, couldn't loosen it. She felt dizzy and nauseated, the horror of the last few seconds replaying over and over. Mitchell's hands shook as he worked unsuccessfully on the tape, murmuring something. She felt his heart galloping, and she knew how desperately he needed her.

It couldn't end like this.

How did he survive? Point blank range!

The thought of his face, the blood, more horror searing her mind, like someone running a broken projector over and over. It made her so sick. She started heaving.

"Calm down, calm down," murmured Mitchell.

She tried, but she couldn't. She couldn't swallow, couldn't breathe, the vomit stuck in her mouth, the panic engulfing her mind. Then finally, she felt the tape coming off, pulling at her hair. She emptied her mouth, lifted her head slightly from his chest, free at last to speak, but the room spun and the blackness started creeping in. *He needs me!* she thought. But she couldn't stop the advancing blackness, every system shutting down, collapsing. She fought desperately against it. She closed her eyes.

He needs me…

Sunday, May 30

MAYBE THE MORENO WOMAN *came to her senses last night*, thought Blaine Richards as he rode the elevator to the eighteenth floor of the GenTech building. She had called early this morning—what time was that? eight o'clock?—and asked for a settlement conference to wrap this thing up. They had decided on ten o'clock. And Blaine had insisted on doing it at his place.

There would be a certain irony, he thought, to wrapping this case up in the same conference room where Dr. Lars Avery had been catapulted through the window less than forty-eight hours ago. Blaine had to hand it to GenTech's facilities manager; he didn't waste any time getting the glass fixed and the room back in order.

It worried Blaine just a little that he had not been able to reach Cameron this morning. Probably just a continuation of her little snit from last night. But everything else was firmly in place. His stock options had done nicely. A few more days and he could cash out just like Cameron had done. Any sooner, and they would accuse him of insider trading.

Win Mackenzie arrived first. Mackenzie looked like the preppy he was—dressed for a day at the country club. White microfiber slacks—pressed, creased, and screaming of money. A beautiful maroon golf shirt with a small but expensive-looking emblem advertising Win's country club membership just above the left pocket.

Richards greeted him at the elevator, handed him the settlement document that he had negotiated with Cameron last night, watched

Mackenzie frown at the notion that Blaine had done this without his lawyer, and then explained that this morning they would apparently be getting the signature of Maryna so they could close the deal.

"She'll probably ask for some additional money for the kid," explained Blaine. "Whatever it is, we'll pay it. Don't act happy about it—but I want this case settled this morning."

Their strategy settled by fiat, the two men went into the conference room, poured themselves some coffee, and waited for Maryna and her legal team. Nearly thirteen minutes later—Richards hated it when others made him wait—he got a call from the security guard announcing that Mitchell Taylor, Nikki Moreno, and Billy Davenport had arrived in the lobby below.

Blaine instructed the guard to send them up, but immediately smelled a rat. "Where's Maryna? How come they didn't bring Maryna?" he asked Mackenzie.

"I don't know."

"And what the heck is Billy Davenport doing here?"

As he walked into the conference room and shook hands with Mackenzie and Richards, Mitchell couldn't believe how calm he felt. He guessed he had just been through so much in the last few days that even the extraordinary no longer unnerved him. And this little "settlement conference" would certainly be extraordinary.

He found himself wondering how much Win Mackenzie knew. Was the lawyer in on this, or was it all just Cameron and Richards? And how much did Richards know about the feigned death of Nathan Brown? Mitchell would soon find out. He placed his Dictaphone on the table and turned it on. "You don't mind if we record this?"

Richards looked at Mackenzie who shrugged. "Probably unnecessary," said Win, "but as long as we get a copy of the tape…"

"Sure."

"Where's your client?" asked Richards.

Mitchell stared him down. This would be Mitchell's first chance to gauge a reaction. "At the hospital, recovering from last night. She went into shock."

Richards did not blink at this news, didn't show even a flicker of recognition. Either he didn't know yet—the police had worked hard to keep this from getting out—or he was very good.

"Dr. Nathan Brown," Mitchell slid forward, leaning on the table, "you know, the deceased doctor, showed up at my apartment last night and took Maryna hostage. He threatened to kill us both, and at the last possible second turned the gun on himself. Maryna was standing right next to him, gagged and hogtied."

Mackenzie's eyes went wide; his mouth fell open. Richards stared in disbelief. "Did you say Nathan Brown?"

"Yeah."

A flabbergasted Richards looked at Mackenzie, "Did you hear that?"

Mackenzie, apparently too stunned to say much, just nodded his head.

Then Mitchell saw it, Richards' tongue moving slowly around the inside of suddenly parched lips. He took a sip of coffee, shaking his head in utter disbelief.

A showman to the end, thought Mitchell.

"That changes everything," sputtered Richards. "This whole case is a...a fraud. I mean...how can this case even..."

Mitchell didn't give the doctor the satisfaction of a reaction. He didn't want Richards to know how well his little act was playing, didn't want the doctor to have time to think—just react.

"Know why he killed himself, doctor?"

Richards grunted his exasperation. "How would I?"

"Because we convinced him that Cameron was not being loyal to him—that you and Cameron were having an affair and using him to get rich. That he was utterly expendable."

Richards leaned back, exasperation turning to anger. "You've been hanging out with these other two fools for too long. That's nonsense. This conference is over."

Richards stood to leave, Mackenzie rising with him. Mitchell just sat there, calling the man's bluff. Richards blew out a deep breath, then looked at Mitchell with patience strained to the breaking point. "What are you suggesting?"

"Sit down, and I'll show you."

They hesitated for five seconds…ten, then Richards and Mackenzie sat back down and looked warily at Mitchell. Richards leaned forward and flicked the cassette recorder off. "If you're going to engage in these flights of fancy, then there's no point in recording this conversation just so you can play 'gotcha' later," he said. Then, looking at Mitchell, "Now, what are you suggesting?"

This is incredible. This man wants to cut a deal. He thinks that he can buy his way out of this one. "I'm suggesting you hear our evidence before you go spouting off or jumping to any more conclusions. Once you consider our evidence, we can talk settlement."

"Exhibit A," piped in Nikki without any further prompting, "is Cameron's trash. If this case had gone forward on Tuesday, I would have testified about everything I found—including used feminine hygiene products. The DNA tests from those products came back yesterday morning. They're a match to the DNA taken from the bloody Band-Aids that Cameron admitted were hers."

"Which proves what?"

"That Cameron never had a hysterectomy. That this whole lawsuit is a fraud."

Richards snorted his disapproval. "I could have told you that when junior here announced that Dr. Brown was still alive."

Nikki smiled a closelipped smile. "You done with your little running commentary? Because there's more."

Richards did not respond.

"Exhibit B," said Nikki, reaching into her pocket, "is this recording made from my cell phone messages. In the middle of the confrontation with Dr. Brown last night, Mitchell managed to call my cell phone number. I didn't answer, so the entire conversation between Mitchell and Brown, the shot, everything, is contained on my voicemail." Nikki placed the tape in the middle of the table.

"The rantings of a madman," suggested Richards. "I didn't even know he was alive."

The denials were still strong, but Mitchell noticed a little less certainty now in the voice. Richards' tongue would make a round after every exhibit. And a bead or two of sweat formed slowly on Win Mackenzie's forehead.

82

NOW IT WAS THE ROCK'S TURN to pile on. "It's over, Dr. Richards. Confronted with this evidence, Cameron has decided to cooperate with the police. I'm representing her, and we cut our deal last night. She told them everything, your little GenTech stock scheme—from which we have the records of every share of stock purchased by her offshore corporations, your little trysts these past few weeks at the beach house …everything. And by the way, I can testify about the beach house myself."

This revelation drained the color from Richards' face and brought a sustained silence to the room. Mitchell could almost see the wheels turning—the unanswered questions spinning inside Richards' mind. Then the man licked his lips and looked down at the exhibits on the table.

"We met a few times to discuss a potential settlement of the case," Richards admitted, choosing his words slowly, carefully. "Unlike the lawyers, we both wanted the case settled—badly." Richards looked at the Rock to judge how well this was selling. "Do you think those settlement discussions on Friday after court came out of the blue? Ms. Davenport-Brown and I had been working on them for days. And as Ms. Moreno knows, we finalized those terms last night. Where else could we meet alone in private—or at least what we thought was private—other than the beach house?"

"You weren't involved with her physically?" asked the Rock. It looked to Mitchell like the little man was ready to jump over the table and attack.

"Of course not."

"And if she says otherwise?"

"No offense, *Dad*"—Richards said the word so sarcastically that it brought the Rock a few inches off his seat—"but it's her word against mine. And she's a little desperate, trying to cut a deal with the prosecutors to cover up *her* little stock-fraud scheme." Now Richards leaned back, the color returning to his face. "Gentlemen and uh…"—he looked at Nikki and smirked—"and Ms. Moreno, do you have any hard evidence linking *me* to any of this? Okay, let's assume that Ms. Davenport-Brown and her husband got a little worried about her chances in this fraudulent lawsuit, which they themselves fabricated—it wouldn't take a genius to set up some offshore corporations and stock up on shares of GenTech and its competitors. If she wins the lawsuit, she wins big. If she loses the lawsuit, the stocks pay off big. The Browns now have a win-win. *But* what does any of this"—he waved his hand dismissively over the table of exhibits—"have to do with *me?*"

What did he just say? Apparently, the Rock had caught it too, and Mitchell smiled as the veteran lawyer leaned forward. "Who said anything about GenTech *and its competitors?*"

The smirk disappeared from Richards' face. He glanced down at the cassette recorder, still in the off position, and seemed to relax just a little. "You did, little man, just a few minutes ago."

The Rock just shook his head.

It was time to wrap this up. "Know what your problem is?" asked Mitchell. "You think it's always about the money. Everybody has a price. But with Cameron, it was never about the money."

Mitchell pulled the plastic bag with the two Band-Aids out of his briefcase, still bearing its exhibit sticker, and placed it on the table.

"Sure, Dr. Avery had his price. And I'm sure that when the commonwealth's attorney charges you with his murder and traces the money, we'll see that he was well paid to falsify the report of Cameron's hysterectomy, to convince Maryna that her baby had Down syndrome, and to set up Billy Davenport for an ethics violation. But you've got to remember, Dr. Richards, that if Avery would sell out to you, he would sell out to others."

Mitchell took a quick glance around the room. How ironic to do this in the very conference room where Avery had met his fate. Almost like Avery could reach out and slap Richards from the grave.

"Those blood tests that Dr. Avery conducted on Cameron and secretly sent you at your request—he also told Cameron that you had asked for those. You're always the doctor, aren't you Richards? Careful and clinical to a fault. Before you slept with Cameron, you wanted to make sure she was safe. But what makes you think Avery was only selling out to you and not double dipping? What makes you think Cameron wasn't paying him a little something extra to falsify blood tests?"

Mitchell watched Richards go white—the realization hitting the doctor a few seconds before the words themselves. "Like I said, doc, with Cameron it was never about the money…it was always about the cure. The blood on these Band-Aids tested positive for the HIV virus. Got it from her husband. And then she figured that her best chance for a cure was to find a way to get lots of money into the hands of one of the top research labs in the country. But she also decided to take it one step further—and give the CEO of that company the greatest possible motivation for finding that cure. A personal motivation."

"Good thing you didn't have sex with her," added the Rock.

Mitchell slid the plastic bag across the table. He watched both Richards and Mackenzie lean slightly away, as if the bag itself contained a poison they would now have to drink.

"Cameron had a nifty little plan," Mitchell concluded. "But she just didn't anticipate that the CEO would have to supervise this AIDS research from a jail cell on death row."

Like a zombie, Richards took his focus from the Band-Aids and stared out the new glass of the eighteenth-floor conference room window at the ozone, his face drained of every ounce of blood.

⊱⋅⋅⋅⋅⋅⋅⋅⋅⋅⋅⋅⋅⋅⋅⋅⋅⊰

A few minutes later, in the lobby of the eighteenth floor, Mitchell took off his golf shirt in front of the Rock, Nikki, and commonwealth attor-

ney Harlan Fowler. A half-dozen Virginia Beach detectives were arrest-
ing Richards and reading him the Miranda warnings, but Fowler, ever
the prosecutor, wanted to check on the additional evidence he had
gained just that morning.

"Nice abs," said Nikki.

"I'm married."

"They're still nice abs."

Fowler stepped forward and started loosening the strap around
Mitchell's chest. "This baby's called a body Nagra," he explained. "Top
of the line. Just got our first one a few months ago."

Harlan removed the Nagra with its attached wires and rewound the
tape. The four of them waited breathlessly until they heard the first few
words of the settlement conference. The tape was perfect. Crystal clear.
Richards' slip-up about Cameron's stock purchases had been indis-
putably preserved on tape.

"These little babies always perform flawlessly," gloated Fowler.

83

THE GOOD PART ABOUT BEING your daughter's lawyer is that you get to visit her in the conference room reserved for attorneys and their clients rather than sitting on the opposite side of twelve-inch-thick, bulletproof glass and talking into phones. The conference-room setting, sterile as it was, sure beat the phones.

"It's too early to tell what kind of a deal we'll end up with," the Rock said as he gathered his papers. "All depends on our continued cooperation in nailing Richards and whether we can convince them that you had nothing to do with Avery. Right now, we're off to a good start."

He took a long, hard look at his daughter. She looked so tough in her orange prison jumpsuit. But at the same time, especially through the eyes, he still saw his little girl, and he thought about how vulnerable she was.

"You'll have to do some time," he continued, trying hard to keep it professional. "These are serious charges...but I'll do the best I can."

"I know." She kept her eyes glued to the table. She hadn't said much the entire visit.

The Rock stood to leave. "Once they take your formal statement and we finalize the plea bargain, I plan on checking myself into rehab. This time I won't leave early." He felt himself choking up a little. *This is not the time—she needs her dad to be strong.* "I don't guess there'll be anybody waiting with bated breath for me to get out anyhow."

The Rock looked forlornly at his daughter, trying hard to think of a profound and fatherly piece of advice. This was so incredibly hard. What could he say to make up for a lifetime of neglect? As usual, words failed him.

"Well, gotta go."

He turned to leave, positioning his crutches under his arms, but Cameron rose as he did so. "I'm sorry, Dad."

He turned back around, leaned the crutches against the table, reached over the top, and gave her a hug. It was just a quick hug, with a few soft pats on the back. But it was a start. And it was more affection than they had shown each other in years.

"I'm sorry too," said the Rock, unable to take his gaze from his daughter for several seconds. Then he turned awkwardly, grabbed the crutches, hobbled to the door, and buzzed the guard to let him out.

— —

Cameron had to hand it to these guys; they really knew how to sell papers. Monday's front page would carry the saga of Cameron, Maryna, Mitchell, and Blaine Richards. CNN was already running the story of her confession, Blaine's arrest, and Nathan's death. But the *Tidewater Times* wanted an exclusive interview. After all, she had been their columnist for several years. They were entitled.

But Cameron wanted nothing to do with fueling the fires of publicity surrounding her own demise. The public didn't need to know every detail of why she had done these things. And any good reporter would have a hundred prying questions that Cameron just didn't want to answer. For some, she honestly didn't know the answer.

They had compromised. She had agreed to write one last column, a confessional, really. The paper got their exclusive, and she didn't have to worry about what some hard-core journalist would ask in an interview. The idea had been approved by her dad. "The cops already have a full confession," he said. "What's the harm?"

At this moment, she wished she had just told everyone no.

The one thing she always hated about writing was the deadlines. Now here she was, sitting in some holding cell in Virginia Beach, separated from the civilized world by twenty-four-inch concrete walls, cast-iron pipes over the windows, eighteen-foot chain-link fences with razor wire on top, and a whole phalanx of beefy sheriff's deputies with service revolvers. She was totally insulated from the world except for the one thing she just couldn't seem to get away from, the one thing that had hung over her head every day of her professional life for the last ten years.

Her deadline.

In less than one hour, a courier from the newspaper would arrive at the jail to pick up her final column.

❦

Tidewater Times

Final Draft, Letter to Readers, Placement in Section A,
Continuation of Front Page Story

CHOICES AND CONSEQUENCES
by Cameron Davenport-Brown

To my loyal readers:

First, you need to hear me say that I was wrong and that I am sorry. As you have undoubtedly read on the front page, I conspired with Dr. Blaine Richards, CEO of GenTech, to defraud the court system into declaring the Bioethics Act unconstitutional. I also conspired to defraud investors by using insider knowledge about this lawsuit to trade shares of GenTech and its competitors. In order to carry out this scheme, I helped fake my husband's death and even reported on the aftermath of that death to you in one of my prior editorials.

All these actions are wrong, and I bring you no excuses, just apologies. I have signed a detailed confession and pledged my full cooperation in making sure that Blaine Richards is held accountable. I am most sorry that I not only misled the court and the investment professionals, but that I also misled you, my readers.

You deserved better.

I also want each of you to know that I had no part in the tragic death of Dr. Lars Avery or the attempts on the life of Maryna Sareth, including one bungled attempt that apparently resulted in the death of an unrelated third party at a Chesapeake hotel. I have answered detailed questions about those events, and I am confident that in the end I will be fully exonerated.

I will not ask you to understand my actions or to forgive me for them. I would ask, however, that you not extrapolate my actions to the causes I have supported throughout my professional career. Do not stereotype those causes just because an advocate of theirs has fallen. It will be easy for the fundamentalists to blame my actions on what they call the "culture of death." "See what happens," they will say, "when you start devaluing life."

Don't believe such talk. It's simply the politics of abortion. To judge the pro-choice movement by my shortcomings is the same as judging the entire antiabortion movement on the basis of the few clinic bombers. To do so is bigotry at its worst. To do so is wrong.

At the end of the day, it all comes down to individual responsibility. I still believe in choice. I just made some incredibly bad ones.

From this day on, I will make better choices and I will accept responsibility. I have chosen to cooperate with the authorities. I will choose to give my frozen embryos up for adoption, hoping they can find a home with parents as committed as Maryna Sareth and Mitchell Taylor. (In an ironic twist, I now have the sole power to decide the disposition of the frozen embryos since my husband's will was a fraud and invalid.) I will choose to bless the adoption of the embryo that was implanted into Maryna Sareth.

Lastly, I will choose to forgive those who have wronged me and will give them the benefit of the doubt going forward.

And my only request is that you might consider doing the same for me.

❦

She looked down at the letter, entirely unhappy with its contents. This *mea culpa* routine didn't fit her very well. But it was too late to go in a different direction now, with her deadline just a few minutes away. And she really did intend to make better choices.

She scratched out a sentence or two, added another, all by hand— how did they ever do this in the old days without computers?—then took a break and stared at the cinder-block wall. She felt so miserable, the entire weight of the world suddenly heavy on her shoulders.

But she would survive. Even in prison. That's what she did.

Back to the letter. She read it again, then with a flourish wrote her closing and printed her name. "Run it just like this," she would tell them. "Absolutely no changes." It would mean so much to him.

To tell the truth, it looked kind of strange, the first time she had signed anything this way in years. But it also felt right. One of those good choices she had written about.

With many thanks and sincere apologies,
Cameron Davenport

No hyphenation this time, she thought. Cameron *Davenport,* daughter of Billy Davenport. An apple that hadn't fallen very far from the tree.

On the other side of the sprawling municipal complex, in the offices of Harlan Fowler, the videotaped statement of Mitchell Taylor was in full swing. Harlan didn't want to take any chances with this case, preserving all the evidence while it was fresh in people's minds.

A weary Mitchell Taylor had already been at it for more than an hour.

"…and then I saw him blink, or flinch, or, you know, close his eyes in the way somebody does when they're anticipating a loud noise or an impact or something. And so I knew I was out of time and I just dove at him, trying to deflect the gun and bust open his head at the same time. And, well…"

Mitchell paused for a moment, closing his eyes, trying hard to run the sequence back in his mind in slow motion. "He swung the gun around like he was going to shoot me, or maybe shoot himself… I really don't know. Because I think he, like, got it partway around so that it was pretty much pointed right at me, but I hit it with my forearm just before it went off.

"This much I know… It went off pointed at his face at point-blank range…just before I nailed him. He was probably dead before we hit the floor." Mitchell looked around the room at the sympathetic faces.

"Do you think it was suicide, or do you think he was trying to shoot you?" asked Harlan, obviously trying to serve Mitchell an easy pitch.

Mitchell thought about this for another painful moment. "I honestly can't say, Mr. Fowler. Does it really matter?"

Harlan looked around the room at the shrugs of the deputy attorneys. Then he turned back to Mitchell, the video camera still running. "Nah," said Harlan, "I don't guess that it does."

EPILOGUE

MARYNA LOOKED AROUND THE HOSPITAL ROOM and thought about how lucky—make that how *blessed*—she was. The monitors beat a steady cadence—strong heart, good blood pressure, breathing easily—basically, she and the baby were fine. She had been through a "little trauma," in the understated words of the doctor, and had probably gone into acute shock. But she would be all right. She just needed a little rest. And fortunately, the hospital knew exactly how much medication she needed to sleep.

So she was blessed to be alive and healthy. But it didn't stop there. Mitchell was alive! And Mitchell had brought flowers earlier that morning and—get this—a CD Walkman with a CD of Beethoven's Fifth. Not her favorite, but still...*classical music!* She couldn't even remember telling him how much she liked classical music.

The nurses and doctors had been great, but she was ready to get out, to go home. She kept telling everybody how good she felt. And she did, as long as she tried not to think about it...how close she had come to dying, how she had almost lost Dara...and Mitchell.

She couldn't wait for Mitchell to come back. She was certain the doctors would finally let him take her home so she could really get some rest. No more needles. No more specimens. No more hospital food.

She made up her mind to stay awake until he came back, but her eyelids already felt heavy. These drugs didn't so much relax her as they did just knock her out. She never felt rested, always tired, and never fully awake. More often than not, Maryna found herself fighting the drowsiness, afraid of the images that would come when she closed her eyes.

Dozing in and out, she saw him at the door. As Mitchell stuck his head in, she couldn't resist a groggy smile.

"Hey, babe," he said, coming over to the side of her bed.

"Hi." She tried hard to sound alert but knew her voice sounded hopelessly sleepy.

"I've got somebody I want you to meet. Said she's been trying to call for a couple days but only had my home phone. Probably left about fifteen messages."

As he talked, he grabbed Maryna's hand and held it. It felt so good to be touching him, but still, she floated in and out, on that thin edge between being asleep and awake.

"Okay," she managed. She saw Mitchell turn to the door and nod. "I think the medication's starting to kick in a little," Maryna said.

She smiled as she looked up at Mitchell, couldn't help but smile, then turned slightly to look at the silhouette approaching on the other side. A woman. Trembling. Hands held to her mouth. Sobbing. "My baby, my baby," she sobbed. Then she stooped and hugged Maryna's neck.

It felt so much like her! But Maryna's mother was dead—had been dead for years. It was the medication, Maryna knew, and when she awoke, as always, her mother would be gone.

"They captured me in Arizona," the phantom sobbed, speaking Cambodian, "Charlie Coggins and his men. Had me deported. It took two years to get back, then another year of working with the Snakeheads to earn my freedom. I've been searching for you ever since. When I saw you on television, well…it took two days to get here from L.A., and I finally found…" Her voice just morphed into the tears, an endless river that soaked Maryna and her pillow.

Maryna looked past her mom at her smiling husband. She couldn't believe this was happening! She returned the hug with her left arm, carefully lifting her wrist with the IV attached while at the same time holding…no, squeezing, Mitchell's hand with her right. She started trembling as the realization hit her and sank in. Her breath came in short bursts—*my mother is back! Alive!*

She squeezed the woman for all she was worth, feeling that somehow if she let go of her, she might never get her back. But this *was* real.

Her mother released her for a moment, stood halfway up. "Look at you, Maryna, you look so tired... We need to let you sleep."

That's my mother, all right. My mother!

"I guess you two have met," said Maryna, trying to smile through the tears. "Oh, I just can't believe this!" She reached out her arm, and her mother hugged her again.

Suddenly, Maryna didn't want to sleep, didn't want to ever again close her eyes and risk losing her mother. She wanted to talk for hours and make up for years of being apart. Maryna held her own for a few minutes but soon realized it was a hopeless task. She dozed off a few times, with Mitchell holding one hand and her mom the other. Each time Maryna woke up, brief little intervals between fitful periods of sleep, her heart would jump as the silhouettes of her mom and Mitchell would slowly come into view. She would squeeze a hand to make sure it was real, smile for a moment, then eventually just start crying when she would think about her mom.

This incredible swing of emotions, the horror of the night before replaced by the joy of finding her mom, finally started taking its toll. A nurse came in, made her take some more medication, and Maryna knew it wouldn't be long.

She looked from Mitchell to her mom, closed her eyes for a few long seconds, and opened them again to find her mom still standing by her side.

"Dara is, um...pretty name," Maryna heard her mother say in hushed tones to Mitchell, as if she were trying not to wake Maryna up. "My name." She watched her mom raise her free hand to her heart. "My honor... But I was hoping that maybe, if not too late, you might consider also another pretty name." She paused for a second, and Maryna couldn't be sure if it was a dream or she actually heard her mom say these next few words, "A name like Piseth."

"Interesting name," said Mitchell. She felt him squeeze her hand and knew that she wasn't dreaming, not yet. She opened her eyes again just long enough to see a smile play on Mitchell's lips, as a knowing look passed from husband to wife. "Piseth, huh? Now, how would you spell that?"

———— ❦ ————

"Wait!" called Mitchell. He stood in the doorway of Maryna's hospital room, calling after Nikki. She stopped and turned, waiting for Mitchell to jog down the hall.

"I just wanted to say thanks again for coming by." Mitchell hesitated, not really sure why. "And thanks so much for everything you've done on this case."

"No problem."

"If I can *ever* do *anything* for you…"

"Now that you mention it… If you could just find me a handsome young lawyer like you"—she took a half step toward him, stood on her toes, and gave him a quick unexpected kiss on the cheek—"preferably not already married, I'd really appreciate it." Her eyes sparkled.

Nikki's contagious smile forced a playful grin onto Mitchell's face as well. "I'll keep my eyes peeled."

Then Nikki turned on her heel and started strutting down the hall. Since she was wearing her standard spaghetti-strap top, it was impossible not to notice that small tattoo on her left shoulder. This time, Mitchell decided to find out.

"Can I ask you a question?"

She stopped a few steps down the hallway and turned to face him again. Her smile said to fire away.

"I've always wondered what that tattoo on your left shoulder means."

Nikki's smile broadened, white teeth flashing, until her whole face beamed. "That, handsome, is an entirely different story."

To learn more about WaterBrook Press and view
our catalog of products, log on to our Web site:
www.waterbrookpress.com